Just for Her

Just for Her

KATHERINE O'NEAL

BRAVA

KENSINGTON PUBLISHING CORP.
http://www.kensingtonbooks.com

BRAVA BOOKS are published by

Kensington Publishing Corp.
850 Third Avenue
New York, NY 10022

All Kensington titles, imprints and distributed lines are available at special quantity discounts for bulk purchases for sales promotion, premiums, fund-raising, and educational or institutional use.

Special book excerpts or customized printings can also be created to fit specific needs. For details, write or phone the office of the Kensington Special Sales Manager: Kensington Publishing Corp., 850 Third Avenue, New York, NY 10022. Attn. Special Sales Department. Phone: 1-800-221-2647.

Brava and the B logo Reg. U.S. Pat. & TM Off.

ISBN-13: 978-0-7582-1062-3
ISBN-10: 0-7582-1062-0

First Kensington Trade Paperback Printing: July 2008
10 9 8 7 6 5 4 3 2 1

Printed in the United States of America

For all the
Femmes on Fire
everywhere

Chapter 1

21 June, 1926
Cap Ferrat
French Riviera

Jules awoke with a start.

Without moving, her eyes scanned the vast bedroom of her hilltop Mediterranean villa. The floor-to-ceiling French doors were open as she'd left them, the breeze billowing the gossamer white curtains into the room, playing with the moonlight that spilled in with a silvery glow. Beyond the windows she could see the conical tops of the cypresses that towered above the gardens below. All was quiet. The world around her seemed peaceful, serene.

And yet . . .

Something had jarred her awake.

She lay motionless in her bed, listening. What time was it? The moon was still high in the sky. She hadn't meant to doze off, but the hours she'd spent waiting the night before had caught up with her. How long had she been asleep? Minutes? Hours? Her brain felt numb, heavy. She couldn't seem to think.

But then she heard the faint tinkle of the tiny bell she'd fastened to her study window before it was abruptly silenced. The hush that followed was dense, fraught with an expectation—a waiting—that throbbed in the air around her. She knew what that brief muffled tinkle meant. Someone had opened the window.

He was here!

And now her mind was sharp, her senses bristling. She lay frozen in her bed.

She could almost see him in her mind's eye—a dark mysterious figure, creeping up to her soaring terrace, finding the window to her study, testing it to find it unlocked. Startled by the bell, grasping it in his fist to silence it. Waiting, breath held, for some evidence of alarm, some movement in the house. And only when he was certain it was safe—only then climbing in through the window to the study beyond.

The study that was next to her bedroom, just on the other side of the wall.

She realized she hadn't been breathing and took a slow shallow breath. She realized, too, that her heart was pounding so violently it hurt her chest. It seemed to her that the sound of it must be reverberating through the night, and that even from the next room, he could hear it as loudly as she could in her own ears.

A cold panic seized her.

What have I done?

When she'd envisioned this scene in the light of day, it had seemed daring and romantic. But now that it was actually happening, everything in her screamed it was a ghastly mistake. The man in that room was no longer a projection of her naïve fantasy, but a living, breathing human being. And a dangerous one, at that.

The Panther!

The notorious cat burglar who'd been terrorizing the villas of the Côte d'Azur these past several months . . .

The audacious thief who'd stolen Lady Westley's ruby ring from her finger as she'd slept . . .

The scoundrel who'd lifted the Duchess of Parma's hundred-carat aquamarine collar from her wall safe without rousing a soul . . .

Like a slide show flickering on a blank screen, the headlines flashed through her mind.

PANTHER ONCE AGAIN ELUDES POLICE TRAP . . .
GUARDS FAIL TO OVERPOWER FLEEING CAT . . .
IN FEAT OF MARKSMANSHIP, STRAIGHT SHOOTING CROOK
EMBARRASSES PURSUING POLICE OFFICIALS . . .

From Menton to Hyères, the idle rich were in an uproar, endlessly retelling the tales of the Panther's exploits in casinos, beneath the striped umbrellas of La Garoupe beach, and all along the circuit of cocktail parties up and down the coast. But as the stories had floated around her like snippets of melodrama from the silver screen, Jules had painted this phantom of the night with an entirely different brush, imbuing him with colors of a larger-than-life character from a storybook. And slowly, the desperate plan had taken shape in her mind.

Two days ago, assured of the brilliance of her scheme, she'd calmly told Lady Asterbrooke, the most notorious gossip in the South of France—a woman guaranteed to blab to the winds—that she had no fear of this bandit. "In fact, Bunny," she'd told the society clarion in a deliberately breezy tone, "I have every intention of wearing my emeralds to the Richardson ball on Saturday. I shall remove them from the Nice vault, and secure them in the wall safe of my upstairs study."

She felt confident the word would reach him. The Panther seemed to have an ear in high society, knowing when people would be out of their villas and even where their jewels were kept. So she'd laid the trap and waited for him to take the bait. She'd stayed awake the night before, certain he would come, excited by the prospect, even disappointed when he hadn't shown.

But now that he was actually in her house . . . only steps away . . . her actions seemed impetuously risky and downright foolhardy.

I must have been out of my mind!

Because the reality was neither daring nor romantic. It was terrifying. Her mouth was so dry she couldn't even swallow.

She listened in the trenchant silence for some indication of his movements. What was he doing? The study wasn't a large room. Once inside, he would look around, see the Fragonard on the far wall, step lightly to it, remove it from its hanger, set it on the floor.

Then he would get to work on the safe. Rolling the dial of the lock back and forth. How long would it take him to crack the combination? From his reputation, not long. Soon, he would pull the door open and see there was nothing inside.

What would he do then? Flee into the night?

I could just stay here, where I am, and he'll be gone. I don't have to go through with it.

But what then? What other choice did she have? There was nothing else she could think to do.

No, she had to go through with it. As demented as it seemed, it was her only chance.

But she'd have to hurry.

Determined now, she reached under her pillow for the pistol she'd placed there. It had seemed so solid and reassuring when she'd taken it from her father's gun collection. Now it suddenly felt flimsy and inadequate. But she gripped it tightly. Then, taking a gulp of courage, she rose from her bed. She fumbled for her robe, but in her agitated state, she couldn't find it. There was no time to search. He could be gone at any second. She'd have to go without it.

Her legs feeling like jelly, she quietly made her way across the darkened chamber to the connecting door. She'd purposely left it open, but it was now closed.

He had closed it. Without her even hearing that he had.

She placed a clammy hand on the knob. Slowly gave it a turn. Silently pushed it open.

And saw him across the room. A dim figure, standing at the safe, working the tumblers.

Once again, panic choked her. Her hand, holding the gun, was trembling uncontrollably.

What will he do when he realizes I'm here?

Her imagination conjured up a swift succession of images. The intruder rushing her . . . overpowering her . . . hurting her . . . maybe even killing her . . .

And she, through self-preservation, forced to shoot him . . .

She'd never shot a gun in her life. She wasn't even certain she knew how.

Unbidden, she remembered Scott Fitzgerald saying, with drunken wisdom, "A burglar is only dangerous when he's been surprised in the act."

Stop it, she scolded herself. *You can do this. You have to. Be firm. Unafraid. You have him in your power.*

Just then, she heard the metallic click as he turned the handle and opened the safe. Within an instant, he would know it was empty.

As he reached inside, she said in French, "You won't find what you're looking for, I'm afraid."

He jerked around, into the moonlight streaming through the window from which he'd entered.

And as he did, she saw him more clearly—a tall figure, clad in all black, the fitted material clinging to a body that was muscular and sleek. A specially fashioned mask, also black, concealed the top of his face . . . hiding his nose and cheeks . . . sweeping over his head to cover his hair . . . The only feature visible was a clean-shaven jaw and the faint gleam of dark eyes through the slits of his disguise. He stood poised and alert, his hands at his sides, ready to pounce. The effect was both masculine and feline, calling to mind images of the jungle cat to which he'd been so aptly compared.

All at once, he darted for the open window. But she was closer. Instinctively, she stepped in front of it, blocking his path, reaching behind her to pull it closed.

He stopped in his tracks.

"I have a gun," she told him, her voice shaky.

She could see his head swivel as he quickly surveyed the room, looking for another escape. Two doors. One, behind him, led to the hallway, but it was closed. The other, the one connecting to her bedroom, was closer and open. He stared at it, then back at her, no doubt wondering if she would really shoot him if he made a dash for it.

Astonishingly, despite her advantage, she sensed no fear in him. His presence sparked and sizzled in the room, sucking the air from it so she could barely breathe. A raw stalking presence, wholly male, predatory and sexual in nature, made her suddenly aware that she stood before him in nothing but a lace and chiffon nightgown. She could feel the vulnerability of her soft female flesh, of the swells and hollows of her body, in a way that made her feel it was *he* who held the upper hand.

For a moment—an eternity—he didn't move. He just stood there, his gaze locked on her. She could feel the heat of that gaze as though his hand was passing over her. She tried again to swallow. Heightened by the danger, it seemed that every pore of her skin radiated and throbbed with her awareness of him.

And then, like lightning—so suddenly, she had no time to react—he lunged across the room and wrenched the pistol from her hand.

For a moment he just stood there, the weapon aimed at her. Her hand aching, Jules could feel the frightened rasp of her breath. Her imagination running wild again, she pictured him pulling the trigger, heard in her mind the roar of the gun's report.

The silence was deafening. Her nerves were raw.

But then—quickly, efficiently—he flipped open the barrel, let the bullets drop to the floor, and tossed the pistol aside. Jules felt a momentary relief. But it was short-lived. Unthreatened now, he skirted around her and started for the window from which he'd come.

In desperation, she sprang to block his exit, flinging herself back against the window, her arms spread wide to prevent his escape.

"Please, don't go."

He stopped at once, his instincts honed. She imagined him grabbing her and hauling her aside.

Instead, with a stealthy grace, he veered to his left and started for the open door that led to her bedroom and the terrace beyond. Realizing his intention, she ran after him.

"Wait!" she cried.

He wheeled on her threateningly, his hand raised. "Stand back," he warned, speaking in Italian—a deep, whispery, dangerous growl.

Switching quickly to Italian, she told him, "I just want to speak with you. That's why I lured you here."

"*Lured* me?" He glanced about warily, as if expecting a contingent of police to burst into the room.

"There's no one here," she rushed to assure him. "I don't want you captured. I just—"

He wasn't listening. She could feel his urgent need to get away. He crossed the room, rounding the bed on his way to the French doors, the terrace, and freedom beyond.

Fueled by despair, Jules shot after him and grabbed him by the arm. Beneath the black sweater, it felt like iron.

He jerked free with a strength that sent her tumbling back. "I don't want to hurt you, but I will."

Jules was past caring. All she knew was that she couldn't let him walk out the door and out of her life.

She grabbed onto him once again. This time he shoved her back onto the bed. "Don't you care what happens to you?" he snarled.

"No," she confessed. "I have nothing to lose."

"You're mad," he rasped.

"Am I?" She stood slowly, careful not to cause alarm. "Perhaps. All I know is that fate has brought you to me."

"Fate?"

"Destiny has sent you to me, Panther. You can't run away now."

"Can't I?"

He turned to leave, but she gasped out, quickly, "I have a proposition for you."

That stopped him. Slowly, he asked, "Now, what kind of proposition could a woman like you have for a man like me?"

Her eyes roamed the feral black-cloaked phantom before her. Unbidden, the first line of Byron's *Don Juan* sprang to her lips: " 'I want a hero.' "

"You want *what?*"

She took a breath and spat out the words.

"I want you to kill my husband."

Chapter 2

The intruder hadn't counted on this.

He hadn't counted on her waking up and catching him in the act.

He hadn't counted on how ravishing she would look in the filtered moonlight: a vision to take one's breath away. The blond hair, falling about her shoulders in slumberous disarray, gleaming like spun gold; the white lace bodice of her nightgown clinging to the voluptuous curves of her breasts; the chiffon skirt swirling gently in the breeze around the slender legs; the pampered skin dewy from Parisian lotions and tanned by the southern sun. Her voice, cultured, silky, carrying the faintest trace of an appealing Austrian accent—the sound of it alone was enough to make any man hard. She had the face of an angel and the body of a Botticelli nymph. With her aura of innocence and vulnerability, he couldn't have envisioned a more ideal embodiment of a fairy-tale princess.

And yet, this delicate beauty was telling him she'd *lured* him here to . . .

"You want me to . . . kill your husband?"

When he spoke, the words sounded as crazed to Jules as they did to him.

"It wasn't my intention to blurt it out that way," she said. "But that is, indeed, what I am proposing."

Slowly, incredulously, he asked, "Why on earth would I want to kill your husband?"

"Because he's a monster." She said this with a sense of poise and delicacy, as if she'd just told him her husband was cutting roses in the garden. "And because I shall compensate you for the service."

He was still staring at her as if she'd lost her mind.

Have I? she wondered.

Deliberately he said, "Let me see if I understand you. You want me to kill the man in cold blood?"

"Of course not. I'm not a murderess."

He shook his head as if to clear it. "What, then?"

"I want you to kill him in a duel."

"What I'm going to do," he told her evenly, "is leave this house and never look back."

He headed for the open doors.

"Do you know who I am?"

He stopped again, in the shadows of the terrace overlooking the gardens below. "I know exactly who you are. The Archduchess Maria Theresa Louisa Juliana von Habsburg. Formerly a royal princess of the Habsburg family, recently dethroned by the Great War and sent into exile. Currently wife of British business tycoon Dominic DeRohan. I make it a habit of researching my prospective—donors."

"Then you know I can afford to compensate you for your trouble."

"On the contrary. I know you have next to nothing of your own except this house and your share of the Habsburg jewels. Not being portable, I care nothing for real estate, but obviously my presence here tonight tells you I care about the jewels. So tell me . . . will you offer a few choice stones as payment for the . . . service? Say, for instance, the Marie Antoinette pearls?"

"I'm afraid I can't do that. They're my—birthright, if you will—all I have left of my family. But I do have some household funds at my disposal."

He considered her for a moment. "Why do you want him dead? To get control of his money?"

"I care nothing for his filthy money. I want him dead because he's the devil himself. Because he killed the two men in the world I cared about. And because I now know it's the only way I can ever be free of him."

He glanced about, taking in the suggestions of furnishings in the darkened room. "If you don't mind, I'll take myself out of the light. An old habit, I'm afraid. Since you insist on this conversation, I take it you won't mind if I avail myself of one of your chairs?"

"Of course. I'm sorry. I seem to have forgotten my manners. But then, the circumstances *are* rather unusual. I was rigorously schooled in every aspect of entertaining, but I was never prepared to—"

"Entertain thieves in the night?"

"You're the first thief I've ever—met, much less entertained."

Suddenly she couldn't believe she was having this conversation with this man. Once again, her heart began to beat erratically.

"And you're the first quarry who ever asked me to do away with her lord and master." He made his way to the far right corner of the room and a padded brocade chair. Once he sat down, he was completely hidden by the shadows. He might not have been there at all, except that his voice floated to her like a murmur from the bottom of a well. "If you hate him so much, why did you marry him?"

"I was forced into it."

"What of it? Arranged marriages are an ancient royal custom, I understand. Particularly in the Habsburg line."

"Except that mine wasn't arranged. It was coerced. By DeRohan."

There was a slight pause. When he spoke, it seemed to her that his tone expressed a more attentive, if still cautious, interest as he asked, "And just how did he manage that?"

"I'd rather not tell you."

"Why not?"

"Because you'll think I'm merely feeling sorry for myself."

"Ah, but you've intrigued me. You wouldn't expect a cautious rogue like myself to join you in such an intimate conspiracy without an explanation, would you?"

Jules hesitated. She felt ridiculous, speaking to this disembodied voice, like a schoolgirl called onto the carpet by her tutor. "I suppose I owe you that much. It would help, though, if I could turn on the light."

He snarled at her from the dark. "Lady, you so much as reach for that light switch and I'll be gone before you turn around."

She froze in place. "Please don't go. I'll tell you what you want to know." She looked about her in the darkness. She hadn't planned for this negotiation to take place in her bedroom. She couldn't very well sit on her bed and talk to him, although she realized the absurdity of thinking anything unseemly at this point. Instead, she began to pace in the moonlight at the foot of the bed, the only glimmer of light in the room.

"You know about my family, so you must know how devastating the war was to us. The empire was broken up, we were ousted from power, stripped of our Austrian possessions, and sent into exile. My brothers and mother all died in one way or another as a result of the war. My father and I were the only ones to survive. All we had left was this house, which my grandmother had built in the last century, and the jewels my mother had sewn into the lining of our corsets and smuggled out of Vienna just before she died."

"Forgive me, but that's more than most people had after the war."

"Believe me, I know how fortunate we were. We had so many friends who'd lost everything. At least we had a roof over our heads. But our accounts had been seized by the new Austrian state. We left Vienna in the middle of the night with what little money we could scrape together. We couldn't afford to run this house, so we boarded up most of it and lived in two rooms like refugees."

"Why didn't you just sell your jewels?"

"To do so would have been unthinkable. They were our link with the past, the symbol of what we'd once been. To lose them would be to lose, finally, everything . . . what was left of our identity. Father always told me, 'Your mother died to save those jewels. You must never part with them under any circumstance, even threat of death.' But ultimately, ironically one might say, even they were threatened by—"

She stumbled on the words. It seemed that she was somehow betraying the father she loved by speaking of such things. Hadn't he suffered enough, without her airing his weaknesses to a perfect stranger?

"By what?" he prompted.

She realized her pride was making her irrational. There was no way to tell it otherwise, so she admitted softly, "Father's gambling. Something I wasn't aware of until we were thrown into such close proximity."

"Another royal custom difficult to give up."

"I'm not excusing him. But you must understand his health and reason had been ravaged by all he'd been through. He desperately needed some diversion, as well as some hope of bettering our circumstances. So I permitted him to indulge his vice under strict limitations. But one week, when I was visiting a cousin in Belgium, he went to the casino at Juan-les-Pains and—despite his promise to avoid the tables in my absence—he was coaxed into a game of baccarat by DeRohan. In half an hour, Father had lost this house. A few minutes after that, in a frantic effort to win it back, he threw a marker for the jewels into the pot and lost them as well."

"Lady Luck is a cruel mistress."

"Luck had nothing to do with it. DeRohan cheated, just as he's cheated in every other venture of his life. He's always hated my family. Like so many people, he unfairly blamed us for the war—"

He cut her off. "After all, it was the assassination of a Habsburg archduke that started the war."

"Was that our fault? That some maniac in Sarajevo gunned down my uncle?"

"Seems to me I recall hearing that certain of your family members pushed for a war for self-serving reasons."

"I'm not here to argue history with you. My point is, DeRohan hated the Habsburgs—and he hated us long before the war. There was something more personal in his prejudice toward us, as if he harbored some private grudge. In any case, he deliberately lured Father into a fixed game so he would lose the few possessions he still had to his name. He wanted to destroy him."

She heard him shift restlessly in his chair. "Where does the marriage come in?"

"It wasn't enough that he had my father completely on his knees. It occurred to him that he could make his defeat even more humiliating. DeRohan—a commoner, scoundrel, and profligate rake—could marry the daughter who'd been groomed to marry a prince. He came to me and coldly told me he would allow us to retain the house and jewels under the condition that I give myself to him in marriage."

"Obviously, you agreed."

"What else could I do? I couldn't allow Father to be thrown into the street like yesterday's rubbish."

"And then, too, there were the jewels."

"Yes, I admit that was a consideration. I've told you what they meant to us. I married DeRohan in a private ceremony. Even Father didn't attend. But in the end, it was all a terrible mistake. Just days later—here, in this very house—DeRohan went into Father's study. He said something to him—I don't know what it was. But that evening, Father shot himself. I heard the shot and ran down to his study. And there he was . . . lying in a pool of his own blood . . . and I felt someone beside me . . . I looked up and there was DeRohan . . . I'll never forget his face. His lips were curled in the coldest, cruelest, most cynical smile . . . it was almost as if he were laughing to himself. My father was dead and this Lucifer I'd married was *smirking!*"

She put her face in her hands, reliving the awful memory. But once again pride rose to the fore. Fighting to control her emotions, she composed her face, then lifted her head. "Later, the authorities told me it was DeRohan's pistol Father had used. DeRohan must have left it there for him when he went in to see him. He must have said something to Father to make him do it."

"With your father dead, why didn't you just leave him?"

"We'd signed a legal contract. DeRohan had agreed to put this house and the jewels in my name and to pay for the up-keep and running of the house until my death. In return, he in-sisted that I make my residence in London. So after Father's funeral, I kept my word and sailed for England with DeRohan. But our agreement failed to specify *where* in London I had to live. So when we arrived at Victoria Station, I informed him that I intended to take my own house in Mayfair."

"He agreed to that?"

"He didn't have much choice. I'd found a loophole he hadn't foreseen. Too, he was so busy in this particular period expand-ing his business empire that he didn't have time to contend with my rebellion. But to keep him pacified, I allowed him to present me as his wife—his Habsburg trophy—at three or four social functions a season. This went on for three years. I ex-pected it would continue forever. I was married to a stranger I detested, but at least I didn't have to put up with him except occasionally in public. I'd long since given up any girlish hopes for happiness. But then, unexpectedly, I met someone I cared for."

"The other man your husband—killed, you said. Your lover?"

She blushed slightly. "His name was Edwin. He was a ten-der, kind man—a poet—who understood the loneliness of my life and befriended me. Gradually, our friendship blossomed into a deeper sentiment. It wasn't lewd or unseemly, I assure you.

It was lovely and pure—a meeting of two minds who cherished poetry and beauty above all else. When we met, we were always careful and discreet. But somehow DeRohan found us out. He goaded Edwin into a duel—poor Edwin, who didn't know one end of a dueling pistol from another. Before he'd even aimed, DeRohan had shot him squarely between the eyes. They say he had a sneer on his face when he did it."

"That's when you left London?"

She brushed away a tear. "Yes. I just didn't care what happened to me anymore. I had to get away—away from that dreary town, away from him. And suddenly all I could think of was Rêve de l'Amour."

"Rêve de l'Amour. Dream of Love?"

So he did speak French. "That's the name my grandmother gave this house. The place I'd come to every winter as a child, the place I loved. Even the fact that Father had died here so tragically didn't spoil my memory of it. He'd been part of this house, as had my mother and my grandmother through the years. It was infused with the spirit of our family. Here I could be a Habsburg once more, instead of a bought-and-paid-for DeRohan. I wanted to be myself again, if only for a week, or a day, or even an hour. I knew it wouldn't last. I fully expected him to turn up at any moment—to take me back, or take the house away from me—something."

"Did he?"

"No. That was the most frightening thing of all. He didn't do a thing. That was a year ago. At first, I lived day by day, always looking over my shoulder, feeling as if I had a sword hanging over my head. But gradually, as the months passed, I began to relax and even hope he'd decided I was more trouble to him than I was worth. I made new friends, built a life for myself here, and found—if not happiness, at least some measure of peace."

"But something must have changed for you to ask me what you did."

"A few days ago, I received a telegram—the first communication I've had from him since I left. He said he was coming here. To discuss our future."

"What does that mean?"

"I don't know. It could mean anything. He's had a year to coldly plot his revenge. He's a diabolically clever man. I don't know what evil sorcery allows him to know the things he does, but he has a way of knowing the exact punishment that will debase his victim most. He could force me to go back to London with him, force me to live under his roof. But I'm very much afraid that what he really means is that he's coming to force me to do the one thing that would disgust and horrify me the most."

"Which would be . . . ?"

She shuddered, feeling mortified. "To . . . give him his . . ." she swallowed, choking on the words, ". . . conjugal rights."

"My, my," he scoffed, "you *are* a damsel in distress."

She whirled toward him, facing the dark corner where she knew he sat, watching her like a phantom. "Please don't make light of me. I've only told you this because you insisted. I don't want your sympathy. I want your help."

For several moments, he pondered her words. Eventually he said, his tone softening, "Look, lady, I'd like to help you. I know who Dominic DeRohan is. I know he's a ruthless, miserable bastard. A man capable of anything—even with his wife. A man who, Lord knows, deserves to be dispatched to his just reward. But I also know he's a spectacular shot. And I have no intention of putting myself in the position of being his target."

"But you're a *marvelous* shot," she cried with new enthusiasm. "That's why I asked you. I heard the story of how you escaped from the Villa Cypress with a detachment of police on your heels. How you shot the hats off the heads of three pursuing gendarmes. They said, when they inspected the hats later, that each bullet hit squarely in the middle of each of the brass badges on the hats. You could just as easily have killed them, but instead you sent them retreating in terror, while at the same time letting them *know* you could kill them. *Nice-*

Matin said the Panther was the best shot on the Côte d'Azur, if not in all of France."

"Keystone Cops, all of them. Not a deadly shot in the bunch. Which, I shouldn't have to remind you, Dominic DeRohan is."

"But I have faith in you," she insisted. "Oh, I know it sounds deranged, and I don't blame you for thinking me mad."

In a bitter tone, he said, "I don't think you're mad. I think you saw an opportunity and took it. After all, I'm just a common thief. What does it matter if I get myself killed dispatching your husband?"

Was it her imagination, or did he actually sound hurt?

"You couldn't be more wrong."

"How am I wrong?"

"To imagine that I think of you as dispensable. On the contrary, it's as if you'd just stepped out of my dreams."

"You must have dark dreams then. I pity you. I know, because my dreams are full of demons as well."

She gazed into the darkness, wondering what he looked like, wondering why, if he was masked, he felt the need for such total blackness in which to hide. "Have you ever read Byron?" she asked.

"Byron who?"

"Lord Byron. He's one of the romantic poets. He created a character they call the 'Byronic Hero.' An idealized but darkly flawed character, brooding, an outcast or outlaw with a lack of respect for rank or social institutions. A loner with a troubled past. But he's also larger than life. A dynamic figure who takes what he wants and sweeps away the obstacles in his path. He defies convention and doesn't care what others think. I've been reading about a man like that for as long as I can remember. But I've never seen such a man in real life. Until tonight. Do you remember what I said when I was trying to keep you from leaving?"

"That you want me to kill your husband."

"No. I said, 'I want a hero.' It's the first line of Byron's *Don*

Juan. Somehow, when I first heard stories of your exploits, I thought *you* might be that hero. That's why I spread the false rumor I hoped would bring you here. I knew you were the one man who could defeat DeRohan. Perhaps the only man."

"A noble epitaph to write upon my tombstone."

Her face, which had been glowing with hope a moment before, fell. "You refuse to help me?"

"You've given me no compelling reason. Not even the prospect of a few meager pieces from your collection of baubles."

"But I've told you I can pay you."

"Thief I may be, but I'd like to think I'm not vile enough to kill a man for money. No, lady. I'm afraid there's only one payment I would consider for my services in this matter."

Her heart quickened. "And what is that?"

"You."

The word he'd spoken hung between them. Suddenly the night air was charged with something raw, something so potent she felt her breasts tighten. "Don't be absurd."

"You think it absurd that I might want your body?"

No man—not even Edwin—had ever spoken to her so frankly before. Taken aback, she averted her embarrassed gaze, attempting to disengage herself from this sticky turn in the conversation with some semblance of grace. "You wouldn't want me."

"Why not?"

"Must I tell you?" she asked helplessly, hoping he'd be gentleman enough to drop the subject.

But he merely responded in an amused tone, "I think perhaps you'd better."

She clasped her hands before her, squeezing the fingers tight. "I'm not . . ." Struggling to find a decorous way to say the words, she finally murmured, "I'm not experienced in such things."

"Come now. DeRohan is one of the—what was it you called him?—profligate rakes of his age. Surely the wife of such a man would learn a few—"

"Our marriage is in name only. I swore to my husband the instant the ceremony was over that I would never allow him to touch me. I've never broken that vow."

"But . . . you had lovers."

"*One* lover. And we only had one . . . encounter before DeRohan found out and killed him for it."

He rose to his feet and started toward her, coming into the dim light. He looked huge suddenly, stalking her way. "You expect me to believe that in your three years of married life, you only got fucked one time?"

The word shocked her, bringing her up short as if he'd just slapped her in the face. "Please do me the courtesy of not being crude."

"I'm a crude man, lady. Answer the question."

"Let's just say—if we must—that I know nothing of the art of . . . love."

"Or sex either, apparently."

"Please, must you—?"

He didn't even bother to listen to her protests. "Are you telling me the truth?"

"I swear it. Every word."

He peered at her for so long, it seemed he would never reply, and she began to squirm beneath his scrutiny. Finally, in a husky voice, he told her, "If you were my wife, you wouldn't be able to give such a testimony. I can assure you that."

She suddenly caught the aroma of night jasmine that perfumed the air. She took a step back, coming up against the bed. "Please . . . don't . . ."

He came closer, treading slowly. "So your husband neglects your education while he whiles away his nights with English whores." He stood before her now. "And meanwhile the fallen princess languishes in her ivory tower, dreaming of an outlaw who takes what he wants and snarls at the uncaring world. Who's man enough to wreak her vengeance for her." He was so close she could feel his breath on her cheek as he spoke. She jerked her head away. But he touched her averted chin with a gloved finger, tilting it so she was forced to look at him. "There's one thing you forgot to take into account in your *fantasia romantica.*"

"What's that?" she gasped.

He took her hand and placed it on his crotch, where a raging erection burned her palm.

"This."

Chapter 3

She tried to pull free, but his hand—massive in its leather armor—tightened on hers as he ground it into his swollen bulge. "Have you ever touched a man before? Of course you haven't. Because you're a lady, and ladies don't sully themselves by taking a man's cock in their hands."

"You animal!" she cried, fighting to push him away, her breath coming in jerky outraged gasps.

His other hand snaked out and grabbed her by the hair. She tried to move away, but the bed pressed into the backs of her knees, halting her retreat. His fist tightened in the flowing locks and slowly, but with unremitting insistence, he eased her head back, holding it pinned as he pressed her hand into him. She felt him lunge and swell beneath her palm, a pulsing, live serpent straining to strike.

"That's right," he growled. "I'm a strong, sex-starved predatory beast who already has the scent of you in his blood. And because you're a lady, you're afraid. Because in your fantasies, your brave, tortured hero bows down and worships at your feet. He brings you flowers and reads you poetry. But he doesn't dare touch you. Woman, you've been living in a dream world. Because no man—not even your precious hero—wants a lady in his bed. What he wants is a shamelessly aroused, yielding bitch—responsive . . . helpless . . . wild—a woman so thrilled by him that she shatters at his very touch."

He bent his head and razed her lips with his, crushing the tender flesh, forcing her mouth open with his tongue.

She felt her head begin to spin, felt herself losing something. It terrified her and she wrenched her mouth away.

"I'll scream," she said desperately. "My butler will come—"

His mouth crooked briefly. "I doubt very much that you'd want your butler to find you in such a compromising position."

Without warning, his gloved hand came to rest on the scalloped lace neckline of her nightgown. With one savage rip, he snatched the flimsy material from her body. It dangled before her scandalized eyes, a frothy piece of white nothing, gently blowing from a clenched black-gloved fist.

As the night breeze hit her, she gaped up at him, shivering with horror and panic.

Dear God! What have I done?

His gaze raked over the body he'd so summarily exposed. Beneath his breath, he swore, "Sweet Christ, you're more ravishing than I'd imagined."

Through her shock, she could feel him studying her trembling body, taking in the sight of it leisurely, hungrily, unashamed, like some heathen warrior accessing his spoils. She sensed, through her panic, that somehow she'd unleashed in him something raw and savage, some primal force she knew instinctively—now, when it was too late—couldn't be controlled or contained.

Reflexively, her hands came up to cover herself, seeking to shield her breasts from his rapacious glare. Even as she did, she caught the flare of something dangerous in the eyes behind the mask.

He twisted the hair in his fist—not enough to hurt her, just enough to emphasize the power he exerted over her—and slowly, deliberately, used his superior strength to move each of her hands stiffly to her sides. The blaze of his eyes warned her not to repeat the imprudent resistance.

"You may think it's poetry you love. Flowers and music and

moonlight walks along the beach. But what you really want is a man who'll rip away the shackles that bind you. The icy shackles of a body that's never been made to feel."

"You're wrong," she cried. "I wanted a champion, not a molester."

Abruptly, he swooped her up in his powerful arms, swinging her around so she felt dizzy and disoriented. She briefly felt the flex of his hardened muscles before he laid her on the bed. As she sank into the softness, he stood above her, a dark feral figure swathed in the light of the sterling moon. She tried to scoot across the bed, to move out of his reach, but he sat down and, reaching out, took her throat in his hand. She felt the leather close around her neck, not enough to choke her, but enough to hold her pinned where he wanted her, lying flat on her back and helpless beside him.

"You want a hero, woman? Then I'll give you a hero." He put his other hand on her abdomen, ignoring the unconscious flinch as she felt the leather on her flesh. "You needn't be afraid. I'm not going to hurt you." Slowly, possessively, his hand began to skim upward, spanning her waist, gliding over her ribcage, coming up to cup her breast. Even through the glove, he must surely feel the hammering of her heart. When she thrashed her head from side to side in protest, he merely tightened his grip on her throat so she was forced to lie still. When she did, he eased the pressure once again.

"A hero wouldn't rape you." His thumb began to toy with her nipple. A current shot through her. Against her will, her nipple hardened. He saw it and the corners of his mouth curled into a slow, knowing smile.

"He'd touch you—patiently—taking his time, showing you what it is to become a stimulated . . . vital . . . *woman*."

"Please," she whispered.

His hand moved on her, awakening responses she'd never felt before—treacherous curls of longing that made her want to hide her face in shame. "Your champion would naturally have your best interests at heart. But he wouldn't be swayed by the pleading of a woman who doesn't know yet what's in store for her." His hand explored her freely, noting how she gave a little jump as he brushed the ticklish underarm, how, despite her desire to resist, she softened and arched into him when he caressed the lobe of her ear.

"He'd permit you no inhibitions, no reservations." His hand trailed her flesh in a downward spiral, causing little shivers to flutter through her. She gritted her teeth, fighting the languorous desire to melt into his words and his hand, keeping her eyes closed tightly as she willed him to stop. But then, they flew open suddenly, because his hand had dipped into the hollow between her legs. He pried her legs open, splitting them wide. When she tried to close them, he pressed his thumb against her throat once again until, with a frustrated cry, she allowed him access. He touched her tender core, stroking gently as shock waves jolted through her. An instant later, he took his hand away, bringing it to her face.

"Put my glove in your teeth," he commanded. She did so because she knew he'd make her if she refused. As her teeth clamped down on the leather, he pulled his hand free. Taking the glove from her mouth, he tossed it aside.

Then she felt his naked fingers playing in the sensitive folds. "That's better," he said. "I want to feel your lust."

"I have no lust," she denied.

"Ah, but you will. It's the hero's mission to incite lust in his lady fair. In short, to teach you to moan and writhe."

As he stroked her with unhesitating fingers, she felt her juices begin to flow, smearing his hand. Her breath began to deepen, to catch in her throat. It became an agony, keeping up her guard, pretending she felt nothing. Because the truth was, he was nearly driving her mad.

"He'd force you to feel. Knowing you'd thank him later for his resolve."

She was in misery, trying to control herself, restrain her body's responses. She'd lost her sense of shock, even of decorum. She couldn't think. All her resistance was being mowed down with the insistent playing of his expert hand. His fingers were carrying her higher and higher, her hips desperate now to lift and arch into his hand. The hunger increasing like a runaway train.

Then, his mouth at her ear, he rasped, "*This* is how you should be touched."

He plunged his fingers into her as he dipped his head and took her nipple in his teeth. She wanted suddenly to throw back her head and scream. She was so famished now, so crazed with need, that she no longer cared what he thought of her. All she could do was feel his fingers in her slippery warmth, his mouth feasting on her nipple and making it hard. She wanted nothing more than to follow where he led, to revel in sensations her body had never known it was possible to feel.

"You can let yourself go," he whispered, his voice hushed and intimate at her ear. "You're being touched by a complete stranger. You'll never see his face, never know who he is. No one will ever know what you do tonight. I swear to you I'll never tell. And if you sell yourself to get what you want, there's no one to judge. Whatever pleasure you give or receive exists in another world."

He kissed her then. A fierce dominating kiss that demanded a response. Without realizing what she was doing, she moaned into his mouth.

But suddenly, his words penetrated the swirling mist in her head. Some last semblance of rational thought whispered that he'd just made a bargain with her. All she had to do was give into his desire, and he could make all her dreams come true.

He could free her from her prison.

Can I do this?

He sensed her withdrawal and put his mouth at her ear. "Don't think. I know your thoughts. What I want—what I demand—is your surrender. Uncontrollable, total, shameless surrender. Because a woman's body is a wasteland unless she can yield to a man's touch with glorious abandon."

There was something exhilarating in the authority he exerted over her. Her body began to move of its own volition as his merciless fingers heated her blood. Some part of her realized that he'd taken his hand from her throat—not needing it now—that it was grazing her body, touching her in ways that made her feel like a hair trigger ready to explode. His hands seemed to be everywhere, in her, all around her, driving her wild. He wouldn't stop. He played with her, with fingers and mouth, forcing more and more pleasure on a body unused to bliss, determined to make her transformation complete. Patiently, relentlessly, leashing his own urges, watching as bit by bit her resistance was whipped like waves upon the rocks. She began to pant, to moan, to make little whimpering sounds in the back of her throat that sounded as if she were begging for more. It was glorious, what he was doing to her. She'd never felt more helpless in her life, more as if she were being sucked down in a whirlpool of sensation that was like need and satisfaction, all at the same time.

And then she felt it rack through her. Lust as she'd never known it was possible to feel. Stark, raw, blistering. Sweeping everything away so she opened her legs wide, bucking now beneath the penetration of his hand, crying out for—what?

As her orgasm blasted through her, she knew. She felt the scream rise to her throat just before his mouth crashed down on hers. Muffling her impassioned shriek, knowing it was coming. Kissing her again, more insistently this time, hurtling her senses out of control as she spun and danced and floated at his command.

As she drifted down, she did so as another self. Gone was the woman she'd been, smashed beneath his hands. The new woman—the joyous wondrous woman whose body was juicy and ripe and knew, only now, that it had been starved—despaired when he began to move away. She clutched at him, wrapping her arms about his neck, seeking his astonishing mouth, moaning, "I had no idea. More . . . I want more."

Slowly, with his superior strength, he eased her away from him, holding her at arm's length. "Do you trust me now?" he asked.

"Yes. Oh, yes."

"And you'll do anything I ask?"

"Anything. Only do stop stalling and give me more."

She preened and stretched before him, seeking his mouth. She sensed his smile, as it was too dark to see him. The backs of his fingers grazed her breasts, dynamite to her already ragged senses. "Hurry," she urged.

He leaned over and picked something up off the floor. She heard the rip of material, then he was winding a torn strip of lace around her wrists. When she flinched, he told her, "I can't take the chance of you—in passion or from other motives— slipping off my mask. You've only had the most basic lesson in surrender. There's so much more to experience and enjoy. A woman only learns true surrender when she's had a thorough . . . and masterful . . . fucking. But to give you that, I must safeguard my disguise. So I ask again . . . do you want to know what you've been missing? And if so, will you trust me enough to surrender yourself completely?"

Did she trust him? She didn't even know him. But simmering in lust, her realities were transformed. She saw silhouetted before her neither thief not hero, but an irresistibly seductive man. A man who knew how to make her body sing.

"Yes," she told him, casting caution aside.

In a trance, she let him tie her hands deftly to the headboard so that she lay stretched out before him, her hands bound above her head, her breasts riding high.

And then he was on top of her, his manly weight welcome, his knowing hands causing her to cry out in need. He touched her, kissed her, licked her flesh like a jungle cat claiming his prize, until once again she felt delirious, tugging at the bonds at her wrists.

"Has anything in your poetry ever been as thrilling as this?"

With a single lunge, he drove himself inside. She cried out

again, but his mouth came down to stifle it. He drove into her hard and strong. Beautifully. Exquisitely. Forcefully. Leaving no question as to who was in charge. Her pleasure was so intense it was almost anguish. Feeling the same catapulting sensation she had before, feeling helpless and deliciously swept away by the magnificent force of his possession.

"Nothing was ever like this," she gasped. "I didn't know anything *could* be like this."

He clutched her face with both hands, looking down fiercely into her eyes. Then he kissed her face, her lips, moving into her with long luscious strokes, his breath one with hers until she felt herself meld into him. Carrying her with him higher and higher, hungrier than before, wild with passion. Sensing her impending climax, waiting for her, urging her on, until at last his patience was rewarded and he could let himself loose. Exploding together with her, clinging to her, catching her cries of passion in his mouth.

It seemed to Jules that the roar of the sea had consumed them. But as she lay spent beneath him and her breath slowed, she realized the roar had been in her head. It was so quiet in the room that his breathing sounded like thunder to her ears. She wanted so to hold him close, to tell him all the wonders a woman wants to tell the man who's shown her what he had . . .

But she couldn't. Her hands were still bound above her head.

"Untie me," she whispered, still simmering in a wondrously joyful satisfaction.

Her voice roused him. He sat up and looked around as if he'd lost track of where he was. But instead of reaching up to free her as she expected, he retrieved his discarded glove, put it on again, then rose, adjusting his clothing. He came to stand beside her, his gaze scanning her prone body, as if looking for one last time.

"And now you know," he said softly, in that husky whisper of a voice.

Yes, now she knew all that she'd been missing. She knew,

too, that she would never be the same. She was about to tell him so when his voice, changed now in some indefinable way, cut her off.

"Even so, it's not enough to convince me."

"Convince you?" She'd been so carried away, she couldn't think of what he meant.

"I'm not going to take on Dominic DeRohan. I have no wish to commit suicide. But thank you, just the same."

He reached up and gave the lace binding a tug, freeing her hands. Then, as quickly as a panther leaping from peril, he stepped onto her balcony and vanished into the night.

Chapter 4

She awoke to the sound of someone moving in her room. *He's returned!*

But, no. She opened her eyes to sunlight streaming in through the open windows and to her butler, Hudson, setting down her breakfast tray.

For a moment, she couldn't quite make the adjustment. She'd been so wrapped up in her dreams. All through the night, she'd been aware of the tingling of her body, of a quiver of excitement in the air, and strangely, of a surpassing peace. It was so unusual that a part of her sleep-drugged mind asked when she stirred: *What is this feeling?* And then snippets of memory would flash through her: The provocative rasp of his voice at her ear, urging her on . . . the feel of his strong fingers amusing themselves inside her as he watched . . . the dizzy, helpless bliss of coming together at last, taking his weight, his size, his very breath as her own . . . She'd never dreamed what ecstasy a woman could feel in submitting to such an enthralling . . . commanding . . . male. And again she would smile that smile of devilish satisfaction and burrow herself deeper into her silk bedding and drift back to sleep.

Even now, the disappointment that he hadn't returned, along with the recollection of his abrupt departure, couldn't dim the radiance that enveloped her. For the first time in more years than she could count, she felt girlish and young, like a sprite who might spring from her bed and dance about the room in the welcoming rays of the sun.

Hudson turned, saw the look on her face, and smiled. It was an odd smile, one she'd noticed from time to time, a secret smile as if thinking thoughts his mistress would never know. But this morning there was something about the smile that seemed faintly impertinent.

Suddenly she stilled. Had he heard the sounds of passion in the night?

But as was his custom, he proceeded to report on the happenings of the morning. "Not much in the post, I'm afraid," he said in the proper English accent assumed by the multitude of butlers in London drawing rooms. "A few invitations to various soirees. The usual solicitations from charities. A thank you note from Mrs. Simpson for the flowers you sent. Oh, and there's a letter from the mayor of Nice inviting you to take part in the dedication of the Great War Memorial on the tenth of September."

There had been much talk about this affair, but Jules had deliberately tuned it out. "That war memorial again. Why is everyone making such a fuss about it?"

"Oh, many reasons, Highness. It's the first to be built away from the battlefields. It's the first to be paid for by subscriptions from all the participating nations of the war. It's a symbol of reconciliation and peace, and a recognition that no one country can be blamed for it—that there were no villains, only victims. The dedication ceremony is going to be an international event."

"Send Mayor Clément my regrets, Hudson. You know how I feel about taking part in anything that even subtly links my family to the war. Is there anything else?"

She sipped the Vienna coffee he handed her, smiling to herself.

"Nothing that can't wait. You look happy this morning, Highness."

She watched him for a moment. He was certainly the

strangest butler who'd ever been in her service. While always maintaining the proper decorum—his butler's sense of propriety insisted on calling her "Highness," though she'd told him her family's titles had been rescinded after the war—he, at the same time, managed to convey a subtle familiarity and a concern for her well-being that was almost personal. Having grown up in the Habsburg palaces in Austria in an atmosphere of staid formality and strictly enforced protocol, Jules found this quality of his to be refreshing. She'd also long since grown accustomed to the fact that he was much too physically striking to be a butler—tall, well-built, with wavy dark brown hair, blue eyes, and a strong matinee-idol jaw. She was so accustomed to him by now that she didn't notice his appearance any more than she took note of the furniture in her house. But her friends found it to be a grand joke. *Trust Jules,* they laughed, *to have a butler who looks like Francis X. Bushman!*

They didn't know the secret sorrow he bore, one he'd shared with her a year ago when he'd happened into her service in such an unexpected way. She'd just left the dreary fogs of London and taken up residence on the sun-bathed South of France. She'd been swimming alone, off the beach at nearby Villefranche, when she suddenly found herself being carried off by a riptide. She was a strong swimmer and was certain she could fight her way back to shore, but instead she found herself weakening and being hurtled out to sea. Her frantic efforts to keep afloat were exhausting her strength. She knew she should scream for help, but her Habsburg pride—the disinclination to make a spectacle of herself—kept her silent long enough to be sucked below the surface before she could utter a sound. She knew then that she'd hesitated too long.

But suddenly, just as her lungs were bursting and she realized through her panic that she was going to die, she'd felt firm hands pull her up and carry her out of the reach of the deadly current. "You needn't worry," he'd told her, as if reading her mind. "No one else saw you." Quietly, efficiently, and with a minimum of fuss, he'd helped her to the shore, away from the crowded center of the beach where she could recover in privacy.

Falling to her knees in the sand, gasping for breath, she'd looked up at him—a muscular man gleaming like a sun God—asking, "Who are you?"

"I'm Hudson, Ma'am."

"No ... *what* are you? To be able to swim like that? A sailor? An Olympic swimmer?"

He'd chuckled. "Hardly, Ma'am. I'm just a humble visitor to this part of the world, accustomed to swimming the Thames each morning. Actually, I'm in service. Between engagements at the moment, I'm afraid. In fact, if you happen to know of any good families in the area looking for a butler, I have excellent references."

She'd eyed him skeptically. "*You* are a butler?"

Stiffly, with a hint of injured pride, he'd told her, "My family has been in service for three generations."

"You'll have to forgive me—Hudson, was it? I didn't mean to sound as if I were mocking you. But I'm very much afraid, Hudson, despite your references, that you're much too, shall we say ... arresting a man for your desired post. The husbands I know would feel most uncomfortable having a butler in their employ who might upset the equilibrium of the ladies of the household. But then, surely you've had this trouble before?"

He'd looked at her for a moment in a most un-butler-like way, an acute sort of look as if carefully deciding upon his next words. Then, lowering his lashes, he'd said gravely, "Should it be necessary, I could put their minds at ease on that score. I was wounded in the war in a manner that would make any question of a dalliance impossible."

Jules's heart broke for him. There was something almost noble in the dignity with which he'd spoken, in the careful tone meant to hide his pain.

"I, too, have a war wound," she'd told him. "Except that

mine isn't physical. It's in my soul. So we're really rather alike, aren't we?"

"I suppose we all of us carry wounds or scars of some sort. All of us who lived through the war."

"I suppose we do. That's why Gertrude Stein calls us the 'Lost Generation.' Because we're so lost inside, and then try to cover it up by chasing bright and mindless gaiety to dispel the gloom."

"Yes," he'd agreed. "Because of course, one soon tires of being lost and wants to find his way to something—more."

She'd felt a bond with him that she'd never felt with any servant, not even the governess who'd cared for her as a child. So she'd confessed to him something she would never have told anyone else. "As it happens, I have need of a butler. I've only just reopened my house. But to be perfectly honest, I'm in a rather fragile state at the moment. I feel the need for someone who might—" She stopped, uncertain how to put it.

"Take care of you?"

She'd nodded mutely because by saying the words, he'd brought the taste of tears to the back of her throat.

"I should consider it a privilege and a pleasure," he'd told her solemnly. "They say when you save a life, that life belongs to you, in a fashion. From this day forth, I shall endeavor to care for and protect my lady to the best of my ability."

He'd reminded her of a knight of Camelot pledging his fealty to the queen. Since then, he'd become indispensable to her, handling everything she threw at him with the same quiet unflappable assurance, no questions asked. But over time, he'd become more than her butler. While always keeping his place and maintaining the proper decorum, he'd become her advisor, her confessor, her friend. The one person to whom she could tell even her most embarrassing secrets, confident that he'd carry them to his grave.

But she hadn't told him anything of her scheme to employ the Panther. He would have gone to any lengths to talk her out of such insanity. But now that it was a fait accompli, she was bursting to tell him. He could do nothing about it now, and he was the only one she could trust with such an explosive confidence.

And yet . . . would it be insensitive to do so? Poor Hudson, to never experience what she had last night. She'd never realized before how dreadful it must be for him, living like a eunuch. She wondered if he'd been able to turn off his desire for women simply because his body could no longer function. She'd never thought about it before. But that was because, before last night, she'd been a sort of eunuch herself.

Still, he knew the one thing about her that she couldn't tell her new modern friends, so cynical and urbane. He knew that after nights in their company, she'd come back home and read romantic poetry late into the night, escaping into fictional worlds where men and women loved desperately and often tragically. Where they found lives not of rote and routine, but of high adventure. They'd even made a game of it. The next morning, she would tell Hudson what had happened to the heroine in her poetry as if it had happened to her.

He always seemed to enjoy the interlude of fantasy before they tackled the daily schedule. But then, it hadn't been real.

While she was debating, he spotted something on the floor by her bed and bent to pick it up. When he rose, he had in his hand the nightgown the Panther had ripped and used to bind her wrists. She'd been in such a tizzy that she'd completely forgotten she was naked beneath the sheet.

"I see we've had a bit of an accident, Highness. Moths, perhaps? I shall see to it that it's disposed of at once. And instruct Denise to be more careful when inspecting your attire."

He was folding the shredded gown in such a serious way. He knew very well moths had nothing to do with its condition, but he would never ask.

Suddenly, she laughed. Pulling the silk sheet to her chin, she said, "I've been a naughty girl, Hudson."

"Have you, Highness?"

"I've done something outrageous. Something so scandalous, you'll never believe it."

"Have you, indeed?"

"I've had a visitor in the night. A man I invited in a cunning sort of way. A most spectacular man."

"Ah, Highness, I see we've been reading Lord Byron again," he said with a twinkle in his eye. "Who was it this time? Childe Harold or Don Juan?"

"No, Hudson, this was real. It happened. A daring thief was actually here, in this room, last night."

"My mistake, Highness. You've been reading stories about the Panther, then?"

She sat up in bed, careful not to let the sheet slip. "Yes, the Panther! He came here last night, looking for my jewels."

He pretended to look around the room. "But of course the jewels aren't here. Did he take anything else?"

"Only me." She giggled, hugging her knees.

"Am I to infer, then, Highness, that the theft was not un-welcome?"

"More than welcome, it was glorious! It was beyond any-thing I've ever imagined. It was . . ." She stopped abruptly, lift-ing a brow. "You don't believe me, do you? You think we're playing our game."

He lowered his gaze so she couldn't see the look in his eyes. "I believe everything Her Highness tells me. And I believe Her Highness deserves whatever happiness comes her way, no mat-ter how it may appear."

Did he still think she was relating a fantasy? Or was this his sly way of acknowledging her truth?

"You're the most exasperating butler there ever was, Hud-son."

With a bow he said, "I don't doubt it, Highness," and left the room.

She wasn't remotely hungry, so she left untouched her breakfast of tropical fruits and fresh-baked croissants and, grabbing the first thing she could find in the line of closets between her bedroom and sitting room, she slipped into a butter-cream summer frock with a low back and a fringed skirt that came to just below her knees. It was a contemporary, flirty creation, very much a product of the Jazz Age in which she lived, strikingly at variance with her elegant eighteenth-century French furnishings.

Eager to be away from the morning household bustle, she left her private apartment on the second floor and went out into the arched columned gallery that ran at mid-length on four sides between the reception hall below and the trompe l'oeil ceiling above, painted to look like a blue summer sky. Peering down, she could see the maids polishing the vast mosaic Pompeii-style floor, dusting the statues and priceless paintings on the walls.

She exited through the two-story staircase enclosed within a half-circular wall of glass that looked out over the green hills and the sea.

Cap Ferrat was a narrow peninsula on which the Riviera's most exclusive homes were located. Once mostly owned by Belgium's King Léopold II, it was the showplace of old money and the long-standing winter abode to Europe's highest ranking aristocracy. Rêve de l'Amour was the largest of its villas and the most spectacularly situated. It was the creation of her grandmother, a Bavarian princess, who'd loved the Mediterranean and had constructed on twelve hectares of barren land atop the highest, narrowest point of the peninsula a sprawling terracotta and white evocation of an Italian Renaissance palazzo. The views from this luxurious perch were breathtaking, with the Bay of Beaulieu and its wedding-cake casino on one side and the Bay of Villefranche with its charming port and fleet of ships on the other. The gardens spread out from the back of the house over four hectares of land, a harmonious counterpoint to the modern hectic world. It had taken her grandmother's workers seven years to dynamite and cart away the original rock and create an oasis of peaceful opulence and exquisite taste.

To visitors who called, her house struck them as a sumptuous, paradisiacal mansion on a grand scale. But to Jules, who'd spent her childhood in palaces with more than a thousand rooms, Rêve de l'Amour was simply a country villa, so named by her grandmother because she'd used it for clandestine meetings with the lover she'd cherished and lost.

Skirting the maids, Jules made her way back through the house to the terrace overlooking the lawns, where no fewer than twelve gardeners toiled to maintain the aura of tranquil retreat. The French garden, the largest of seven with different themes, stretched before her in the morning sun, the cypresses and Aleppo pines and palms swaying in the ever present breeze from the sea that kept the property cool, even in the most scorching summer heat.

Going down the steps, she passed between the smaller fountains on either side to the large central fountain, where a row of water sprays shot up and danced twenty feet in the air. From there, a rectangular pool extended some two hundred feet between the manicured lawns, like the pool at the Taj Mahal, where it met a stepped waterfall spilling into it from the high hill on the far side. She made her way alongside the pool, climbing the stone steps of the hill, the sounds of gently rushing water and birdsong sweet in the morning air. At the top, she came to the Temple of Venus, a circular columned open gazebo with a domed roof fashioned from marble, in the center of which stood a graceful statue of Venus, Roman goddess of love.

This focal point could be seen from the house, but the trees and luxuriant plants that surrounded it on three sides gave it an air of privacy, a sanctuary Jules had always loved. She'd come up here as a young girl to read her treasured books of heroes and their lady loves, to dream her own personal dreams, away from prying eyes.

But today, as she sat on the marble bench facing the temple from the side, she drank in the familiar surroundings with a new sense of wonder. However briefly, she'd lived her secret fantasies for one enchanted night. She was no longer merely the barren, bartered wife of an insufferable fiend. As she hugged herself, her body tingled anew with the memory of what his hands and tongue had done to her, and she blushed like a new bride. It seemed that she could still feel him inside, so large and hard that he'd fit her like the last missing piece of a puzzle. She smiled dreamily, feeling altogether different than she had the day before. She'd been swept away by a man who in her mind was not a wanted thief, but who'd taken on the proportions of a reckless hero, casting the world's conventions aside. A man who was like no other she'd ever known in her sheltered life. He'd taken her girlish dreams and given them a raw sexual edge that was far more thrilling than her own arid notions had ever been. Because he'd forced her to face an aspect of herself that she hadn't known was there, she felt strangely stronger, capable of handling whatever came her way.

It didn't even matter that the Panther had turned down her proposition. It was a desperate idea, born of panic upon learning of her husband's intention to reenter her life. She probably couldn't have gone through with it anyway. Despise DeRohan as she did, she didn't have it in her to be a party to his murder, however cloaked it might be by the pretense of a duel.

No, she would have to think of another solution. But in some mystical way, the Panther had made her feel she could. As if she'd absorbed some of his courage and audacity and made it her own.

She wondered suddenly who he was. He'd given her no clue. He spoke Italian in a whispery tone surely meant to disguise his true voice. His Italian was perfect, but it was a vernacular form, not the more cultured language she'd learned from her tutors. She couldn't tell whether it was his native tongue or a second language he'd perfected. She didn't even know what he looked like.

Not that it mattered. She'd never see him again. But she'd always treasure the memory of the gift he'd given her. For showing her that the life she'd been living, the persona she'd adopted, had been a lie. He'd made her feel there was more to her than what her battered ego had supposed.

Someday when I'm an old woman, I can look back on that one moment of insane rebellion against everything I am, and it will give me some strange comfort.

But while she felt changed inside, her circumstances hadn't altered. Unwanted, the words of DeRohan's telegram ran through her mind. *Arriving Cap Ferrat last week of June to discuss our future . . .*

The last week of June. Just a few more days of freedom.

She shuddered, cursing him for intruding on her happy mood. Well, he'd find a more formidable opponent this time around. She'd see what he wanted, inform him that she had no intention of falling in line, and send him packing, leaving her in peace once again.

It struck her then how odd it was that the Panther's domination of her had thrilled her so, while her husband's left her feeling abused. But then, the Panther had sought to give her pleasure, when all DeRohan wanted was to crush her spirit.

Before she realized it, the sun was high in the sky. The faint growl of her stomach made her realize she'd had no breakfast and it was nearing noon. She left reluctantly, taking the path down the steps, but when she reached the bottom, she saw the garden staff rushing about the grounds, gathering armfuls of cut flowers with uncharacteristic haste.

What was going on?

As she crossed the lawn alongside the long pool, she saw Mimi, one of the housemaids, rushing toward her, flapping her hands in agitation. "Madame, Madame . . ." She stopped before her, wheezing.

"What is it, Mimi?"

The maid struggled to catch her breath, then gasped out in French, "Monsieur has arrived."

"Which monsieur?"

"Why, the master, Madame. Your husband. Monsieur DeRohan."

Jules looked up at the villa, her happy mood vanished.

Mimi rushed on, "He arrived half an hour ago. We did not expect him so soon. And even then, we were told his visit would be brief. But Madame, he has come with many, many trunks. He has been moving in since he arrived, ordering us about, taking over the house. The staff is in a tumult, Madame. We did not know what you would want, so naturally we've done as he instructed—"

Moving in . . .

Taking over the house . . .

Her house.

She'd just see about that.

Chapter 5

She retraced her steps back into the house feeling heavy with dread, as if she were climbing into a pit she knew to be full of snakes. She tried to remind herself that she was stronger than when she'd seen him last, when he'd lacerated her with the announcement that he'd just killed her lover—coldly, unfeelingly, ever in control. Taking a malicious pleasure in being the bearer of this news.

Just speak to him calmly and find out what he wants. Don't let him goad you into losing your temper.

But what of his *temper?*

Inside, she was greeted by pandemonium. Servants scurried to and fro, carrying suits to be pressed and shoes to be polished, carting trunks up and down the stairs. They bobbed hasty curtseys to her when they saw her, then dashed off with the harried look of subordinates who'd just had the whip cracked over their heads.

It helped to anchor Jules, to solidify her resolve. She wasn't about to behave like one of DeRohan's hired help, cowering at the sight of him.

She crossed the reception hall beneath the towering gothic arches and took the stairs up to the second floor of the east wing. There, in the sitting room of the guest apartment, she saw her husband, conferring with Hudson as several maids unpacked the trunks that cluttered the tapestried Louis XVI room.

Dominic DeRohan had always been an imposing man. Well over six feet in height, he was nothing like the aristocrats of her acquaintance: soft, well-mannered, schooled in the art of dance and social graces. She hadn't actually known him before their marriage, but he owned the Carlton Hotel and was a frequent presence on the Côte, so she'd inevitably caught the snippets of gossip that followed in his wake: How he'd grown up poor in the streets of London, but through ruthless determination, an inexhaustible capacity for work, and an unflinching readiness to bully his competitors, he'd built a business empire from nothing and amassed a fortune that put most of his contemporaries to shame; how he'd been a decorated pilot in the war, gunning down enemy planes with the same pitiless relish with which he destroyed his business rivals; how this combination of war hero and cold-blooded raider made him a source of dark fascination to the women who brazenly solicited invitations to his bed. But Jules knew these two seemingly contradictory aspects of his character were one and the same—fueled by his need to crush anything in his path.

He was dressed as always in a dark suit, even in the heat of the season, but despite the expert tailoring and unmistakable aura of wealth, there was something craggy and rugged and raw about his appearance. He reminded her of a Scottish warrior accustomed to roaming the Highlands who'd stuffed himself into a Saville Row suit and was passing himself off as a gentleman.

When he sensed her presence and turned to look at her, she nearly flinched at the stark look in his fierce eyes. She'd forgotten that intimidating, penetrating stare, how, with a furrow of his heavy brows, he could make even the most hardened negotiator squirm in his seat. She could feel his daunting energy from across the room, a force that allowed him, without seeming to try, to beat people down until they acquiesced to his demands.

He stared at her long enough that she was able to note the

changes since she'd seen him last. He was thicker about the middle—the result, no doubt, of too many business dinners, unless his mistresses had been spoiling him in his wife's absence. The beard and mustache he wore, dark like his hair, were closer cropped than she remembered. But there was no mistaking the possessive cruelty that came to his eyes as he took in her appearance.

He waved an imperious hand at the servants. "Out. All of you," he ordered.

The maids scampered away as though shot from a cannon. Hudson followed more slowly, but Jules put her hand on his sleeve as he passed, saying in a gentle voice, "It was good of you, Hudson, to offer your assistance to Mr. DeRohan, but in future I should be grateful if you remember that you answer to me."

Hudson cast a quick glance at DeRohan, who didn't bother to look at him, then said, "As you wish, Highness," and left the room.

DeRohan raised a brow and addressed her. "I begin to understand the charms of the South." His English accent was properly aloof, but the guttural undertones of his voice hinted at the pains he'd taken to banish a rougher form of speech. "It seems it isn't the sunshine that keeps my wife a fugitive, but a butler much too eye-catching for his own good. Is he even a butler? Or is this merely a clever way of camouflaging your latest paramour?"

Twenty-four hours ago, Jules would have been outraged by such a suggestion. But today she flushed with the knowledge of what she'd done the night before. She must handle him carefully, but not too meekly. If she backed down without demur, he might suspect his accusation was warranted, albeit with another man.

"I'd expect that from someone who sees the worst in human nature. But I won't have you maligning Hudson with your indecent suppositions."

"My indecent suppositions have proved only too accurate,

as I recall. Why should I suppose otherwise when you so clearly want him for yourself and hasten to defend his honor before even bothering to greet your long-lost husband?"

"You must take my word for it."

"You'll forgive me, I'm sure, but the word of an adulterous wife is hardly meritable proof."

"Very well," she sighed, hating to betray Hudson's confidence, but badly needing to derail DeRohan from this train of thought. "If you must know, Hudson would be incapable of living up to your allegations. He was injured in the war."

"How convenient for him."

She felt her temper flare. He was the only person she'd ever known who could anger her as he did. She'd been brought up to be seen and not heard, to hold her tongue even when she disagreed, to be pleasing and gracious and avoid confrontation at all costs. She knew how to be a princess, a hostess, a slave to duty. But she'd never learned how to be in the same room with DeRohan and keep her composure.

"I'd naturally assumed that you'd stay at the Carlton," she said to change the subject.

"Why should I, when I have a perfectly good home right here?"

"*My* home," she corrected.

"That, Juliana, depends on my good graces. Technically, you violated our agreement when you moved back to France, which means this house belongs to me. I could go to my solicitors and they would have the title out of your hands in five minutes flat. Everyone knows you've been living here. It's easy enough to prove."

"I left London because you murdered someone near and dear to me. What decent woman wouldn't?"

"If you were a decent woman, you wouldn't have had a lover, now, would you? Besides which, I murdered no one. I dispatched that sniveling bastard in a duel of honor."

"Honor!" she cried, losing her battle with self-control. "The best shot in London against a gentle soul who never fired a pistol in his life. You goaded him into that duel with the intent of murder and you know it."

"Did you really think I'd let you make a fool of me?" he snarled. "Allow everyone in town the spiteful pleasure of gossiping that my wife was tarting around on me? No, Juliana. I protect what I own."

"You don't own me."

Calmly, almost as if he were moving in slow motion, DeRohan reached out and grabbed her arm, jerking her close and piercing her with an unflinching glare. "You fancy yourself independent because I've allowed you to run free for so long. But that's an illusion that ends now. You came to me bought and paid for. Yes, I killed your precious Edwin. And I'd do it again. I will, in point of fact, destroy any man you foolishly choose to take up with. You may not warm my bed, but by God, you'll warm no one else's either. Know it, Juliana. Remember it."

Once again, despite her resolve, she tasted her fear of him. She swallowed, trying to dispel it, and said with all the dignity she could muster, "Take your hand off me."

For a moment, she thought he'd refuse. Then, just as abruptly as he'd taken hold of her, he dropped his hand and turned away.

"I've come to tell you," he said conversationally, "that your happy little sojourn has come to an end. I can see that I've been too lenient. I allowed you to live apart from me in London. I have courteously—some might say indulgently—given you time to lick your wounds. I've been as patient and understanding a husband as ever there was. But now my patience is at its end. From today forward, you're going to start living up to your agreement. For the time being, I'm establishing my residence here. I have a specific mission that's vital to me, and as it happens, I need your help."

"Help with what?"

"Two years ago there was a revolution in Persia. The new leader—they call him the Shah—has voided all the country's previous oil concessions. He's shopping around for a new recipient for those concessions. I intend to be that recipient."

"Why oil?"

"The man who gets those concessions and has the ships, as I do, to transport the oil around the world, will become the richest—and most powerful—European of the Machine Age."

"What do I have to do with that?"

"It seems the Shah is an admirer of the fallen Habsburg Dynasty for the same reason the rest of the world hates it. A family that managed to rule most of Europe for more than six hundred years—two hundred years longer than Rome did. The fact that I have a Habsburg wife has intrigued the Shah enough that he's agreed to come and discuss the possibility of a partnership. So you see, my dear, you will be an enormous help to me in the competition to acquire those unimaginably lucrative contracts."

"And if I tell him what a blackguard you really are?"

"Don't even joke about that. You don't have any idea what I can do. Go out and ask some of my competitors just how unpleasant I can be when I'm crossed."

She believed him. There was a ferocity in his eyes she'd never seen before.

"I want this," he ground out. "I *will* have it. These contracts are more important to me than you are, but I need you in order to get them. So listen carefully to how things are going to be. Not only will I live in this house, I will be master of it. You will play the role of my devoted wife and helpmate, and will obey my every whim. Because if you don't, you'll lose the house and jewels you love so well."

"You've always wanted them," she accused. "This house, the jewels. It isn't enough that you took my father from me. But you're not going to take them, too. You say you have a mission, well so do I. All you care about is raking in more and more money until you don't even know how much you have. But I care about more than that. I've been given a sacred trust, to safeguard all that's left of my family, of our old way of life, of everything we stood for. I swore to my father that I would protect the Habsburg name with my life. I even sold myself to you. All to keep the last meager remnants of what's left to us. So don't think I'm going to let you take them from me. You'll have to kill me first."

"Then you had better start acting like the wife you agreed to be. Because you're wrong, Juliana. I don't have to kill you. All I have to do is assert my legal rights. So long as you play the role I dictate and stay in line, I shall keep the house and jewels in your name. But the minute you give me any trouble, I shall seize this house and level it into the rock heap it once was. And I'll melt your precious jewels into scrap metal."

The reality of her situation had never been more plainly stated. If she'd had a knife in that moment, she'd happily have plunged it into his vile heart.

"As soon as the bulk of my things are unpacked, I'll be off for four nights on business. I suggest you use the time to think over what I've said. And get some rest. You're looking a trifle ill, for all that you're as brown as a gypsy. That won't do. By the time the Shah arrives, I expect you to be looking your best. Thank God you haven't bobbed your hair in that ridiculous fashion. That's something, at least."

She was burning under his scrutiny. Between clenched teeth, she managed to ask, "Am I dismissed, then?"

His gaze flicked over her. "For now."

She stormed off, racing through the house to the west wing and the sanctuary of her own apartment, slamming the door behind her. Tears were streaming down her cheeks. Tears of anger, frustration, and fear of living under the thumb of this deranged sadist. She sank onto the velvet stool before her vanity and put her head in her hands on the table, wracked by sobs, her eyes stinging with hot tears. What would the rest of her life be like? How could she bear it, living under the same roof with him?

But it wasn't long before the helplessness was replaced by a growing sense of rage. She looked up, catching sight of herself in the vanity mirror. Her face looked pale, her eyes red and swollen, her blond hair falling in tangles about her shoulders. *At least you haven't bobbed your hair in that ridiculous fashion...*

In a fury, she rifled through the drawers until she found a pair of scissors. Grabbing a handful of hair, she began to hack at it with violent strokes. Again and again, until the carpet at her feet was littered with strands of severed golden hair. She looked again at herself in the mirror, surging with satisfaction, vindication, revenge. The face that looked back at her appeared altered suddenly. She felt younger, lighter, freer somehow.

But the sense of emancipation was short-lived. When the dust settled, it was futile, the rash rebellion of a child. The loss of her hair would change nothing. DeRohan would return and already she could feel the life draining out of her.

What can I do?

Through her despair, the memory of her adventure of the night before came floating to the surface of her mind. Once again, that same impulse seized her. This midnight specter ... this Panther ... she sensed again that he was the one man who was more than a match for DeRohan. The man who could set her free. He was clever and brave, and from all accounts, afraid of nothing. And the truth was, she could make all the resolutions she wanted, but if she was going to come out of this in one piece, she would need help. Somehow, she felt certain the Panther could think of a way out of this awful mess.

But how?

She'd lured him to her once with the false bait of the Habsburg jewels. She could do it again. But this time, he wouldn't be fooled. She'd have to put the goods on the table.

The corners of her mouth began to tug into a smile as a new plan began to unfold.

Her mind racing now, she went to the buzzer and pushed

the button. In a few moments, Hudson entered. He stopped short when he saw her, startled as he took in the mass of hair on the Savonnerie rug.

"Highness?" he asked, uncertainly.

"Hudson, call Monsieur Philippe and ask him to come as soon as he can to give me a proper trim. I've decided to cut my hair."

"Very well, Highness." He paused briefly. "The master intends to remain, I understand."

"Don't call him that," she snapped irritably. "My husband is not my master. We won't discuss his plans at present. I'll give you instructions as they're needed."

"As you wish, Highness."

His sudden stiffness jogged her. What was she doing? Treating Hudson as if he were just one of the hired help, when in reality he knew of her feelings for DeRohan and her dread of what she'd thought was but an impending visit. More gently she added, "With any luck, Hudson, the situation will prove temporary."

"Then we'll hope for good fortune, Highness."

Dear Hudson. He always knew just what to say. "The Clews's masked ball is the night after tomorrow, isn't it?"

"It is, Highness."

"I've decided to go after all. Have Madame Giverny bring by a selection of costumes this afternoon for me to choose from."

"I shall telephone her immediately I've rung up the hairdresser."

Jules played with the fringe on her dress as she thought. "And Hudson, I'd like you to make some other calls this afternoon. And have the Rolls washed and ready in the morning. I'll want you to drive me."

"Where are we going, Highness?"

"To Nice."

"May I ask the nature of our outing?"

"We're going to pay a visit to the bank vault."

"I see. And may I be so bold as to ask what Your Highness is planning?"

She turned to him with a twinkle in her eye. "Planning? Why, not a thing, Hudson. I've just decided the Clews's ball would be the perfect opportunity to show off some of my jewels."

Chapter 6

Monsieur Jarot, the manager of the Nice Banque de Marchés, pulled out the oversize safety deposit box and, with some effort, walked it across the floor of the vault to a table where Jules waited with Hudson standing behind her.

At her nod, Hudson lifted the metal lid as three eager faces crowded around to gawk, then retrieved the various sized deep blue velvet boxes, laying them on the table.

Jules could feel the nearby reporters holding their breaths. Pausing momentarily to build the suspense, she opened the lids one by one, displaying a dazzling array of gems. It was a small collection—a mere portion of the pieces that had been passed down through the Habsburg family for generations—just four matched sets of necklace, bracelet, and earrings. But they were crafted by some of the most celebrated eighteenth and nineteenth century jewelers in Europe, and the stones were some of the finest their audience had ever seen, gleaming seductively, even in the harsh overhead light.

The gasps of the audience were audible. Only Hudson kept an impassive face. He was well acquainted with the gems.

Jacques Ronin from the *Cannes Soir* asked, "Which of these magnificent pieces belonged to Marie Antoinette?"

"These." Jules held to her throat a string of massive creamy pearls. The clasp was fashioned from a large emerald surrounded by sixteen diamonds. "As you may know, Antoinette was exceptionally fond of pearls. This necklace was one of her favorites."

"May we take a picture of you with them on?"

"Of course." It was exactly what she wanted. Hudson quickly fastened the clasp, brushing aside the chic new bob that framed her face in soft golden curls. She'd worn an unadorned platinum dress, something that would offset, but not contrast with, the jewels. When she was ready, the photographers came forward from the rear of the immense vault. Several bursts of flash powder blinded the spectators and sulfur smoke tinged the air.

"Exactly what relation do you bear to the tragic queen?" asked the reporter from *Nice-Matin*.

"She would be my aunt, four generations removed. After the Revolution, the pearls were saved from the mob by her daughter and eventually returned to the family. My father gave them to my mother as a wedding present."

"I understand, Madame DeRohan, that the Austrian State confiscated all your family's property. How then did you get these jewels out of the country?"

"My mother sewed them into our corsets."

She was about to change the subject when another reporter asked, "Your mother was killed trying to leave Vienna, is that not correct?"

"Yes, that's correct. Perhaps you'd like to see—"

"Stoned to death, they said. Is there any truth to the story?"

"Unfortunately, it's true."

"Could you tell us how it happened?"

"I really don't see—"

Hudson stepped in. "Gentlemen, surely this has nothing to do with the subject at hand. These memories are quite painful for Madame DeRohan. I feel certain you wouldn't wish to cause her undue pain."

"It seems to me that the story of the smuggling of the jewelry out of Vienna gives them the element of tragedy and romance an eager public would greedily gobble up. If you wish to call attention to the pieces, as you so clearly do, what better way than to break the public's heart with the glamorous tale?"

Hudson was about to argue, but Jules put her hand on his sleeve and said quietly, "It's quite all right. I shall tell these kind gentlemen what they wish to know." It wasn't something she cared to talk about, but if it was the only way to get them to print the story, she was resolute enough to do even that. She began softly, "After the war, all the members of my family were given the option of either renouncing any claim to the throne or going into exile. Some of my relatives decided to stay and sign away their claim, but my father chose to go. We were the last to leave. We were being watched by the authorities, but my mother had known this was coming and secretly hid what jewels she could and sewed them into the linings of our corsets a little at a time. The public had turned against the family. They blamed us for the war . . . for so many things. There had been riots all day long, so we'd decided to wait and leave late at night. But some of the mob had been watching for us. As we came out, they began to throw rocks, yelling obscenities. My father hurried me to the auto to shield me, but as he did so, the crowd closed in on Mother, hurling more and more rocks at her. We were able to get her into the car and speed away, but she died that very night."

A silence followed. Each of the men stared at her, moved by the quiet dignity with which she'd told her tale.

"And these jewels are all you have left of her," one of them said at last.

"That and my house. And my memories."

"One could say that your mother died saving the jewels."

"Yes," Jules said. It was what her father had told her numerous times.

Hudson picked up one of the velvet boxes and passed the sapphire and yellow diamond necklace before them. "But you gentlemen haven't even seen the rest . . ."

So effortlessly they didn't seem to notice, he steered their attention away from Jules and back to the gems, detailing each of the pieces, telling them the carat weight of the rubies, informing them that the emeralds had once belonged to the Maharaja of Rajasthan. Holding up a thirty-six inch strand of three-carat diamonds strung together like pearls, Jules felt a rush of gratitude. She could always count on Hudson.

As the photographers took their pictures, a reporter said, "There has been such interest in these pieces, and yet this is the first time you have ever cooperated with the press to show them. Why now?"

"As you know, the Clews are holding a charity masked ball tomorrow night at the Chateau de la Napoule to benefit wounded war veterans who have been forgotten. The public isn't invited, but donations would be most appreciated. It's my intention to raise interest in such a worthy cause by wearing some of the jewels publicly for the first time."

"Which will you wear?"

She considered. "You have a picture of me in the pearls, so perhaps I'll wear them."

"But Madame DeRohan, are you not apprehensive to put these irreplaceable stones at risk when this Panther criminal is plundering the villas of the coast?"

"*Oui, oui,* the Panther. Do you not quake to wear them while the beast still prowls?"

Jules waved a dismissive hand. "The Panther, from all accounts, sneaks into homes when all are asleep and there's virtually no chance of detection. I daresay a man as cautious of his liberty would hardly be so foolhardy as to risk exposure in such a public setting. No, gentlemen, for all his reported bravado, I wager this Panther is in reality a cowardly creature of the night. He's not going to come anywhere near my pearls."

One of the reporters gulped. "May we quote you?"

Jules lowered her lashes so they couldn't read the triumphant gleam in her eyes. "By all means."

With Hudson at the wheel, the white Rolls Royce convertible eased through the gothic arched stone entry of the front wall of the Chateau de la Napoule, an estate that had once served as a fortress in the fourteenth century. An eccentric American couple, Henry and Marie Clews, had rescued the crumbling edifice destroyed during the French Revolution, and had lovingly restored it to its original medieval splendor, complete with turrets and towers, creating a fantasy world of their own where peacocks, swans, ibis, and cranes pecked freely about the grounds. To visit the chateau was to take a journey back to the time of Sir Walter Scott, where troubadours sang and knights jousted to impress the ladies of the court.

The perfect setting for a masquerade ball.

As they pulled up to the front courtyard with its cloistered façade, Jules took a gulp for courage. She'd decided to dress as Marie Antoinette with a heavy white powdered wig. But instead of costuming herself as the queen holding court, she'd chosen instead to replicate her ancestor's more playful disposition by wearing the flouncy eighteenth-century shepherdess attire the queen had favored while cavorting at Versailles. The white dress had a voluminous skirt with a low décolletage and frilly peasant sleeves that bared her chest and shoulders and afforded a blank canvas for the showcasing of the Antoinette pearls.

"It's peculiar, Hudson," she said, putting her hand over her pounding heart. "We've played our game so many times, imagining all sorts of adventures where I was a woman of intrigue, much bolder and more courageous than I could ever really be. Harmless stuff and fancy. Yet here we are, about to embark on an adventure that has the potential to be far more daring than anything we ever concocted. Never once in all our imaginings did I foresee how nervous I would be. I swear my heart is about to take flight."

"We could always call it off, Highness."

"Oh, I couldn't do that. It's my only chance of contacting the man. I think I'm more nervous for him than I am for myself. It's only just occurred to me the risk I've asked him to take. Of course, there's no guarantee that he's even seen my challenge, or that he'll take the bait if he has, but if he *should* come, and should be caught because of me—"

"I hope Her Highness knows what she's doing. It's not my place to approve or disapprove, but I can't help worrying that—"

"Please don't try to talk me out of it. I'm doing what I must. He's the only man I can think of who is capable of standing up to DeRohan. I have to take the chance."

"Very well. Your Highness knows best."

She didn't notice the tautness in his voice as he pulled to a stop. She was already gathering her skirts as the doorman opened the car door. She looked up at the façade of the castle, wondering again if the Panther would dare brave such a risky venture. It was thrilling to think of him finding a clever way to sneak—costumed—into this private party and cheekily mingle with the people he was bent on robbing.

Now that it was upon her, she began to feel all shivery inside at the thought of seeing him again.

The Clews met her at the front door over which was carved the phrase "Once Upon a Time . . ." They were dressed as usual in rich medieval velvets, Marie attempting to resemble the Virgin Saint. A steady stream of costumed guests flowed into the house and mingled with drinks in hand in the cold stone rooms that, with their vaulted ceilings, beehive fireplaces, stained glass windows, and heavy carved doors from Spain, resembled the interior of an antiquated church more than it did a home.

She followed the sounds of music into the long hall with its high arched windows and red stone floor that tonight served as a ballroom. As she roamed through the crowd, some dancing, some conversing in small groups about the perimeter, she noted the eclectic mix of the guests. It seemed that the entire history of the region was represented here tonight.

The Côte d'Azur—Blue Coast—had once been a sleepy, barren stretch along the Mediterranean inhabited by a few local fishermen. All that had changed when Lord Brougham, former Lord High Chancellor of Great Britain, had been stranded in

Cannes in 1834, and had fallen under its spell of unspoiled beauty and luminous climate. His wealthy English friends quickly followed, building fabulous villas and chateaux in the hills that resembled their palaces back home, or fanciful replicas of structures they'd seen on their travels to exotic corners of the globe. They transported plants and flowers and transformed the rocky shores into lush green gardens. The Russian aristocracy turned up in their wake, and soon all the crowned heads of Europe had brought their great fortunes and settled the area. Emperors, tsarinas, kings, queens, princes, grand dukes, lords, and wealthy bourgeoisie all flocked to the Côte in winter months to take advantage of the sunshine beneath their parasols and partake of the festival atmosphere of parties, dances, and casinos. But they'd always left in April, when the sun grew blinding and the heat became oppressive to their Victorian sensibilities.

All that changed in 1922 when Erich von Stroheim directed the first million dollar moving picture and set it in Monte Carlo. *Foolish Wives* created the legend of the reckless decadence of the moneyed classes, idling away their days amidst the palms and sunshine of a golden coast, gambling with abandon through the long, sultry nights. Americans began drifting into the area, lured by their fascination with the film, a favorable exchange rate that allowed them to live beyond their means, and the refreshing absence of Prohibition. With that, the summer season was invented. They called the area "the Riviera," and brought with them a new fresh informality, introducing such novelties as cocktails, jazz phonograph records, and corn on the cob. Since then, increasing numbers of bored American millionaires, frustrated artists and writers, and glamorous sirens and swashbucklers of the Hollywood silver screen were baking themselves on the beaches and showing off their tans in colorful summer dresses, revealing bathing suits, and shorts worn with sailor caps and sweaters. A new era had arrived, and the old guard aristocracy, though they now stayed through the summer, still weren't certain what to think of this uninhibited new generation of hooligans who were gradually overtaking their hallowed coast.

Tonight they mingled warily, the Americans drinking heavily on one side, the British, French, and Italians more discretely on another, the titled Russians—mostly impoverished since the overthrow of their Romanov tsar and living off the charity of their friends—huddled together in a less conspicuous corner, as if embarrassed by their humbled circumstances. The hum of various languages and accents competed with the orchestra.

Nodding greetings to people she knew, Jules wandered through the room, surveying the crowd. The colorful costumes were expensive and elaborate, spanning the centuries. The women she dismissed, concentrating instead on the men. Kings, courtiers, jesters, clowns, cardinals, musketeers . . . So many of them wore masks that she felt a moment of discouragement. If the Panther had dared to show up, how could she possibly guess who he might be? He could be any one of them.

She took a breath, trying to calm herself.

What do I look for?

She'd caught only glimpses of him in the moonlight. She didn't know what color his hair was—the bandana had covered it completely. But he was tall—six feet, perhaps more—broad shouldered, leanly muscular. Athletic, certainly, which meant he couldn't be more than thirty-five at most. That would rule out anyone short or portly or old. He was clean shaven, which would discount anyone with facial hair, unless he used a false beard or mustache tonight as a disguise. She remembered her first glimpse of him in her study, how he'd moved with such masculine grace, something that would be difficult to conceal.

So that narrowed her choices considerably.

All at once, someone swooped down on her, took her in his arms, and proceeded to Foxtrot her around the floor. He was dressed as a Jacobean revolutionary with a tricolor emblem on his hat. His eyes glared at her through the mask holes with a dazed wildness.

Could it be . . . ?

"How do you like my getup? I'm Danton, or maybe Robespierre. One of those guys anyway." The voice was distinctly American.

"Scott." She couldn't disguise her disappointment.

He was gawking at her necklace. "So those are the famous goose eggs. I saw your picture in the papers. Lucky girl. Must be nice to be rich!"

She could see he was already well in his cups.

F. Scott Fitzgerald was a young American author who'd been a fixture of the American colony on the Riviera for the last few years, most of whom were free-thinking writers who'd come to France to escape what they called the commercialization of America and the killjoy aspect of Prohibition.

She was looking for an avenue of escape when Booth Devlin tapped Scott on the shoulder and cut in. He, too, was an American writer, though without the sort of success Fitzgerald had. He'd published a crime novel two years ago which had never sold well, but that was before Jules had met him, and she'd never read it. A tall man with short brown hair, he wasn't classically handsome, but he had a craggy face that was full of character and interesting to watch. And he had wordly grey-green eyes that often hinted at some hidden sadness she found intriguing.

"I thought you might need rescuing," he told her.

"Don't we all need rescuing when Scott's around?"

But she wasn't really paying attention. She was scanning the room for likely candidates. She spotted a man sitting down, dressed as a musketeer. The breadth of his shoulders looked likely, and he was masked and clean shaven. She tiptoed, peering over her partner's shoulder. But when the musketeer stood, she saw that he wasn't nearly tall enough.

"You seem far away," Devlin commented. "I'm not sure my ego can take the rejection. Looking for someone special?"

She vaguely caught the teasing tone and glanced at him apologetically. "Forgive me, Dev. I promised to speak with Nikki. Will you excuse me?"

"Sure. Go ahead. Break my heart."

Just then, Fitzgerald's wife Zelda came floating up, asking, in her Southern drawl, "Have either of you dahlin' chickadees seen Scott? I checked the bar where, by all rights, he should be. But nary a trace. My heavens, Jules, what *is* that necklace you're wearin'? I've never seen pearls like those in all my days!"

"Let's go find Scott," Dev said, steering Zelda off and giving Jules a wink.

Jules headed in the direction of Nikki Romanov, a childhood friend, in case Dev should happen to glance her way. But as she went, she continued to search the crowd. She passed Father Siffredi, an Italian priest and one of the organizers of tonight's event. She didn't know him personally, but it was well known that he loathed her husband and denounced him at every turn. She thought fleetingly that they had a great deal in common, except that the priest didn't know it. But it wasn't the priest himself who was the focus of her attention. He was talking to a tall man dressed as Cardinal Richelieu. Could that be the man she was looking for? Surely he wouldn't be so bold as to be speaking to a priest!

As she came around the front of him, however, she saw that he had a massive stomach beneath his long red robes. And he wasn't masked.

But even as she searched for the Panther, she realized it was just as crucial that he see her. She'd purposely not worn a mask so he'd recognize her, but now she pushed her way into the center of the party where the band was playing, greeting people she knew, laughing, letting herself be seen. She wondered if he was watching even now from some shadowed corner. She could almost feel his eyes on her.

She didn't stay with one group long, but greeted and moved on, covering as much ground as she could. As always, she received offers she'd turned down a dozen times before. Rex Ingram, the movie director who had his studio on the coast, called to her, "I still want to make that movie about you—Norma Talmadge wants to play the role."

She laughed him off. "You never give up, do you?"

"Think of it! *The Last Habsburg!* The audience will eat it up with a spoon!"

The Spanish painter, Picasso, overheard and said, "Forget the cinema, *mon petit chou!* Let me paint you. Only my canvas can do you justice."

She shook her head. "You want to paint me with three eyes."

"I want to show the real you."

She pushed on.

The mayor of Nice blocked her path, saying, "Madame DeRohan, I really do wish you'd reconsider and make an appearance at the Great War Memorial dedication. It would mean so much—"

"Forgive me, Mayor Clément, but I'm really not good at such things. Will you excuse me, please?"

More people were dancing now, although the older guests sat around the ballroom in Spanish leather chairs.

She'd been so busy looking around that she literally bumped into Nikki Romanov—a tall, dark, attractive but indolent looking young man who carried himself like the prince he was. Realizing that she was on the verge of becoming conspicuous, she asked him to dance. They were playing a waltz and Nikki guided her gracefully about the floor. He was a grand duke of the exiled Romanov family—a cousin to the overthrown tsar—and understood, more than any other friend, her sense of exile. She'd known him since she was a little girl—before the war, their families had both wintered here—and he was more like a brother to her than anything else. With him, she didn't have to put on an act. She could use him as a screen to view the incoming guests.

He let her dance in silence for a time, then said in her ear, "This waltz reminds me of the old days. Remember, Juli, how we used to dance?"

"It's best not to think about the old days," she said distractedly. His hand on hers tightened and she felt something press into her, hurting her. Looking to see what it was, she spotted a ring on his pinky finger with a magnificent star sapphire. She'd never seen it before.

"That's a bit out of your price range, isn't it?"

Nikki, like most of the Russians, had escaped without any money of his own. He'd actually been on the verge of humbling himself by pleading for employment and a place to live when a friend had inquired about his villa.

"What villa?" Nikki had asked.

To which the friend had cried in astonishment, "Why, your villa above Cannes!"

Nikki had bought it on a whim before the war, and had forgotten all about it.

He lived there now, but without any source of income that anyone could discern. He never said how it was that he still managed to live the privileged life he did.

He smiled at her slyly now. "Don't think, little Juli, that you're the only one with admirers." He fingered her pearls. "Ah, but my ring is a mere trinket compared to these. They really are spectacular. My grandmother had some similar, though smaller. Do you recall? I used to pull on them as a child. But she never scolded me. She told me they'd be mine someday, to give to my wife."

She caught the grief in his eyes. "Poor Nikki. If I thought they could bring back the past for you, I'd almost give them to you."

He chuckled, dispelling the gloomy mood. "Don't tempt me. I'm cad enough to take them."

Jules was discouraged. Hours had passed and still there was no sign of the Panther. No masked man had contrived to get her alone. She hadn't even seen a likely candidate. She'd even stood outside on the terrace, hoping he might slip away and come to her.

Nothing.

The entire evening had been a waste of time. It was madness to think he'd show up here. Once again, she'd retreated into a world of fantasy that had no bearing with reality.

Feeling hot and tired, she wandered down the terrace stairs, to walk around the side of the house and into the gardens. As she meandered along the curved paths, she found herself in a secluded half-circular alcove. It was dark and she could barely make out the shapes of the two Roman columns that led to a stone wall where a double-arched Gothic window overlooked the rocks and sea below.

She went to the window and leaned her head on the wrought iron railing in front of it, listening to the thrash of the surf against the rocks. The night was cool, as usual, a welcome relief after the cloying heat of the ballroom. In the moonlight, the Mediterranean shimmered with shifting facets, as if sprinkled with diamonds.

She took a deep breath, trying to squelch her disappointment. What was she going to do now that he'd ignored her call? What else could she do to attract his attention? She'd been so certain the Antoinette pearls would lure him out of hiding.

If not that, what?

What an idiot she'd been to think of something so desperate. But what else could she do? DeRohan would return in two days. The thought of that reptilian ogre taking charge of *her* house, sleeping in her linens, forcing her to serve his imperialistic interests . . . it was enough to make her flesh crawl.

Realizing that her last futile grasp at a straw of escape had failed, a curtain of despair began to crush in on her.

But all of a sudden, she felt a presence behind her. Before the realization could register, a hand came round to cover her mouth. It was large and strong, muffling any startled sound that might be tempted to escape her lips.

"Cowardly creature of the night, am I?"

The voice in her ear was once more a sultry whisper, as if he were attempting to disguise his true inflection. Again, he spoke in Italian.

She squirmed, trying to disengage his hand and turn to him as her heart swelled. He'd come after all! But his hand on her mouth tightened while the other came up to her shoulder, securing her. "Don't turn around," he commanded. "Don't cry out. Can I trust you?"

She nodded. When he took his hand from her mouth, she made a movement toward him in eagerness, but he gripped her other shoulder, keeping her with her back solidly to him. She accepted the condition and said, "I have to talk to you."

She felt his breath on her ear. "Talk? You mean the way we—*talked* the other night?" He began to nibble her ear. "As I recall, you're a most scintillating conversationalist."

"Let's go somewhere where we can sit down . . ."

He tightened his hands on her. "I said don't move." He sucked her earlobe into his mouth, causing a jolt of desire to shoot through her. As she squirmed, trying to move away, his mouth moved lower, kissing the long column of her neck.

"I didn't summon you for this," she protested.

"Oh, did you summon me?"

His fingertips were trailing her bare shoulders, one hand playing with her shoulder blade, the other tracing a tempting path down her front, dipping toward the ruffled décolleté of her shepardess gown, causing her to quiver.

"Of course I did. What did you think those newspaper stories were for?"

Distantly, she noted the breathiness of her tone.

Once again he was nibbling at her ear, exploring it with his tongue in a way that made her feel as if she were beginning to melt into a puddle at his feet. "I don't read the papers," he told her. "Except for my own notices."

His hand came up to cup her breast. It felt so good, so treacherously welcome. Against her will, she felt herself leaning back into him, feeling his erection against her derriere. "Please," she sighed, "I'm drowning." It was all she could do to get out the words. His touch was playing havoc with her designs. "You must listen to me. Please. I beg you."

She felt him pulling up the back of her skirts. "Very well," he said. "Tell me."

"DeRohan has come back early. He's moving in. I've had a few nights reprieve, but he'll return the day after tomorrow. He's taking over my house and my life. I just don't know how I can bear it. I can't—"

All at once she stopped. She had no idea how he'd accomplished it, but somehow, as she'd been trying to concentrate on what she was saying, he'd managed to slide her panties down. Now his fingers were playing with her clit in a most deliciously wicked way, chasing the words from her head.

"Are you sure that's why you *summoned* me? It couldn't be that you wanted more of this?"

He shot into her from behind. He was so big, his entry so unexpected, that she gasped aloud. Once again, his hand came round and clamped itself on her mouth.

He plunged into her, thrusting hard, pulling her back against his cast-iron chest to anchor her. His mouth nuzzling her ear, making her head spin.

She reached up and ripped his hand from her mouth. "You're insane! Someone could come upon us at any time."

"Now you know what it feels like to steal into houses in the dead of night. The danger . . . the risk of discovery . . . the thrill of getting away with something daring and forbidden. It's the danger that gives it the spice."

And all the while, he drove himself into her, his fingers playing with her in front, wracking her with shudders of reckless lust, propelling every thought from her brain. Her body on fire, hurled to the brink of madness by the astonishing force of his seduction, thoroughly swept away.

"Once in your life, you should taste the thrill of danger," he told her. "It electrifies the senses like nothing else. Do you feel it? Give yourself up to it. Feel the cock of a wanted criminal who's crashed the party beneath the very noses of those who most want him caught. Because that's what you really wanted, wasn't it?" He shook her roughly. "*Wasn't it?*"

"Yes," she cried, the agony too much, the pleasure too intense. She could no longer think, she could only feel his stiff erection pumping inside, his hands on her, cupping, grasping, causing her hunger to spin out of control. His lips mouthing words that fired her imagination, while tasting her flesh and whipping her into a frenzy.

It was too much. She exploded in a vortex of sensation, leaning back into him, giving herself to him completely. Spinning defenselessly in his hands, trusting him to keep her from tumbling from her dizzying height.

She was so befuddled with pleasure that she fell forward against the window when he pulled out of her, gasping for air. Her skirts fell back to graze the brick walk at her feet. She still felt as if she were soaring, her body throbbing in a way that made her feel lusciously fulfilled. And slowly, a dazed sort of somnolence began to steal upon her. It was as if she were a part of the sky and the sea and the very night.

But slowly, the silence changed. It was *too* quiet. There was no sound, no movement behind her. She reached her hand back, seeking him. When she felt nothing, she swiveled around.

She was alone.

She put her hand to her heart. Once again, he'd vanished into the night. She recalled, as if from a dream, all the things she'd wanted to say.

But then . . . slowly . . . she became aware of a sense of lack . . . of a weight that wasn't there . . . of something missing. Gradually, her hand moved up her chest to her collarbone. With rising horror, she realized her neck was bare.

The Antoinette pearls were gone.

Chapter 7

Jules left the gathering in a stupor. Not wanting to see anyone, or answer any questions, she went through the gardens to the front courtyard, where the autos were waiting. Finding the Rolls, she saw to her dismay that Hudson wasn't there. He had no way of knowing when she'd want to leave, but in her present state it made her feel frantic to find him gone. She wanted to get away, and fast.

She reeled toward a group of chauffeurs playing cards in the cloistered portico, asking if they'd seen him. They shook their heads dumbly, embarrassed at having been caught at their sport. No one had seen him.

She returned to the car and banged her open palm against the window. *I have to get hold of myself.*

Just then, she heard hurried footsteps and turned to find Hudson sprinting her way. "Where were you?" she demanded.

"Highness, what's happened?"

"Don't ask anything," she told him shortly. "Just take me home."

As he opened the car door for her, the inside light illuminated her. "Highness, your necklace—"

"Hudson, I swear if you ask me any questions, I'm going to scream."

He knew when to keep his peace, so he helped her inside

with solicitous care. "You close your eyes and rest, Highness. We'll have you home in no time."

As he drove along the coast road in the dark, Jules laid back her head and closed her eyes. She couldn't believe what had happened. He'd actually taken the necklace! Played her for a complete and utter fool.

I am a fool—a stupid romantic imbecile!

The worst of it was that he'd been right about her. She knew that now. Oh, she'd wanted him to help her with DeRohan, certainly. But she'd also wanted—without admitting it to herself—to see him again, to feel his touch, to experience the wild ecstasy she'd found with him that first night. He'd been able to dupe her so easily because her treacherous body—starved for so long—had craved that riotous bliss. The danger. The excitement. And yes . . . even the temporary rebellion against everything she was—her background, the expectations on her, the farce of a marriage.

She'd behaved like a whore and now she was paying the price.

She slept fitfully that night. The next day, her stomach in knots, she refused breakfast and lunch. The smell of the food made her feel nauseated. She couldn't seem to keep still. She paced the Louis XVI salon like a caged animal. The sounds of the maids working grated on her nerves, so in the afternoon, she walked in the gardens, filled with self-recriminations.

That evening, she still couldn't face the idea of food. She told Mimi to inform the chef that she would skip dinner as well.

Finally Hudson, who'd been quietly keeping an eye on her all day, and who seemed to understand what had happened, approached her, saying, "Highness, I know you've had a blow—a loss—but you must eat."

She ran her hands through her shortened hair, brushing it back off her face. "Oh, Hudson, why didn't I listen to you? I've let my romantic fancies get the best of me and—because of it—I've lost Antoinette's pearls. How could I be so irresponsible? I'm only glad Father isn't here to witness my shame."

Carefully, Hudson asked, "Do you wish me to call the police, Highness?"

The police? It would serve the Panther right if she reported the theft. He was probably smiling confidently to himself even now, certain she would hold her tongue.

If she told the police, the story would be plastered all over the newspapers and would increase the pressure to bring the Panther to heel.

But even as she considered it, she knew she'd never do it. Because she really was a fool. Taken in as she may have been, she still didn't want him caught. And she didn't even know why.

"No, Hudson, we'll tell no one. I shall write it off as the cost of a valuable lesson learned."

The next morning, she awoke to the sounds of angry male voices—an argument flaring somewhere in the house. She pushed herself up and peered at the clock across the room. It was past ten.

She rose and padded groggily through her sitting room in her nightgown and bare feet, coming out into the hallway. One of the voices booming from the reception hall below belonged to DeRohan. He must have returned in the night.

Jules went to the upper gallery where, running the entire length of the second story on four sides, twenty-four columned arches—six on each side—enclosed a carved, filigreed marble balcony that topped the larger arches around the perimeter of the reception hall below. Looking down, she could see her husband arguing with Father Siffredi, the priest who'd been at the La Napoule ball two nights before. He had a rolled-up scroll tucked under his arm. It was clear from the rigidity of their stances that both men were furious.

"How dare you invade my private quarters!" DeRohan

snarled. "Who do you think you are, the Spanish Inquisition? You have no authority here and your turned-up collar means nothing to me. If you don't remove yourself from these premises, I shall personally throw you out."

It appeared to Jules as if that might not be an easy task. The priest was a solidly built northern Italian of the same height as DeRohan, with dark blond hair and blazing blue eyes. There was nothing meek or liturgical in his manner. He glared at his opponent as though he might be on the verge of charging him and seizing him by the throat.

"I have brought with me a petition signed by every family in Cap Corse," he said in Italian-accented English. "A thousand signatures imploring you to do the right thing."

"Haven't you caused enough trouble?"

"It is *you* who have caused the trouble, my friend."

"Me?" DeRohan cried. "I've been nothing but reasonable in the matter. You've organized a strike that's closed down my Corsican gold mines—the most valuable property of the mining division of DeRohan Enterprises. You've initiated a lawsuit in the names of the miners that's prevented me from selling the ore that's been excavated there for the past year—a stockpile that's collecting dust in a warehouse in Bastia. My prestige and the public's confidence in my company has been shaken everywhere I do business—and you call *me* unreasonable."

Siffredi hurled back, "Your company is systematically exploiting the people of northern Corsica. They work for a fraction of the wages miners get in other parts of Europe. The conditions are unsafe, and the work shifts punishingly long. The housing you provide is unspeakable. You may have a piece of paper giving you mineral rights to their land, but in the eyes of God and all reasonable men, you have no justification whatsoever to exploit them as you do. That gold represents their heritage and their future—and you're stealing it from them. How can even *you* be so heartless?"

DeRohan was unmoved. "The lawsuit will eventually come to trial. You will lose, I shall win—and then you will see how heartless and vindictive I can be."

"Yes, you may win because you will bribe the French officials and courts, but you will still not get your gold. These people are Corsicans—and now that they have been mobilized, they will fight you to the death to keep it on their island. And then, my friend, you will see what it is to be at the receiving end of a Corsican vendetta."

"Even Corsicans have to eat. I shall merely wait them out."

The priest pointed the rolled-up petition at his hostile host. "I happen to know that you do not have that luxury. All three divisions of your business empire—mining, real estate, and shipping—are in jeopardy. You desperately need the infusion of cash and renewed business confidence that will come with the sale of that stockpile of gold ore, and you need it quickly. You cannot afford to outwait us."

DeRohan smiled cagily. "That may have been true a few weeks ago. But things have changed. I now have a deal nearly in my pocket that will ensure my future and catapult my company into an entirely new league of global power and influence. So you and your Corsican Bolsheviks can all go to hell!"

Dramatically, Siffredi threw the petition at DeRohan's feet, saying, "Hell, sir, is where you belong."

DeRohan picked it up, ripped it to shreds and said, "And when I've won, Siffredi, I'll not forget your part in this—nor all the other actions you've initiated against me. I'm not without friends in the Vatican. When this is over, I intend to make sure you spend the balance of your career converting cannibals on some godforsaken island in the Indian Ocean."

Squaring his shoulders, Siffredi told him, "If that happens, I will leave the Church. Because come what may, for the rest of my life, I intend to devote every breath I take to fighting your incomparable evil."

He stormed out.

Jules returned to her suite, stirred and inspired by the priest's fiery resistance. Too, she realized now why DeRohan was so intent on this deal with the Shah: His empire was troubled. He desperately needed those oil leases. And since—to get them—he needed her help, maybe—just maybe—she could use this need to her advantage.

She dressed in a pale pink summer frock, and then, because she didn't want to antagonize DeRohan, wrapped a silk scarf about her hair so he wouldn't know she'd cut it. She went downstairs, made arrangements with Hudson, and put on a sober pleasant face. Then she entered what had once been her father's study, a smaller salon where DeRohan had set up headquarters, with Hudson following behind, carrying a tray.

DeRohan looked up from the desk, where he'd been reading his mail. "Ah, my loving wife," he drawled.

"I heard you'd returned. Since it's such a hot day, I thought you might like some citronade."

Hudson laid the tray on a crescent-shaped table below her father's portrait, then left quietly.

DeRohan was watching her with the trenchant glare that always made her want to turn her back, lest he see too much in her eyes. "To what do I owe this extraordinary reception?"

"I'd like to speak with you. Calmly, unemotionally."

He tossed his mail aside. "That should be a novelty. I've had my fill of histrionics for one day."

She poured him a drink from the icy pitcher, then turned to find him standing by her side. Repressing the instinctive urge to draw back, she handed the glass to him, and indicated the formal sitting area, offering, "Please, have a seat."

He dropped into one of the petit point chairs, took a sip, then looked over at her as she sat across from him on the settee. "I confess, you've piqued my curiosity."

Jules sat with her back straight, folded her hands in her lap, and took a deep breath for courage. "DeRoh—" she began, then corrected herself carefully, "Dominic."

She waited to see if the never-before-used familiarity aroused his cynicism. It didn't. He seemed poised to listen.

Heartened, she continued. "I've done a great deal of thinking since you arrived the other day. And I've decided to do what you've asked. I shall help you with the Shah."

His eyes narrowed. "Will you now?"

"Yes."

"You will willingly help me."

"Yes."

"But you want something in return."

"I do."

"And what is that?"

"My freedom."

"Your . . . freedom." The ice tinkled in his glass as he swirled it in his hand. He took another sip, idly, then set the glass on the table next to him.

Jules rushed on. "Somehow, through no fault of our own, we've fallen into a tragedy. I don't have to tell you this so-called marriage that's existed between us for four years is a cruel farce. It's never been consummated. It's been a prison for the both of us. Surely your feelings for me have been every bit as acrimonious as mine have been toward you. There's no use raking over the past and hurling accusations at one another as to how we fell into the situation. None of that matters now. What matters is that we end it. Peacefully. Amicably."

She looked up to see that his face hadn't changed. He considered her words for a moment, then asked, "How would you suggest we do that?"

"A simple annulment."

"I see," he said quietly. "You want me to admit, for all the world to know, that our marriage was never consummated."

"A divorce, then. I'm certainly willing to protect your reputation in return for my freedom. I don't want anything from you. I shall take my house and my jewels. Only what's truly mine. We've been apart for a year now. Surely during this time you've come to realize that we have no future." She leaned forward, pressing her clasped hands together. "Please, Dominic. Can't you be reasonable and see that this is the only solution for us?"

For an entire minute, he didn't move. Then he reached over, took another sip of the citronade, and sat back in the chair, thinking deeply about all she'd said. Another interminable time passed as Jules pressed her hands together so tightly, they went numb. She forgot to breathe. She waited, encouraged by his thoughtful silence, but afraid to hope.

Finally, his eyes turned to her and he said, "Never. Not in a million years."

All her hopes came crashing in around her. "You cad! You let me go on, knowing you never had any intention of—"

"You listen to me carefully, Juliana. I—will—never—let—you—go. You made a bargain with me. I've coddled you long enough. You've had your year of ridiculous mourning. Now you're going to start living up to your responsibilities."

"My responsibilities," she spat out at him, "ended when you pushed my father into blowing out his brains with the gun you left for him in this very room. Our end of the bargain was paid for with his blood."

"Whatever your father did—and why—has nothing to do with the bargain you made with me. You belong to me. And you always will."

It was too much. Vaulting to her feet, she ripped the scarf off her head, displaying the bobbed hair that was the symbol of her rebellion. "I don't care what you do or what you say. I will *never* belong to—"

He rose up and sprang on her, gripping her arm and wrenching it until she cried out, cutting off her words. "What did you do to your hair?"

"I cut it not two minutes after you praised me for not having done so. I hope you hate it. Every time you see it, I hope it will remind you that all your wife wants in all this world is to be free of *you*."

He twisted her arm. "Your Habsburg fairy tale is over. You're no longer the spoiled and pampered princess. You're my wife, and by God, you're going to start acting like it. So let me tell you what you're going to do: In two weeks—on the ninth of July—I'm giving a reception for the Shah. You will plan it. To give face to the man, you will see to it that every one of your titled friends who happens to be anywhere near this coast is present. I want none of your flighty American friends in attendance. And if it isn't the most lavish gathering ever seen on this blasted coast, you will answer to me. Throughout this bacchanalia, you are going to be hanging onto my arm, smiling adoringly up into my face, and oohing like a smitten schoolgirl at every word that ruddy Hottentot says to you. I don't care if it kills you."

She pulled on her arm. "I won't. I don't care what you do to me. If you think you're going to waltz into *my* house and give me orders, you're even more demented than I thought."

"Demented?" he snarled, his face black with fury. "I'll show you demented." He dropped her arm, picked up the glass of citronade, and hurled it with all his might. It shattered against her father's portrait, ripping a tear across the canvas.

She stood staring at it, shaking uncontrollably. It was the only portrait she had of her father. And now, like the man, it too had been destroyed by DeRohan.

She couldn't find the words to express her revulsion. After several moments she settled for a whispered, "I despise you."

In a flinty tone, he replied, "Hate me all you want, so long as you do as I say."

"You can't even conceive of the depths of my hatred for you."

He yanked her around to face him. "And if you ever again think to defy me—if you cut your hair or shave your head or whisper something you shouldn't to the Shah—I may just have to punish you in such a way that you'll understand I'm not to be crossed again."

"And how's that?" she asked scathingly. There was nothing he could possibly promise that could be worse than what he'd already done.

"You've broken your word with your rebellion. I may just have to break mine."

"Meaning?"

"Meaning, Juliana, that I may just decide you're right. This charade has gone on long enough. It may be high time that I claimed my true rights as your husband by taking my lawful place in your bed. Not because I especially want you. But because I know how it would make your flesh crawl."

Chapter 8

Jules was so shaken, she couldn't stop her hand from trembling. Numbly, she summoned Hudson, who faced her with the same unruffled expression as ever. "Did you hear any of that?" she asked.

He lowered his gaze, saying nothing.

"I suppose the rest of the staff heard it all, too."

"I don't think so, Highness. I sent them to other parts of the house with various duties."

"That was good of you, Hudson. Look what he's done to my father's portrait."

He glanced at the desecrated painting. "A pity, but perhaps not irreparable."

"You think it can be restored?"

"Oh, I think so, Highness. There's an artists' supply store in Mougins that specializes in mending canvas tears. I'll ring them up to come around and have a look."

She breathed a little easier. "Thank you, Hudson. I can always depend on you." He was heading for the telephone when her voice stopped him once again. "Oh, and Hudson. One more thing. I shall be needing the strongest bolt available installed on my side of the doors to my private apartment. I don't care what it costs, but it must be done by nightfall."

He shot her a concerned look, as if he knew exactly why

she'd made the request. But he only said, "Very well, Highness. I'll see to it at once."

She passed the rest of the day in a state of sustained shock. Rêve de l'Amour was no longer a sanctuary. She could feel DeRohan's dominating presence everywhere. She had to get away.

All at once, she had an idea. One of the tightly kept secrets of the estate—one not even Hudson knew—was the fact that it contained a network of secret underground passageways. When her grandmother had built the villa in the 1860s, she'd insisted on the feature, and also insisted that the builder keep it off the official blueprints. Her stated reason was to guarantee escape in times of trouble or war, but the true motivation was that it allowed her lover unseen access to the house from the private beach at the bottom of the steep hill.

One tunnel ran from behind a false cabinet in the basement several hundred yards under the rear gardens that led to the Temple of Venus. Below it, her grandmother had constructed a hidden room to accommodate her clandestine rendezvous with her lover. From there, a second tunnel led straight down to an inconspicuous cave-like opening behind a cluster of boulders overlooking the beach.

Today, because a delivery man was loading stores of food and household supplies in the basement, she instead went to the gardens and climbed the hill to the temple. Making certain no one was nearby, she found the small cleverly disguised doorway at the back of the base of the rotunda-like structure. She flicked the mechanism, opened the door, and slipped inside.

Taking a flashlight from its holder on the wall, she descended a spiral staircase to her grandmother's amorous hideaway. As a child, Jules had often come here to play, her girlish reverie heightened by the knowledge that, since her grandmother's death, she alone knew of its existence and what it had meant.

She passed through the room to enter the second tunnel, and hiked its downward path to emerge on the beach.

At sea level, cut off from the criss-cross breezes that cooled Rêve de l'Amour, she could feel the summer heat. She spent most of the afternoon there, hugging her knees on one of the rocks—watching the glisten of sun on the water, listening to the cry of the gulls circling overhead, gazing across the bay at the ships of the American fleet anchored at Villefranche. All familiar, comforting sights. But somehow they looked different today. They made her feel like a stranger.

She eyed her sailboat bobbing at her small private pier, and wished suddenly that she could sail away. Escape. Her thoughts drifted back to that romantic spot on the Italian coast she'd stumbled upon with her father after the war—the place that, in another century, had been the refuge of her beloved Lord Byron. An enclave of harmony and simplicity that had become her fantasy sanctuary. There she would be safe. Away from her responsibilities . . . her troubles . . . DeRohan . . .

If I lose everything else, I can go there . . .

But it was only a fantasy. And DeRohan would be looking for her. So she rose reluctantly to go back. But instead of returning through the tunnel, she trekked up the hill and back through the gardens. When she reached the back terrace that ran the width of the house, she was glad she'd taken the precaution because DeRohan was standing there with another man.

As she approached, she recognized Booth Devlin. Though the two men were about the same height, DeRohan's immaculate suit made the tan cotton trousers and casual shirt Dev wore look shabby in comparison.

"Ah, there's the missing mistress of the house now," DeRohan's voice rang out.

"Hello, Dev," she managed.

"We've been enjoying a jolly chat, your American friend and I." He pronounced the word "friend" with some sarcasm.

Dev told her, "You left the party the other night so suddenly, we were a little worried about you."

"I wasn't feeling well, I'm afraid," she said.

"But she's better now," DeRohan chimed in. "Aren't you, darling?"

The American looked at him with some distaste, then back at Jules. "Anyway, I brought you a copy of my book. You mentioned that you didn't much like Scott's literary ramblings, so I thought you might get a kick out of this. No one could ever accuse it of bearing literary pretensions."

He handed it forth. But DeRohan intercepted it, gave its cover a cursory glance, and handed it back to him. "A thoughtful gesture, no doubt. But I'm afraid my wife will have little time for reading in the coming weeks. She'll have her hands full with other matters."

Dev looked to Jules for confirmation, and she nodded in agreement. "I'm afraid he's right. But I will have time later in the summer, so if you don't mind—" She took the book out of DeRohan's hand. "I'll look forward to it, Dev. Thank you."

DeRohan turned a territorial gaze on the writer. In a stern voice, he said, "You might inform her other American admirers that my wife will be out of their social whirl for the foreseeable future."

Once again, Dev's worldly grey-green eyes glanced her way. To cover the awkward moment, Jules smiled her agreement. "I *shall* be busy for a while."

Dev looked at them both in turn, then said, "Well, if you need anything at all, you know how to get hold of me."

"Thank you for coming, Dev. Really. And thanks for the book."

With that he nodded and said, "I'll be going then. Don't bother to show me out. I know the way."

When he left, Jules turned to DeRohan, the slim volume in her hands. "Are you dictating what I may read as well as whom I may see?"

"You may read whatever you like. I don't give a hang. But your days of entertaining men in this house are over."

*   *   *

When she reached her rooms, Jules found that Hudson—with that miraculous efficiency that never let her see how he accomplished his tasks—had already mounted a heavy sliding bolt on her door. So heavy it looked as if it would withstand the attack of a battering ram. The first measure of comfort Jules had felt all day.

For dinner, to avoid DeRohan, she left instructions for him to be served alone while she dined in the sitting room that, with her bedroom and spacious bath, formed her personal suite of rooms taking up the entire back west wing of the house. Hudson laid out the dishes of filets de sole poêlés meunière and tomato and basil coulis before her. She picked at the food automatically but tasted nothing. Her sense of security had been summarily smashed in a single afternoon and she felt herself a prisoner of DeRohan's malevolent will.

Putting up a front before the servants, she drifted through her late night routine as if nothing untoward had happened. She stepped into the steaming bath her maid Denise had drawn, enveloped by the heat and aroma of white gardenias, listening as if from the other end of a tunnel to the girl's steady stream of French chatter.

"I have always wondered what the master would look like. He is a most striking man. And so virile! I confess, when he looks at me—ooh la la!—he makes me quake in my shoes."

Jules said nothing. The silly twit actually found him attractive!

She allowed Denise to dry her, then sat on the padded stool while the maid cut and filed her toenails.

"And his eyes!" Denise gushed on. "I have never seen that exact color before. They are not blue, they are not green, they are not aquamarine. They are the color of . . . what?"

"Ice."

"*Oui, Madame.* Ice! One freezes in their glare."

It was clear from the way she said this that DeRohan's air of ruthlessness excited the girl. Was it possible that he'd made some advance toward her? After all, if the gossip could be believed, he rarely missed an opportunity to bed a willing young wench.

A curious idea began to form. Could she deflect her husband's amorous new attentions toward the maid?

She stood thoughtfully while Denise slipped a gold satin negligee over her head, automatically put her arms through the long belled sleeves of the marabou-trimmed peignoir, and stepped into high-heeled satin slippers.

"You know, Denise, the monsieur and I live together in name only."

Denise blushed. "Oh, Madame . . . I did not mean to . . ."

"So if the monsieur were to show an interest in you, it would not be disloyal of you to respond to that . . . interest."

"Madame, surely you do not think that—even if he were to ask—do you think he might—?"

"In fact, Denise, I would go so far as to say that I would not take it amiss if you were to instigate some manner of . . . special attention to the monsieur's needs."

"Are you serious, Madame?"

"You might even find a bonus in your pay envelope for such a valuable service."

The maid followed her to the vanity table, seeming to mull over the proposition as she brushed Jules's hair. Her eyes, in the mirror, were glowing with animation.

But the girl's next words surprised even Jules. "And if we were caught, Madame . . . and if I were to testify . . . there would perhaps be an even more generous bonus?"

It hadn't occurred to Jules. She looked at the girl in the mirror and caught the shrewd gleam in her eyes. French women were so practical.

"I would never ask such a thing, Denise."

"But certainly not, Madame. However, a servant may give freely that which is not asked, no?"

"You would do that, Denise?"

"You have been good to me, Madame. To do such a service in repayment would be a pleasure. And if I can receive even more pleasure in the bargain . . ." She shrugged.

Again, Jules found it incredible that the girl could take any pleasure in the prospect of giving herself to such a man. But clearly, the possibility—beyond the promise of reward—titillated her.

Was it fair to ask such a thing?

She began to feel guilty about even considering it. But before she could comment further, Hudson entered the room with her cocoa and the maid put down the brush and left to iron Jules's dress for the next day.

"Oh, Hudson, I've just done a dreadful thing. I've conspired to throw that innocent girl at DeRohan like a piece of meat to a lion."

Hudson flashed one of those impertinent smiles that occasionally cracked his façade. "That innocent girl has been with the footman, the chimney sweep, and half the gardening staff. So I shouldn't be too concerned about protecting her virtue."

She turned to him, amazed. "How do you do it? You always know just what to say to make me feel better."

The moment was interrupted by the sound of the door opening, then a voice drawling, "Well, well, well. Isn't this is cozy scene?"

Jules whirled around like a rabbit caught in a trap. DeRohan stood in her doorway, filling it, looking like the wolf who'd swallowed the canary. Without thinking, her hands came up to pull together the marabou of the peignoir, covering her cleavage. His eyes flicked to it, showing his scorn.

"I find it worthy of comment that you hide from me what your butler feasts his eyes upon nightly. Am I to be jealous of everyone, even the help?"

Hudson stood rigidly, staring straight ahead as if he hadn't heard. Jules could feel him bristling inside, but he merely said, "Your cocoa, Highness," and handed it to her.

She took it automatically, demanding of DeRohan, "What are you doing here?"

"I came to ask the meaning of that meager supper you left me."

She strained to keep her tone light and matter-of-fact, to keep her hands from shaking. "Since you've shown up on my doorstep with your buttons nearly bursting, I thought consommé and toast a fitting repast. You should be more mindful of your figure, DeRohan. If you're not careful, you'll run to fat before the summer's through."

His eyes narrowed. "While we're on the subject, I've allowed you your sulk this evening, but in future, I expect to dine with my wife sitting across from me. In the dining hall, or here in your rooms, since you seem to prefer it. The location makes no difference to me."

"Then I'm afraid you'll be disappointed. I've decided to reduce and shan't be eating dinner. Unlike you, I take pains with my appearance."

His eyes did, indeed, look like ice as he glared at her. "You try my patience, Juliana. You'll see to it that—on the odd occasion when you *do* deign to have a meal—you do so in the dining hall with me. And I'll not be served bread and water like an inmate. Kindly pass on the word to the kitchen."

She gave a sarcastic curtsy. "No bread and water for the self-appointed master of my house. Will poison suit your palate?"

When she straightened, he was watching her with wintry unfeeling eyes. She could feel her hatred of him burning through her gaze. But still her mind struggled to understand why he was here, in her private domain. Not because he cared about such trifles.

Because he wanted her to see him in her rooms.

He wanted her to know he could enter if and when he chose.

Without another word, he turned to leave. But abruptly he

paused, coming up short at the sight of the new steel bolt on the inside of her carved rococo door. The room seemed to shudder as Jules waited, not daring to breathe. He stood looking at it, his back straight, arms hanging stiffly at his sides. Then, slowly, he turned to look at her. He didn't say a word. He just lifted the corner of his mouth in a contemptuous sneer.

His cold and silent disdain frightened her more than anything he could have said.

When he'd gone, she stood rooted where she was, trembling. The rooms seemed suddenly to throb with the hushed aftermath of his departure. The cup began to rattle on the saucer she held. Gentle hands took it from her. She looked and saw Hudson setting it aside with an averted gaze, no doubt as embarrassed as she.

"Are you all right?" he asked.

She didn't notice the personal quality of his tone, or his lack of the use of the ubiquitous "Highness." She just nodded her head, saying numbly, "I'm fine. My head aches a bit, that's all."

"Perhaps a candle would be more soothing to the eyes."

He went to her bedside table and lit the candle they kept at the ready when the mistral wreaked havoc with the electricity. Then he crossed the room and turned off the overhead chandelier. The flicker of the candle cast a faint distant glow that threw shadows upon the wall and onto the ceiling by her bed, but darkened the room enough to bring a welcome sense of anonymity. He could no longer see the telltale flush of her cheeks.

"Is there anything else I might do for you?"

"Thank you, Hudson, no. There's nothing anyone can do."

"Would you care for some company, then? I could read aloud from your Lord Byron."

She smiled at him sadly. "I think reading Byron has caused me enough trouble for the moment."

She wanted to apologize for what DeRohan had said, but was afraid that to mention it would embarrass him all the more. So instead, she walked with him out into the sitting room so she could bolt the door behind him. Once he'd passed the threshold, he turned and looked at her oddly for a moment. "Rest easy, Highness," he said kindly. "No one will pass through these doors without your consent."

"Thank you, Hudson."

"I shall wait to hear the bolt slide home before I retire."

She had to turn away to hide the tears that sprang to her eyes. She closed the door, slid the massive bolt, then crossed to her bedroom and closed the connecting door behind her. Despondently, she sat down once again at the vanity and put her face in her hands, still feeling DeRohan's domineering presence.

What was she going to do? How long would it be before he took the bolt at her door as a challenge to be overcome? Hudson would help as much as he could, but he was obviously no match for a brute like DeRohan.

She felt the hopelessness welling up inside. She was running out of time, and there was nowhere to turn.

As if to emphasize the point, she slowly became aware of the delicate ticking of the Empire clock in the dense silence of the night. It started as a small distraction, but gradually began to take on a rhythm of its own inside her head, blending with her despair to numb her battered mind. She concentrated on it to keep from thinking, just listening as the minutes passed, one after the other. Tick, tick, tick . . . lulling her into a sort of trance until something began to shift inside. It seemed to her as if she were floating free, looking down on herself, a woman trapped in convention despite the defiance of newly shorn hair, her face in her hands, praying without words, with her body, her breath, for some sort of miraculous deliverance.

Knowing it wouldn't come.

"You cut your hair."

The voice came from behind, soft, whispery, speaking in Italian. Slowly, thinking she must be dreaming, she lifted her head from her hands and looked into the mirror. In the dimly dancing light of the candle far behind, she could make out the figure of a man standing behind her, his face masked, looking at her in the glass.

The Panther.

Chapter 9

He was dressed as before in formfitting black, his face and head masked by his bandana, his hands gloved—mysterious phantom of the night.

She whirled around, casting a panicked glance toward her bolted door, then to the other side of the room where the French doors stood open, though they'd been closed only moments before. She hadn't even heard him enter.

"Are you mad?" she hissed. "DeRohan's just down the hall."

Ignoring her words, he merely touched the blunt ends of her hair. "I like the change. It suits you."

All her bottled up feelings came rushing to the surface. Standing, she reached for the light switch, but he moved swiftly, putting his hand on hers. "Uh-uh, lady. No lights. Darkness is the world I inhabit."

She jerked her hand away. "Where are my pearls?"

He reached into a pouch he wore at his belt and withdrew something, holding it toward her in his palm. In the faintly flickering candlelight, the rich creamy gems gleamed softly against the dark leather of his glove.

Antoinette's necklace.

Suspiciously, she asked, "You're returning them to me?"

"I am."

"What kind of game are you playing?" she demanded.

She heard the click of the pearls as he laid the necklace on her vanity. "I didn't come to play games." Despite the gravelly whisper, there was something serious—almost dire—in his tone.

Suddenly, her mind cleared and she raised her gaze to his shadowed form, hope glistening in her eyes. "You've come to help me."

"Kill your husband?"

"Free me from him."

He stepped closer and trailed a gloved finger down her cheek. "What you don't seem to realize, *Cara*, is that freeing you from your husband won't really liberate you at all. Your bondage to him is only a symptom of the bondage of your life."

"What are you talking about?" she asked impatiently.

A trace of remembered passion flared at his touch. But she had too many emotions warring inside to give into it. She was angry with him, distrustful of him, and—Lord help her—in spite of everything, still treacherously attracted to him. But she'd been stung by him before. And overriding all of it was her desperation and fear. She was more frightened of her husband than she'd ever been. All she could see at the moment was that she had to free herself from him. Now. Before it was too late.

"I mean that your attachment to the past is the hold your husband has over you. You have to stay under his thumb in order to cling to these symbols of a past that is dead—the jewels and this house. Once you let go of that compulsion—once you no longer care about possessions that keep you tied to a past that will never come again—you can simply walk away from him. So you see, *Cara*. No one can free you but yourself."

His words infuriated her. "You're talking rubbish. I told you, I was entrusted with a sacred duty: to protect the last remains of a noble line. Maybe you can't understand what that means. Our traditions go back nearly seven hundred years. All those centuries of history, of art, of glory—all of it wiped out with the stroke of a pen. But it wasn't just history to us. It was our family. A family I loved and lost. The only thing my father ever asked of me was that I protect what little is left. Don't you see? I can't neglect that duty. It would be like . . . giving up *everything*."

He cupped his large hands on either side of her face, stroking the cheeks with his thumbs. "They're just things. They only assume the importance you give to them. Let your husband have them, and you'll be free for the first time in your life. Free to live for yourself."

All at once, she wanted to cry in frustration. "I can't. I've tried. But I'm not equipped for this. Habsburg women were taught everything but how to think for ourselves. We've only been good for one thing: to make marriages that would expand the Empire. But the war changed all that. There's no Empire, I'm no longer an archduchess, and I've been left in a world I don't really understand."

"And so you hide away here, in your Habsburg fortress, where the world you don't understand can't touch you."

"I've tried to break away. I've told you that. I tried to find happiness with Edwin, but DeRohan killed him. I tried to run away. But he's back, and I'm terrified of what's going to happen to me under his thumb. I'm afraid—"

She broke off, feeling humiliated.

"Afraid of what?" he asked gently.

"I'm afraid that all my old training will win out in the end. And maybe, despite all my best intentions, I'll finally decide it isn't worth the effort. That it's my fate, after all, to be the pawn I was trained to be. That I shall give in, from sheer exhaustion, and let DeRohan win. And then, where shall I be?"

He let out a slow steady breath. "I know you think I can't possibly understand," he told her, "but in my own way, I do. I, too, am trapped in a world I didn't choose." The sorrow in his voice mirrored that in her heart. "But you've sold yourself short. You're capable, you're inventive, you're more courageous than you know. I wouldn't be surprised if you relished facing down DeRohan every bit as much as I do climbing rooftops at night. Your hatred of your husband doesn't weaken you, it makes you strong. And if you're a Habsburg, you're like the original outlaws who defied the world and established this dynasty—not the corpulent inbred sleepwalkers who ended it. You can do anything you set your mind to."

She turned her back to him. "You're wrong. I'm cursed. All the Habsburgs are cursed."

He came up behind her and took her shoulders in his hands. "Then break the curse," he whispered fiercely. "It's not the being, it's the *doing* that defines you. In your own way, you're as much an outlaw as I am."

His hands felt so strong, so warm on her. She felt the desire to lean back into him and let his strength seep into her. But her urgency propelled her to turn on him. "Then help me. If you're right . . . if we really *are* alike . . . couldn't we perhaps help each other?"

"No."

"Why not?"

"Because I'm not the man you think I am."

"Who are you, then?"

"A tortured empty man. A man who has grown to despise what he's become. I would like nothing more than to help you in this rebellion you're mounting, this—journey to self. To be your guide. But I can't. Because I'm in a prison of my own. I became a thief as a way of trying to wrest myself from that prison. But I've come to realize that the mission of the so-called Panther has failed."

"Failed? You mean . . . because it's become too dangerous?"

"No. Because I know now what I wanted to do cannot be done. It was selfish vanity on my part. So the Panther has no more reason to exist. He is simply going to disappear into the night."

Something stilled inside her. "Disappear?"

"His last act is to return what he took from you, and to tell you—simply and sincerely—that he believes in you. You have within you the resources to free yourself from this evil man. But more importantly, to free yourself from the curse history has foisted upon you. This is your fight. And I know, as I've known nothing else in my life, that you *will* triumph."

"*How* can you know that?" she croaked. "I don't even know it myself."

He took her face in both hands. "I saw it when you called me back that first night. When you asked me to kill your husband. When I saw that defiance, that willingness to break the conventions of your world *that* drastically . . . when I saw that . . ."

"What?" She could scarcely breathe. It seemed to her in some strange way, that the next words he uttered would be the most important she would ever hear.

His gaze behind the mask bore deeply into her eyes. "I fell in love with you. In that instant."

The breeze fluttered the curtains, nearly extinguishing the candle's flame, shifting the light and shadows in the room so she could barely see him in the darkness. Outside, from somewhere far off, she heard the cry of some night bird, calling for its mate.

"You love me?"

"As I never thought I *could* love."

She felt her heart turn over.

"I suppose it seems sudden to you, that a man could take one look at a woman and lose the heart he never knew he had. It wasn't your beauty I fell in love with, or your pedigree, or even the fact that you were so unattainable—something I could never have. It was your *spirit*. When I saw that stark rebellion in your eyes, I felt . . ."

When he paused, she prompted breathlessly, "What did you feel?"

"That I'd somehow always known you. And that loving you could make me a better man."

Something died inside Jules. She put her hands on his chest, feeling the flexing of lean muscle against her palms. "If you love me, you won't leave me alone with this. You can't."

"I can and will. You must trust me, *Cara*, when I say there is a reason why we can never, under any circumstance, be together. A reason that has nothing to do with our stations in life, or the fact that I'm a thief. But a reason that is absolutely insurmountable nonetheless."

"Nothing is *absolutely* insurmountable," she said desperately, even though she knew it wasn't true.

"This is."

Why did the finality of his conviction tug at her heart so? She'd never expected it to be anything but temporary between them. It shouldn't matter in the least. But for some reason, it did. After a moment, she asked, "Will I ever see you again?"

"I hope not. I will do everything in my power to resist coming to you, no matter how deeply my heart yearns to do so. But know that I will always be close—just around the corner—a shadow in the night."

The despair in his whispered voice cut her like a knife. *I will always be close . . .* Something about the way he said this, something in the tone, or the cadence, or the very phrasing, sounded strikingly familiar. Then a thought—an incredible thought—occurred to her. "Do I know you?" she gasped. "Not as the Panther, but as your real self? Had our paths crossed before the night you first came here?"

He parted the marabou-trimmed robe with his hands, sliding them inside to graze the curve of her waist. "What difference does it make? If you *had* known me, you wouldn't have looked at me twice."

His evasion told her it was true. Their paths *had* crossed!

But when? And in what guise? The familiarity, whatever it was, seemed very distant. Almost like something out of a faintly remembered dream.

"None of this matters," he continued. "What does matter is that you find it within yourself to break the bonds that have imprisoned you."

"Alone."

"Yes, *Cara*. Alone."

His hands moved up her ribcage, brushing her breasts. She knew he wanted her—she could feel his desire emanating like sparks of electricity to every corner of the room. But she also had the feeling that the purpose of his touch was not to possess her, but to memorize the feel of her body, to create a memory that would last him a lifetime.

"And if I hate you for abandoning me?"

She felt him flinch, but he answered in the same earnest whispered tone, "I'll have to live with that, as I live with all my other regrets. But know this. Whatever happens in the long stretch of your future, whether you hate me or not . . . know that there is somewhere in this bleak world a man who, though he can never see you like this again, will love you—and believe in you—for the rest of his life."

She yanked away. "How can you say you love me when you'll do nothing to help me? Don't you know that man down the hall is threatening me in every conceivable way? Physically . . . emotionally . . . sexually . . . I desperately need help! You'll brave danger, you'll risk your life for a mere bauble, yet you won't lift a finger to help *me!* Instead, you spout platitudes about self-reliance and loving me from afar. They're only words, Panther. But your words won't help me. I need *action!*"

"Then take action."

In a rush of anger and frustration, she turned her back on him, no longer able to bear the sight of him—so large, so strong, radiating the power of possibility—and refusing to come to her aid. "How could I have been so deluded? I thought you were a hero sent to me by Providence, and in the end, you're just one more face at the party. Well, if that's all you're good for, you might just as well go. Get out!"

Her last words reverberated through the room.

Suddenly, she realized, with rising horror, what she'd said. She hadn't really meant it at all.

She whirled around, appalled regret burning her eyes. But he wasn't there.

Searching the shadows for him, she could already feel the emptiness of the room.

She was alone.

She raced to the French doors and out onto the terrace. Far below, she saw a dark figure skirting across the lawn.

She gripped the stone rail of the terrace, hearing as never before the lonely melody of the night, standing like a specter as the breeze gently swirled the pegnoir about her.

Too late, she understood why the words he'd said had cut so deeply.

She hadn't loved Edwin after all. He'd been nothing more than one more way to get back at DeRohan.

She'd never really loved anyone before this moment.

But she loved him. This mysterious, tortured man.

She wished she'd told him so.

Chapter 10

Jules didn't sleep that night. She sat in her bed, her back propped against a mountain of pillows, hugging her bent knees, staring out the open French doors into the sterile night. Hearing over and over all the things he'd said.

I fell in love with you . . . in that instant . . .

How could she have said the horrid things she had? How could she have hurt him that way? He'd only come one last time to tell her he loved her . . . that he believed in her. When no one had ever believed in her before.

And how had she repaid him? By making him feel that his love—his sacrifice—was nothing more than something she could use.

She'd never hated herself as much in her life.

She was so numb, she didn't notice the passage of time. She barely moved. She just felt wretched. Achingly conscious that she'd lost something she hadn't known she'd had.

He hadn't treated her like a whore at all. He hadn't wanted anything from her. He loved her . . .

When Hudson knocked on her outer door, bringing her breakfast, she was startled to realize it was morning. She hadn't even noticed the brightening of the sky.

Always sensitive to her moods, he asked, "Had a restless night, Highness?"

"Restless . . . yes," she murmured, still in the clutches of her dejection.

"I'm very sorry, Highness."

Something in his tone penetrated her dazed state. "You needn't apologize, Hudson. You didn't do anything."

"Still . . . I do hate to see you so troubled. Perhaps I could be of some assistance."

For once, even the prospect of unburdening herself to dear, loyal Hudson was no comfort. Her feelings were too brittle even to share with him.

"Thank you, Hudson. Perhaps later."

She scarcely touched her breakfast of scones with Corinthian raisins. She said nothing else to him as he moved about, quietly tidying up, until the telephone rang and he held it out to her. "For you, Highness. Mrs. Murphy."

She took the receiver reluctantly. "Darling," said her friend Sara in her breathless American accent, "Gerald and I just *this minute* got back from Paris. We saw Dottie Parker and Dos Pasos and had the most splendid time making the museum rounds. Gerald's full to the brim with new ideas he wants to put on canvas. I'll tell you all about it when I see you. Ernest is coming back from Pamplona and we're going to make a day of welcoming him back. I'm in Nice now, and I'll swing by to pick you up in about an hour. I can't wait to see you, darling. I hear you've taken the plunge and bobbed your hair!"

Jules couldn't seem to concentrate on what her friend was saying. "No, Sara, not today. I'm not up to it."

"Not up to it? Since when is our jewel not up to anything? Darling, are you all right? You sound positively *alarming*."

Jules closed her eyes, feeling the dull throb in her head. She couldn't very well tell Sara the truth, but there was one thing she could confess. "DeRohan's back."

Sara deepened her voice sympathetically. "Darling, I know all about it. Dev met us at the train and told us about his ghastly meeting with the brute. Oh, you *poor* dear. But never fear, we're coming to the rescue. You need your friends around you at such a time. I won't be long. You can have that lovely butler of yours collect you tonight. Bring your swim things, and something to go to the station in, and something sparkly to wear to the casino tonight. No arguments, now. I simply *won't* take no for an answer!"

The line went dead before Jules could protest.

Resigned, she rang for Denise to help her get ready. What did it matter? If nothing else, it would get her away from DeRohan. And perhaps, surrounded by her friends, she could forget for a time the awful mess she'd made of her life.

Sara was true to her word. When Hudson opened the front door, carrying the straw bag Denise had packed, she flew past him and took Jules in her arms. "Your hair! It's precious! Chic, sassy . . . Why, my dear, you've become a flapper!"

Sara had a golden presence. She was a true beauty, with wavy dark golden hair and a special aura that captivated everyone with whom she came into contact. She took artists under her wing, supported her friends both emotionally and financially, and despite her youth, served as a radiant mother hen to a pack of insane bohemians.

Jules felt her friend's affection soothe her throbbing nerves. But just then, a hated voice sounded behind her. "Going somewhere?"

Jules froze and Sara jumped as if Quasimodo had just bounded into the hall.

DeRohan was standing there, blocking their path to the door.

In a tight voice, Jules answered him, avoiding his eyes. "Yes. A friend is arriving from Spain and we're welcoming him home."

He continued to stand there, arms crossed over his chest, saying nothing, looking truly frightening as his gaze pierced her.

The words he'd said to Dev the other day came back to her: *You might inform her other American admirers that my wife will be out of their social whirl for the foreseeable future.*

What was he going to do?

Would he physically detain her? Throw Sara from the house?

For an agonizing minute that seemed an eternity, he continued to stare at her, stroking his close-cropped beard. Then he
stepped aside and said, "Have a good time."

His acquiescence was more frightening than his open hostility. She was learning that he was most dangerous in repose.
Like a sleeping lion, he'd let her have her year of freedom only
to come back pouncing with claws unsheathed. Would he do
the same after allowing her this day of liberty?

She brushed past him and they made their escape.

Once ensconced in the backseat of Sara's Isotta, Jules laid
her head back wearily as the driver put the auto in gear. She
could feel DeRohan standing in the doorway, looking after
her.

"Oh, my!" Sara sighed. "He *is* a hulking brute, isn't he?
Rather a magnificent specimen, in a Machiavellian sort of way.
A little thick around the middle perhaps, but not unhand-
some."

The unexpected praise reminded her of Denise's similar ap-
praisal. Jules wondered if perhaps DeRohan had had the maid
in the meantime. Did that explain his sudden docility in the
face of her rebellion?

"I've seen pictures of him in the papers, of course," Sara
rambled on, "but nothing quite prepares one for that *presence*
of his. I declare, I couldn't seem to catch my breath. I felt like
a hapless ladybug caught in the spider's web, with the spider
stalking in upon me. That, my dear, is one scary man! Exciting
in a curious way, and yet..." She fanned herself with her
hand. "I do believe the sight of him has just taken five years off
my life!"

Gerald and Sara Murphy were a wealthy American couple
who'd taken a villa on Cap d'Antibes, which they'd re-christened
Villa America. They were the major trendsetters of the new
generation of American Riviera expatriates, and the sun around

which the artistic avant-garde revolved. Along with their friend Cole Porter, they were credited with having invented the summer season. It was Sara who'd made wearing pearls to the beach fashionable.

It was also these breezy Americans who'd given Jules her less formal nickname. Previously, she'd been known to the world as Juliana and sometimes to her closer friends as Juli.

At La Garoupe, on a patch of beach Gerald had rescued from dried seaweed debris and religiously raked everyday, they found a handful of friends sprawled in the sand beneath the huge umbrella the Murphys had purchased from a market in Sienna: Anita Loos, who wrote for the cinema and had authored a book everyone was talking about called *Gentlemen Prefer Blondes*; the playwright Charles MacArthur; Archibald MacLeish's wife Ada, the soprano; and rounding out the group, a trio Jules knew better than the others: Booth Devlin, Scott Fitzgerald, and his unpredictable wife Zelda, who'd come down from their rented villa in Juan-les-Pins.

When the two women showed up, the well-tanned group, slick with coconut oil, jumped up in their bathing suits and rushed forward to inspect Jules's bobbed hair. Ada cried, "What *have* you children done?"

Zelda pronounced in her Southern Belle drawl, "Smart, smart, smart. I simply adore it!"

Her husband Scott, who hadn't risen, reached for his flask, lifted it in a silent toast, then poured himself another drink.

Sara raised a hand, calling for silence. "We come bearing news. Jules's bully of a husband has invaded the homefront. Come, everyone, we must do what we can to put her in good spirits."

Gerald Murphy approached and handed her a glass of iced sherry. "Here's all the spirits you need."

Jules drank it down in a gulp, hardly feeling it.

They did their best to amuse her, making up scathing puns from the names in the newspaper of passengers arriving on ships at Marseille. For a time, it helped. She genuinely liked these people. For the past year, she'd been very much a part of their circle. They knew her story and were protective of her. She felt nourished by them, accepted. They represented a new kind of artistic rebel: young, good-looking, privileged, talented, acidly witty, madly brilliant, with a glorious future before them. They'd adopted her in spite of her title, not because of it—simply because, in the year they'd known her, they'd found her fun to be with.

But as the morning wore on—a morning of endlessly acerbic conversation, refreshing dips in the blueberry sea, of sun and sand and the white-hot glow behind closed eyelids—her spirits began to wilt. Despite their best efforts, she couldn't escape the heaviness that had settled upon her. She was relieved when Gerald, like the ringmaster of a circus, waved his hand in the air and said, "Time for the station, kiddies. We don't want to keep Papa waiting."

They dressed in the cabanas, coming out in a parade of twenties fashion—wide-leg pants, slim dresses with waists at the hip, cloche hats, and espadrilles—and hiked back to the cars, carrying all the beach paraphernalia, to drive in a caravan to the nearby Antibes train station. They were just in time to see the object of today's celebration step onto the platform.

He was the magnetic young American author Ernest Hemingway, who'd just returned from one of his periodic trips to take in the bullfights. Jules watched as both his wife Hadley, and his secret lover, Hadley's friend Pauline, rushed to hug him. No one else knew about the clandestine affair, least of all Sara, who abhorred marital infidelity. But Jules had a gift for keeping people's secrets, and because of this, they confided to her things they wouldn't tell their more puritanical hostess. In his cups one evening, Hemingway had told her the whole story.

When it was her turn to be greeted, he flashed his teeth at her and winked. "Hiya, Princess. Cute hair. But you're looking a little piqued. You okay?"

"The prodigal husband has returned," Sara explained.

"Ah. Then I'll tell you all about the matadors. That will take your mind off your troubles."

The caravan went to the Murphys' villa where they lunched on the terrace, then went their separate ways: to walk through the gardens or along the beach, read, take naps. Booth Devlin, who'd driven ambulances with Hemingway on the Italian front during the war—and who wasn't particularly fond of the man—had wandered down to the beach by himself.

Appreciative of his attempted gallantry the day before, Jules walked down to join him. She'd often found comfort in his quiet company. He was the only one who didn't drink or smoke. And while the others bathed every utterance in sarcasm and brittle wit, Dev chose his own words carefully, and carried in his soothing grey-green eyes an air of sadness that he masked with friendly dignity, which touched her. His wife had died three years ago, and everyone assumed that was the source of his sadness, but no one asked. For all their outward gaiety, there was a great deal of turmoil floating beneath the surface that was never voiced aloud.

He'd been sitting in the sand with his elbows resting on his drawn-up knees, gazing at the ocean with a faraway look in his eyes. When Jules sat down beside him, he glanced at her and smiled ruefully, as if she'd caught him in an unguarded moment.

"I wanted to apologize to you for my husband's rudeness," she began, digging the toe of her espadrille into the sand.

"Think nothing of it. If I've made things worse for you—"

"You haven't. His possessiveness has nothing to do with you. It was kind of you to think of me."

He let a silence drag between them as he once again looked out toward the horizon. Finally he said, "You know, Jules, it's impossible to go through life without finding your back to the wall every so often. But even if things happen that we can't control, there *are* ways to live with our circumstances and do what we must. Unconventional ways, sometimes. But with a little initiative, we can live with heartache and turn it into something creative."

It seemed an eerie rephrasing of what the Panther had said to her the night before. But she was distracted from the thought by the flash of pain in Dev's eyes when he glanced at her. She wondered if he was still grieving the loss of his wife. She wanted to ask, to console him if possible, but there was something about the set of his shoulders that told her such an intrusion would be unwelcome.

She understood the need to keep one's troubles to one's self, so she only said, "Thanks, Dev. You're a good friend."

She reached over and took his large hand in hers. He gave an involuntary start and, after a moment, pulled his hand away. As if even this small intimacy might be a betrayal of his dead wife.

That night, they were joined by more of their circle at the casino further up the coast in Juan-les-Pins for a champagne and caviar party: the official celebration of Hemingway's home-coming. Caviar was unheard-of in the summer, because it would spoil on the journey from Russia, but Gerald had the brilliant idea of having it flown in from the Caspian Sea—the kind of extravagant gesture that had made him one of the Riviera's most legendary hosts.

But the party was doomed from the start. Apart from Jules's lack of enthusiasm, Scott had been drinking all day and showed up already drunk. Zelda wasn't speaking to him, except to say, "All you ever do is drink." As Sara tried to convince "Gross Patron," as she called Hemingway, to tell them about Spain, Scott began to pout. He'd been Ernest's mentor in the early days when Hemingway had been an aspiring writer penning dispatches for newspapers, but with the impending publica-tion of his much anticipated novel, *The Sun Also Rises,* the spotlight began to shift from Scott to him. Scott—who, along with Hemingway, Picasso, and a host of others, was half in love with Sara—showed his displeasure over her fawning of

"Gross Patron" by first hurling ashtrays off the casino terrace, then putting a throw rug over his head and crawling from room to room moaning, "Sara's being mean to me."

Fuming, Gerald accused Fitzgerald of ruining the *fête,* and the two men exchanged heated words.

Jules had had enough. The antics of her friends, which she usually found amusing, seemed suddenly, in the light of all that had happened, shallow and frivolous. Especially once Booth Devlin left the party. Taking a glass of champagne with her, she went down into the garden below and sat among the ashtrays Scott had hurled from the terrace above.

She felt closer to Dev than to any of the others today for she, too, was brooding over something she couldn't share. She'd been willing herself all day not to think about the Panther. But now, alone, exhausted from her sleepless night, her defenses loosened by champagne, other things he'd said began to float to the surface of her mind.

I'll always be close . . . just around the corner . . . a shadow in the night . . .

He'd known her before. Not as the daring and glamorous cat burglar, but in some other guise.

If you had known me, you wouldn't have looked twice at me . . .

No one she knew well, then. No one from her vast circle of acquaintances. Someone on the periphery, perhaps? Someone she'd brushed up against without realizing it?

And yet, she was sure of it now, there was something vaguely, hauntingly familiar about him. What was it? She couldn't put her finger on it. Like a strip of film going through a projector, she ran the scenes of her life through her head, searching for him. But she couldn't find him.

If only she could figure out who he really was . . .

Oh, what was she doing? Harboring some fantasy that she could somehow discover his secret? And then what? Try to make it up to him for all the awful things she'd said?

Tell him she loved him? That whatever it was that lay between them *could* be overcome? Somehow . . . despite everything . . .

Despite DeRohan?

A breeze blew up suddenly, chilling her. What did it matter *who* he was?

He was just a phantom in the night . . . as much a fantasy as any Byronic hero she'd read about through her long lonely nights. And now she was alone, once again, just as she'd been before he'd so dramatically swooped into her life.

Alone and faced with an impossible situation.

DeRohan.

What was she going to do?

Once again the Panther's words came back to her. *You have to free yourself. You're more courageous than you know.*

But how could she do it?

As she slowly sipped her champagne, she became aware of voices from the terrace above, drifting down to her. Two men moved closer to the rail. Gradually, she recognized the voices as belonging to Scott and Gerald.

"I'm telling you, Gerald, she's having an affair."

"You don't know that."

In a slurred voice, Scott whined, "How many years have I been married to her? I *know* Zelda. I know when she's just restless, and when she's infatuated with someone else."

"Scott, you're dreaming. You're a writer. That's what you do for a living, you invent things. Your imagination is running wild."

"It's that aviator. That damned frog flyboy. I know it is. And I know how I'm going to get the goods on them."

"Oh? And how is that?"

"I will partake of the services of Emile the Snake."

A slight pause. "Emile Gréoux? You have to be out of your mind."

"They say he's a whiz."

"Scott, you're talking about the slimiest character on the Côte."

"The guy specializes in this sort of thing. Remember that Olympic tennis player? Maria What's-her-name? The Snake got the goods on her philandering husband in one weekend. That's how she got her divorce. A *Catholic* divorce at that!"

"Do you really know anything about this character?"

"I know he can ferret out any secret, if you pay him enough."

"Well, I *do* know a few things. And listen: First of all, you have to go to him. He won't come to you. Second of all, he hangs out in the worst section of the Toulon waterfront. You risk life and limb just going there. Thirdly, even with *Gatsby*, you don't have enough money to pay this guy what he'll ask."

"But you'll lend it to me, won't you, Gerald?"

"No, I won't. Not for this. And you don't want to divorce Zelda anyway. Just forget it Scott. What you're talking about is dangerous. Honestly, kiddo, you don't have the guts."

They moved away, leaving Jules's mind in a whirl.

I can't help you. You must help yourself.

Suddenly, she stood up and flung her champagne into the bushes.

Very well, Panther. You want me to handle this alone? Well, just watch me!

Chapter 11

The train rounded the bend. Ahead, Jules could see the first outskirts of the port of Toulon come into view. A major French naval base since the seventeenth century, its reputation surpassed even those of Marseille and Naples as the Mediterranean's most sordid den of iniquity.

She took a breath, feeling nervous but excited. She realized she'd never been alone on a train before, indeed, had never done much of anything by herself, much less anything as daring and reckless as the mission she was on today. All her life, even during the most desperate trials, she'd been surrounded by a protective entourage.

Today she was completely on her own.

Hudson had made the arrangements through an intermediary and had tried his best to accompany her. "Highness, this Snake fellow insists you come alone. But I can't allow it. The Toulon harbor is a dangerous place for anyone, much less someone of your inexperience in such matters."

But she'd refused. She wasn't about to risk alienating the man they called Emile the Snake. And besides . . . as irrational as it may be, she wanted to show the Panther—whoever he was—that his faith in her was warranted. That she *could* do this by herself.

So she'd told Hudson, "I need you to stay here and deflect DeRohan. If he asks where I am, you must convince him I'm off with my American friends, but you don't know with whom or where. That way he can't call and check up on me."

This would all be unnecessary if DeRohan would accommodate her by jumping to the bait of Denise the maid. But Hudson, who knew everything that went on in the house, was adamant that, despite Denise's numerous coy advances, DeRohan hadn't shown the slightest interest—indeed, had sent the poor girl sobbing from his room with a gruff rebuke. No, it had been naïve of Jules to think such a clever man as her husband would allow himself to be so easily trapped.

Once again, she felt inside the purse she carried, fingering the diamond bracelet. It was a relatively newer piece and therefore less valuable than the others, so it wouldn't pain her as much to lose it. But it would certainly be enough to buy the services of the scoundrel who, by all accounts, was sneaky enough to outwit even the likes of DeRohan.

The train pulled into a decrepit station, and she disembarked amidst the pushing and shoving of departing and boarding passengers. The heat was stifling. To dress down she'd worn her simplest summer frock, chicly cut but unadorned, but she could see instantly that even with those pains, she was the best dressed person by half.

Outside the station, the scene was even more hectic and the sun bore down mercilessly. The setting had none of the Belle Époque splendor of the train stations of the eastern Côte d'Azur. Everyone was shabbily dressed and the faces looked haggard and soulless. The men, idling on street corners with cigarettes hanging from their mouths, looked her up and down as if she were a slab of beef in a butcher shop. Several of them had lost limbs in the war. Women with deeply lined faces seemed to snarl at her as if resenting her pristine appearance. Mangy dogs fought in the street over a scrap of sausage thrown by a bystander, their snarls eliciting howls of laughter from a gang of filthy urchins playing in a puddle. As Jules moved on, she began to feel dizzy and disoriented, and to fear she'd taken on much more than she'd bargained for.

She had no idea in which direction to head. Looking about, she spotted a more congenial looking boy selling newspapers. "I beg your pardon, could you please direct me to the old port?"

"The old port? Straight that way." He pointed. "But, Madame, they'll eat you alive in the old port! It's not pleasant like it is here."

Not pleasant like it is here? She gulped, but was determined to push on.

She proceeded to wind her way down a series of narrow cobblestone streets. By an alley that reeked of stale urine, a small beggar boy walking with a crutch approached her with his hand outstretched. "If you please, Madame."

Her heart went out to him. She reached into her bag to give him a coin. His eyes widened greedily at the sight of it. As she tried to move away, he followed, dropping the crutch in his eagerness and trotting alongside of her. "Please, Madame, more. Surely you can spare . . ."

Wanting to get rid of him, she reached into her purse again and gave him another coin. But it didn't dissuade him. He began pulling on her dress, leaving a grimy stain on her peach colored skirt.

"I gave you two coins, now please leave me alone," she requested.

But he kept pulling at her. Soon, he was joined by another beggar, seemingly from out of nowhere. Then another. And another. They were all shouting and pulling on her. She began to fear they were plotting to snatch her purse.

The bracelet!

Thinking fast, she reached into her bag, grabbed whatever coins she could find, and flung them into the air. As they clanked against the cobblestones and the boys scrambled after them, she ran as rapidly as she could to make her escape.

She continued on in the direction the newsboy had indicated, struggling to catch her breath, until she came to a group of heavily made-up women perched on a corner. Prostitutes.

She'd never actually spoken to one before, but once again she was feeling disoriented and in need of directions.

"Excuse me, *mesdames,* but I'm in search of the Rue de Faron in the old port. Could you help me, please?"

"The Rue de Faron?" cried one. "A pretty young thing like you? They'll throw a hood over your head and you'll be on the next boat for Tangiers. Better to stay here and work with us, *ma petite.*"

"The Sultan of Tangiers would pay a pretty sou for *this* choice morsel!"

Most of them cackled with delight, but one sympathetic redhead said, "If you must, Madame, the Rue de Faron is three blocks that way."

Smiling her thanks, Jules proceeded on until at last she came to a square that faced the waterfront. Suddenly she knew what the newsboy had meant. The stench was overwhelming. Even in the blinding sunlight, it was seedy, sordid, and dangerous. Thick-necked sailors and brawny fishermen drank absinthe in a rundown sidewalk café. Her presence caused a stir. Sailors whistled openly, pimps called out lewd comments and invitations. One particularly disreputable looking character without any teeth ambled up to her, looked her frankly up and down, then unbuttoned his trousers and proceeded to urinate against the side of the building.

She was a long way from Schonbrunn Palace.

Some part of her mind was screaming at her, *Turn around and get out of here as quickly as you can.*

But she couldn't turn back.

Go back to what? DeRohan?

Whatever was ahead couldn't be as bad as that.

Taking a gulp, she scanned the row of dilapidated establishments facing the water until she spotted the Café de la Midi. Emile Gréoux was supposed to meet her here at exactly one o'clock. Five minutes from now.

Ignoring the catcalls that followed her, she made her way toward it. Its outdoor tables were half-filled with sailors eating bouillabaisse, washing it down with cheap wine. As she found a table, she was shocked to hear a familiar voice call out, "Juli, good God!"

She spun around to see Nikki Romanov standing not five feet away.

"What in the world are you doing *here?*" he cried, rushing to her.

What do I do? What can I do?

Turn it on him.

"What are *you* doing here?" she asked.

He gave a vague shrug. "Slumming, naturally. The healthy exercise of a young man. But not a young woman."

"Slumming?"

"Well, after all my sweet, you may think of me as the little boy you used to play with, but I'm not as innocent as you like to think. And don't think I haven't noticed that you never answered my question. What in the name of Creation are you doing in a place like this—and *alone?*"

She didn't know what to say. To even begin to explain would take too long, and the Snake had stipulated that she must be alone. "Nikki, I'm having an adventure, and you must leave me."

His brow creased. "Adventure? Are you mad? What kind of adventure would take you into *this* seventh level of hell?"

"Nikki," she repeated, "I don't have time to explain. But it's very important to me and you're only going to impede my success by staying here."

He pushed her down into a chair and sat across from her. "I'm going to sit right here and I'm not going to move until you tell me what's going on."

She glanced about, exasperated, not knowing what to do. Even now, the Snake could be watching her. Would he assume she'd disobeyed his stipulation and leave?

Somehow, she had to get Nikki out of here.

But just as she was opening her mouth to speak, she heard the screech of tires and saw Nikki's concerned eyes jerk to the distance. With lightning speed and all his might, he raised his foot and kicked her chair, sending her tumbling backward just as a hail of gunshots ricocheted all around them.

She felt a ripping pain on her temple and the blazing sun began to go out like a lantern being slowly turned down.

The last thought that occurred to her before she passed out was that never, in all the years she'd known him, had she seen Nikki Romanov behave in such a swift, heroic manner.

It was almost as if he'd moved like a panther.

Chapter 12

Jules opened her eyes to a splitting headache and the sight of Nikki's troubled face gazing down upon her. She thought she was lying beneath a café table on the Toulon waterfront, but she quickly realized she was back in her bedroom at Rêve de l'Amour.

"Nikki . . ."

"Juli, thank God you're awake."

"What happened?"

"You were nearly killed."

It began to come back to her. The look of panic in Nikki's eyes. The gunshots. His quick reflexes.

"You kicked me over."

"It's the only thing I could think to do. I heard an auto careening around the corner and I looked up to see two pistols pointing our way. All I could think was to get you out of harm's way."

"Pistols?"

"The Toulon police think we must have wandered into the cross fire of two warring waterfront gangs. Luckily they were fast on the scene and helped me get you out of there."

She reached up to rub her aching head and her hand came in contact with a bandage. "I was hit?"

"A bullet grazed your forehead. The doctor says it's not serious. But if you hadn't moved when you did, we'd most likely be planning your funeral right now."

"Then . . . you saved my life."

He averted his gaze. "Just a reflex, I'm afraid."

She stared up at him wondrously. And all at once she saw him as if for the first time. He wasn't little Nikki, the companion of her childhood. He was a man. A very striking man, at that, with his tousled black hair and lean muscular body. She'd always thought him lazy and indolent, and yet . . .

She remembered the image that had crossed her mind in that moment before she passed out.

He'd moved like a panther.

You wouldn't have looked at me twice.

Of all men, Nikki most perfectly fit that description. Of the same age, they'd known each other since they were three, when their parents had first brought them to the Côte. She'd always looked upon him with the dismissive affection one gave a tagalong brother. In their childhood games of make-believe— when he'd joined her and her brothers in acting out scenes from stories of *Robin Hood* or *Camelot* or *Bluebeard the Pirate*—he'd played the role of confidant and best friend, but never leading man. Yet, when she'd been in danger, he'd come to her rescue with a dash and flair worthy of any Dumas hero.

Was it possible?

No. It was ludicrous. This was Nikki she was talking about. It must be the effects of her injury.

Once again, she fingered the bandage on her temple.

The room was silent for some time. When she finally opened her eyes and looked at him, he was sitting with elbows resting on his thighs, his head in his hands. All she could see was the luxuriant black locks of hair.

"Jesus, Juli, I'm so sorry."

"You have nothing to be sorry for."

He looked up at her and she read some torment in his eyes. But he masked it quickly, saying, "No. I suppose not." After a moment, he asked in a voice that to her imagination seemed quite unlike his own, "What were you doing there?"

"I wanted evidence I could use against DeRohan in a divorce action. I was trying to engage the services of a man named Emile Gréoux."

Nikki lunged out of his seat. "Emile the Snake!" Raking a hand through his hair, he paced a few steps up, then back. "I suppose if I were any kind of friend at all, I'd find a way to help you myself." She held her breath. "But I can't."

"Nikki . . . what are you saying?"

He turned and looked at her. "Nothing, Juli. I just wish I wasn't such an ineffectual twit. But in any case, you'll never do this again, will you? I don't think I could stand it if anything ever happened to you."

Just then, Hudson rapped softly and entered. "Excuse me, Highness. There's a gentleman from the police here to see you."

Nikki bent, brushing a kiss on her forehead. "I'll leave you, then, and call in a day or two to see how you're feeling. Take good care of her, Hudson."

As he closed the door behind him, Jules turned her gaze to Hudson. "Did you tell anyone that I was going to Toulon?"

"Of course not, Highness."

"You didn't mention it to Nikki?"

"I had no conversations with the Grand Duke before he brought you here."

"It certainly was odd, him turning up there like that. Don't you think?"

"Perhaps. But then, it's not uncommon for young gentlemen to go there seeking exotic pleasures they can't find in Nice or Marseille."

For a moment she wondered what those exotic pleasures might be. If Nikki were secretly masquerading as the Panther, could that explain how he'd learned to be such an inventive lover?

But it couldn't be. She couldn't be in the same room with

the Panther without feeling that stark sexual presence, without her body leaping with longing. She was in love with the Panther. But she'd never—not once—been attracted to Nikki in any way. The whole notion was madness. And yet . . .

You'd never have looked at me twice . . .

She shook her head and tried to clear it, and feeling a stab of pain, turned to Hudson. "Who is this policeman who wants to see me?"

"He's British, Highness, from Scotland Yard. One Inspector Ladd. You may recall reading in the papers that he's been called in by the Nice police to act as a special consultant in the Panther matter. Apparently, society burglaries are his forte."

Her heart skipped a beat. "Why does he want to see me? Do you think he—"

"I don't think so, Highness. His interest seems to be in your unfortunate incident in Toulon. Apparently, he thinks it might be connected to some other case he's investigating in England. Shall I tell him you're not up to it?"

"No," she decided. "Show him in. I might as well get it over with."

Hudson vanished, then returned a few moments later with a smiling middle-aged man who had the ruddy complexion of a weekend cricket player.

"Good afternoon, Mrs. DeRohan. So sorry to hear about your accident." He glanced at the chair so recently vacated by Nikki. "May I be seated?"

"Yes, of course."

It occurred to her that this man's primary purpose in life at the moment was to hunt down the Panther. Was it possible that his prey had just passed him in the hall?

She couldn't resist saying, "I've read about you in the papers, Inspector. How you've come here to track down our notorious Panther. Have you had any success in that matter?"

"You can be sure that rascal is in my sights—and will soon be under lock and key—but I didn't come here to talk about him. I'm most concerned about your little mishap in Toulon. Might I ask you some questions about it?"

"Certainly, Inspector."

Awkwardly, he began, "First of all, if you'll forgive the intrusion, I must ask *what* a young woman such as yourself was doing in that little corner of Sodom and Gomorrah in the first place."

No handy excuse leapt to mind, so she decided to just tell him the truth.

"Oh, I see," the inspector said. "Well—hrumph—I'm certainly not here to involve myself in any domestic conflicts. But this Emile—What's-his-name—I can never pronounce these French names—he knew you were coming and was expecting you?"

"Yes. We had an appointment."

"And on the journey there, did you have a sense of anyone following you, by any chance?"

"None at all. Of course, I wasn't looking for it. Why do you ask?"

"Well, Ma'am, the Toulon police believe you just happened to wander into a territorial dispute between two gangsters. And I suppose that is the logical explanation. But, given that you're a Habsburg, there is another possibility."

"What is that, sir?"

"Have you ever heard of the Verdun League?"

"Verdun? As in the Battle of Verdun? I'm afraid not, Inspector. Why?"

"You do know that the former Archduke Matthias was attacked in London last year, do you not?"

He was a distant cousin she couldn't remember ever having met. "Yes, in the Strand. I read about it. But it was never revealed who did it, or why."

"And another cousin of yours, Prince Otto of Saxony, drowned two years ago crossing the English Channel."

"Yes, a boating accident. What are you inferring, Inspector?"

"That maybe it wasn't an accident. I've investigated both these cases and I have evidence that they might have been carried out as part of a conspiracy that blames the Habsburg dynasty for the Great War—and is determined to punish them for it. The Verdun League."

"You think I was the target of these people? I can hardly credit such an outlandish supposition."

"Outlandish, perhaps. I don't really know, Ma'am. And I don't care to unduly alarm you. These people, as far as I know, have only operated in England, and have only attacked the men of your extended family. I have no real reason to believe they might be after you. Most likely, the Toulon police are correct in their analysis of the situation. But under the circumstances, I would implore you to take no more personal risks. I've instructed your husband on certain precautions he might take for your safety. That should be sufficient."

Precautions . . . what did that mean? Was she to be even more of a prisoner now than she was before?

She laid her head back in the pillows and for a moment thought of the mess she'd made of everything. She'd taken a bold action to free herself just as the Panther had said she must—and look what had happened!

The policeman soon left, but the door didn't completely close behind him. After a moment, she heard the inspector speaking back and forth with DeRohan down the hall.

Any minute now, DeRohan would make his appearance. What would he say to her? Would he perhaps, at last, show her some small sympathy?

Momentarily, she began to hear his distinctive heavy footsteps. Then the door opened and he entered the room.

He stepped over to the bed and looked down at her with an expression she couldn't read. The air in the room was suddenly charged as she waited.

Finally, in a voice that sounded like ground glass, he said, "How dare you?"

"I beg your pardon?"

Now she could see the fury in his eyes. "How dare you put yourself in such jeopardy at a time when you know I need your help?"

His uncaring hostility was more than she could bear. She'd almost been killed and it mattered not at all to him. All he could think of was the inconvenience it would be to his precious plans of preserving his business empire. To be hated that much—for nothing she'd done, just because of who she was—was truly unsettling.

"Oh, go and leave me alone," she said wearily.

"You *are* a pathetic fool. Did you really think you could employ the services of Emile Gréoux without me knowing about it?"

She gasped her surprise. "How could you know?"

"I know everything. I'm always one step ahead of you. I could hear your mind ticking: *I can collect irrefutable evidence of his infidelities.* First you throw your silly little maid at me. Then, when that doesn't work, you get a better idea: *I can get Emile the Snake to track down the lovely ladies who have graced his bed in my absence and bribe their sworn testimony in a court of law. After all, it worked for the Marquis de Riquier and Lady Silvia Bentley, why shouldn't it work for me?* But what you don't know, wife of mine, is that Emile the Snake has been on my personal payroll for the last three years. And even if he weren't, don't you know there is no court on this continent that I couldn't manipulate into preserving our *sacred* marriage vows? So get this through your head once and for all, Juliana: There will be no divorce. Not now. Not ever. I—will—never—allow—it. Do you hear me?"

As he said this, his voice cracked, as if with some emotion other than hatred. It shocked her. But if she thought for a moment that she'd witnessed some unexpected rupture in his wall of hatred, she soon found she was mistaken.

He reached down, gripped her chin in his hand, and turned her to face him. "Furthermore, now that we know it's not safe for you to be running around loose, I suppose I shall have to add to our security staff and put a few more locks on the doors. After all, as every good businessman knows, one must protect one's investments."

At that very moment, some two hundred miles away, a stooped balding man entered a nondescript London pub and walked slowly to the rear, where another man sat nursing a pint with an angry expression on his raw-boned face. As he sat down nervously, he said in an upper-class English accent, "I've bad news to report, I'm afraid."

"I have heard," the second man responded. He spoke English with a Hungarian accent.

"It was no one's fault. They managed to fire off several rounds, but the police came before they could make sure the job was done."

"And who's idea was this? No one from the central board issued a strike order."

"The decision was made on the spot. The opportunity presented itself, and our man there had to seize it. You don't know how rare it is for the target to expose herself in that manner. We had to act."

The Hungarian fumed for several moments, then exploded. "You idiot! What possible good do you think it would do our cause for this woman to be gunned down in some dark alley of the armpit of the Mediterranean? What attention would that give us? The decision was made after the obscure death of Prince Otto to make our revenge public, to capture the eyes of the entire world. When this woman dies, people will know by whom, and why."

"We know that is the ideal. But you must realize, old chap, that this woman is difficult to catch in such a situation. And our people are unfamiliar with the terrain, so—"

"I care nothing for your rationalizations of what happened. It is a botched job all the way around. And now it will prove even more difficult to corner the woman in the way we require."

The Englishman lowered his head. "I assume full responsibility. If the League has lost confidence in me, I shall willingly step back and—"

"What the League wants is this: On the tenth of September, the city of Nice will inaugurate an unusual war memorial that will stare down on the Riviera from the hills above. Unlike the other memorials in France, it will commemorate the losses of *all* the nations involved, and is designed to be a symbol of reconciliation that will bring together the former combatants and look to the future with a forgiving eye on the past. We happen to know that, as part of this conciliatory spirit, the committee behind the memorial has been attempting to lure their resident Habsburg to be one of the speakers. Do you see the beauty of what I am proposing?"

"Indeed. If we could get her there, and somehow gun her down as she presents herself to the forgiving public, it would be like grabbing the world by the collar and telling it we will *never* forget!"

"Precisely."

The Englishman considered the plan. "But the woman is likely to refuse their invitation. She is, by all accounts, a proud young woman who, like the rest of her cursed breed, has never acknowledged her family's guilt."

"Your job is to get her there. This inside man—the one you call Dante—how good is he?"

"He's excellent, but . . . he's grown more reluctant. His heart has never been in it. He's not one of us. We've had to force him."

"Can we rely on him, then?"

"I believe so. We know a secret about him that he would do anything—and I do mean anything—to keep from coming to light."

The Hungarian took a gulp from his beer. "Then squeeze him. Squeeze him as hard as you must. But make it happen. The Great War Memorial. September."

Chapter 13

Two days later, Jules was still in bed. It wasn't that she was suffering the ill effects from the accident. The doctor had come earlier that day and removed the bandage, saying her wound was healing nicely. She was young and healthy and had been made strong and athletic from hours of swimming, walking, and playing tennis. Her body had recovered quickly.

But she was suffocating in feelings of hopelessness, failure, loss. She couldn't seem to think what to do next. And so she did nothing.

Even her suspicion that Nikki might be the Panther had waned. He hadn't even called or come by to see her. What had seemed an epiphany in her confused state gradually lost its force. The more she thought about it, the more difficult it became to merge the two figures in her consciousness. It now seemed like one more subconscious urge to transform this creature of the night into a storybook hero—and keep him in her life even when all the evidence pointed to the fact that the phantom had vanished forever.

It was 1926, a modern age of jazz and aeroplanes, in which women had forsaken their corsets, were smoking openly in public, drank as much as men, and kicked up their heels all night long to syncopated rhythms. But while Jules outwardly embraced the new age, she still secretly felt like a princess in her ivory tower, looking for a champion to come to her rescue.

Even when he'd told her he couldn't.

Or wouldn't.

Momentarily, Hudson returned for the tray he'd left earlier. When he saw she hadn't touched it once again, he frowned. But as he picked it up, he only said, "Your American friend Mr. Devlin just dropped by to see how you're doing, Highness."

"He did? Why wasn't I told?"

"The master is turning away all well-wishers at the door."

The insufferable swine!

The news reinforced the bitter fact that she was now more of a prisoner than she'd ever been. Three additional security guards had been added to the staff and were now patrolling the grounds at regular intervals. But she had the feeling they weren't there so much to keep intruders out as to keep her in.

Then a thought hit her. "Has Nikki Romanov been by to see me by any chance?"

"I don't know, Highness. I was away on an errand much of the morning."

Had he come to see her and been turned away at the door?

Was she wrong to think he hadn't cared enough to come see her?

"Do you plan to spend your life in bed?"

Startled out of her thoughts, she looked up and saw DeRohan standing in the doorway, his arm above him, his fingers resting on the jamb. Filling it with his massive form, like a warden checking on his convict.

"Perhaps I shall," she replied, utterly disinterested.

"The hell you will." His eyes were cold and fierce, piercingly her. "I should think, what with that precious Habsburg upbringing of yours, you'd be made of sterner stuff. You've better things to do with your time than feel sorry for yourself."

"Such as?"

"Such as preparing yourself for the Shah's arrival. This afternoon, I've arranged for several Parisian couturiers to come down on the Blue Train and show you their collections. You have a blank check. Buy something to wear that will please the Shah. What, I shall leave to you."

"So long as it's alluring enough to do the job? Perhaps I should consult a streetwalker to ascertain what would be best."

He was quiet for a moment. She could feel the hair on her neck bristling.

Then, slowly, he came closer. As she watched in growing horror, he sat beside her on the edge of the bed. She could feel her body jump at the close proximity and instinctively pulled back. But he reached out and, with the back of his finger, traced a path down the line of her arm. "If anyone is going to partake of your services, it's going to be me."

She recoiled beneath his touch, her heart pounding like a jackhammer. When he saw her appalled expression, he merely laughed, as if enjoying the sense of power his threatening presence gave him.

In a strained voice, she said, as calmly as she could manage, "Take your filthy hand off me or I shall spit in the Shah's eye when you present me to him."

The laughter vanished. He studied her for a moment, then withdrew his hand and stood. "You do, Juliana, and mark my words: you'll live to regret it."

Alone again, she sat up in bed. Her hand was trembling, but for the first time since Toulon, something was stirring in her.

The Panther was right about one thing.

Your hatred of your husband makes you strong.

She rose and rang for Hudson. When he arrived, she had him get on the telephone and track down the whereabouts of Nikki Romanov. After a few minutes, he told her, "His valet informs me that the Grand Duke is presently at a beach party at Villefranche."

It couldn't be more perfect!

"Hudson, bring me a swimsuit and a sundress to wear over it. I think a swim might be beneficial to my health."

"But, Highness . . . you do realize there are guards posted all over the grounds poised to prevent you from leaving the premises. You'll never get past them."

She turned her back, smiling to herself. "Oh, won't I?"

The long crescent of sandy beach—one of the few on the rocky Côte d'Azur—was nestled below a ridge of rocks in the curve of the coastline between the charming medieval fishing village of Villefranche and the jutting peninsula of Cap Ferrat. Across the dirt road to the back and supporting the train tracks high above, the towering wall was draped for a quarter mile with lush purplish-pink bougainvillea, creating a backdrop of flowers that dazzled the eye.

It was one of the loveliest beaches on the Riviera, but few people knew about it, so it was often possible to share it with just a handful of children. The sailors of the fleet spent their time drinking or smoking opium with the artist Jean Cocteau at the nearby Welcome Hotel, and the local families of fishermen found it incomprehensible that anyone would want to bake themselves in the sun.

But today, the beach was littered with the paraphernalia of an afternoon beach party. A portable phonograph sat in the sand, cranking out bubbly tunes from a scratchy record while the young revelers danced the Charleston in their beachwear. Jules, dressed in a white one-piece backless bathing suit that would seem scandalous anywhere except the Riviera, put up a hand to shield her eyes from the blinding sun and spotted Nikki frolicking in the water with some of his society friends.

She'd walked the half mile from her own private beach below Rêve de l'Amour. This was the first time she'd had to use her grandmother's tunnels to escape the house. She'd merely crept her way unseen to the basement, found the hidden opening behind the false cupboard, and followed the hidden route down to the safety of the beach some two hundred feet below the estate, and well out of view. Hudson would be scratching his head trying to figure out how she'd managed it. She felt guilty about not telling him, but she didn't want to share the secret with anyone, even him.

It was good to be away, comforting to know there was at least one advantage she held in the face of DeRohan's malevolent power over her.

As crazy as it seemed in the full light of day, the notion that Nikki might be the Panther was simply not going to go away. If it were true, she wasn't sure how it would affect her situation—or her feelings for him. But one way or another, she had to know.

When he noticed her standing at the edge of the water, the tide tickling her toes, he abandoned his friends and began to trudge her way through the waist-high water. As he rose from it, she noted for the first time the chiseled muscles of his chest, the lean yet sculpted arms. How was it that she'd never noticed before what a magnificent physique he had?

"Well, you're the last person I expected to see. You seem to have made a remarkable recovery. And the bandage is off. Let me see it. Ah, only a scratch after all. *Brava*."

Was it a hint—some sort of tease—his using the Italian word? To test him, she responded in Italian. "Two days was long enough to lie about in bed under the menacing eye of my husband."

He peered at her for a moment. Then, glancing away, he said in English, "I stopped by this morning to see you, but he turned me away at the door. Wasn't very nice about it, either, I might add."

If he *was* the Panther, he wasn't going to make this easy.

"In any case," he added, "it's marvelous to see you up and around. I love your bathing suit, by the way. Why don't you come in the water? Unless you're too debilitated from your injury. You are, after all, just a girl."

His eyes twinkled when he said it.

She put a hand on her hip indignantly. "I can still swim faster than you, even with a bum head!"

He moved a little closer and kicked a spray of water her way. Some of it splashed against her legs. It was so cold, she gave a mock shriek. "Why, you devil!"

He grinned at her. "And what are you going to do about it?" he taunted.

It was as if they were suddenly ten years old again.

"I'll tell you what. You see that raft out there? I'll race you to it. Last one to the ladder has to do whatever the other asks."

She saw his hesitation. "That depends on what's asked."

"Oh, no. The winner gets to ask whatever she wants."

"Then I suppose I shall have to make sure I win."

With that, he leapt into the air and swerved like a dolphin in a single motion, diving into the surf. She dove in after him. At first contact with the water, her healing forehead stung from the salt, but she ignored it and it soon passed.

They were both strong swimmers and made quite a spectacle surging through the water like two Olympic competitors after a gold medal. But Jules's determination gave her the added incentive that won the race. She grasped the ladder just an instant before his hand did the same.

Panting, laughing, she cried, "Now I have you in my power."

She heaved herself up the ladder and he followed. The large rectangular float was empty at the moment, so they were able to stretch out on it, lying on their backs in the sun. Jules could feel his body close to hers. While she was panting, he was barely breathing hard.

She let the companionable silence stretch between them for a bit, then said, "Nikki, I wanted to be alone with you to thank you for what you did for me the other day."

He swiveled his head toward her, his gaze inquisitive. "What I did for you?"

"You saved my life. Have you forgotten?"

"Oh, that. I told you before it was nothing. As you know,

I'm a coward by nature. I could just as easily have run the other way."

She looked into his eyes. In the dazzling sun, they looked like turquoise pools in the shallows of the sea. She'd never seen the color of the Panther's eyes in the dark. Was she looking into them now?

"Or perhaps you like to play the coward because it suits your image."

He looked away, smiling. "Perhaps you think too highly of me."

"Just as your hanging about these sort of people suits your image. These distant cousins who were fortunate enough to be on the winning side of the war. In your heart, you don't think much of them, do you?"

He sighed. "Not really, Juli. They're a pretty shallow lot, when you get right down to it. Even before the war, you were the only one of our people I ever felt really drawn to. Just being away from them now is sheer Heaven."

He moved his arms over his head, arching luxuriously.

As she listened to his Russian-accented English, she searched for clues, wondering what his voice would sound like if he were whispering Italian. His voice didn't sound as deep, yet it carried a rich timbre that could well be deepened if he made the effort.

"If you feel that way, Nikki, why do you always hang around them? Why not strike out on your own? Put it all behind you?"

"Because I can't. It's the only life I know. I have no money. No profession. Unlike my fellow fallen countrymen, I don't have it in me to be a taxi driver or washroom attendant at the casinos where I once lost a hundred thousand francs without batting an eye. So all I can do is exist on the crumbs that spill from the tables of my so-called friends. I've tried to free myself from it, but nothing I've tried has worked."

The mission of the Panther has failed . . .

And yet . . . being in the company of his society friends

would have given him the perfect opportunity to determine who had what jewels and when they would be most vulnerable.

He sat up, presenting his back to her. His discomfort was palpable. They weren't accustomed to having such serious conversations, but she wasn't about to let it go when she'd come this far.

She sat up beside him, feeling the water from her shorn hair drip onto her back. "You could marry money."

He gave a rueful smile. "What? When *you* are already taken?"

His voice sounded teasing, but there seemed to be something serious underlying his light tone.

"Nikki, look at me."

He did. His gaze met hers briefly, blazing like the sunlit sea, before being masked again by his lowered lids.

"Ever since I've known you, long before the war even, I've sensed that you've been haunted by something. Something that's made you embrace a frivolous life and has kept you from giving your love to any one woman. Am I wrong? Is this my delusion?"

She felt him stiffen beside her. His shoulders tense, he stared off into the distance. "Everyone is haunted by something, Juli."

"Please don't evade me. Please honor me with your trust. We all need one person in the world to whom we can tell anything."

"I'd like to have one person like that. But there are some things you can't tell anyone."

"It's a lonely life when you can't trust anyone."

"But then we know about loneliness, you and I."

"Trust me, Nikki. Let me in. I can be that one person you can tell anything. You don't have to carry this burden alone."

For a long time, he didn't say anything. Then, she caught a glimpse of moisture in his eyes as he said, "I'm cursed, Juli. My blood is tainted."

"Tainted?"

"The royal disease. Surely you know about that."

"Hemophilia? But you don't have it."

"No, but I carry it. It skipped my generation, which means it will appear in my children, just as it appeared in two of my uncles."

"But Nikki, you don't know that for certain."

"I know it. I've always known it. I feel it. I think about it every day of my life. I can never have a family. I will never foist this burden on a woman. So you see, Juli, I am doomed to spend my life alone."

"But you could be wrong. It might not show up in your children at all. This exile you've imposed upon yourself could be so . . . unnecessary."

He turned to her so suddenly that she jumped. With a ferocity she'd never seen in him before, he cried out, "No, Juli. My exile *is* necessary. It is the one good thing I can do for this world. Nothing will ever change my mind about that."

Her heart aching for him, she put her hand on his warm tanned back. But he flinched at the contact. "I shouldn't have told you this. You'll never think of me the same way again."

"You're right. When I look at you now, I'll think how brave my Nikki has always been . . . and I never knew it."

He raised his gaze to hers, holding it for one long moment. A moment in which she thought she saw something unreadable flash in the depths of his eyes.

"Very well," he said in a lighter tone. "You've had your prize, such as it is. Now I demand a rematch. A race to the beach. First one back gets a kiss."

She smiled. "Aren't you stacking the deck just a bit?"

"I don't intend to lose this time, either way."

He stood, grinned at her, and dove in with princely grace. She raced after him. Though she tried her hardest, this time he triumphed. He stood in the shallows, waiting for her as she scampered through the waves.

"You win a kiss," she told him, her breath in her throat.

It seemed to her that he studied her for just an instant.

Then, leaning, he brought his mouth to hers and barely grazed it with his lips.

Not enough of a kiss to give away the masquerade.

But if he *was* the Panther, she knew now the obstacle that lay between them. An obstacle he thought insurmountable, but that she knew in her heart she could overcome.

Because it couldn't be about marriage and children between them anyway.

It could only be about love.

When she reappeared in the front reception hall, DeRohan was just coming down the stairway with a puzzled expression on his face. She expected an outburst of blind fury, but she felt empowered by her new certainty and could face anything he handed out with aplomb. But he merely looked at her as if she were a conjurer who'd just performed a magic trick and he couldn't for the life of him figure out how she'd done it.

With more wonderment than anger in his voice, he asked, "Where have you *been?*"

She shrugged airily. "Just out with a few friends."

"How did you get out? I've got guards posted all around this place. None of them saw you."

She hid the smile that tugged at the corners of her mouth, her secret power over him. "Perhaps you should purchase some spectacles for them. I just walked out the front door."

He continued to peer at her as if not believing her, but was at a loss for a rational explanation. After a moment, he asked, "What's wrong with your hair? It looks as though it's been wet."

"Oh, that. We ran into a brief rain shower this afternoon."

"There was no shower here."

"That," she said breezily, "is why Cap Ferrat has the best weather in Europe. Because it can rain a mile away and not touch us here."

He glowered at her, his heavy brows coming together. "Do you realize that you've left the most important couturiers in Paris standing about twiddling their thumbs all afternoon?"

She feigned ignorance. "Oh, did I? I forgot all about it."

"You forgot! I finally had to make the selections myself."

"Then you've wasted your time. I've told you, I have no intention of attending your reception."

"And I've told you that you will." He looked at his watch. "We're having guests for dinner. Go upstairs and change."

"What guests?"

"Some business associates."

"Then you don't really need me there. I know nothing about your business dealings. And I care even less."

His face hardened and she caught the twitch of a muscle in his cheek beneath the close-cropped beard. "You might as well get used to it, Juliana, because your life is going to be full of it from now on. Now get upstairs and make yourself presentable. If you're not down here in one hour looking fresh and ready to welcome my guests, I shall come up and drag you down."

Dinner was an ordeal. The guests were the two men who managed the Corsican gold mines that had been closed down for over a year by the strike orchestrated by the activist priest, Father Siffredi. The subject dominated the dinner conversation, and from what Jules could tell, the problem had become a cancer that was gnawing away at the mining division of DeRohan Enterprises and beginning to undermine the confidence of his other divisions as well. It was a serious problem, and the men were deeply concerned, demanding to know what DeRohan was going to do about it.

At one point, one of them said, "If we could just make this meddlesome priest disappear, it might very well solve the entire problem."

"Do you think I haven't thought of that?" DeRohan snarled. "The problem is, he has his own allies in the Vatican and he's managed to resist every move I've made against him."

They were at an impasse.

But Jules wasn't listening. She was thinking of Nikki—of how difficult it was to reconcile the two images in her mind. As she pondered the dilemma, however, she was struck by a thunderbolt of an idea. If she was right, then the Panther was the *real* Nikki—not the other way around. He was the Nikki she'd never known. The one he'd hidden from the world, even as he'd hidden his secret pain. No, it wasn't Nikki who was real. It was the Panther!

And *if* this was all true . . . this afternoon must have been a torment for him. He'd told her the obstacle that, in his mind, separated them—why? Because he'd realized what she was doing and had taken pity on her? Decided to tell her the only way he could? To help her understand?

But having seen her again—having confessed his soul— could he really stay away as the Panther?

I will do everything in my power to resist coming to you, no matter how deeply my heart yearns to do so . . .

It was a terrible question. But she didn't have to wait long for an answer.

As the men adjourned into the drawing room for brandy and cigars, she went back up to her room. She dismissed the servants, even told Hudson to leave her alone. She felt empty, as if something had been stolen from her, and she wanted no prying eyes to witness her vulnerability. Having dressed for the night in a ciel blue satin nightgown and flowing matching robe, she stared at herself in the mirror with haunted eyes.

What had he thought when he'd seen her standing on the beach? Asking all those questions. Selfishly pushing him to a confession it pained him to reveal. Had he any idea what was going through her mind? Or had he thought her innocent, merely showing concern for a man she thought of as a friend?

Her heart heavy, her motions forced, she walked to her bed like a sleepwalker to pull back the covers.

And then she saw it.

A white card with black lettering in a bold hand.

She picked it up. And as she read it, her heart began to race madly in her breast. The hand that held the card shook uncontrollably. And all at once, she couldn't seem to catch her breath.

Chapter 14

Her eyes filled with grateful tears.

Come to me in the wisteria garden at midnight.

The only wisteria on the property was in a self-contained Florentine garden on the level some fifteen feet below the main garden, with its own panoramic view of the sea. A stranger was unlikely to know about it, but she and Nikki had played there as children. It was an inspired choice—so secluded, the guards may not even know it was there.

Come to me . . . come to me . . .

So he couldn't stay away after all!

But how had he possibly managed to get the note into the house? He would have to have crept past the sentries, climbed up her terrace without being seen, and laid it under her covers while they were dining below.

The absolute wonderful cheek of the man!

Her hands were trembling so badly, she dropped the card. But she picked it up again, holding it to her heart. Hastily, her pulse racing, she glanced at the Empire clock. Eleven fifteen.

Forty-five more minutes.

A lifetime.

The impulse to dash out to him was overwhelming. But she

had to wait. At eleven thirty, she went out into the hall and—thank Heaven!—heard the guests taking their leave below. She returned to her rooms.

Eleven forty . . .

She paced the floor.

Eleven forty-five . . .

She took the note he'd left her and, kissing it joyously, hid it beneath a stack of scarves in her vanity.

Eleven fifty. Finally time to move.

She crept into the hallway and tiptoed down the darkened stairway. When she reached the foot of the stairs she saw something that caused her to pause in her tracks. The light was on in her father's study, the room DeRohan had commandeered for his business command post. The route to the basement went directly past it. He must be in there nursing his brandy and brooding.

There was no way she could risk going by it. She'd have to take her chances with the guards in the garden.

Making an about-face, she headed in the opposite direction through a side hallway and out onto the back terrace. As she stepped into the suddenly blissful night, she could hear the dancing waters of the fountain. Then, somewhere close by, muffled voices. She went to the balustrade, peering out into the darkness. Two guards were chuckling over some ribald joke. One took a flask from his pocket and drank, then handed it forth and waited while the other did the same. Her heart beating a frantic rhythm, she willed them to be gone.

Hurry you fools. Be on your way.

Come to me . . .

Beyond them in the night was the man she loved. Was he as impatient as she? She could feel his presence, feel him waiting for her. Waiting . . .

At last, the guards parted, heading around the perimeter of the terrace on both sides, walking their regular route to meet up once again at the front of the villa. She stayed where she was, counting the seconds with her erratic breath, desperate to go to him, but loathe to chance his discovery by any hasty move.

Remembering all too keenly that DeRohan had killed her lover once before.

Finally, when all was still again, when she could hear the quiet croaking of the frogs in the pond, she could wait no longer. She ran down the steps, holding up her hem, all but tripping down the lawn. And then she raced on bare feet through the damp grass, skirting the main garden, finding the stone path that led to the lower level. She passed through a series of Romanesque arcades and finally came out into the Florentine garden with its rectangular pond, stone columns, and central vine-covered pergola. From there, it opened onto a small lawn stretching out toward the cliff and the sea.

In her haste to find him, she ran almost to the cliff, her gown flowing behind her like a train. She stopped, the roar of the sea in her ears, the rhythm of it corresponding to the thrashing of her heart. She stood in the darkness, looking frantically for him. Fireflies blinked like tiny beacons, like hundreds of pinpoints of candle flames. Even the evening breeze had ceased, as if the whole world held its breath.

She turned a circle beneath the stars. Where was he?

Then she heard a soft whistle. She whirled in its direction and it sounded once again. Slowly, her toes damp with dew, she walked toward it, feeling the enchantment of the night saturate her soul.

The whistle seemed to be coming from an arched pergola, thickly draped with dangling wisteria and honeysuckle that overlooked the sea—a haven of privacy and shade during the summer heat. She moved toward it cautiously.

And then she saw the figure of a man, powerfully built and commanding beneath the bower of blossoms. She stopped as her breath left her completely, filling her eyes with the miraculous sight. Masked and virile, he looked like an avenging hero from another, more romantic age.

He opened his arms. Her heart leaping, she rushed across

the velvet lawn to throw herself into them. He scooped her up, his arms like a vise, and twirled her around. Her head began to reel with a rush of emotions that once again brought tears to her eyes. Her senses heightened, she could smell the sugared scent of honeysuckle all around them.

This wasn't Nikki. This was the Panther.

No matter what her eyes and reason might tell her in the logical light of day, the darkness told her this was a different person, with no relation to Nikki or anyone else she'd ever known. More god than human.

"I thought I'd never see you again," she cried. "Not like this."

He answered with a kiss, cutting off her anguished cry, crushing her mouth with a longing that mirrored her own. His hands, gloveless, found her face, stroking it lovingly, then thrusting his fingers into her hair to clutch her head. She melted into his mouth, swooning with pleasure so great that tears spilled onto her cheeks.

She clung to him, covering his jaw and lips with kisses of mad exultation. Then she felt herself falling, his arms locked around her, into the welcoming grass at their feet. And he was on top of her, moving over her, his hands caressing her, his lips tasting her flesh like a man starved beyond the point of no return. She arched up into him, her body singing, rejoicing in a way that seemed to burst open the very star-filled sky with her joy, feeling his warmth, his strength, flow into her, nourishing her. His mouth on hers was hot with unleashed desire, thrilling as only that which is forbidden and denied can be. She tasted him greedily, ravenously, feeling her heart gloriously filled.

But there was something left unsaid. The words that had haunted her, when she'd thought he'd never hear them, ruptured to the surface in the hushed and mesmerizing night. Tearing her lips from his, she opened her eyes and looked up at him, at the cloaked mystery that was the answer to her every prayer.

She could only vaguely see him in the misty dreaminess of her gaze, sheltered by the wisteria that fell like a waterfall on three sides. The fireflies, all around them now, briefly illuminated him to her eyes, flickering, lending a magic all their own. She couldn't see his face but she could feel the light of love blazing from his eyes.

"I adore you," she whispered. She'd never said it to another man, realized that until now, she'd never even known the meaning of the words. "I don't know how or why, but I think I've loved you—waited for you—all my life."

He dropped his head, resting his forehead against hers. She could feel his body trembling.

"If you only knew—" he began.

But there are emotions too deep for words to blight. She felt it in the clutching of his arms, in the shudder of his body over hers. His silent reverence touched her more deeply than any words he could have said.

And then he was moving on her again, grazing her with his massive body, touching her with large expressive hands. Casting from her any need for words as the physical jolt of his longing shot into her like a bolt of lightning, charging her, electrifying her. Kissing her now with a mounting desperation that matched her own, sweeping away any thought of what lay behind or what was to come. Moving as if in slow motion, shoving aside the satin of her gown, seeking bare, quivering flesh. His mouth at her breast, feasting, sending shock waves of desire into her very core.

Then she felt him, rigid as steel, graze her moist and hungry clit. Rubbing himself against her, inciting her need, back and forth, back and forth, building her craving until her desperation overflowed. The anticipation mounting, her breath like fire in her lungs. Famished now, riotous with passion, with the need for the joining that made her shiver helplessly in his arms.

He shot inside her. Jolting her alive, as if every moment leading up to this had been nothing more than waiting for him. As if only now, with the mighty span of him filling her to the hilt, was she whole.

He moved in her, his hands grazing her, his mouth kissing her fiercely, capturing her sighs. Then he withdrew again, rubbing himself upon her, rugged staff teasing the moist softness that opened itself to him. Then again coming in, loving her with long, lusty, manly strokes that sent her heart slamming in her throat, then withdrawing again to tease her once more. Building the suspense each time, as if understanding that the waiting was almost as delectable as the fulfillment.

And then, after the waiting, plunging inside once again, the delicious friction filling her so completely, bringing with it an earthy sweetness that was agony in itself. Her hands flew to his head, seeking an anchor to her swirling senses, feeling the suppleness of the mask. But he lurched away, grabbing her hands, entwining her fingers in his, pushing them inexorably into the grass, pinned on either side of her head, ordering her with his grip, with the renewed force of his kiss, to obey his command. To honor his disguise.

When he was sure of her, he let her go, moving his hands to the underside of her knees, hiking them back over her shoulders so he filled her more deeply still. Then he thrust into her, powerfully, concentrating all his focus, his attention, his energy on her, his fingertips trailing her flesh in a way that made her arch up and gasp. And all the while, the sumptuous, unending friction, driving her on and on—her head spinning giddily as she lost the battle for conscious thought. All she could do was feel—feel him in her, all around her, possessing her in every way that it was possible to be possessed.

She was losing her mind. She clung to him, biting his shoulder because the pleasure was too intense. Not knowing what she was doing, not even caring. Feeling reckless and gloriously free. She felt the need to rip off his mask, to let him know she knew, and that it didn't matter. But every time she moved her hands toward his face, he took hold of them once again, forcing them to the ground, denying her access to that which cloaked his identity, forbidding her without words to breach his self-imposed mystery. His virile hands dominated her will to explore, but lovingly, patiently. Instinctively understanding her need, but denying her nonetheless.

Somewhere, in the still of the night, with the crash of the sea sounding in her ears, it ceased to matter. Somehow, beneath the bower of ambrosial flowers, amongst the twinkling of the fireflies, she lost her need to strip him of his anonymity and became one with him. Giving all of herself, her heart, her soul, as her body gave its ripening fullness to him.

And she knew, as they came together as one, that come what may, whatever the future held, she would love this magnificent, tortured man for the rest of her life.

"Don't ever leave me again," she beseeched him. "Swear it."

But he clamped his mouth on hers, silencing the plea.

And as he did, in the midst of their bliss, she felt a stab of fear.

Chapter 15

Slowly, she became aware once again of the bouquet of honey-suckle and wisteria and damp earth scenting the night around them. He held her to him cherishingly as his labored breath slowed. But there was something desperate in the way he did so that reminded her too keenly of the night when he'd come to say good-bye. She tightened her arms about his back, wanting to hold onto him forever, not wanting him to speak.

But at last, as if remembering where they were, and the peril that lurked in the shadows, he raised his head and looked around with the alertness of one accustomed to sniffing out traps.

"We have to talk," he told her softly. "But not here. It's too close to the house. Is there someplace where we won't be seen or heard?"

She hesitated for a moment, then said with an excited smile, "I know just the place."

They stood and smoothed their clothing, then he kissed her, took her hand, looked outside the pergola to make certain no one was around, and said, "Lead the way."

Hand in hand, they stole along the cliff overlooking the sea, watchful for guards, until they came to a stone stairway that led up the very back of the main garden to the Temple of Venus at the crest of the hill. Then, making certain once again that no one was watching, Jules felt around in the dark for the small doorway at the back of the rotunda and opened it.

"Ingenious," he whispered.

"Just wait," she promised quietly.

She led him inside, secured the door behind them, then located the flashlight on the wall and wound down the spiral staircase to the sanctuary below. "Close your eyes," she told him.

Crossing the room, she lit one of the candles set on a small serving table, then turned off the flashlight. As the candle's flame flared, she told him, "All right, you can look."

He opened his eyes. She watched with delight as he took in the marvelous sight with an astonished smile. "My God, it's beautiful!"

"This room was built to be an extension of the temple above—its inner sanctum. The walls and encircling columns are fashioned from the whitest Carrera marble. The mosaic on the floor was taken from a villa in Pompeii. The bed is modeled after the couches the Romans used to lounge on during banquets."

"But we must be twenty feet below ground, and yet the air is fresh. And it's spotless in here. I don't see a speck of dust."

"That's because there are five air ducts leading to the surface, each with its own filtering system. All of it cleverly disguised."

He was strolling through the room, looking at the antiquities—the friezes, the statues, the segments of ancient columns used as bases for glass tabletops—totally captivated by the unlikely grandeur of it all. "I feel as if I'm in the Emperor Hadrian's palazzo. Who built this? And why?"

"My grandmother. She was a Bavarian princess, married to my Habsburg grandfather by arrangement, and the marriage was never happy. When she was in her forties, she fell madly in love with a French cavalry officer while wintering one year in Menton. She built this house to be near him. That's why it's called Rêve de l'Amour—Dream of Love. This sanctuary was built for her private trysts. And because she couldn't afford for even the servants to know, or for word to get back to her husband, she also built a system of secret tunnels so they each had private access. One tunnel leads from the basement of the house to this room, and the other from this room down to the beach."

He turned and looked at her. "Amazing! Who else knows about these tunnels?"

"No one. Only me. And now you. Because my grandmother used the tunnels only for the purpose of romance, she told me when I was a very little girl, 'Juliana, someday this will be your special place, just as it was mine. You must only share this secret with the man you truly love. A man worthy of your trust.' "

For a moment, he didn't react. He just stared at her. Her confession of the depth of her feelings echoed in the hush of the room.

Then, he crossed the distance between them like a shadow in the dim light of the chamber. He took her shoulders in his hands and said softly, his voice full of emotion, "You honor me."

Slowly, he took her face in his hands and pulled her toward him, kissing her with a depth and commitment he hadn't shown before. Telling her with his kiss all that her trust meant to him.

But as he held the kiss and his fingers lovingly explored the contours of her face, he touched the still tender forehead and she involuntarily winced.

"Does it still hurt?" he asked at once.

"It's nothing."

He pulled her close and gently kissed the spot where the bullet had grazed. "I'm so sorry for what happened to you in Toulon."

"It wasn't your fault."

"I heard just last night. I came to you as soon as I could."

She stilled. What was he saying?

Slowly, she pushed back from him. Though the candle was across the room and they stood in shadow, she tried her best to search his face. The mask was formfitting, molding itself over his nose so that the shape was camouflaged. All she could see of him was the indistinct outline of his jaw and mouth.

He'd only just heard. Was it true? Or was it his way of preserving the façade? Of convincing her that her suspicions about Nikki were false?

Growing uncomfortable beneath her scrutiny, he put his hand to the back of her head and pulled it to rest on his shoulder. "Besides which," he continued, "it *was* my fault. I didn't do you any favors saying what I did that night."

She shook her head beneath his hand. "What? That you believed in me? I loved that you said that. No one has ever believed in me before. I took a chance and it didn't work. But I'll try again. And again, if need be. I can't use the Snake—he's on DeRohan's payroll—but I can find some other snake, some other way—"

"No," he cut her off. "I was wrong. You are the prisoner of an evil man. You *do* need help in freeing yourself from him."

"I don't want you to kill him. I never really meant it. It was just my desperation talking when I heard he was coming after me."

"We're not going to kill him. But we *are* going to destroy him."

"Destroy him? How?"

"By taking away the source of his power."

"I don't understand."

"Come, let's sit down." He put his arm about her shoulders and walked with her to the bed, then sat down so his back was to the candle's glow, leaving his face in shadow. When she sat beside him, he turned to her.

"Since I saw you last, I've spent some time learning everything I can about the business empire of Dominic DeRohan. And I have to tell you, it's an even seedier affair than the world knows. The man is a true gangster. His empire is a house of cards built on a foundation of intimidation."

"What do you mean, intimidation?"

"Most of the remarkable success he's enjoyed over the last five years has stemmed from the inexplicable support he's received from the Rothschild banking interests."

"The Rothschilds?"

"Why do you suppose this conservative and proper family has time and again bankrolled even the most dubious of his business initiatives? At the lowest imaginable interest rates? Never once foreclosing when, time and again, he has failed to meet his obligations to them?"

"I don't know. I suppose because they've made money off of him. After all, everything he touches turns to gold."

"No. They've done it because they have to. Because he has acquired a letter written by one of their more prominent members that, if given public exposure, would so embarrass the family that they would do *anything* to keep that from happening."

"He's blackmailing them?"

"Exactly."

"But . . . how did he acquire the letter?"

"He got it the same way he gets everything. He stole it."

She thought about that for a moment. She certainly wouldn't put it past DeRohan to bully the Rothschilds into feathering his nest. From the very first day of their marriage, he'd taken twisted pleasure in bullying her. And as for resorting to theft to get what he wanted . . . hadn't he stolen *her*? Hadn't he blackmailed her into marrying him?

She looked down at her lap. "I wonder where he keeps that letter?" she mused.

"I think I know where he keeps it."

Slowly, she lifted her gaze, looking at him in awe, beginning to understand.

"As you know," he went on, "his company owns the controlling interest in the Carlton Hotel."

"Yes, of course. It's where he used to stay before we were married, his quarters away from London."

"When he bought it, he lavishly remodeled the penthouse suite, turning it into his showcase residence on the Côte. As part of that renovation, he installed a new wall safe and the most elaborate security precautions ever seen in the South of France—or anywhere else in his empire for that matter. I believe the Rothschild letter is in that safe. It's so important to him, he wouldn't risk keeping it anywhere but in the most secure of his vaults."

Jules was sitting up straight now, all but vibrating with excitement. "You're going to rob him!"

"Not I. *We.* Think of it, *Cara!* If we could get that letter and destroy it—or better yet, return it to the Rothschilds—it would cut him off completely from his source of easy credit. And the Rothschilds, out of vengeance for all he's done to them over the years, would demand payment on all his outstanding loans. The whole deck of cards would come tumbling down."

She jumped up, twirling in exhilaration. "It's perfect! It's brilliant! Oh, you lovely man!" Stooping, she grazed his cheek with an elated kiss. "Just think! I'm going to be a cat burglar. Or does one call it a burglaress, if she's a woman?"

He laughed. It warmed her heart. She went to him, plopping herself on his lap.

"But, how do we do it? You yourself said he had the most elaborate security—"

"Last night, after I heard what happened to you in Toulon, I decided to go to Nice and pay a little midnight visit to the office of the venerable Swiss security company that did the job for DeRohan. That's why I couldn't come to you at once. I was able to find the plans and specifications for the job. Admittedly, the heist still seems a formidable—perhaps even impossible—task. But armed with this inside information, I think I know a way that it might—just might—work. But the scheme requires a great deal from you. It will require more cunning, stealth,

courage, and resourcefulness than you've ever had to summon."
He held out his hand. "So think hard, think deeply about it,
before you give me your hand."

She didn't have to think. She placed her hand in his. "Oh,
thank you, *thank you*. It's perfect. We shall use a thief to catch a
thief. And then, when we've destroyed DeRohan, then what?"

He put the fingers of his other hand on her lips, cutting off
the words. "Hear me well, *Cara*. I will do whatever it takes to
help free you from this bondage. But once the job is done—
once we've brought DeRohan to his knees—the work of the
so-called Panther will be finished. And I will disappear forever."

He could say that, but she didn't for a moment believe him.
He'd proved tonight that he couldn't stay away from her. She felt
certain now that it would be impossible for him to leave her
once this new mission was accomplished.

She'd see to that.

Somehow, she would find a way to do what had to be done.
To free the Panther from the prison of Nikki.

Just as he was freeing her.

"Whatever you say, darling."

"I mean it."

"I know you do. But we don't have to think gloomy thoughts
tonight, do we? We have this delightful room that no one knows
about all to ourselves. Everyone thinks I'm in bed asleep. So
we may, if we wish, amuse ourselves until dawn."

She squirmed about in his lap, and felt him harden against
her.

"What did you have in mind?" he asked.

"Well . . . you've shown me a little of what I've been missing
all these years. But you said this was just the beginning. Teach
me some more. I promise to be an apt pupil."

His mouth crooked in amusement. He bent, taking her nipple into his mouth through the blue satin gown. She shivered
with pleasure. "You make a remarkable pupil," he told her

huskily. "More eager, more insatiable than I would have guessed. I wonder if I would ever tire of teaching you."

She smiled at him sassily, like a girl bent on mischief—a defenseless, shimmering smile that lit up her face—a smile she'd never given to a man in her life. She could feel the glow of it all around her. Bringing her mouth close to his, she challenged, "Try it and see."

Chapter 16

The next morning, Jules lay in bed sipping her first cup of Vienna coffee of the day. She'd slept wonderfully, more soundly than she could ever remember. Thoroughly spent—drained of any trace of tension—by their lovemaking the night before. He'd taught her such shocking things! She'd never imagined that people did such things behind closed doors. Even now, she blushed to think of them. But with him, they hadn't seemed smutty or depraved. They'd been absolutely delicious. He'd demanded of her—in that commanding way—a trust she hadn't known it was possible to feel. And because of it, they'd achieved a closeness—an intimacy—that she would never have thought possible between a man and a woman. It had seemed the most natural thing in the world—a creative and imaginative expression of their love.

Then, too, there was the peace that came from knowing she was going to be engaged in a decisive action. A heist! She, a royal princess who'd been confined behind palace walls for most of her life, was going to become—at least for one night—a cat burglar! She supposed she should be frightened, intimidated by the immensity of the task she'd undertaken. But she felt instead, as she sipped the hot brew, an odd sort of confidence. It was the excitement, of course, the anticipation of doing something that could have been lifted right out of the pages of the romantic adventures she'd always loved to read. Now she would be living an adventure of her own.

But it was more than that. It was knowing her extraordinary lover would be by her side every step of the way. If she had any doubts about her ability to carry out this audacious mission, she had nothing but faith in him.

There was the one caveat, of course. *Once the job is done . . . I will disappear forever.* But the threat seemed empty.

You may think that. But once you've freed me from this monster, there's no force on this planet strong enough to keep me away from you.

Suddenly she heard the sound of gunshots. She bolted up in bed. Were the guards shooting at someone? The Panther?

For a moment her heart froze. But no, she reminded herself. He only came in the night.

And then she realized the shots were coming at regular intervals, like someone shooting at a target.

She went out onto her terrace and looked down to see DeRohan, standing on the lawn with a shotgun in his hand. He was shooting skeet. He had Hudson operating the mechanism that catapulted the clay disks high into the air. Her immaculate lawn was covered with bits of shattered clay.

The sight of her husband so vilely desecrating the peace of Rêve de l'Amour—and commandeering Hudson in the process—filled her with blind wrath.

But as she was charging through her room, determined to vent her feelings on him, she brought herself up short. No. Things had changed. She had a plan now that must supercede any other considerations. She must keep that plan in mind, remember her true objective, and conduct herself accordingly.

She took a moment to draw a calming breath, then put on her satin robe and went down to meet him with a cool, self-possessed air.

As she crossed the lower terrace, his gaze flicked to her for an instant, but didn't acknowledge her presence.

"Pull!" he called to Hudson.

The butler pulled the lever, sending a disk soaring into the air.

Barely bothering to aim, DeRohan pulled the trigger and shattered the projectile in mid-flight. Three more times, in rapid succession, he repeated the process, splintering the quiet morning with the roar of his spitting gun. He seemed lost in the rhythm of destruction. He was such a master shot that twice he closed his eyes, as if to show that he could hit the target in his sleep.

She called to him, her voice but a murmur against the rude blast of the gun. Eventually it penetrated. He lowered the weapon and turned to look her up and down. "Up already? It's only half past eleven."

His mouth was a tight drawn line within the frame of his close-cropped mustache and beard. Then, without waiting for a reply, he looked at Hudson, held up three fingers, and ordered, "Pull!"

Three clay birds rocketed into the sky and DeRohan, barely looking at them, pulled the trigger three times in swift succession, exploding each with a cold precision that chilled her.

She'd been in a dreamy state, relishing the adventure to come. But in her excitement, she'd forgotten something.

DeRohan was a deadly shot. And once before, he'd killed a man who'd dared to come close to her.

She forced the thought from her mind and assumed the role she had to play, following the Panther's instructions.

"If you're not too busy littering my lawn, I've come to tell you that you win."

He turned and looked at her. "What is it that I'm so fortunate to win from you?"

"I'm going to do what you want."

"I want a great many things."

"I shall give your precious Shah the party of his life. I shall assemble every titled character in the South of France to welcome him. I shall charm him to the point that, when I'm done, he'll be eating out of your hand."

"Why the sudden turnaround?"

"I'm tired of fighting you. I'm hoping that, when you have what you want, you'll go back to London and leave me alone."

"By all means, then, let's get on with it."

"It won't be inexpensive."

"Money is no object. Spend what you will. I'll arrange a line of credit."

"Where is the Shah staying?"

"At the Carlton, of course."

"Splendid. We shall hold the party there."

He mused for a moment, then said, "No. Hold it somewhere else."

"Where, for instance? We could certainly have it at the Grand Hotel here in Cap Ferrat. But do you really want him thinking there's a finer place than the Carlton? That the only reason you've put him up there is that you own the hotel and it's the cheapest thing you can do?"

His hooded eyes narrowed on her. "All right, then," he relented grudgingly. "The Carlton it is."

"Very well. When do you expect him?"

"His yacht will get in on Friday—six days from now. He'll be well rested, so we can hold the reception that very night. But let me caution you, Juliana. If you are hatching some scheme to embarrass me in front of the Shah, I can think of any number of ways to cause you to regret it. Pull, Hudson."

A clay pigeon once again shot into the air. Turning his back on her, DeRohan pulled the trigger. The projectile exploded, emphasizing his threat.

"If you want my word, you may have it," she told him. "I promise not to publicly humiliate you during the course of the evening. Will that satisfy you?"

"It will more than satisfy me. It will be a refreshing change. If," he added, with a cynical smile, "I can trust you."

She turned and walked toward the house. "Oh, you can trust me."

You can trust me to do whatever it takes to wipe that smile from your face forever.

"*Rien ne va plus!*"

The croupier sent the ball rolling in the roulette wheel on the intricately carved wooden table of the Casino de Monte Carlo. It was midday and the vast Belle Époque chamber with its gold fixtures, rococo ceiling, and bohemian glass chandeliers was mostly empty of gamblers, except for a small fashionable crowd gathered around this one spot.

The ball landed in a red slot. "*Neuf, rouge.*"

"Drat," said a matronly fleshy woman in her sixties, stuffed into the latest Lanvin day frock and sitting in the prominent position at the end of the table, opposite the croupier. "I lose again."

The woman was the Duchess of Olifant. She and her late husband were two of the oldest titled residents of the principality of Monaco. They'd begun coming from their native home in England in the 1880s. For the past forty years, her grace had been the social doyen of the area's aristocratic émigrés.

Normally, the Duchess of O, as she was called, had a soft spot for Juliana von Habsburg. But a string of losses here today had put her in a sour mood and she was resisting Jules's entreaties with all her patrician stubbornness.

Once again, Jules gave it a try. "But Fanny, dearest, surely you don't want to miss what will positively be the event of the season."

"My dear, should I choose not to attend, how could it *possibly* be the event of the season?"

"Well, of course it couldn't. Which is why I'm endeavoring to make you change your mind. You know I don't throw parties very often. Couldn't you, for the sake of friendship, bless it with your presence? Without you there, it couldn't possibly succeed."

"Naturally I should like to help you, pet. But four days from now! It's too soon. How does one get a dress made in four days that's worthy of being displayed?"

"Anything you wear will be the grandest thing at the ball. That's why you are who you are."

"But a party hosted by your husband . . . a man who—forgive me for saying it, my child—is considered unacceptable in decent London society . . . why should I want to lend myself to anything with which *he* is associated?"

"As a favor to me. Is that too much to ask of my dear friend and mentor?"

"But my dearest girl. A gala honoring some wog from . . . where did you say?"

"Persia." It was beginning to look hopeless. When the duchess got her back up, nothing could change her mind. If she didn't come through, none of the old aristocracy was likely to come on board.

"Persia, of all places. Why would that possibly interest me?"

"Because, my dear lady," said a male voice from behind, "Persia is the land of scorching desert sands, of towering citadels sporting mighty stone lions. Of Suza and Persepolis. Of Xerxes and Darius. When their armies of millions marched across the lands, they drank the rivers dry. Persia is the land where romance began. Haven't you read your Herodotus?"

As one, the women turned to see Nikki Romanov standing there, his hands thrust in his pockets, a persuasive smile on his handsome face. He gave Jules a quick wink.

"You naughty boy," the duchess scolded, "you know I don't read anything but Mr. Dickens and the *Times*. Herodotus, indeed!"

Her manner was petulant, but her rheumy eyes had begun to sparkle the moment she'd recognized him.

Nikki bent over her, putting his mouth close to her ear. "I don't know about you, but I can't wait to meet the Shah of Persia. Think what stories we'll be able to tell in Biarritz this winter."

"I hardly think my friends shall be impressed with another potentate from the East. Biarritz is crawling with maharajas as it is."

Nikki took her hand and kissed it, then sat down in the vacant chair beside her. "Then I suppose I shall have to be all alone at the impromptu party of the season. And I was so looking forward to having you on my arm with that gown you wore at the Deauville ball last April." He wagged his finger at her playfully. "You know the one I mean. That stunning cranberry brocade with the feathers—the one that made you look like a temptress of the Nile."

She couldn't help but smile. "That *is* a smashing gown, isn't it?"

"Smashing? A gown fit for the king of Persia. Wouldn't it just knock out his eyes to see how our fairest maidens of the West can outshine those Persian harem girls?"

She swatted him with her closed fan. "You scoundrel. Stop tempting me."

He edged his chair closer and put his arm about her waist. "Surely, sweet Fanny, you're not really going to deny us your presence at Juli's gala. You couldn't be that cruel. I'm going to sit right down here and weep until you change your mind."

"Oh, very well," she acquiesced wearily, though clearly she was delighted by his flattery. "If I must, I must."

For a moment, Jules just sat there watching him continue to charm the old woman. He was on his feet now, acting out some battle between the Greeks and Persians. She remembered when they were children, he'd acted the same scene for her. What was it? Thermopylae. Three hundred doomed Spartans holding off Xerxes' invading hordes.

As he darted about, brandishing his invisible sword, she thought of what a sly devil he was. Appearing here in his other guise, at just the right moment to make sure this party happened as planned.

When he could steal away for a moment, she said to him, beneath her breath, "Isn't this fun?"

"Isn't what fun?"

"Pretending this way."

"Oh, like when we were children, you mean?"

She peered at him for a moment. "Something like that."

"Well, you might think it fun. But now the old bag is insisting I go see her new bulldog pup."

"Oh, you poor thing," she laughed.

"Actually, I was looking for you. Hudson told me you were here. I wanted to ask you something."

Still smiling, her hands placed coyly behind her back, she cooed, "I can already tell you the answer is yes."

"You'd better hear me first. This is a subject on which you have some strong feelings. I've been approached by Mayor Clément to be part of the Russian delegation at the opening ceremony for this new war memorial. You've read about it in the papers, I'm sure. Anyway, it's being unveiled in September. People are coming from all over Europe to take part in the ceremony and they really want a Habsburg presence—perhaps even a speech. So he petitioned me to ask you if you could be persuaded."

Her face fell. "Nikki! How can you even ask me such a thing? You know very well that if I took part in something like that, it would be like bowing to all those people who say the Habsburgs caused the war. This *can't* be why you came looking for me today."

"I don't know," he shrugged. "I thought it might do you some good."

At that moment, the duchess called shrilly, "Nikki Romanov, stop your dawdling this instant! We don't want to keep Daisy waiting."

"Duty calls," he told Jules with a grin. "But think about it, won't you?"

As he left, Jules stared after him. It seemed an odd request, particularly at such a time.

What was he up to?

*   *   *

That night, after the rest of the household had gone to bed, Jules crept out of her room, hurried down the stairs, crossed the vast reception hall, and went down into the basement.

Within seconds, flashlight in hand, she was traversing the long tunnel toward her secret love nest. This would be the third night in a row that she'd met him here since hatching their scheme. As she drew closer, she could see the faint light of the candle already lit, indicating he was already there. Her heart pounded with anticipation.

Finally, she reached her destination and saw him sprawled casually in one of the Roman emperor chairs. He rose to greet her and she flew into his arms.

In a frenzy, with no words spoken, they undressed each other, their lips locked all the while. Still standing, he cupped his hands beneath her thighs, lifted her legs to wrap around his waist, and entered her with a single thrust, supporting her back against the white marble wall as he slammed into her again and again with savage ferocity. As his tempo increased, his voice against her ear said huskily, "Tell me you love it! Say it!"

"Oh, I love it," she cried. "I love it, I love it!"

Somehow the verbalizing of it—something she'd never done before—was tremendously exciting.

"Tell me you love me fucking you."

When she hesitated, he slammed her back against the wall, thrusting deep. "*Tell me,*" he demanded.

Her body spiraling out of control, she gasped, "I love you—fucking me."

"Tell me again," he insisted, pounding harder. "Tell me." Again and again, until his heated decree became a pounding rhythm in her brain—telling her the lusty words he wanted her to say, making her repeat them, firing her to a mad abandon, pushing her to the brink—until she was joyously babbling words she'd never thought she'd say, telling him what he did to her in the language he taught her. The voices of their duet—the give and take, his commands and her compliance—were more electric, more lyrical than any poetry she'd ever read. By the time he'd made her explode on his thrusting cock, she was hot and damp, intoxicated by the taste and feel and scent of him swirling through her senses.

"Oh, my God," she gasped, clinging to the wall behind her. "That was the most enthusiastic welcome I've ever received! And the finish—!"

He was still stiff inside her. At her ear, he rasped, "Who said you were finished, woman?"

He swung her around, carrying her—legs still wrapped about his waist, his staff still buried deep inside—toward the bed. There, he took one of the large pillows in hand, tossing it to the hard mosaic floor.

"What's that for?" she asked.

He slowly slid out of her and set her on her feet before him. "There's more for my eager pupil to learn."

She clapped her hands. "I love learning!"

"Good," he said sternly. "Now get on your knees."

Chapter 17

After her third orgasm, she rolled off him and collapsed onto her back on the bed beside him. By now, the bedding was in total disarray, some of it dangling onto the floor. The candle had burned down so that only an inch of wax remained.

"Where did you ever learn *that?*" she gasped, still swooning after the scrumptiously wicked things he'd shown her—and her last mind-blowing climax.

He, too, lay on his back with his arms flung wide. "You don't really want me to talk about other women, do you?"

She felt a pang of jealousy. She swiveled her head, looking over at him, naked except for the headgear that masked his face and hair. His body, too, was damp from exertion, the chiseled form glistening faintly in the firelight.

"No," she answered.

A long silence passed. Then, in his gentle voice, so different from the masterful tone of the commander in bed, "Besides, from now on, there will be no other women but you."

"Never?"

"No, *Cara*. Never again."

It heartened her to hear it. It almost sounded like a promise. As if already he were reconsidering his vow to leave her.

Seized by an impulse, she rolled onto her side. "DeRohan's

gone for the night on business. Let's get out of here. Let's go have some fun."

"I was under the impression that was just what we were doing. Or were those cries of pleasure merely a pretense?"

"With *you?* I think you know better than that. No, I mean let's behave like normal people for a change."

"You want me to take you dancing perhaps, in this mask?"

"No, silly. Let's go sailing."

"In the dark?"

"I often go sailing at night. I have a small boat moored at the pier on my beach. I want to be out in the open with you, beneath the sky and the stars. The only way we can. You say I can only see you at night, and I accept that. But while we're cloaked in eternal darkness and danger, allow me the slightest touch of normalcy this one time."

"You want, in short, for us to go on a date."

"A date. That's it exactly! You do know how to sail, don't you?"

A slight hesitation. Then, "Yes, I know how to sail."

"Then let's go. It will be fun. We'll take the tunnel to the beach and no one will see us."

They dressed and, taking the flashlight in one hand and his palm in the other, she went with him down the branch of the tunnel that led to the beach: the same tunnel he'd used to meet her in their room. They came out into the night and climbed down from the rocky opening to the small pier where a single-masted sailing skiff was tied.

"Our magic carpet awaits us," she said.

He helped her aboard and within minutes he'd raised the sail and caught the wind, expertly steering the rudder to take them cruising into the starry night. As they headed further out to sea, the lights of the coast sparkled in the distance. The hills behind were but the faintest of black silhouettes.

The breeze against her face was cool and fresh and wonderfully invigorating. The sound of the sail flapping overhead was lulling and serene in the quiet night, cutting a wedge in the canopy of twinkling stars.

All around her was beauty and splendor, a night such as there had never been, with the man she loved at her side.

A trio of seagulls floated with them on the breeze, symbols of the delectable freedom she was feeling.

"Let's swim," she suggested.

"That's one of the things I can't grant you, I'm afraid."

They hadn't brought any form of light, so he, like the hills, was a dark figure in the night with no distinguishable features. "Why not?" she asked. "You could take off your mask. I can't see my hand in front of me, much less your face."

"That, I'm afraid, would be asking for more trust than I can give."

She sighed, feeling suddenly sulky. What difference did it make anyway? She knew who he was.

To change the subject, he asked, "Did you sail with your husband?"

"God, no. As far as I know, he doesn't even know how. Too busy making his precious fortune. Besides, I never did anything with him. I told you that."

"Then I pity him. To have a wife such as you without being able to enjoy your many talents."

The tenor of his tone, though smacking of amusement, was blatantly sexual.

But she was still feeling petulant. "We didn't come out here to talk about my husband, I hope."

"No. It would be a pity to spoil such a pleasant night."

The seagulls squawked, then veered back to shore. Jules, watching them disappear, became aware once more of the enchantment surrounding them, and realized her folly at casting a blemish on their bliss.

"What, then," he was asking, a gravelled whispered voice in the dark, "*did* we come to talk about?"

She shook off her peevishness. "Oh, I don't know. You."

"Ah. There you have me at a disadvantage. There's not much I can say. I thought you understood that."

"I do. But surely there *are* things you could tell me."

"For instance?"

"For instance . . . how did you become a cat burglar?"

"How?" he repeated.

"The ways and means. It isn't, after all, something just anyone can do. I imagine it requires a singular training."

"You could say that."

"Well? I mean, one doesn't merely wake up one morning and say, 'I think I shall become a cat burglar today.'"

He laughed. "Actually, that's just about how it happened. I'd become a man I didn't much care for anymore. I wanted to leave the anger and bitterness of my past behind me. To try and regain something that had been taken from me. But I couldn't figure out how to go about it. And then one day it hit me. A way to remove the obstacle in my path. I would become a thief. I'd take the things that would open the door for a new life."

"Did the morality of it never trouble you?"

"The stealing of baubles from spoiled rich women who were insured? No."

"Women like me, you mean."

He ignored her comment. "Once I'd made the decision, I spent nine months training myself for the task."

"Learning to climb walls . . . to dance across rooftops . . . that sort of thing," she offered.

"You make it sound more romantic than it really is." Once again, she heard the amusement in his voice.

"Did the heights not bother you?"

"I've always loved heights. The thrill of being high above the world, looking down on it from afar. I'd never felt so free as when I was in the air. It seemed a natural transition. I had a specific goal in mind. But then, once I'd begun, I found that I enjoyed the challenge of it. The danger added spice to my otherwise lackluster existence."

"And will you not miss it all, when you're finished—the danger, the spice?"

A brief pause. "When I'm finished, I will miss many things."

She mulled over his words. "I understand that. Sometimes I think my life is so sterile. There seems to be no purpose or meaning to it. I envy you. If only I could find some specific purpose—I might make something of my life after all."

"The answer lies inside, I think. To take your pain and find a way to use it, to do something with it."

"Is that what you did?"

"It's what I tried to do. What I'm trying to do now, by helping you."

"That's something, at least," she said. "I've been too selfish, too wrapped up in my own troubles to help anyone."

"As have I. But people can change."

"Can they?"

"I've changed. Because of you."

That surprised her. "Of me? How?"

"When I saw the pain you were in, when I really understood it—it became more important than my own."

She looked up at the stars, and the small crescent of a moon hanging in the sky. "You make me feel ashamed."

"How so?"

"I've told you. Because I've been so selfish."

"You have a kind heart, *Cara*. You can do much with it."

"Can I? How?"

"By taking your pain—what's haunted you most—and redirecting that energy toward something . . . or someone . . . you care about."

"Then we've come full circle. Because my pain has been my husband."

"Has it?"

"You know it has."

"But I've told you before. Your husband is only a symptom. Your pain has a deeper source."

She shifted impatiently. "You're doing it again."

"What am I doing?"

"You think my pain comes from being a Habsburg."

"I think that's the guilt you carry."

"Why should I feel guilty?"

"That's for you to say."

She leaned over the side of the boat and trailed her hand in the chilly water.

"Tell me about your life in Vienna," he suggested.

Jules tried not to think about the old days. She and Nikki had rarely spoken of the past. They'd had similar experiences, and there'd been no need.

But he'd been open with her—as open as he felt he could be—and she wanted to repay him in kind. So she looked back at the road behind her.

"There were two Viennas. Before the war, of course, I lived with all my relatives in our various palaces—one for the summer, one for the winter. Hundreds of us, roaming about the thousand rooms. It was a regimented life in many ways. Strict protocol, endless lessons to be learned. Deportment, manners, languages, how to address various heads of state, what to say, how to behave in any given circumstance, how to entertain. Well, you know about that. All the usual things meant to groom me for the place it was assumed I'd take."

"To marry a prince."

She smiled slyly. "Or a grand duke, perhaps. But Vienna in those days was much like St. Petersburg must have been. Full of light and laughter and gaiety. There were dazzling balls with thousands of guests, all decked out in jewels that took one's breath away. There were picnics along the river, and riding in the parks, drinking coffee in bistros. Outings to the races, the theater, museums. We were surrounded by such beauty, such grandeur. Music everywhere. And dancing—always dancing. Waltzing until dawn. It was a city where even the horses danced."

"You were happy."

"I never thought about it. I enjoyed my life. I did what I was told. Like all of us, I thought it would go on forever. But then the war broke out and everything changed. It wasn't Vienna anymore, it was the Austrian State. Food grew scarce. There were long lines of gaunt people, hoping for a crust of bread. All around us, entire families were starving. The maimed and wounded poured into the city. People came from all the corners of the Empire, desperate to try and eke out any kind of living they could. And all the while, the secret police were turning them into suspicious, hunted creatures. They warned of traitors in out midst. Neighbors turned against their oldest friends, reporting imagined infractions to keep themselves alive. Our beautiful city became a cesspool of mistrust and greed. And of course they blamed the Habsburgs for all of it. They hated us more each day."

"I'm sorry," he said. "The war did awful things to us all."

"Yes. But it's the past now."

"Not so long as you cling to the trappings of that past."

She sighed, exasperated. "I'm a product of my past. You suggest I take that pain and do something good with it. But how?"

"That is for you to discover. When you see the opportunity, you'll know."

She suddenly remembered the proposal he'd made as Nikki that very afternoon. Was this all part of the same conversation?

She challenged, a little crossly, "Like you saw the opportunity to become a cat burglar?"

But he answered her in the same quiet tone. "Like I saw the opportunity to become a cat burglar."

Once again, the enchantment of the night had seeped away. She sat with her hands in her lap, feeling confused and strangely dejected.

He adjusted the sail. "But that can wait," he told her. "In the meantime, there's fun to come."

"The caper, you mean."

"That, too."

She caught the faint flash of his teeth as he grinned.

"Is there other fun to come?" she asked.

He leaned forward, took hold of her arms, and with one sudden forceful yank, brought her into his lap. "The best kind of fun."

He kissed her, dizzily, insistently, enfolding her in arms that were strong and stirring. Until the resistance in her body gradually loosened its grip, dissolving all the disquiet inside, reminding her of the present moment that was theirs to take.

He loved her. He was with her. That was all that mattered for now.

"Are you not tired from your earlier exertions?" she teased, feeling suddenly absurdly lighthearted.

"I'm making up for lost time."

He laid her back on the polished deck of the boat. And there, beneath the flapping sail and the moon and the stars, with the lights of reality far away on shore, he showed her what he meant.

Chapter 18

The beachfront main street of Cannes—the Croisette—had been decked out for the Shah's arrival with a splendor unseen since the days when Queen Victoria was the area's most celebrated winter resident. Luxuriant flower baskets decorated every lamppost. Persian flags caught the sea breeze from a dozen impromptu flagpoles assembled along the promenade. The hundred-piece Nice Symphony Orchestra had been bussed in and was playing Rimsky-Korsakov from a grandstand erected on the Carlton's private beach. And leading to the front entrance of the hotel was a deep aromatic carpet of fresh red rose petals brought in from the perfume capitol of Grasse, emulating the manner in which the Ephesians had welcomed Cleopatra and Marc Antony.

On the dock, Jules stood beside DeRohan, watching as the Shah was escorted down the gangway of his lavish yacht onto the waiting tender. It was cloudy, but the clouds were high, making the sky look misty. She could see the harsh sun behind them, still brilliant, still hurting the eyes despite its veil. But even with the clouds, it seemed sunny below, as only it could in the South of France, a placid yellow light. Across the bay, the Esterel hills looked indistinct, like a mirage. The water was such a light green that it was almost colorless as it drifted in ripples toward the west, where the terra-cotta buildings and rampart walls of the old town on the hill served as a reminder of its medieval past. Yachts lay at anchor in the bay, modern playthings bobbing gently with the tide as if sleeping, preparing for the evening festivities to come. The whoosh, whoosh, whoosh of the pounding surf could be heard even over the traffic at their backs.

It was warm and humid, with a hint of impending rain in the air. But the weather in Cannes changed every ten minutes, so Jules wasn't concerned.

As the tender chugged its way toward them, she could feel her husband's tension beside her. She'd thrown herself into this occasion: dressing in the ball gown DeRohan had chosen—a surprisingly tasteful sheath of shimmering dark blue satin—wearing the sapphire and yellow diamond suite of jewels retrieved from the Nice vault. To impress the Shah, she wore her father's Habsburg garter with its royal emblem as a broach. She'd made the arrangements for the reception herself, with Hudson's help, lining up all her aristocratic and royal friends. But DeRohan still seemed suspicious, as if she might be playing along so she could pay him back with some epic personal embarrassment once she was in the presence of his precious guest.

The Shah stepped from the tender, a man of thirty-eight with greying hair worn close to his head, a dark charismatic face with large brown eyes and a bushy mustache. He was dressed in his gold-braided military uniform, with his many medals and decorations displayed prominently on his tunic. When DeRohan had shaken his hand in welcome, Jules stepped forward, gave the man her most beguiling smile, and said, giving a slight bow of her head, "Your Imperial Majesty, King of Kings, Light of the Aryans, welcome to our coast."

"Dear lady!" he beamed. "You know all my titles!"

"Your illustrious titles don't prepare one for the magnetism of your presence. You honor us with your visit."

She offered her hand with the regal grace that had been bred into her from the cradle. He took it, raised it to his lips in tribute, then, still holding it, extended his arm so he could step back and give her a long appreciative look.

"It is you, Your Royal Highness, who honor me. I am but a humble desert chieftain, come to worship at the shrine of the greatest ruling dynasty the world has ever known. Your beauty shines with the centuries of the Habsburg reign. This is, without question, the most auspicious day of my life."

"I am no longer a royal highness, Your Imperial Majesty."

"So they tell me. But to me, you will always be a royal princess of history's most esteemed line."

Jules deepened her smile, saying, "I suspect, Your Majesty, that we are going to be good friends."

He squeezed the hand he still held, so tightly that it cut off the flow of blood to her arm. "We will, dear lady, most assuredly."

Jules glanced at DeRohan, who stood watching at her side. He was visibly pleased, and seemed finally to lose his edge.

They walked the rose petal path to the Carlton with its molded white façade and distinctive black domes on both seaward corners, reputed to have been fashioned to resemble a Belle Époque courtesan's breasts. The staff, who'd been instructed to display particular deference, made a great show of bowing as they passed through the high-ceilinged marble lobby with its stately columns, grand arched doorways, and sparkling chandeliers. Down the left hallway, in the Grand Salon ballroom, several hundred people in formal attire were assembled, awaiting the arrival of the East's most powerful sovereign. This was the cream of the Riviera's aristocratic residents, dukes and duchesses, counts and countesses, Indian maharajas and dethroned princes from half a dozen Middle European countries, all here at the approving nod of her grace, the Duchess of Olifant.

They led the Shah across the ballroom—decked out like a turn-of-the-century fantasyland—to a place of honor where the crowd, in a long reception line, snaked its way to meet him. For the next hour, the guests moved slowly before them as Hudson, who'd been stationed there waiting, announced the titles.

"His Majesty, the King of Sweden."

"The Marquis de Rethel."

"The Duc de Vêndome."

"Princess Mafalda."

"The Grand Duke Dimitri."

"Her Majesty, Queen Margherita of Italy."

On and on it went. Any other man might have tired of it in ten minutes, but the Shah was like a small boy in a confectionary. His eyes widened at each new face, as if he were consciously trying to store them in his memory to look back over and cherish. When it came time for Fanny, the Duchess of Olifant, to come forward, Jules experienced a moment of trepidation. Fanny had no escort, she looked to be in a foul mood, and seemed capable of unleashing one of her legendary snubs.

But as she took the man of the hour's hand, she smiled as courteously as the others. "Lovely country, Persia. I have a relative who lives in Cairo. Count DeBrazie. I don't suppose you know him?"

Without bothering to inform her that Cairo was nowhere near Persia, he responded, "I am afraid not, dear lady. But I would be most eager to make his acquaintance."

As she passed, the duchess pulled Jules aside with a sour face. "That Nikki! Wretched boy. He coaxed me into coming to this cattle show, and at the last minute, he conveniently gets a toothache and has to beg off. I could simply thrash him!"

Jules tried to look sympathetic, but inside she was gleaming.

Of course he begged off. He couldn't very well come here as Nikki and do what he had to later tonight.

As the line progressed, DeRohan put a hand to Jules's elbow and gave her a queer look, as if trying to penetrate the workings of her mind. "I must say I'm surprised. For once, you seem to have come through with your part of the bargain."

"You wanted royalty, I delivered it. Unlike some people,

when I give my word, I keep it. In fact, as you shall soon see, there's a great deal more to come. A private performance by the Ballet Russe, an epicurean feast catering to all the Shah's favorite dishes, and dancing—which he particularly enjoys. Capped off by the most spectacular pyrotechnical display ever seen on the Côte in the man's honor."

DeRohan frowned. "You said nothing about fireworks."

"I said nothing about rose petals either, but that doesn't seem to bother you. Really DeRohan, you are too suspicious. What do you think I'm going to do with those fireworks? Blow up the Shah? Or better yet, you?"

"It just occurs to me that you quite pointedly did not tell me about them."

"Very well, then." Raising her voice a notch, she said to Hudson, who was standing on the other side of their guest, "Hudson, tell the hotel manager, Monsieur LeFarge, that the *feu d'artifice* are to be canceled."

Hudson appeared nonplussed. "Including the display of the Persian flag, Highness?"

"Sadly, yes."

"What?" the Shah interjected. "But I *adore* fireworks! Don't tell me, lovely lady, that you went to the enormous trouble and expense to custom order a representation of my country's flag especially for me?"

"I thought it might please you, but my husband seems to think—"

"A minor misunderstanding," DeRohan cut her off, stepping between them. "Of course we're having fireworks. In fact, the balcony of your suite should provide the perfect vantage point from which to view them in private, away from the other guests."

Jules stepped around him. "But surely the penthouse suite would be more suitable. It's one floor higher and its balcony has a more sweeping view of the harbor."

"Better yet," DeRohan suggested, "we'll go to the roof. It has the best view of all."

Jules gave her husband a sweet smile. "But mightn't it be windy up there?"

The Shah was shaking his head emphatically. "One does not come to the Riviera to be blown off the roof."

With two sets of eyes on him, DeRohan gave in with a shrug. "Very well. The penthouse it is."

It was a long evening. Throughout, Jules was the perfect hostess, subtly flattering the Shah, laughing at all his jests, listening attentively during the ten-course banquet as he spoke of his plans to westernize Iran, as he called Persia. But as the ballet was drawing to a close and the more hazardous business of the evening neared, she began to feel nervous. It was a simple yet tightly constructed plan. There were a dozen places where things could go wrong. Timing was crucial.

Finally, she looked at her diamond watch and announced, "We'd better be going up. The fireworks are scheduled to begin promptly at midnight."

DeRohan shot her an irritated look. Boor that he was, he'd been using the party to make his business pitch to the Shah and clearly didn't like being interrupted. But their guest, who still seemed somewhat resistant to his overtures, cried, "Splendid! I am most eager to see how you can possibly light up the sky with the likeness of my country's flag."

Jules looked around for Hudson, intending to have him inform the other guests that they should file out to the viewing area that had been set up on the hotel beach. But he seemed to have already left to oversee the staff on the beach, so she rose to her feet and made the announcement herself.

Turning to the Shah with a smile, she asked, "Shall we proceed, Your Imperial Majesty?"

He offered his arm and the three of them followed the crowd in the direction of the lobby, then veered off to take the elevator to the top floor.

As the door closed behind them and the cage began to rise, Jules felt her mouth go dry. DeRohan had picked up the conversation where he'd left off, so she didn't have to participate. She heard the Panther's voice in her head.

When you get to the top floor, there will be a guard stationed by the elevator. DeRohan always has one there, twenty-four hours a day.

The door opened and they stepped out. There, as promised, she spotted a burly uniformed Basque with a holstered pistol on his belt. He was seated, but he leapt to attention when he saw DeRohan. Jules eyed him tensely. He was as big as an ox.

DeRohan didn't even spare him a passing glance as they continued down the hallway.

It will be sixty paces from the elevator to the door of the penthouse. It should take you about a minute, give or take a few seconds.

She counted the paces as they walked with DeRohan's voice droning in her ears. At the door, he reached into his pocket and withdrew a key. She noted that it was a different lock from the others in the hotel, specially crafted by the Swiss security firm.

He opened the door to expose a sumptuous corner suite with a staggering view of the Mediterranean. She caught glimpses of Aubusson rugs scattered on the parquet floors, a Chippendale writing desk, a refectory table and Italian chairs, and on the walls, drawings by Watteau, Fragonard, and Lorrain. Beyond the sitting room was a dining area with a table that could easily seat sixteen guests.

When you get inside, wait until you're certain he's not looking at you, then locate the fireplace on the north wall. It's not real. It's just a casing that conceals the safe.

She found it as DeRohan threw open the glass doors of the balcony, then turned to usher them outside. The night was dark now, and the Esterel hills were black. The clouds obscured the stars, appearing dark grey against the murky night. Looking down, Jules could see her guests seating themselves at the tables on the beach across the Croisette. Although there were lanterns on the beach, she'd had all the lights outside the hotel extinguished on the pretext that they would detract from the drama of the exhibition. A strong sea breeze cooled her hot brow. And then, the orchestra on the beach began to play and a rocket streamed into the air, bursting into thousands of red and orange spheres that floated gracefully down to the midnight blue of the water. The appreciative cries of the guests mingled with the music.

The display continued for the next half hour, each portion more spectacular than the last, until it climaxed with the *pièce de résistance*, a synchronized, twenty sky-rocket concoction that gave an impressive pyrotechnic version of the Persian flag. At that moment, the orchestra, which had been playing Handel's *Water Music,* struck up the Persian national anthem. Jules had spent twenty thousand pounds sterling of DeRohan's money for this one bit of flattery alone.

The Shah was beside himself. With tears in his eyes, he turned to Jules. "What a magnificent moment! A moment that will live in my memory forevermore. A thousand thanks, dear lady." Then he turned to DeRohan with undisguised envy and asked emotionally, "Where does one acquire such a wife as this?"

DeRohan stepped over to Jules and put his arm about her with possessive affection, ignoring the way she stiffened under his touch. "Think what partners we shall be, the three of us. My ships, your oil, and Juliana's support and inspiration."

The Shah beamed at Jules, but his smile, when he turned to DeRohan was more noncommittal. "Inshallah," he murmured, dodging the issue. "If Allah wills it."

Jules wriggled free of her husband's show of domination and stepped over to take the Shah's arm. "But the evening is not half done. There is much more entertainment to come. I've engaged the services of a syncopated American dance band. I'm told you have a particular interest in all things modern. I thought you might like to learn to dance the Charleston. Unless, of course, some other more fortunate hostess has beaten me to it."

"But, no!" the Shah declared with a delighted grin. "I was waiting for you!"

"I couldn't be happier," Jules assured him. "We'll have such fun!"

Hands on his heart, the Shah declared, "I am speechless. Cyrus the Great himself could not have been more lavishly fêted than I have been this night."

DeRohan leveled a look at his wife, as if he couldn't believe how magnificently she was bringing off this extravaganza. But she turned from him, saying, "Shall we go down?"

As the three of them started for the door, she deliberately didn't pick up the small sequined evening bag she'd set down on the desk. With a proprietary air, DeRohan opened the door to let them pass. But as she stepped into the hall, and before he could close the door behind them, Jules said, "Oh, I forgot my bag."

Leaving them in the hallway, she quickly reentered the suite to fetch it. With her back turned to him, she reached beneath the dangling thirty carat sapphire of her necklace and pulled off the small piece of bandage tape she'd placed there earlier, sticking the end to her finger. Then she turned again for the door.

We'll need a bit of luck here. If he steps back into the suite after you, and insists on closing the door himself, our entire scheme will be thwarted.

DeRohan was still in the hall, talking quietly to the Shah, but his eyes shot suspiciously her way. Was he going to step in so he'd be the one to close the door? He made a motion in its direction, but the Shah said something and he turned back to his guest.

She hurried to the door, stepped so that she was between it and DeRohan, reached behind her to secure the tape on the latch—as she'd practiced on her own lock many times over the last few days—and, in the same motion, closed the door behind her.

DeRohan glanced sardonically down at the bag in her hands, but he was more interested in the conversational point he was trying to make with the Shah. She followed them down the hall, resisting the urge to break into a triumphant smile.

I did it!

But this was only the beginning.

As they approached the ballroom, they joined the crowd that was returning from the beach, gushing over the fireworks display, ready to dance until dawn.

You'll dance with the Shah for a time. But keep your eyes open for a chance to slip away from your husband. This is where you'll have to be inventive, because his instincts will be set on fire if you tell him you need time alone.

A band of black American jazz musicians who'd been brought over from Juan-les-Pins had taken their places on the raised platform and were awaiting Jules's signal. She held her hand out to the Shah. "Shall we?"

"With the greatest of pleasure!" He glanced at DeRohan. "And you, Dominic, will you join us on the dance floor?"

DeRohan raised a hand in negation. "Not me. I'm going to find a quiet corner as far away from that noise as possible. You children come find me when you're done playing."

Jules couldn't believe her luck.

She smiled at the Shah. "My husband doesn't know how to amuse himself. But we do, don't we?"

"I have never been so amused!"

Jules gave the signal and the band struck up a lively number. As the aristocrats looked askance among themselves, she led the Shah out onto the floor. "It's easy, really. Here, I'll show you. Step, step, kick, step, step, kick. Now you try it."

He did. Giggling, he followed her lead, picking up the steps. Soon enough, he was moving in rhythm with the tempo of the music. "It certainly gets the heart pumping!"

Before long, others began to join in, encouraged by the gleeful demonstration. Then more, some coming up to Jules and watching as the Shah had, then tentatively trying out the steps.

Soon the entire dance floor was crowded with formally attired ladies and gentlemen kicking up their heels in joyous abandon.

She danced two more dances with the Shah, showing him the Black Bottom and Turkey Trot, all the while keeping an eye on the time and scanning the room to make certain DeRohan wasn't watching. She didn't see him. The time was approaching when she'd have to leave. She was going to have to do something with the Shah. As the music died for the third time, she spotted Carlotta, the eighteen-year-old daughter of the Spanish consul and the prettiest girl in the room. Excusing herself briefly, she went to her and said conspiratorially, "The Shah has worn me out. I need a rest. Be a love and keep him occupied for a while, will you?"

"Me? But what am I to do with him?"

"Just keep him dancing. He can't seem to get enough of it."

Accustomed to such requests, the girl agreed and Jules walked her back to the Shah, who was sipping water from a goblet. He was delighted when he saw his new partner and eager to return to the dance floor. Once she was certain he was settled, Jules checked her watch, scanned the room one more time to make sure DeRohan wasn't in sight, then walked as calmly and inconspicuously as she could out of the ballroom.

Making her way toward the lobby was more nerve-wracking. She jumped as a bellboy barreled past her, thinking at first that it was DeRohan. For all she knew, he might be wandering about the hotel and could pounce upon her at any moment. If he caught her betraying him in this way, there was no telling how brutal his response might be. She remembered the story of how, when they were first married, he'd discovered an indiscretion by Franklin, his most trusted assistant, and had beaten him black and blue. What then would he do to her, she whom he loathed, for an infinitely greater infraction?

Taking a breath to steady herself, she headed for the elevator, but continued past it down the hall until she came to the service stairs. She paused and looked at her watch. One o'clock.

What's most imperative is that you reach the top of the service stairwell and be waiting at exactly five minutes past one. If you're even a second late, it could all go wrong.

She had five minutes, so she began to climb slowly. But halfway up, she realized it was taking her longer than she'd thought, so she increased her speed. By the time she reached the seventh floor, she was winded and had to pause to catch her breath. But she'd made it with thirty seconds to spare. At the door, she watched as the second hand on her watch moved around the dial.

I'll be waiting on the roof. I'll have a heavy rock attached to the end of a rope. At exactly five minutes past, I'll swing it down to break a window at the opposite end of the corridor from the penthouse. The guard is sure to go charging down to investigate. I'll sprinkle a few feathers down to the window ledge, so hopefully he'll assume—as sometimes happens—that a seagull flew into the window.

She put her ear to the stairwell door. She heard nothing. What if something went wrong? What if he wasn't able to get there on time? What if he was spotted?

Momentarily, she heard the distant sound of breaking glass. Relieved, she then heard the surprised curse of the guard.

You should have about sixty seconds to get around the corner and down the hall and into the penthouse—that's how long it will take the guard to get down there, inspect the broken window, figure out that there was no intruder, and return to his post to call maintenance.

She charged through the door and, without even looking to see if the guard had done what he was supposed to, she swerved around the corner and down the hall, counting in her mind, *sixty . . . fifty-nine . . . fifty-eight . . .*

The passage was longer than she remembered. By the time she'd reached the count of ten, she was running as fast as she could. At last her extended hand reached for the doorknob. Would the tape do its trick?

It did. The door opened and she slipped inside, glancing

back down the hall to see the guard inspecting the broken windowpane. She removed the tape from the latch and closed the door behind her.

Inside, the suite was dark, deserted, and eerily quiet. She rushed to the glass doors, banging her leg on a chair along the way.

All the French doors in the suite are made of unbreakable glass and will trigger an alarm if anyone even tries to open them from the outside. The only way to open them is from within.

Carefully, she opened one of the doors. Now all she had to do was wait. He would crawl down from the roof onto the balcony to join her.

But suddenly a flash of light blinded her. Panicked, she flattened herself back against the wall. What could it be?

DeRohan must have figured it out.

We've been caught!

Chapter 19

Adrenaline raced through her veins. Then there was another blinding flash of light. She turned cautiously to the open door again, peering around the jamb. All at once, she realized what was happening. A pair of mammoth searchlights were crisscrossing the façade of the building. They were imported from Hollywood and sometimes used to give a dramatic touch to special occasions. She hadn't ordered it. The hotel manager must have arranged it on his own.

This would ruin everything!

The plan was for him to drop a rope ladder from the roof and climb down to the balcony where she'd opened the door for him. Then, once they had the letter, the two of them would climb back up the ladder. But the huge lights were sweeping the front of the building from corner to corner, so they would be spotted by anyone down on the Croisette who happened to look up. Her own guests and other late night revelers from the Carlton and other hotels had spilled out into the night and were strolling the beachfront.

Would he risk lowering the ladder and climbing down? If he did, he'd surely be seen from below. If he didn't, she'd be trapped up here. The plan hadn't included any way to divert the guard a second time.

Momentarily, she heard his whistle. She looked up. And as she did, she saw a dark figure fall from the sky. With the grace of a trapeze artist, he broke his fall by grabbing onto a flagpole that jutted out perpendicular to the balcony, swinging around in a complete circle, and flinging himself feet first onto the balcony where she stood.

The entire maneuver took only a few seconds and was perfectly timed to miss the next glare of the spotlight. As it swept toward them, he grabbed her and pulled her back into the suite. She gazed up at him with all her love for him shining in her eyes, marveling at his daring.

But how would the two of them ever get out of here?

If he shared her trepidation, he didn't show it. Below his mask, his mouth formed a devilish grin. He wrapped his arms about her shoulders and jerked her to him to give her a heady kiss.

It was like something out of a Douglas Fairbanks movie.

"Well done," he told her. "Now let's get what we came for."

Taking a small flashlight from the pouch at his belt, he flicked it on and crossed the room, going directly to the fireplace. He pulled open the false front, exposing the thick steel door of the safe with its intimidating combination lock.

She joined him as he knelt before it. "The manufacturer says it's burglar-proof," he whispered, flashing a grin. "But not if the burglar happened to steal the combination from the manufacturer's files."

She watched him play with the tumblers for half a minute. Then he jerked the handle. Nothing happened. He pursed his mouth in irritation. She felt a rush of affection. Nikki used to give a similar grimace when they were children and he came up against some obstacle he couldn't immediately overcome.

He tried the combination again, and once more the handle wouldn't budge. She sat back on her heels, her fingernails biting into the palm of her hand. With the party looming, had DeRohan been clever enough to change the combination in the last few days? Had he outsmarted them? Was it possible that *he* had brought in the searchlights to trap them up here?

The Panther began to move the dial once again, more slowly

this time. Left. Right. Left. A third time, he grasped the handle and gave it a jerk.

This time the door swung open.

The safe was empty except for a single envelope resting in the dead center. He snatched it up. It was unsealed. He removed a single sheet of paper, scanned it in the beam of the flashlight, then whispered, "This is it." He offered it to her. "Would you like to see it?"

For a moment, she looked at the sheet of paper that represented the evil hold her husband had on the Rothschild family. She shook her head. "We'll let it be their secret."

She thought she detected a flash of admiration in the eyes behind the mask. He reached forward and slid his gloved thumb down her cheek. "I'll make certain it gets back to its proper owner."

Just then, the French door banged against the wall, causing them to jump. The wind outside had kicked up suddenly, coming off the sea. Jules could hear the echo of it in the suite, like a mournful whine. And then it sounded outside the room, behind them, as if the wind was roaring through the halls.

It reminded her that they were now trapped up here. "How are we going to get out of here? With those lights, they'll surely see us from down below. The Carlton is the showcase of the Croisette. Everyone looks up at it as they pass."

He was glancing about the suite. "Yes, I hadn't counted on the lights. Let me think. We'll have to improvise. I could try to shoot out the lights, but the gunshots would be heard. There's no way of overpowering the guard, because he'd see me coming and gun me down before I had a chance to get close to him. We could wait here until they turn out the searchlights—whenever that might be—but the instant you're missed downstairs, DeRohan may remember how eager you were to come up here and charge upstairs to investigate. So the way I see it, we have just one hope."

"What's that?"

"The glare of the searchlights doesn't reach the far end of

the building, so there's a blind spot there. Since this suite takes up the west corner of the building, we might use that to our advantage. The balustrade of this balcony runs the length of the entire seventh floor. The balconies of the suites on this floor don't connect, but the balustrades do. The width of the top of the balustrade is about a foot and a half wide—enough to walk on, though admittedly challenging to one unaccustomed to heights and wearing an evening gown. But if you're game, we could step onto that ledge and walk around the corner of the building and all the way down the west façade. Around the back of the building there's a service ladder used by the window washers, which will take us right up to the roof. The west side of the hotel will be dark, so nobody will spot us."

To make the prospect even more terrifying, a flash of lightning split the night and all at once the sky opened and a heavy rain began to fall.

Everything seemed to be falling apart.

"It's starting to rain. Won't it be slippery on the marble ledge?"

"We'll have to be extra careful. But I'll help you."

"What if you took that route of escape while I go back the way I came? After all, the guard isn't going to shoot me—"

"No. But he'll tell your husband you were up here by yourself. DeRohan will come straight here, see the letter's gone, and have a little reception party waiting for me when I finally get down from the building—or more likely, he'll shoot me off the west façade."

The image of DeRohan gunning her lover down was more agonizing than the prospect of stepping onto the ledge. Jules swallowed hard. "Very well, then. Let's go."

He stowed the letter in his pouch, returned the empty envelope to its place in the safe, closed the door, and gave the dial a spin. Then he replaced the false front of the fireplace, took her by the hand, and led her to the balcony.

But along the way, the room was suddenly illuminated by a massive flash of lightning, instantly followed by the loudest crack of thunder she'd ever heard in her life.

She halted abruptly, pulling him up short, her hand in his beginning to tremble. "I can't do this," she told him. "I'm terrified of thunder. I'll freeze out there. I won't be able to move. There has to be another way."

He put his other gloved hand over hers. "*Cara,* there *is* no other way."

"You don't understand. It was the war. For years, we lived in fear that the enemy would come into Vienna at any moment and destroy us. So every time there was thunder, we thought it was their cannons and we died a little. But for me, there was more. One of the servant's children told me that everyone hated us, that they were going to come and rip us from our beds and tear us apart for all we'd done. So I used to cower in my bed during thunderstorms, certain the end was near, envisioning a mob like that of the French Revolution coming for us. I know it's irrational—a silly, childish fear. But I can't help it. I become so afraid when I hear thunder, I can't function."

He squeezed her hand. "I understand your fear. But listen to me. I can get you through this. All you have to do is put your faith in me. Can you do that?"

She looked up at him. "I want to."

"Trust me, *Cara.* Nothing else matters. Don't think of the thunder or the ledge. Don't think of anything at all. Just know that I love you. And loving you will allow no harm to come to you."

She felt some of his certainty seep into her. Could she do it?

"You must decide. We're running out of time."

She closed her eyes and for a moment felt the strength and security of his touch.

"I can do it," she said.

They stepped onto the balcony into a shower of cold rain. The force of the wind was increasing. Below them, the surf was rushing into the shore in furious volleys, pounding the sand. She could see, in the next flare of lightning, that the palms along the Croisette were blowing like hula skirts in the gale. At the east end of the harbor, the emerald green beacon of the lighthouse blinked in regular flashes, like Gatsby's green light at East Egg.

He waited until the full force of the searchlight illuminated the balcony, then, as it moved back the other way, he pulled her to the part of the balcony that rounded the corner of the building and looked out on the dark west wall of the hotel. There, as the lightning flared again, she could see the narrow ledge leading like a white ribbon into the darkness beyond.

"Here's what you're going to do," he told her in a confident, soothing tone. "First, take off those heels and give them to me." She did so, and he hooked them into his belt. "Now, I'm going to help you up to the ledge. This far out, we won't have anything to hold onto, so you're going to hold onto me. I'll lead the way. You just step when I do. We'll take it as slowly as you need. It's vital that you don't look down or think about what we're doing. Do you understand? Think about the look on DeRohan's face when the Rothschilds tell him to go to the devil. Feel that satisfaction now, and hold onto it."

Listening to his voice, she could feel it. It *was* a glorious prospect. "All right, I'm ready."

Easily, he leapt up to the ledge topping the balustrade, then held his hand out to her and helped her up. Suddenly she was exposed, unprotected, with nothing to grab onto except his hand, all too aware that if she leaned even a few inches to the side, she could lose her balance and send them both hurtling to the ground. She looked up and saw the outline of the black dome on the roof soaring above. But the rain blinded her. She was already drenched. The wind swirled around her, making her sway, almost causing her to lose her balance. She felt his hand tighten, anchoring her, and curled her bare toes inward, trying to find a secure grip on the slick stone beneath them.

"All right, let's take a step. Slowly. Take your time."

She shook the water from her eyes and took a tentative step, following his lead. Suddenly there was a flash of lightning and a deafening roar of thunder. Her body went rigid with fear.

"*Cara*, look at me." His voice penetrated the panicked screaming inside her head. It took every ounce of willpower she had to swivel her head in his direction. "You can do this," he assured her.

She felt the gentle pull of his hand and felt her foot move the slightest bit. "*Brava*. Just like that. Now another."

The wind was whipping her long skirts about her. She was afraid they would act as a sail and blow her off. But she did her best to concentrate on him instead. She slid her bare foot along the parapet, holding her other arm out for balance. Again he gave her a gentle tug and again she took a step. Soon they were making their way slowly down the perilous route. Another step. Then another. And another. She thought of DeRohan's face, fuming when he heard the news.

"I see the edge of the building now," he told her. "We only have another ten or fifteen meters to go."

She was shivering with cold. The bodice of her satin ball gown clung clammily to her skin. She was being battered by the wind, but she clung to his hand.

And then, there came a quick succession of lightning bolts, one after the other, splitting the vast extent of the sky with its forked shafts of fire. And on its heels, the rumbling of thunder, rising with such intensity that it seemed to shake the very core of the building. It boomed down on them like the roar of a hundred cannons, again and again and again, sounding as if the world were coming to an end.

Recoiling from the shock of it, her foot slipped off the marble.

And then she was falling, tumbling in space. In an instant of horror, she knew she'd killed them both.

But her fall was abruptly broken by the grip of his gloved hand. Somehow he'd managed to keep his footing and hold her weight. Her arm tearing in its socket, she dangled high above the street, the wind whipping her back and forth on her precipitous perch.

She was too petrified even to scream. He had nothing to hold onto. She knew that at any moment, she would pull him down with her.

The thunder boomed again. She was shaking uncontrollably. She felt her wet hand slip a little in his.

In the aftermath of the boom, she heard his stern voice. "Look at me, *Cara*."

Propelled by the command in his tone, she looked up through the rain and saw him crouched on his haunches to bear the weight of her body with his one hand. "I have you. I'm not going to let you go."

She could only see his hunched outline in the darkness. But she could hear the confidence in his tone.

"Trust me."

Suddenly she did. Completely. Devotedly. And in that instant, even the thunder lost its terror. Dangling seven stories above the ground, a straining handgrip away from death, she'd never felt more protected in all her life.

"I'm going to lift you," he called down. "Don't move. Let me do the work."

Slowly, the muscles of his arm vibrating from the effort, she felt herself rising. One inch. Then another. Her hand slipped once again in his. But she wasn't afraid. She knew now there was no force on earth strong enough to make him let her go.

He pulled ever upward. Inch by torturous inch. Until at last he'd lifted her high enough so that he could grab her wrist with his other hand.

A final lunge, and she felt the ledge beneath her feet once more.

She fell into his arms, her heart soaring, feeling liberated from all trace of fear.

When the thunder came again, she looked at him and smiled. It had lost its power over her.

He returned her smile. The he readjusted his grip on her hand and they continued their trek to the ladder. Safety was now in sight. Yet she felt so secure, so close to him, that she almost didn't want this to end.

Soon, his voice said, "We've made it, *Cara*."

He helped her up the cast-iron ladder and onto the roof. She didn't know it was possible to feel so exhilarated, so wildly happy.

They scampered across the flat surface behind the hotel's façade to the spot where he'd left a long rope attached to a grappling hook—which he'd used to scale the back wall earlier that night. Finding a secure spot for the hook, he let the rope drop down the dark rear of the building.

"All you have to do now is wrap your arms around my neck and hold tight while I slide us down the rope."

She did as instructed, wrapping her arms about his neck, feeling the wall of his chest crushing her breasts. He put an arm about her waist and took hold of the rope in his other gloved hand. Then, leaping off the building, he slid down the rope in one breathtaking sweep, like an elevator broken loose from its cable.

By the time they landed on their feet on the ground, her head was spinning. Stepping away from her, he gave the rope a jerk that sent a wave up to the top, dislodging the grappling hook, sending it tumbling toward them.

Then he handed forth her shoes. "Time is of the essence. You need to go around the building and reenter the party as quickly as possible."

"But I'm soaked."

"Everyone on the Croisette got caught in the rain, including a number of your guests. You can use that as an excuse." He came closer and took her face in his hands. "You've made me proud."

She still felt dizzy. But she beamed, basking in his praise. "Now I know why you love this. It was such fun!"

He was gazing down at her. "You realize this is good-bye?"

"Is it?"

"You know it is. I've told you so."

The rain was washing down on them. "I don't believe you. After all we've been to each other—after *tonight!* You won't be able to stay away."

"But I must, *Cara.* Please believe me."

She felt like scolding him, the way she had when they were young. *Very well, Nikki, have your little game. But this isn't good-bye. Because I know your secret. And I'm not going to let you go.*

"If you're really bent on leaving, then kiss me one last time."

He did. Enfolding her in his arms, he gave her a scalding kiss that set her shivering body to flame. He kissed her the way a man would kiss a woman he would never see again.

She smiled inwardly. *You're a better actor, Nikki, than I gave you credit for.*

Should I tell him I know now . . . or wait until tomorrow?

Better tomorrow. I'll show up on his doorstep and say: I have a surprise for you, Nikki. I know who you are. Now, enough of this nonsense. I'm yours.

She couldn't wait to see his face.

He tore himself away. "Now go. Quickly. Don't look back."

"So long, then," she told him with a coy smile.

So long until tomorrow, when we can stop playing this charade!

She turned and ran with a light step back around the side of the building to the front entrance, where other guests were drying themselves with towels provided by the hotel. Jules took one inside with her. She didn't care that she was dripping water on the gleaming floor. She didn't care what DeRohan said when he saw her. She didn't care about anything. It seemed as if the whole world had suddenly opened at her feet.

As she went down the hallway toward the Grand Salon, dabbing at her dripping hair with the towel, she began to hum the song the band was playing.

> *I'm sitting on top of the world . . .*
> *Just rolling along . . .*
> *Singing my song . . .*

She entered the ballroom, floating on air.

And stopped cold.

Because dancing with the Duchess of Olifant was a late arrival to the party.

Bone dry, resplendent in black tie and tuxedo.

Nikki Romanov.

Chapter 20

Two days after the Carlton heist, just after luncheon, Baron de Rothschild, two of his sons, and three of their attorneys appeared at the doorstep of Rêve de l'Amour, having made the journey down from Paris on the Blue Train.

DeRohan met the delegation in the Louis XVI salon with his customary arrogant assurance. "And whom do I have to thank for this unannounced personal visit?"

Jules, who'd been informed of the visit by Hudson, stood in the doorway, watching the scene.

The baron nodded to one of his lawyers who handed forth a document. "I merely wanted to see for myself the expression on your face when you received this."

DeRohan's eyes quickly scanned the legal document. "What *is* this?"

"I'm calling in all our loans to you, DeRohan. Every one. Furthermore, I've spread the word throughout the international banking circles that DeRohan Enterprises is no longer an acceptable risk for any further loans it might seek to finance its survival."

"Are you out of your mind? Have you forgotten—"

"The letter? I haven't forgotten about it in the least. It's simply no longer a consideration. You see, it was returned to me by a Good Samaritan."

"Returned?"

Contemptuously, the baron sneered, "You didn't even know it was missing, did you? And they call you DeRohan the Invincible." All the years of suppressed hostility from being under this man's thumb seethed in the baron's voice.

The impact of the Rothschild action was swift and catastrophic to the DeRohan empire. The financial press speculated that, with not even half the cash reserves to pay off the loans and its credit rating abruptly reduced to nearly zero, it was going to be a scramble to survive. To weather the storm would require a massive campaign of selling off assets and conniving to withstand the continued assault of the Rothschild family.

Passing by his study the next morning, Jules overheard DeRohan talking to someone on the telephone. "No, I don't know how they got the goddamned letter . . . all I know is they did . . . Yes, of course it's bad . . ." A brief silence. Then, "What the newspapers don't know is that I still have an ace up my sleeve—the prospect of the deal with the Shah. If I can secure those oil leases, it will make up for the Rothschild treachery. Once I get his signature on paper, every other bank in Europe and America will be falling over themselves to give me money."

There was a pause as he listened. Then he said, "He's still at the Carlton. He *wants* to make the deal. I've impressed him to the point that he's going to wait to see if I can ride out the storm. So what we have to do is sell off whatever we have to and scrounge up cash in any way we can to stay alive. If we can do that—if we can stay afloat for . . . I don't know how long—just so it's clear that we're not going to fold overnight—then I'm telling you, that man is going to come to my rescue."

In this campaign to stay solvent, he was working nonstop, tying up the phone, firing off telegrams. All day long, there was a steady stream of people coming and going, all with grave expressions on their faces. The once peaceful house began to resemble the war room of the admiralty in the midst of a great sea battle.

That afternoon, Inspector Ladd paid him a visit. They met

in the study, but standing just outside in the hallway, Jules could hear their conversation.

"It appears your instinct was correct, Mr. DeRohan. When we questioned the guests at the hotel, we found two people who claimed to have seen someone walking along the row of balconies on the seventh floor that very night."

"I knew it!" DeRohan exploded. "Did they get a description?"

"Not much of one, I'm afraid. It was pouring down rain and dark to boot. But in the flare of lightning, each man thought he saw two figures."

"Two? But I thought the Panther worked alone."

"He does, by all accounts. Apparently, this is a first for the dashed fellow."

DeRohan's voice trembled with rage. "I want that man's scalp."

"I assure you, sir, we're putting forth our best efforts to bring the rascal to justice."

"Your best efforts be damned. I intend to put up a reward for his capture—dead or alive. Fifty thousand pounds. No, a hundred thousand. It's more than I can afford at the moment, but I don't care."

"That may not be prudent, sir. That sort of money could only create a mob mentality and hamper our efforts."

"You may think that, but I don't. The one thing I believe in is human greed. No man is an island. He must know someone, somewhere. A friend, a relative, a servant, somebody. And for that kind of money, that someone will sell him out."

The evil determination in her husband's voice—the image of someone turning in the Panther for his filthy money—gave Jules a stab of alarm.

At that moment, the two men came out of the room. DeRohan, seeing her standing there like a spying school brat, stopped in his tracks. As the inspector found his way out by himself, DeRohan peered at her. "Why do I get the feeling that, in some way I can't yet imagine, *you* are responsible for all this?"

She said nothing.

Stepping closer, he ground out, "If I find out that you were, everything you've experienced from me so far will have been but a mere prelude to what your life is going to be like."

But it was an empty threat. The next morning, he packed up and left for London, where his advisors warned him he needed to be if his businesses were to have any hope of surviving the next critical month.

Suddenly, Rêve de l'Amour was free of him. Even the security he'd added after the Toulon incident was gone. Blissful silence lingered in the halls. No one came and went. The servants once again relaxed. But Jules felt no relief, no satisfaction. All she could feel was a crushing sense of regret and self-recrimination.

What have I done?

Thinking he was Nikki, she'd answered the Panther's farewell with thoughtless flippancy.

But he wasn't Nikki. He couldn't be.

And now he was gone.

She couldn't accept it. She had to find him, tell him why she'd acted in such a fashion, how she'd deluded herself. But how *could* she find him?

There was nothing she could do. Nothing but relive the awful moment again and again in her mind. Trying to rewrite it as one might tear up the false start of a letter and begin anew.

And so she drifted through her days numbly, like a ghost.

A week passed. The silence of the house began to seem oppressive. Friends, hearing of DeRohan's departure, called to invite her out, but she didn't have the heart and had Hudson stall them with one excuse after the other.

At one point, compelled by some insane impulse, she went to see Nikki at his home above Cannes. As he chatted away about the party at the Carlton, he seemed once again the boy she'd known. She scrutinized him bleakly. He suddenly didn't even seem to be the same height . . . the same build . . . he didn't move with that masculine feline grace. His hands, she noticed now, were soft, almost feminine—not the large hands that had so often cupped her face in passion, or driven her to ecstasy with their masterful touch. He whined about how the silly duchess had monopolized his time. She couldn't believe she'd ever convinced herself that he might have been capable of transforming himself into such a bold and seductive character.

I must have been out of my mind!

So she closed herself off once again. She slept late, ate fitfully, and spent hours each day wandering aimlessly through the gardens in her hilltop hideaway. When Hudson was out of the house on one of his frequent errands, she would often descend into the basement and walk the tunnel to the secret room. There, she would lie on the bed where they'd shared such impassioned love, remembering everything they'd done, every word they'd said.

Then, one night, lying in her own bed, the idea seized her that he might secretly return to the room and just sit there, reliving the memories as she'd done. The next day she put fresh candles on the tabletops, a vase of pink roses picked from the garden, and left them with a note that said:

Please come to me. I must speak with you.

But every day, when she checked, the note was still there, and the flowers were a little more wilted than the day before.

Her mind was in turmoil. The newspapers were full of stories about DeRohan's offered reward—a king's ransom for the head of a panther. Meanwhile, the police—embarrassed by the added publicity—were stepping up their efforts, vowing to bring the clever fugitive to justice at any cost. Inspector Ladd rang up to tell her they were receiving more than a hundred calls a day from people claiming to have information on his identity.

She hoped—prayed—that he was as far away from this as possible.

And yet, as foolhardy as it might be, she also desperately wished he would appear in their room so she could see him one more time. If only for a moment. Achingly, she longed for the touch of his hand against hers, a whiff of his breath against her lips, the whisper of his voice when he said the word *Cara*.

Even if it was only to say a proper good-bye.

One afternoon, she found herself sitting on the bench by the rotunda of the Temple of Venus when all at once she realized she didn't know what time it was, or when she'd come here. She'd been wandering about in a kind of fog.

It was a beautiful day. As she looked back toward the house, all was quiet and serene. The birds were singing softly, and the dancing waters of the fountain below sounded soothing. The cicadas chirped in the pines.

Her personal attorney in Nice, Monsieur Breton, had called that morning to update her on DeRohan's continued ill fortune. He couldn't raise any money, his businesses were collapsing left and right, and the Shah had returned to Tehran. But she needn't worry, he'd hastened to assure her. The villa was in her name, the taxes were paid, and there was enough money in the household fund he managed for her to carry the estate for several years to come.

She suddenly realized that she had what she'd asked for that fateful night when the Panther had first entered her life.

Freedom from DeRohan.

But it meant nothing without the man she loved. She realized, sitting by the temple of the goddess of love above the room where they used to meet, that she would never get over him. She'd lost the only thing that really mattered.

As the shock began to wear off, her despair got the better of her and she began to cry.

Momentarily, she felt a movement beside her. Startled, she looked up to find Hudson standing there. She hadn't even heard him approach.

Embarrassed, she swiped at her tears with her fingers. Hudson, reaching into his pocket, offered his handkerchief. She took the freshly laundered square of linen, dabbing at her eyes.

"Thank you," she sniffed.

He must have been in the middle of some task when he'd looked up the hill and noticed her, for his jacket was off, the knot of his tie was loosened, and the collar of his crisp white shirt was unbuttoned.

Uncharacteristically, he sat down on the bench beside her. "You can't go on like this."

"I'm sorry, Hudson. I just can't quite get a grip on myself."

"It pains me to see you in such misery. Is there anything I can do?"

"No, nothing. There's nothing to be done."

"It's not my place to ask, Highness, but I must. Has this . . . man you've been seeing done something to harm you?"

"No. It's I who've done the harm. He's given me my freedom, but it means nothing without him."

He thought for a moment. "He's left, then?"

She found herself pouring out the whole story, from the beginning, filling in the details she'd never divulged to him. Everything but the tunnels and the secret room.

"I'm so very sorry," he finally said. "And there's no hope for the two of you?"

"He says there's some insurmountable obstacle that separates us. But I can't accept that. I refuse to envision an obstacle that can't be overcome."

"I'm afraid there *are* such obstacles."

She realized he was talking about himself. "Forgive my insensitivity. Of course you're right. I just wish I could find him, to tell him that whatever obstacle he sees, I don't care. I just want to be with him, under any circumstances. If that means he must place limitations on our meetings, I'll accept them. Even if I can't see his face, or know who he is. Even if I *never* can. I'd accept even that. But I can't find him. I don't know where to look."

"I imagine it's as difficult for him as it is for you," Hudson told her in a faraway tone.

"Is that supposed to make me feel better? That he suffers? That he's causing both of us pain? I suppose he thinks he's being noble, sacrificing himself this way. But it's an empty sacrifice. It doesn't have to be."

"It may seem so, to you. Yet you say you trust this man with your life. You said yourself, when you were hanging from the roof in his hand, that you had never felt more safe. If that is so, how can you not trust him now? How can you not accept that what he tells you has to be?"

"Because he's not trusting *me*. He's not trusting that I have it in me to accept him under any conditions. When I know I can. I *must*. Because life without him is no life at all."

Abruptly, Hudson rose to his feet. "There are just some things you have to accept." His adamancy surprised her. She looked up at him. He stood above her, fists clenched tightly at his sides. As a gentle breeze rose up from the sea, she noticed, distractedly, that it ruffled the thick hair peeking out above the open collar of his shirt. Instantaneously, he amended his tone. "Can't you see? You're doing yourself such damage. You must give this up."

"How can I?" she asked miserably. "The only thing I know for certain anymore is that if I give up hope, there's nothing left. I must find him. Somehow."

He watched her for a moment, weighing his words. "And what if you did? What if you learned his secret? What if you didn't like what you found?"

She stood, lifting her chin a defiant notch. "There is nothing in this world that I could find out about him that would be so awful, I couldn't accept it. *Nothing*."

More days passed. Try as she might—at Hudson's urging—she couldn't pull herself out of the abyss in which she was steadily sinking. She'd instructed him to tell anyone who called that she wasn't at home. But one day, against her orders, he handed her the candlestick telephone, dragging the long cord behind him.

"Mrs. Murphy to speak with you, Highness."

She shot him a scathing look. But with him holding the receiver in front of her, she couldn't very well tell him to say she wasn't here.

Reluctantly, she took the phone. "Hello, Sara."

"Hi, hun. You're going out with us tonight."

"Sara, no. I'm—"

"Dev sold his book to the movies! Got a hefty price for it, too. We're all going to dinner to celebrate."

Jules was happy for Dev, but she couldn't face the prospect of a celebration. "Please give him my congratulations. But I'm afraid that—"

"Now Jules, you shush," Sara interrupted with a reproachful note. "You know how that big lug dotes on you. This is the biggest thing that's ever happened to him. Honestly, if you don't show up, why—it will positively *ruin* his entire evening."

Jules knew she was trapped. "All right, Sara. I'll try to be there."

"Oh, no you don't. You're not getting off that easily! We're picking you up at six."

With that, she clicked off.

As he took the phone from her, Hudson said, "It will do you good, Highness."

She sighed. Where would she ever find the strength? What's more, she'd have to take a look at the book Dev had given her. It wouldn't do to admit she hadn't even cracked it open. Where had she put it? It seemed a lifetime ago that he'd brought it for her to read.

She had to think for a moment before she realized she'd placed it in her bedside drawer. Going upstairs, she retrieved it and went out onto her terrace to sit in one of the oversize rattan and cushioned chairs. Tucking her feet under her, she glanced at the title: *Man on the Roof*. "A mystery with comic overtones," the cover told her. She vaguely remembered overhearing some derisive comments from Scott and Ernest and some of their more literary-minded friends—something about Dev having squandered himself on a potboiler. And there was something else they'd said—what was it? Some cryptic comment about life imitating art.

Opening to the final paragraph, she saw that it was only two hundred pages. She glanced at her watch. It was only two. If she skimmed it, she could surely manage to finish it by the time Sara arrived. Enough to find something to say, anyway.

Perhaps it was for the best. It would help take her mind off her troubles—temporarily, at least.

Wondering what it was about, she turned to the publisher's description on the inside flap of the dust jacket. And nearly choked.

Because this book Dev had written—the one she'd tossed into a drawer without so much as a glance—was about a gentleman thief who mixed in high society.

A modern masked bandit who defied gravity with his daring aerial heists of Park Avenue apartments and the corporate headquarters of Manhattan skyscrapers.

The world's most glamorous cat burglar!

Chapter 21

Inspector John Curtis Ladd sat in the back of an inconspicuous black Peugeot parked on the Rue de la République in central Marseille.

Across the street, his gaze was fixed on a prosperous-looking establishment with a small display window filled with various items of jewelry and a simple sign identifying it as "Maison de Louis Cerrel, Bijoutier."

Back in Nice, the inspector's life had become an ordeal of impatient accusations—"When are we going to see results in this investigation?"—and endless futile chasings down of worthless tips telephoned in by charlatans eager to collect DeRohan's obscene reward leveled at the Panther's head.

He cursed the day he'd ever accepted this assignment and longed to be back in England.

But he had no intention of returning in defeat. And he was convinced now that his best chance of success rested here in Marseille—sixty miles east of the glittering center of the Riviera, and the largest city in the South of France.

He reasoned that the Panther wouldn't be so amateurish as to try and fence his ill-gotten gains in Nice, so close to the scenes of his crimes. Nor would he go to Paris, where the underworld was so well organized that the disposal of such a large volume of precious gems would arouse unwanted attention.

He also reasoned that the Panther wouldn't go to a professional fence who would give him only a fraction of the value of the stones. Instead, he would more likely try to find a shady legitimate jeweler through whom he could sell the pieces intact—and at closer to full value.

So Ladd had been canvassing all the jewelry stores in this city, which was a legendary haven for all manner of disreputable characters.

Momentarily, the door of the establishment opened and Ladd's confederate—an enthusiastic young French policeman named Gaston—started toward the auto at a more rapid than usual clip.

As he slipped in next to Ladd, he said, "I think we may have something this time." He reached into his pocket and handed forth a small maroon velvet box. "The man seemed overly cautious, almost nervous about the sale. It was necessary to pay more than you wanted, but I deemed it worth the risk."

Ladd opened the box. For the first time in months, he felt a swell of excitement. Because resting in a lining of black satin was a paraiba tourmaline and platinum broach in the shape of a peacock. It belonged to the actress Gloria Swanson and had been stolen from her suite in the Grand Hotel Cap Ferrat.

By the Panther.

Ladd finally had his break!

"Bloody good show, Gaston. In we go, then."

They left the auto, signaled to another Peugeot down the street containing several other uniformed French policemen, and as a group, they charged into the store, frightening Louis Cerrel half to death.

Ladd flashed his badge, then set the broach on the glass counter before the terrified jeweler. "Where did you get this?" he demanded.

Cerrel was shaking visibly. "Just a routine consignment, *monsieur l'inspecteur*."

"It's stolen property. Part of the stash of jewelry pinched by the notorious burglar known as the Panther."

Cerrel's eyes widened at the word "Panther." "But monsieur, you must believe me, I know nothing of this!"

"Nothing my foot. You just told my undercover officer here that you had to be very careful about this transaction. Now, why would you tell him such a thing if you didn't know you were doing something illegal?"

"But I merely thought it was a husband in financial distress selling his wife's jewels without her knowledge!"

"What man?"

"I do not know the man. He merely came in off the street."

"Well, I feel for you then, old chap. Because in a case of this magnitude, it will most certainly be Devil's Island for you."

"L'île du Diable! Mais non!"

"I see only one chance of salvation for you, my friend. If you can give us this man, we will be inclined toward leniency."

"But *monsieur l'inspecteur,* I tell you I do not know the man!"

"Very well, then." He turned to Gaston. "Put him in cuffs. Confiscate all his property. Board up the shop."

"But the man said he would return," Cerrel screeched.

"When?"

"Soon. As I said, I took this only on consignment. So he said he would return in a week or so to see if I had sold it."

Ladd offered up a silent prayer of thanks. After all this time, he finally had the Panther in his sights.

In a stunned trance, Jules read *Man on the Roof* word for word in a single sitting.

It told the story of a young New York newspaper reporter and would-be novelist who, to research a book he wanted to write about a jewel thief, became a jewel thief himself. In the process of his research, he found that he enjoyed being a thief more than he enjoyed being a writer. At the end, when he was caught, he confessed to the police, "I never felt more alive than when I was climbing rooftops, high above the world."

The narrative was a witty satire of Manhattan society, and yet, save for the setting, everything the fictional thief did eerily reflected the career of the Panther.

Could it be . . . ?

She realized her wounded spirit was once again grasping at straws. Still, such a coincidence was impossible for her to blithely ignore.

With the book still in hand, she ran what she knew through her mind. Dev was a rugged American—a far cry from the distinctly European persona of the Panther.

But he'd served in Italy during the war and there could easily have learned the vernacular form of Italian that the Panther used.

When he wasn't writing his novels, Dev freelanced for the Paris *Herald,* and frequently wrote articles about the Côte d'Azur and its society—so he had access, from time to time, to it grand villas.

He was roughly the same size and build, though he moved with a slower, more cautious gait.

Once again she tried to drive the notion from her mind—it was Nikki all over again. Besides, if he was the Panther, what was the irreconcilable thing that would keep them apart? She'd always felt in Dev's presence that he carried some secret sadness, but she couldn't envision anything in his spartan widower's life that would definitively preclude a future with her.

But then again . . . sometimes, when he looked at her in his quiet, thoughtful way, she had the sense that Dev had feelings for her that went beyond friendship. She remembered Sara's words that very afternoon. *You know how that big lug dotes on you.*

And he'd wanted her to read his novel. He'd made a point of bringing it to her himself. Was this his confession?

As much as she castigated herself for jumping to the conclusion that Nikki was the Panther, she still felt as strongly as ever that she knew him in some other guise.

Dev?

But, as senseless as it seemed, if he *was* the Panther, wouldn't the publicity of a movie version of his book put him in danger of exposure? Their friends had already noticed the parallel, with their comments about life imitating art. How long would it be before the police noticed the similarity?

Yet, even as she worried, she could feel a renewed sense of hope boiling up inside.

Booth Devlin.

Could the Panther have been under her nose all this time? Had he been trying to reach out to her even as she'd been off chasing butterflies?

At six sharp, Sara, Gerald, Scott, and Zelda were waiting for her in the drive in the big Isotta, the top down, calling to her gaily. Zelda was sitting on top of the backrest of the rear seat, waving a bottle of champagne.

Jules joined her and Sara in the rear as Gerald, at the wheel beside Scott, slammed down his foot and the car took off in a shower of gravel.

"Dahlin'," cooed Zelda, "a moving picture! Isn't it wild? Here. Have some bubbly."

"You'll never guess who's directing the picture," Sara called into the wind. "Our old friend, Rex!"

Rex Ingram was the Irish-born director who made showy Hollywood-style movies with American stars at his own studio in Nice. It was he who'd been after Jules for months for the rights to her life story.

Over his shoulder, Gerald called back, "They're going to switch the setting and film it all here. Maybe he'll put us all in a crowd scene as extra players."

"And you'll never *guess* who Rex has signed to play the part of the gentleman thief," Sara added. "*Valentino!*"

Valentino. That meant the eyes of the world would be on this story. The news dampened her suspicions somewhat. Surely the Panther would never expose himself to such an extent.

"Those Hollywood types," Scott grumbled. "Can't you see what they're doing? They don't really care about Dev's book. They've just found a way to cash in on the Panther."

"Still," said Gerald, "it's a good book, and Dev deserves a little success."

Scott shrugged. "If you like that sort of thing."

Zelda looked at Jules and rolled her eyes at her husband's pettiness.

Heading to St-Paul-de-Vence, a medieval village in the hills above Antibes, Gerald drove fast around the hairpin turns. Jules let the wind blow back her hair, using it as an excuse to keep silent, unsure how she felt about any of this.

At La Colombe d'Or, a pastoral inn high on a hill overlooking a sheer two hundred foot drop into the Loup Valley below, the large party was seated at a long table by the stone rail of the terrace. The entire American artist colony seemed to be there, all those Jules knew—Ernest Hemingway, John Dos Passos, Archibald MacLeish, Dorothy Parker—and many she didn't.

Dev sat in the place of honor in the middle of the table. As the latecomers joined the others at the table, his eyes followed Jules across the room. She was shown to a seat across from him, several places down. As rambunctious greetings were called all around, she smiled at him and said, "I read your book, Dev. I really enjoyed it."

It seemed to her that there was a special light in his eyes as he said, "Thank you."

Dos Passos stood, raising a glass of vermouth and bitters high in the air. "It's not easy to toast a man who doesn't drink, but I'll give it a try. We'll all carp about him on the way home, but we're all secretly green with envy. To you, Dev, and may we all follow in your footsteps and move in beside you in Beverly Hills."

Beneath his breath, Scott, who was sitting next to Jules, mumbled, "I wouldn't be caught dead in that no-man's land for writers."

But the rest of the party let out a rousing cheer, banging their drinks on the tables, then downing them in hearty gulps.

Hemingway said, "Scott, you're just jealous."

"Jealous? I suppose you've forgotten that at this very minute, Paramount is making a moving picture out of *Gatsby?*"

"Yeah," Zelda deadpanned. "With Warner Baxter in the lead."

Scott hissed at her, "What's wrong with Warner Baxter?"

In a singsong voice bubbling with champagne, she inserted the knife blade. "He's no Valentiiiino!"

Some of the men, already well along in their drinking, started chanting, "Warner Baxter, Warner Baxter, Warner Baxter!"

Scott turned red in the face. "Warner Baxter is a great actor!"

Recognizing Scott's flash point, Gerald seized the conversation. "Come on, Dev. Tell us. How did you come up with this character, anyway?"

Dev was looking increasingly uncomfortable. "I don't know," he shrugged. "I suppose, like all characters, he's a fantasy projection of the author. The man I'd like to be."

Or perhaps the man you really are, Jules thought, watching him closely.

"You know what *I* think," said Dottie Parker, leaning over the table in a conspiratorial manner. "I wouldn't be a bit surprised if this Panther fellow who plagues our hallowed coast hadn't taken his inspiration from your book."

Scott mumbled, "Maybe you should ask him for a cut of his proceeds."

"Warner Baxter would," Zelda jibed.

To which Dottie Parker quipped, "I've always said a girl's best friend is her mutter."

There was a general laughter, but Dev was concentrating on the glass of citronade in his hand.

Once again seeing the blood in Scott's eyes, Gerald quickly declared, "I found the character development to be quite fascinating. He starts out trying to learn how the mind of a crook might work, and then—what happens to him?"

"Well," said Dev, "he gets sort of addicted to it. He finds it more satisfying than the writing. I suppose, in a way, he finds that being a man of action is more entertaining than sitting in a room behind a secondhand Olivetti."

"But it's more than that, isn't it, Dev?" Jules asked, still watching him. "He becomes more than what he was before—a different man in almost every way."

"That's true," Dev admitted. "He finds that when he puts on a mask, all the inhibitions that made him a small, average man disappear. Behind the mask, he *is* a different man. But only behind the mask."

"But isn't the man behind the mask the *real* man—not the reporter?"

He considered her. "That's an interesting question. I hadn't thought about it."

"The ending confused me," chimed Hemingway. "One might infer that he deliberately set out to be caught. Was that his intention?"

"Yes, I believe it was. In their heart-of-hearts, don't all crooks want to be caught? Even *need* to be caught?"

Those words sent a chill through Jules.

"I enjoyed the book," Archie MacLeish commented. "But I must confess I found his motivation somewhat lacking."

Dev smiled. "You've got me there, Archie. After all, this isn't *Gatsby*. It's just a piece of fluff."

Despite the effort to soothe Scott's feelings, Fitzgerald continued to glower.

Jules interjected. "I disagree. I sensed the presence of some great unspoken motivation. Some secret sorrow he found difficult to face, that inspired his life of crime. I could feel it between the lines of every page."

Dev leveled his worldly grey-green eyes on her. "That's perceptive of you, Jules. He does have a motivation that I couldn't share with the reader. And with that admission, I believe I need another citronade."

The evening wore on. The meal consisted of seven courses. Everyone at the table drank heavily and chain-smoked Turkish cigarettes except for Jules and Dev. The conversation shifted from bullfighting in Spain to skiing in the Alps, to the new plays on Broadway, to the latest absurdities of the Dada movement in Paris, to the newest innovations of Cubism being explored by Picasso and Braque.

Jules wanted to talk to Dev in a more personal way, but it was proving impossible. Every once in a while, however, she would feel his eyes on her. But when she looked up, they always darted away.

As the night wore on, and some of the guests took their leave, she thought she might have the opportunity to go over and sit by him.

But Scott had grown progressively surly, pouting over the lack of attention he'd been afforded and Zelda's continual digs. And just as Dottie Parker left and the chair beside Dev was empty, someone said, "Oh, look, there's Isadora Duncan."

They all turned to look. The legendary dancer sat at a table with three male admirers. She was grossly heavy—a far cry from her svelte youth—and sported a shock of hennaed hair. "God, she's magnificent," Scott slurred. "I have to go worship her."

With another sip of Pernod, he rose, stumbled over to her table, and flung himself into a kowtow position at her feet. Startled at first, then charmed, the object of his reverence began to run her fingers through his hair, clucking, "Ah, my brave centurion."

At which point Zelda stood abruptly on her chair and leapt over the table, over Gerald on the other side, over the terrace rail, and into the dark void beyond.

Even for Zelda, it was such a bizarre occurrence that for a moment, her friends all sat gaping at one another in horror.

"She's dead," Sara whispered. "I know she's dead. It's a two hundred foot drop."

But moments later, Zelda appeared at the top of the stone staircase, which had broken her fall, her torn dress stained by her bloodied knees. Jules and Sara shot up and ran to wipe the blood from her with their napkins.

Zelda's scrapes were superficial, but her stunt had summarily ended the party. Gerald said, "We must get her home and put some iodine on those cuts."

Dev had come around as well to help. "Do you want me to come back with you?" he asked.

"No, there's no need, Dev. Scott's useless to me, but between Sara and Jules, we'll be fine. We've handled Zelda before. You stay. Enjoy a last citronade to your success."

Zelda draped her arms about Jules's neck, so that it was impossible for her to have even a final moment alone with Dev. He smiled at her and said, "Thanks for coming, Jules. Having you here tonight meant a lot to me."

Jules nodded to him mutely, then shifting the burden of Zelda's weight, walked her toward the door.

Zelda, swaying on her feet, leered at a waiter as they passed. "We can't find the door, honey. You know why?"

"No, Madame. Why?"

She threw back her head and roared with laughter. "Because we're the Lost Generation!" Then she called back to her wobbly husband, "Come on, Scott, you ole spoilsport, you. Warner Baxter's waitin' for us in the car."

As they were driving home in the dark, with the occasional lights of other autos flashing by, the Murphys fell into a drained silence. But Zelda was singing "Ain't We Got Fun?" to herself over and over again. And Scott was babbling at Jules as he continued to drink from his hip flask. She'd completely tuned him out until something he said roused her from her own ruminations.

"You know, JuJu, you were dead-on with that business about Dev having a secret motivation. There's something about that guy that just isn't right. Have you ever noticed that when we're at the beach, or at someone's house, or—anywhere—he always vanishes for a few hours in the late afternoon? Where does he go? No one knows. Not to his flat, because once or twice I've been by there when he's disappeared, and he's not there. I'm telling you, there's something that man is hiding."

Zelda chimed in. "Could it be, I wonder, that maybe he goes somewhere to *write?* Unlike *some* people I might name, maybe *he* doesn't drink his afternoons away."

"No," Scott insisted. "He's hiding something. My writer's instinct can smell it. He may even be . . . musical, for all I know."

"Musical" was Scott's colloquial euphemism for any man he suspected of preferring men to women.

"Oh, Scott, really—you think everyone's musical," Zelda accused. "If you ask me, *you're* the one who's musical."

That shut him up. But Jules was intrigued. The Panther made his raids only at night. So where did Dev go with such regularity in the afternoons?

Could it have something to do with the irreconcilable obstacle the Panther had spoken of?

She needed to find out.

Chapter 22

From the backseat of the Rolls, inconspicuously parked in the rear of the lot of the Victorine Studios in Nice, Jules's eyes were trained on the front steps of the administration building. Sitting behind the wheel in the front seat, Hudson drummed his fingers against the steering wheel. They'd been sitting out here for over an hour.

Finally, three men emerged and stood talking on the front steps. One of them, seeming particularly antsy and eager to get away, was Booth Devlin. Talking to him was the movie-star-handsome director, Rex Ingram. Standing to the side listening was the Italian-American actor who, over the last few years, had set the world on fire with his smoldering portrayals of exotic sexual heroes—Rudolph Valentino. It was Rex Ingram who'd insisted on Rudy for *The Four Horsemen of the Apocalypse,* and had made him a star.

Devlin kept trying to leave, but each time he did, the director asked him another question and held him there a bit longer—until at last, he grabbed Ingram's hand, gave it a pump, and pushed off.

As he hurried toward the front gate, Ingram ambled toward the Rolls. Jules rolled down the window to talk to him.

He shook his head. "I kept him as long as I could. But, as you can see, he was in a big hurry."

"Thanks, Rex. I owe you for this."

"If you really want to repay me, you could sell me the rights to your life story. It would make a hell of a photoplay."

"I'll think about it, Rex. I promise. But I really have to run."

"Give my love to Sara."

"I will. And thanks again." Then to Hudson, she said, "Let's go. After all this, I don't want to lose him."

Outside the main gate, a road ran about a quarter mile down to a larger street. Dev had walked down it most of the way by the time they pulled out. Hudson crept along, keeping well back so Dev wouldn't know he was being followed, letting him turn the corner before proceeding to the main boulevard.

There, a streetcar was just stopping and Dev hopped on and made his way to the front of the car. Hudson turned to Jules and said, "The streetcar will zip right through the traffic. We shall never be able to keep up with him."

"Then I'm getting out."

"Is there anything I can do to discourage you, Highness?"

"Not a thing, Hudson. I shall see you at home."

"Please be careful."

She quickly jumped out and raced across the street, her head lowered. She managed to leap onto the back step of the streetcar just as it was pulling away.

She found a seat in the back, from which she could keep an eye on her prey. But momentarily, the conductor came back and held out his hand. She'd never been on a streetcar before, and she had no idea what he wanted.

When he saw her puzzlement, he said, "Fifty centimes or a jeton, Madame."

She had neither. She opened her handbag and rifled through it, looking to see what she had. She rarely carried money, and she hadn't anticipated needing any today. But in a small satin pocket on the side, she found a folded hundred franc bill. She handed it to him.

His eyes widened. "But Madame, I have no change for this."

He spoke with a raised, annoyed voice. People around her

were beginning to turn and stare. If this went on any longer, Dev might hear and turn around in curiosity like the others.

"Keep it, Monsieur," she told the conductor.

"But Madame—"

"Donate the change to the fund for the widows and orphans of streetcar conductors."

He winked his understanding of the bribe. "With enthusiasm, Madame."

The streetcar traveled several miles along the Boulevard Victor Hugo, then turned sharply to the left to climb the hill to the Cimiez district.

It proceeded for some miles along the Boulevard de Cimiez, stopping several times. Through the crush of boarding passengers, Jules could catch glimpses of Dev up front, sitting hunched forward with his elbows on his knees, his large hands gripped together, staring straight ahead with an oddly grim focus.

Because of the shifting of passengers, she almost missed it when he got off. The streetcar had already started to leave again when she spotted him walking in the other direction. She quickly stood and pushed her way through the throng, jumping off just as the car picked up speed.

She waited behind a news kiosk for him to get a little distance on her, then she followed, keeping well behind. The road skirted the old Roman ruins at the top of the Cimiez hill. He continued for perhaps half a mile, then turned off to the left and soon vanished into a large mustard colored stucco building. When she reached the front door, she noted the brass sign: St-Maurice Hôpital pour Convalescence.

A convalescent hospital.

Was this the place he vanished to *every day?*

She peered through the small window in the entrance door and watched him step into the elevator. As its doors closed, she entered the lobby and was hit by the smell of antiseptic. The lobby was eerily empty. No one manned the functional front desk. Most hospitals were teeming with activity, but this place was infused with an air of hopelessness and abandonment.

Watching the arrow make its sweep above the elevator door, she saw it stop on the number five. She pushed the button and watched the arrow slowly return to zero. Its doors opened and she stepped in, stabbing at the button with a faded five printed on it. The elevator jerked upward.

As she neared the end of this covert journey, she was suddenly seized with doubts. Clearly, she was invading this man's privacy. It sickened her a bit to think what she might find.

I shouldn't be doing this.

But whatever it is, I have to know . . . for both our sakes.

And if he isn't the Panther . . . if all this has been for nothing . . . I have to know that, too.

The elevator opened to reveal an empty corridor with a row of rooms on each side, the doors of which were all open, except for one on the right. She started slowly down the hall, looking in the open doorways as she passed. Each room was empty. She began to feel as if she might be in some sort of morgue. There was no movement, no sound of any kind.

Finally she stood in front of the single closed door. She felt a constricted feeling in her throat, as if it were closing up with dread. Her hand, as she reached for the doorknob, hesitated. Again, some instinct told her not to look. But she knew, having come this far, that she couldn't turn back now.

Slowly, she turned the knob and pushed the door open.

Inside, the room was dim and cool. As her eyes adjusted, she could see Dev sitting in a chair with his back to her beside a hospital bed. Beneath a summer-weight blanket lay a woman with long, frizzled blond hair. Her eyes were closed and she appeared to be sleeping. A tube led from a machine beside her bed into her mouth. It seemed to be pumping air with rhythmic whooshes.

As she stepped toward him, he jerked, then turned around and saw her. "Jesus Christ!" he swore. His eyes were wild.

"I followed you, Dev," she told him softly.

"Jules . . . you shouldn't have done this."

"I wanted to see your character's motivation."

He turned from her again and slumped in the chair. Noise-lessly, her espadrilles making no sound on the floor, she went to him and put her hand on his shoulder. The muscles were hard and clenched.

"This is your wife, isn't it? She isn't dead, after all."

In a hollow voice, he said, "I did this to her."

"No," she whispered.

He leaned toward the bed, resting his elbows on its side, putting his face in his hands.

"It's true," he told her in a haunted monotone. "It hap-pened in Paris three years ago. We'd only been married a year and Gracie was six months pregnant. We were living on the Rue de Vaugirard on the left bank and I was working full-time for the *Herald*. I drank a great deal in those days—way too much—and Gracie was always on my case about it. But you know, I didn't care. A man's entitled to a few drinks."

She glanced again at the woman lying in the bed, noticing now that her face and arms were hideously scarred.

"One night I was out drinking with the boys. We hit every spot in Montparnasse and I was drunker than a skunk when I came home. Gracie, being the dutiful wife she was, got me un-dressed and put me to bed. We both went to sleep. But some-time in the night I woke up, still dead drunk, and decided I just had to have a cigarette. So I did. I lit it up, took a few puffs, and went right back to sleep. Then I awoke with a start. The room was full of smoke and there was a flame on the bed. In a stupor, I got up, coughed my way to the door, opened it, and—not even thinking about Gracie—went tumbling into the hall-way, where I promptly passed out again. The next thing I knew, I was down on the street and some fireman was trying to force coffee down my throat. Then I saw them bring Gracie out on a stretcher. The fire had swept through our whole floor, killing three people. But Gracie wasn't that lucky. She'd taken a bad fall while trying to get out. There were burns over eighty per-cent of her body. She lost the baby, of course. And her body suffered such shock that she went into a coma. She's never come out of it. The doctors don't think she *ever* will. She could live to be an old woman . . . like this . . ."

"Oh, Dev."

He'd been speaking in that same dull monotone, but now a sob cracked his voice. "I'm not angry at you for coming here. But I can't talk to you anymore right now. If you'll just leave us alone, I'll come see you in a day or two, and we can . . . talk then."

She kept her hand on his back for a moment more. "I'm so sorry, Dev. Please don't hate me for doing this. I only—"

"I don't hate you. But I can't talk to you now. Please leave."

She stumbled out of the room. In the hall, she nearly plowed down a nurse carrying a tray.

"Madame, what are you doing here? This is a private—"

But Jules just barreled past, tears streaming down her cheeks.

The taxi pulled into the half-moon driveway of Rêve de l'Amour. On the fifteen mile return from Cimiez, Jules had replayed the haunting scene over and over in her mind.

It had been heartbreaking. She felt so sorry for him, so sad for that poor woman. But she couldn't stop the chain of thoughts that tried to make sense of it all.

After Nikki, she wasn't going to delude herself. She couldn't be absolutely certain that Dev was the Panther.

But he fit the criteria. The money it must have cost him to keep his wife in that place for three years with round-the-clock care had to be crushing for a struggling writer. If he'd turned to crime as a means of obtaining the needed funds, who could blame him?

And God knew, this was as strong an obstacle as she could have envisioned. His guilt was so raw and overwhelming that he could only escape from it in a few stolen moments behind the anonymity of a mask—exactly as Dev had described his character doing. She knew without asking that Dev would never give up his loyalty to his sleeping wife. She wouldn't ask him to.

And yet, in a strange sense, she felt relieved. She'd seen the worst. She'd looked the obstacle in the face. And despite the tragedy of the circumstances, she felt that even they could be overcome. Somehow, she felt she could pull from this ravaged man the secret part of him that was the Panther and find a way to have a life with him. And if his wife lived as long as they did, and he spent hours with her every day, she'd accept that, too.

Hudson was standing on the front steps as the taxi came to a halt. Without a word, Jules went inside, leaving the butler to pay the fare. She went straight up to her room and closed the door behind her.

After a few minutes, Hudson tapped softly on the door.

"I don't feel like talking right now," she told him.

"You were unsuccessful, then?"

"No. I was successful. I just have to figure out what to do about it."

"I shall leave you to it then."

He folded the newspaper in his hands.

"What's that?" she asked.

"It's something I thought you might wish to see. But you can look at it later."

"It's all right, Hudson. I'll look at it now."

It was the financial section of the *Times of London* from the day before, folded to showcase a column with the headline: "DON'T COUNT DEROHAN OUT JUST YET."

She scanned it quickly, an analysis of the state of DeRohan Enterprises. It said that, only a week ago, the City had written the epitaph for this always-controversial consortium. However, the announcement three days ago that DeRohan Mining had struck a spectacular new coal vein in Scotland—perhaps the largest ever found in Europe—had given the troubled company a slight glimmer of hope for survival. Then yesterday, the financial markets were flooded with rumors that the Shah of Persia was favoring DeRohan as the likely recipient of the coveted Persian oil leases that were still up for grabs. Apparently, the Shah had told an American reporter in Tehran that if

DeRohan survived his crisis, he was still in the running. And based on that report, certain American banks which a week ago had closed the door on DeRohan, were now in discussions about restoring a portion of his credit. Whether or not it was a case of too little, too late, only the future would tell. But perhaps reports of the tycoon's demise were premature.

She dropped the paper into her lap, realizing she hadn't even thought about him for days, assuming he was a specter that had vanished from her life forever.

But he was a tough man to kill.

And if he survived, how long would it be before he returned to make her life miserable again?

Chapter 23

The Hungarian stepped out of the taxi in the St-Philippe district of Nice and looked up at the six onion domes of the pink brick and grey marble Russian Orthodox Cathedral. Built in 1912 by Tsar Nicholas II himself, it was the largest orthodox church outside of Russia.

He paused a moment on the steps, gazing up at the blinding midday sun. This was his first trip to the South, and everything seemed lush, exotic, and astonishingly beautiful. No wonder people came here to escape the real world.

He went inside. The interior—which took the form of a Greek cross—was vast, cool, and lavishly decorated with frescoes, plasterwork, and rare icons. Painted saints on rich wood panels looked down on him from their lofty perches.

At this time of day, it was deserted except for one lone figure sitting in the middle of a pew in the center of the sanctuary. He sat hunched forward with his elbows on the pew in front of him, his hands clasped together as if in prayer.

Dante.

The Hungarian watched him a moment, then slowly headed his way, his footsteps echoing throughout the cavernous space. He took a seat in the pew directly behind the man and said in a low voice, "At least you are prompt."

Without looking back, the man code-named Dante said, "Let's just get this over with."

"Then tell me, have you any success to report?"

"None. Several people have been urging her to attend the War Memorial ceremony and she is adamant in her refusal. She considers her presence there an admission of family guilt. I don't think that anything—"

The Hungarian cut him off. "She *must* attend. The leadership is unanimous on this point. Never again will we have such an opportunity to capture the eyes of the world. The notoriety of the event has been increasing by the day. It now appears that it will be covered by every major newspaper in the world."

"That may be," Dante argued, "but her mind is made up, and she is not one to sell out on principle."

"Do I sense a weakening of your resolve in this matter?"

"Despite what she represents to you, she is a good and noble woman."

"Good and noble!" the Hungarian exploded. "This woman is the corrupt end product of an inbred clan that exploited the world for over six centuries and led it into a war that decimated the finest young men of our generation!"

His angry outburst reverberated through the chamber. Dante glanced about warily to make certain they were still alone. He let the silence settle once again, then asked in a pained tone, "How can you blame a sheltered young woman who never harmed anyone in her life for what you perceive to be the sins of her fathers?"

The Hungarian leaned forward in his pew, hissing, "I am not here to have a debate with you. I am here to inform you that if this woman does not appear at the ceremony, we will ruin you. We will make absolute certain that this thing you are so desperate to conceal is made public in such a way that you will never be able to show your face again. Now, let us begin anew. Can you give me a guarantee that the woman will be at the ceremony, or can you not?"

The figure in front of him slumped once again. After a drawn out silence, he finally ground out, "I'll get her there . . . somehow."

*   *   *

Two days after following Dev to the Cimiez hospital, Jules was pacing restlessly outside on her bedroom terrace. She paused every once in a while to look across the expansive outlook of the gardens to the focal point of the Temple of Venus on the hill. From here, she had a soaring view of it, and of the fountains, pool, and trees that bowed like supplicants at the goddess's feet.

But today she wasn't admiring the view. She was thinking of Dev.

He'd said he would come to her. But *how* would he come? As Booth Devlin? Or—if she could believe the accumulation of evidence—would he realize she'd deduced the truth and come as the Panther?

She'd gone to their room the night before, lying on the bed, staring at the candle's dancing flame for hours, waiting. But he hadn't shown up.

Or had he now had second thoughts about coming at all? Had he, on consideration, decided that her action had been an unforgivable violation of his privacy?

She had no way of knowing.

She had no intention of giving up, but she didn't know what to do next.

The question was answered for her when Hudson appeared, and with a stone face said, "Your friend Mr. Devlin is here to see you, Highness."

She exchanged a knowing glance with him. But all she said was, "Thank you, Hudson. Please tell him I shall be down directly."

Then she hurriedly put on some lipstick—realizing the feminine foolishness of it—and, smoothing her dress, went down to meet him.

He was standing in the salon with his back toward the room, looking out the windows over the gardens beyond. When he heard her enter, he turned, hat in hand, and gave her a sheepish smile. He looked big and rumpled and awkward.

"Well, I said I'd come and here I am. A little embarrassed, admittedly."

"I'm glad you did, Dev. I was hoping you would."

"Would you mind if we get out of here? It's a gorgeous day. I thought we might take a drive. Rudy lent me his Duesenberg for the day."

"What a lovely idea."

"It's a convertible, so you might want to take a scarf."

Hudson, who'd been lurking in the hall, said, "I'll fetch it for you, Highness." When he returned, it seemed to her there was a slight hesitation before he handed it forth. But she ignored it, saying firmly, "Thank you, Hudson." Then, to Dev, "Shall we go?"

Outside, Valentino's bright yellow Model J Victoria stood gleaming in the drive. Jules settled herself in the passenger seat, tying the scarf about her head as Dev started the auto and took off down the long, winding drive, past the gatehouse and onto the road below.

"Well, Jules," he said as he turned away from the village of St-Jean-Cap-Ferrat, "you now know something about me that no one else does."

"I'm sorry to be so deceptive," she told him. "But I had to know."

"Now that someone does, it's kind of a relief. But it doesn't make it go away. Of course, Jules, you have to know that I'm flattered by your interest."

"Of course I'm interested. I care about you, Dev."

He glanced at her quickly, then away. "You have to know that I care about you, too. But I have to be honest. I could never abandon Gracie."

"No one would ask you to," she replied carefully.

"She has to be my highest loyalty. Can you understand that?"

"Naturally. But I don't understand why there can't be room for something else in your life. Look at the resourcefulness you've shown. Your struggle to take care of her has brought out the best in you. This stronger you deserves more in life than you've allowed. Can't you see that?"

He nodded thoughtfully and fell into silence.

At the northern end of the peninsula, he swung onto the Lower Corniche toward Nice.

"Where are we going, by the way?" she asked.

He smiled at her. "It's a surprise."

After a mile or so, he turned off toward Plateau St-Michel. From the corner of her eye, Jules quietly watched him. As they began to ascend a network of dirt roads that wound their way to the hills above Nice, she noticed he was driving carefully, his hands tightly gripping the steering wheel. As they reached the Great Corniche, built by Napoleon along the old Roman road that led from Rome to Arles, the views were stunning. From this dizzying height, she could see the expanse of the white buildings and red rooftops of Nice, the bay of Villefranche, all of Cap Ferrat, and the meandering coastline past Monaco toward the Italian border. The hillside dropped steeply on the left side. The oncoming traffic whizzed by, but as they rose higher still, Dev slowed his speed perceptibly as if worried that a flying rock might dent the borrowed car.

Jules enjoyed having the top down, the sun on her face, and the wind sweeping through the open car, but it made conversation difficult, so they drove along in a pleasant, companionable silence. After a few more miles, the Corniche neared the top of Mont Gros—the most prominent mountain overlooking the city of Nice—and Dev turned off onto a dirt side road, traveling for about a hundred feet before he pulled to a stop.

Before them was a construction project: a half-completed monument with a large square base supporting a central tower that would ultimately look over the entire expanse of the Côte d'Azur. All around was scaffolding, cement mixers, and various masonry tools, abandoned for the Sunday. To the side was a large board tacked up on a post, with a painted depiction of what the finished project would look like come September. On top of a two hundred foot column would stand the statue of a mother with a fallen soldier in her arms—a modern postwar Pietà.

The Great War Memorial.

Jules instantly chilled. "Why did you bring me here?"

"I just thought it would be interesting for us to see it. There's been something about it in the papers every day this summer. Come on, let's have a look."

He came around to open the door for her, and she climbed out uneasily. "I don't think we're supposed to be here. Perhaps this isn't a good idea."

He smiled. "I don't think anyone's going to arrest us. Not for this, anyway."

She looked at him closely. Was that some sort of acknowledgment?

"I really don't want to be here, Dev."

"Come on, it'll be fun. We'll be the first ones on our block to see the place."

He took her by the hand and pulled her toward the imposing memorial-to-be.

"You know," he said, "I usually don't think much about statues and monuments to the brave dead. But the idea behind this one appeals to me. The theme is that there was no right or wrong in that ghastly war, that everyone involved was its victim. As an ambulance driver, God knows I got to see my share of victims."

She watched him, wondering what he was doing. Did he know there'd been pressure for her to attend its dedication? And that she'd been resisting that pressure?

They climbed the steps to the top of the base and walked around the circular column. The view up here was even more spectacular than from the road. It was such a clear day, they could see the black dot across the panoramic sweep of the Mediterranean that was the northern tip of Corsica.

Was this journey here as innocent as Dev let on? Or had he brought her here for a purpose? She had a strange sense of déjà vu. She remembered her conversation with Nikki when he'd tried to talk her into speaking at the ceremony.

Why was it that everyone seemed to want her to give up her identity?

The central massive column of the memorial seemed to be only about half-completed. But it was surrounded by scaffolding and a staircase the workmen used to reach the top. To try and get away from her thoughts, she impulsively decided to climb up.

Within a few minutes, she'd walked up the rickety steps about a hundred feet to where a platform marked what would be the halfway lookout point.

Up here, high above the ground, a warm breeze caressed her face and she suddenly felt free, unburdened of troublesome thoughts. From down below, Dev was looking up at her, as if concerned. She remembered the magical night of the Carlton heist, dangling from the Panther's clasped hand, how in that moment she'd never felt so close to anyone in her life. And all at once, she wanted to feel that again.

She called down, "Come on up, Dev."

He kept peering up at her, his hand shading his eyes. But he didn't move.

"Come on," she repeated. "It's marvelous up here!"

After a hesitation, he started toward the steps. But as he reached them, he stopped and called up, "I don't think so. Why don't you come down and we'll continue our drive?"

"No, please, come up. This is the most majestic view I've ever seen of the Mediterranean. I want to share it with you."

He took two steps up, gingerly it seemed to her. But once again he stopped. Looking back toward the Corniche, he pointed to a black coupe that had turned off and was coming their way. "I think someone's come to chase us away," he called up. "You'd better come down."

"Oh, fine. Everyone wants to try and get me here, and now that I'm here, I get chased away!"

But she climbed down obediently. When she reached him, however, she noticed something odd. His brow was dotted with sweat. He actually looked relieved to see her.

"Are you all right?" she inquired.

"I'm fine. But we now have company. Why don't we go?"

Something was wrong. The prospect of climbing that column had clearly intimidated him. Was this real ... or something he'd put on to throw her off track?

She decided to find out.

When they reached the Duesenberg, she grabbed the keys from his hand and said, "I've never driven a movie star's automobile before. You don't mind, do you?"

"Can you drive?" he asked.

"Of course I can drive, silly. I only let Hudson drive to make him feel useful."

She jumped into the driver's seat, pulled out the starter, and turned the key. As the engine fired, Dev took his place in the passenger seat, still looking vaguely uncomfortable.

As she pulled onto the Corniche, she said, "Why don't we take this high road to Èze and then to La Turbie and circle around to Monaco and go back that way?"

"Really? That's kind of a perilous route, don't you think, for someone who doesn't drive much?"

"I'll be careful," she promised.

As she proceeded down the Great Corniche toward the Col des 4 Chemins, she drove slowly and carefully. Unlike the northwesterly journey here, they were now traveling east on the cliff side of the road. The shoulder had no railing and Dev's seat often looked down on a sheer thousand foot drop.

As they passed the Col and headed toward the Belvédère d'Èze, the road became increasingly windy, with one hairpin turn after the other. But instead of slowing down, she pressed her foot down on the accelerator.

Dev's hand crept over to the armrest, as if to hold onto it for security. She watched him from the corner of her eye and pushed down even harder on the pedal. The auto surged ahead.

"Don't you think you ought to slow down a little?" he called over to her.

"No! This is fun! I never get to drive like this with Hudson. He's such an old fuddy-duddy."

Up ahead was the sharpest hairpin turn they'd encountered. Instead of slowing down to maneuver it, she maintained her speed and took the corner with a spin, spraying a rooster tail of gravel in their wake.

"Watch it!" he cried.

Their angle of ascent became near vertical as they reached the Belvédère. There was no shoulder at all to the road. If she swerved over even a few more inches, they were likely to go tumbling off the precipice. She looked over at him and commented, "Quite a drop, isn't it?"

"For God's sake, watch the road!"

His hand was gripping the armrest so hard it had cut off the circulation. It was dead white.

As they passed below the perched village of Èze, the road suddenly began to descend, but the drop from the passenger side was just as soaring. Dev was closing his eyes now to keep from seeing it.

"The road ahead is straight," she called to him. "I think I shall see what this baby can do."

She put her foot to the floor. The speedometer read: sixty . . . seventy . . . eighty . . . ninety . . . Occasionally she would swerve over to the side of the road, to the point where part of the wheels were nearly to the edge, then veer back to safety.

She looked at him. He was bathed in sweat. Finally he cried, "Stop . . . please stop!"

She slammed her foot on the brakes, slowed down, then pulled over to the turnoff of a vista viewpoint. Setting the hand brake, she turned to him.

"You're afraid of heights!"

"All my life," he gasped. "Since I was a kid."

"But . . . your character . . . he never felt more alive than when he was in the air!"

"I *told* you," he stammered, "he's a fantasy projection of me."

"Oh, my God," she said. "I've done it again."

She rested her head briefly on her hands at the wheel. Then, suddenly remembering the hell she'd just put him through, she lifted it and looked at him.

"I'm so dreadfully sorry," she told him sincerely. "You poor, poor man."

Chapter 24

As the Marseille-to-Nice Express chugged along the coast near Ste-Maxime, Inspector Ladd sat in the second-class compartment and inconspicuously watched a tall dark-haired man eating an apple as he read his newspaper.

So *this* was the notorious Panther, the man who'd eluded them for so long and had made his life a living nightmare.

For the past week, the inspector had been ensconced in Marseille, staking out the jeweler and waiting for something to happen. Finally, it did. This fellow they now had under surveillance had entered the establishment two hours ago. After he'd left, the owner had come out, stepped into the street, and waved his hand excitedly.

Ladd and his two plainclothes subalterns had followed the suspect directly to the Marseille train station, where he'd promptly boarded this train to return to Nice. Ladd barely had time to call the Nice *poste de police* to arrange a reception, buy tickets for him and his men, and board the train before it departed.

It was a risk not to nab the rascal at once, but Ladd had to make certain this was the Panther himself and not some go-between. If possible, he also wanted to track him directly to his lair, which was sure to be full of incriminating evidence, as well as at least some of his stolen loot.

The train hugged the coast, offering views of the Maures

and Esterels on the landward side and flashing glimpses of blue water and pristine sandy beaches on the other. It made stops in St-Raphael, Agay, La Napoule, Cannes, Cagnes-sur-Mer, and finally Nice Ville. When they pulled into the station, the terminal was peppered with plainclothes French policemen, all endeavoring to look as inconspicuous as possible.

The suspect left the station and hailed a taxi. As it pulled down the street, five unmarked police cars zoomed to the station exit, and Ladd and his legion of officers piled into them to trail behind.

The cortege followed the taxi through the palm-lined streets all the way down to the beachfront Promenade des Anglais to the old section of town. As the taxi stopped and the suspect got out, Ladd felt a momentary panic at the thought that he might quickly vanish into the casbah of narrow streets.

On foot, they kept an eye on the man through a succession of winding streets, past the immense outdoor market with its fruits, vegetables, and foodstuffs for sale, until he lighted at a small apartment building directly across from the church of St-Augustine.

The man entered the apartment. After a few moments, they saw shutters open on a third-floor window and a brief glimpse of the man as he turned back into the room.

Finally.

The Panther in his lair.

At Ladd's nod, a dozen of the officers drew their concealed pistols and moved toward the building to make the arrest.

The next morning, Jules's attorney, Monsieur Breton, telephoned with alarming news.

"I regret to inform you, Juliana, that your husband is presently on his way back to Cap Ferrat from London. He may arrive later this very day."

Jules's hand gripped the phone. "But why?"

"As you may have heard, there has been a modest improvement in his financial situation. But he knows his only hope of survival rests in acquiring the Persian oil leases. Apparently, the Shah is also returning here in a few days time, and your husband hopes to continue to press his case with the man."

"So he's planning to move in here again."

"Yes, but I am afraid that is not the worst of my news. In his desperate search for cash to stay solvent, he has informed me that he intends to take possession of the house and the jewels."

"But he can't do that!" she cried.

"Not immediately, perhaps. However, Juliana, I must warn you that you violated your agreement with him by living here in France—which according to the terms of your contract, gives him repossession of those properties which he originally won from your father. Once he decides to press the suit, I am afraid there is nothing to be done."

Her heart sank. She was right back where she'd started.

She thanked the lawyer and replaced the receiver. *Presently on his way . . . later this very day . . .* She glanced at her watch. It was midmorning. The overnight Paris train would be arriving within the hour.

She had to get away from here. She couldn't bear the thought of seeing him once again unloading his trunks and assuming possession of her house like Caesar marching into Gaul. She had to find Hudson.

He'd been gone all day yesterday, and hadn't returned by the time she'd gone to bed. This morning, it had been Denise who'd brought her breakfast tray. When Jules questioned her about the butler's whereabouts, the maid had shrugged her shoulders in that way the French have of making a question seem unimportant. "But I have no idea, Madame. He never tells me where he goes."

Jules searched the house now, asking all the servants if he'd returned, but no one had seen him.

In despair, she went out into the back garden.

Where can I go? What can I do?

Suddenly, she stopped at the boundary of the hill overlooking Beaulieu. And all at once, this situation that had seemed so dire just a moment before began to rearrange itself in her mind.

She went inside, retrieved a sun hat from the front hall closet, then left the property by the front drive, walking slowly, thinking through this fresh perspective.

If DeRohan was once again coming to reclaim her . . .

If he was, indeed, in the process of saving—perhaps even expanding—his empire . . .

The Panther was certain to hear about it.

It was the one thing that would force him to reenter her life!

She walked all the way to the end of the peninsula by the Grand Hotel Cap Ferrat and back again in the July heat. But she barely felt it. The more she thought about it, the more excited she became by the idea. If she couldn't find *him* . . . perhaps now, through this odd twist of fate, he would come to her!

When she returned to the house and saw DeRohan's trunks strewn about the reception hall, waiting to be carried upstairs, she almost welcomed the sight.

But as she passed the tray table by the front door, her attention was caught by the morning newspaper that had been left there. Its front-page banner headline was the boldest she'd seen on a newspaper since the end of the war. She stepped closer to have a look.

It read:

PANTHER CAUGHT!
POLICE OUTWIT DARING BANDIT!

Feverishly, she seized the paper and read the story. The infamous cat burglar had been nabbed after attempting to sell a stolen broach to a Marseille jeweler who'd heroically alerted the police.

The Panther was a gypsy from the Carmague, an untamed

region of western Provence. His name was Juan Cubatta. He was being arraigned at the Nice Palais de Justice at two o'clock that very afternoon.

Forty minutes from now.

In a daze, she raced to the garage, looked around for the keys to the red Austin Clifton roadster, and drove at a suicidal speed into Nice. Four blocks from the courthouse, the crowd of spectators, eager to catch a glimpse of the celebrated desperado, was so thick she had to abandon the auto and push her way on foot to the courthouse steps.

She arrived just as the paddy wagon from the city jail honked its way through the crowd. The door opened and two officers escorted a tall man in prison grey from the van. His feet and hands were shackled together. He was solidly built with a scar on his forehead, and a shock of jet-black hair, worn rather long above eyes that were dark and fearless. He didn't look as she imagined he might. His face was browned to a leather-like consistency, and he was more rough-hewn than she'd expected, but he exuded a defiant charisma.

A man next to Jules muttered, "The mockery he's made of those flics, it will be forty years on Devil's Island for that one. If not the guillotine."

She left the man, elbowing her way to the front of the throng. As the prisoner passed her, his eyes glanced her way. But only for a second. Then he was marched up the steps.

She watched him go, her heart in her eyes. She had to do something! But what? She couldn't very well go in there, demanding to see him. Perhaps she could watch from the gallery. She had to know what was happening to him.

As the crowd began to disband, she raced up the steps and opened the front door. But a guard inside held up a hand. "I am sorry, Madame, you are not permitted to enter."

"I only wanted to watch the proceedings."

"The hearing is forbidden to the public. Move along, please."

Numbly, she retraced her steps back to the roadster, unsure

what to do next. She'd never felt more devastated or more helpless in her life. She could see it all: the sensational trial, the parade of testifying victims, the guilty verdict. All the while, she would be unable to see him, touch him, get word to him.

She cast about in her mind for some way to help him. She could go to the police, tell them she'd been robbed by him and had seen his face and this wasn't the man. But no, they'd only ask why she hadn't reported the robbery earlier. What then?

There was Monsieur Breton, but he wasn't a criminal lawyer. He could recommend someone else perhaps, but how could she explain it? And if she hired another solicitor, how would she get the money without DeRohan knowing?

For hours, she walked the streets around the courthouse, trying to figure out what to do. The heat was sweltering by now. The soles of her feet began to burn in her shoes. She sat down at a café and ordered coffee, but was so wrapped up in her dilemma, she forgot about it. By the time she remembered and took a sip, it was cold and bitter.

Sometime later, she looked up to see the sky was now dark. She'd sat there for hours without noticing the passage of time. She rose stiffly and retraced her steps, walking back to the roadster, which she'd left on the Rue de la Préfecture, and drove home.

The thought of facing DeRohan was more than she could stomach. But she couldn't think of anywhere else to go. When she entered, the trunks were still where they'd been before, and Hudson wasn't there to greet her. She found Denise, who told her, "No one is here, Madame. The master is taking dinner with some business associates in town, and Hudson has still not returned."

"Very well, Denise. I shall be in my rooms. I'm going to bed, and I don't want to be disturbed by anyone."

"As you wish, Madame."

With heavy feet, she trudged up the stairs, entered the dark room, and collapsed onto the bed.

For a moment, she just lay there thinking of the man she loved, rotting in that jail cell with no hope—abused by the police he'd humiliated, facing an unthinkable future. Was he thinking of her now?

I have to find some way to help him!

Then she heard a slight shuffle from the recesses of the darkened room.

And then a voice.

"Are you going to lie there all night? Or are you going to come over here and give me a proper greeting?"

Chapter 25

In one swift motion, she flung herself across the room and into his arms, landing on his lap. Joyously, she rained kisses on his jaw. "You escaped!" she cried feverishly. "All day, I've been trying to think of a way to get you out, and you did it yourself!" She clutched his head with her hands, feeling the soft silk of his mask beneath her fingers, and kissed his mouth, all her relief and exultation pouring into him.

His arms went round her, holding her close, deepening the kiss. And as his firm mouth moved over hers, his bold tongue setting her on fire, she wondered how she'd ever mistaken him for her two more timid friends.

She would have gone on kissing him all night, too happy to let him go, but soon, he gently pushed her away. She heard the deep chuckle emanating from his chest.

"You don't seriously think I'm that gypsy pickpocket?"

"Aren't you?" she gasped.

He laughed. "Of course not. But I must say, it was convenient of him to get himself caught in my place."

"Who is he, then?"

"A mere copycat."

"I don't understand. They said he had some of the Panther's loot."

"Juan Cubatta is a petty thief and pimp who got the idea from my success that the villas of the Côte d'Azur are easy pickings. He did two or three of the jobs for which the police so generously give me credit. Then the idiot marched right into a jewelry store and thought he could fence his takings at full price. Anyone that stupid deserves to be caught."

"So where does the Panther fence *his* takings?" she asked coyly.

He kissed the tip of her nose. "Professional secret."

She settled deeper into his lap, laying her head on his shoulder, feeling his warmth and strength envelop her. But gradually, the events of the last weeks without him came back to her. Softly, she asked, "If you're not this gypsy copycat, as you call him . . . who *are* you?"

She felt the slight stiffening of the arms that held her. "I've told you, that's something you can never know."

She sat up straighter, trying to make him out in the darkness. "I've been wracking my brain trying to figure it out. Trying to find you."

"Then you've been wasting your time."

"I thought you were Nikki. That's why I was so callous when you said good-bye at the Carlton. I thought—"

"Nikki Romanov? Good God, woman! I don't know whether to laugh or feel offended."

"And then I thought you were Dev."

"Dev who?"

"Booth Devlin. An author friend of mine who wrote a book about a cat burglar."

"I should read it sometime. I might pick up a few tips." His voice was mockingly amused.

"Don't make light of me," she pleaded. "You don't know what I've been through."

"Poor *Cara*. Perhaps it would be better if I'd never returned."

"Don't say that. Not even in jest. Having you with me, even for an instant, is more precious to me than you can possibly imagine. I don't care who you are in the other world. Because however you may disguise yourself there, I know this is the real you."

His hand came up to cup the back of her head, laying it again on his shoulder as he stroked her hair. "Not many men have had such unconditional acceptance. God knows, I've never had it—never even dared to dream it was possible. I cherish that. I cherish the look of love I see shining from your eyes every time you look at me. I don't want to lose it. I'm a selfish wretch, I know. I have no right to it. But if I do lose it, it's not going to be because I've told you something you can never accept. I can bear not having you for more than borrowed snatches of time in the dead of night. But what I can't bear is to see the love in your eyes turn sour. I never want to look at you and see betrayal or disappointment in your eyes."

"I could never be disappointed in you," she told him vehemently.

Just then, before he could say anything else, they heard footsteps approach her door. In an instant, he went rigid, poised to strike.

"Don't worry," she whispered. "It's bolted."

Momentarily, they heard someone try the door handle.

"It must be DeRohan," she groaned softly. "He's back."

But after one try, whoever it was gave up, and they soon heard the footsteps retreat back down the hall.

"Maybe it was Hudson," she said, as much to convince herself as him. "He's been gone and I've been looking for him all day."

He put his mouth at her ear so she could feel his breath tickle it when he spoke. "I find," he told her, "the prospect of being in a woman's bed with her loathed husband just down the hall to be curiously stimulating."

She felt him swell against the curve of her buttocks on his lap. "So I see," she grinned.

"Knowing that he's blithely going on about his business a few dozen feet away while I'm doing this to his wife." He unbuttoned her dress, then reached inside, clasping her breast with his hand, taking the nipple between his fingertips, massaging it.

She gave a luscious moan.

"Right now, the bastard is probably brushing his teeth, looking at himself in the mirror, longing for just a brief touch of the beautiful princess who's locked herself behind her fortress door . . . having no idea that right now a thief is in that very room, doing this to her . . ."

He reached beneath her skirt, his hand grazing up her thigh, making her breathless as he nudged her legs apart with his fingers. Digging into her panties, finding her already wet and ready for him. Stroking her with a compulsive rhythm that shot intoxicating thrills to every inch of her body.

"And now he's gone over to his bed and taken off his robe, and he's laid back to think about how much he wants to possess her. He's touching himself . . . dreaming of it, envisioning breaking down the door . . . grabbing her up in his arms . . . flinging her on the bed . . . ripping off her clothes . . . spreading her legs . . . and forcing himself upon her."

He put one arm behind her back, the other beneath her knees, and with a single lunge, stood with her in his arms.

She felt herself swept up by some primal, feral force that was not to be denied. That she didn't want to deny.

"And all the while, he has no idea that under his very roof, just a breath away, a rogue of the night is doing just that to the woman he *thinks* he owns."

Like a ravaging pirate, he flung her on the bed, unbuckled his belt, stepped out of his pants, leaned over her, and took the neckline of her dress in his large fist. With one violent yank, he severed the seams and tore it from her. Then he sat on the bed beside her, leaning over her, nuzzling her neck as his hand slid her panties off and tossed them aside.

"Never even dreaming that an infamous outlaw has invaded his territory and claimed his 'chattel.' That he's about to spread her open and fuck her as she's never been fucked in her life."

"Oh, God!" she gasped.

He was on her in an instant, shoving her legs back, spread-

ing them wide, entering her with a mighty thrust that caused
her to cry out with the sheer rapture of it all, not even caring
who heard.

In the aftermath of their fierce lovemaking, they lay in each
other's arms silently. The minutes ticked by, but neither moved.
Jules didn't want to break the sweet spell that enveloped them.
Just the intimacy of his powerful body beside her, the scent of
his spent manliness, the sound of his satisfied breath as it
moved his chest beneath her hand was enough to make life
seem sublime.

But inevitably, thoughts of that other world—that world
that wasn't theirs to share—began to creep into their self-made
paradise. She furrowed her fingers in the thick hair of his
chest, then trailed them downward, resting her palm on the
flat iron of his stomach. "You've heard, I suppose, that
DeRohan is trying to crawl back to power."

He kissed the top of her head. "I've heard. The bastard may
be cursed in love, but the gods of fortune favor him in business. It's one of the reasons I've come back to see you."

"It's worse than you know. My attorney says DeRohan's
trying to regain title to this house and the Habsburg jewelry."

"Can he do that?"

"Monsieur Breton thinks he can."

The Panther silently took this in. After a moment, he said,
"He's not going to get your house *or* your jewels. I'm going to
see to that."

"But how can you possibly stop him?"

"I think I know a way. If you'll help me."

"I'll do anything."

"All right," he said, pushing himself up to sit against the
headboard. "Bear with me a moment."

She shifted her position, laying her cheek on his sinewy
thigh.

"At the present moment, your husband is desperately attempting to stay solvent in the hopes that if he does, he can still convince the Shah to give him the Persian oil leases. Correct?"

"Yes. It's his only real hope of survival. That's why he's come back, because the Shah is returning this week."

Idly, his fingers played with her hair. "What if the Shah told him that he would give him those leases if he came up with a substantial signing bonus—for him personally? Say, ten million pounds in cash. By . . . say . . . the eighth of August. That gives him . . . ten, eleven days. So he'll have to come up with it fast."

"Why would the Shah want to do that?"

"Because in his heart, he wants to make the deal with DeRohan. The ten million would prove his worthiness and go straight into the Shah's pocket. And he might just be made to think he had an even more compelling reason for doing so."

"What's that?"

"You."

She lifted her head and sought him in the darkness. "Me?"

"The promise of you, anyway. With his fascination for all things Habsburg—you being the shining light of the line—he has to be completely smitten with you. You could make him think he has a hope of knowing you even more intimately. A hope that will never be realized."

She laid her head back down, nuzzling his thigh with her cheek. Thoughtfully, she said, "Yes, I could do that. He's certainly interested. But why would I want to? It would be doing DeRohan a favor. And he'll come after the house and jewels even more forcefully to come up with the money."

"But if he only has ten days, he'll be in a real bind. Any legal proceeding to take the house and jewels out of your name will take months. And no bank is going to lend him ten million pounds sterling to pay a bribe—particularly with nothing guaranteed on paper. So he'll be just as stuck until we give him a way out."

"And what is that?"

"All that gold ore that's been impounded in Corsica for the last year. Since the war, there's been an international shortage of gold bullion. Its price has been skyrocketing, and the Americans have been particularly desperate to get their hands on as much of it as they possibly can. I should think the stockpile of ore that's been held by the Corsican strikers would easily be worth that much to them."

"But those Corsican miners are on a vendetta against DeRohan. There's no way in the world they're going to allow him to waltz in there and take it away from them."

"They might if he gave them some inducement, and the strike's instigator, the priest Siffredi, told them they must."

She thought back on the morning when she'd seen the priest defy DeRohan. He'd seemed more like an avenging angel than a man of the cloth.

"Would he do that?"

"Let's just say he knows who I am, and has some small reason to trust me."

Her head jerked up. "He *knows* you?"

"In a manner of speaking." He pushed her head back down. "So the Corsicans release the gold ore, the American agent in Ajaccio buys it, the ore goes to America, and the cash is shipped here to give to the Shah."

"Wouldn't DeRohan just wire him the money?"

"It's a bribe, remember? The Shah isn't going to want a paper record of the transaction. DeRohan will insist the Americans pay in pounds sterling, which he'll ask them to gather up quietly from a number of London banks. They'll realize some sort of shady transaction is in the works, but they'll want the gold so much they won't care. They'll send the money down to Corsica, the exchange will be made on the spot, and DeRohan will then ship the money here and hand it over to the Shah personally."

She chewed on her lower lip, trying to follow. "I still don't understand how this is going to hurt him. The money comes here, he gives it to the Shah, he gets the oil leases—"

"Keep thinking," he told her. "The money arrives. Mind

you, this is ten million pounds—trunks and trunks of the stuff. He's not going to instantly hand it over to the Shah. They'll have to sign the agreements for the oil leases first, which—considering his bad press of late—will surely involve a ceremony of some kind, with the press in attendance. Meanwhile, he can't take the money to the bank because—again—no one wants a paper record of it. What is he going to do with it?"

"Bring it here."

"Now you're getting it. And where would be the least likely place a thief might get to it—the place where it would be most easily guarded?"

"Well . . . DeRohan would think it was the basement."

She felt a swell of excitement, already anticipating what was to come.

"And . . . ?" he prompted.

"We're going to steal that money!"

He dropped his head back against the headboard. "Think of the beauty of it. They're having a fancy ceremony on the lawn with the press boys frantically scribbling away. During which time, I calmly walk through the tunnels to the basement, transport the trunks of cash back through the tunnels and down to the water, where a ship will be waiting to carry it back to Corsica. There, under the auspices of Father Siffredi, it will be dispersed among the people from whom it was stolen in the first place. DeRohan will have nothing to give the Shah, he'll look like a complete bumbler, and he'll never recover from the debacle."

"You're an absolute genius!" She began raining kisses on his thigh. "You *are* my hero, do you know that? I'm so sorry I ever said those awful things to you—"

"Hush, *carissima*. None of that matters now. What matters is that we decimate DeRohan once and for all. It won't be easy. It will require more from you than the last job. The arrangements for this will have to be made during the day, and I'm a creature of the night. So, much of the success of the plan will rest on your carrying out my instructions."

"I'll make the arrangements for you."

"It may be dicey. You're going to have to be the spy in the enemy's camp. Somehow you're going to have to get the confidence of DeRohan, as well as the Shah. Your husband may be down, but he's no pigeon for the taking. He'll likely watch you like a hawk. You'll have to be just as clever—and careful—to keep him from guessing what you're up to."

"I'll be careful. I promise."

"Can you follow my instructions?"

"To the letter."

"I'm glad to hear it." His hand moved to the back of her head, guiding her further up his thigh. "Then forget about your husband for a few minutes and suck my cock."

The next day, Jules sat opposite Father Siffredi in a rectory office of Monaco's St-Nicolas Cathedral. For the past half hour, she'd been outlining his part in the plan the Panther had proposed. He'd listened carefully, showing no surprise at the audacity of the scheme—indeed, showing no emotion of any kind. Now, his fingers steepled before him, he was deep in thought.

She recalled again the morning he'd so dynamically flung the petition at DeRohan's feet. Up close, his presence was equally powerful but more contained, giving the impression of discipline and self-mastery. Still, he looked more like a man of action than a supplicant who spent his off-hours kneeling in a monk-like cell. With his northern Italian good looks—swept-back dark blond hair, cornflower blue eyes, and a charmingly accented, melodious voice—she could well imagine the ladies of his congregation fanning themselves discretely during mass.

While he continued to ponder her proposition, her gaze drifted out the window, which looked down on the forecourt of the cathedral and the street where Hudson waited with the Rolls. He was leaning back against the side of the car, his hands behind his head, his face tipped to the sun. His hat was off and the sunlight glinted on his wavy brown hair. At ease this way, he appeared more strapping than subservient. He seemed a different person altogether—not a butler, but a man.

That morning, when he'd brought her breakfast, she'd confronted him about his absence the day before. But he'd shown little contrition, merely commenting that he'd been on a matter of personal business. And when she'd more jokingly prodded him on the matter, he'd snapped out, "Is a servant's personal life not his own?"

His sharp reaction had startled her—even hurt her feelings a little. But he was right, of course. He was entitled to some privacy. It was thoughtless of her not to consider that he might have some sort of life outside of Rêve de l'Amour.

Her thoughts were drawn back to Father Siffredi, as his hands dropped to the desk in front of him and he looked at her with a concentrated stare. "You must know, Signora DeRohan, that this is an extraordinary thing you ask of me. You are, after all, the wife of a man I have dedicated my life to opposing."

"I realize it may be difficult for you to believe, Father, but I despise Dominic DeRohan even more than you do. The hatred we share so intensely makes us natural partners."

"Still, to simply throw in the towel of a struggle that so many people have given themselves to for so long—on the nebulous notion that it will provide the bait by which DeRohan will be trapped . . . Signora, you must admit—"

"I admit it would require a great deal of faith on your part."

He smiled at that. "In whom, Signora? You?"

"No. In the man who has brought us together. The man who has proposed this daring plot. A man who, if I'm not mistaken, you have learned to trust."

The priest rose and took a thoughtful turn about the room. As she waited for his reply, Jules thought again of what the Panther had said the night before.

Let's just say he knows who I am, and has some small reason to trust me . . .

What could the relationship between the Panther and this idealistic priest possibly be? Unless . . . She'd never really considered before what he might be doing with all those jewels he was stealing. Could he be giving them to Father Siffredi? Like a sort of modern-day Robin Hood? Funding his many charitable endeavors? Even perhaps his fight against DeRohan?

And if so . . . if the Panther had been after DeRohan from the start . . . was there more to his first midnight visit to her villa than she'd known? If she hadn't lured him, had he intended to come anyway?

Stop it!

Once again her mind was running away with her.

The priest was speaking again. "There is a great deal at stake here. I will have to give all you've said my deepest consideration."

She stood. "Don't wait too long, Father. Time is of the essence. Just remember, our friend tells us this is our only hope of stopping DeRohan once and for all."

She had an odd feeling that his hesitancy was more a matter of show, of going through the motions that any thoughtful man would take before plunging into such an ambitious—perhaps even dangerous—endeavor. In fact, she found it remarkable that the priest had shown so little surprise when she—the wife of his blood enemy—had come toddling in here with such an outrageous proposition.

As he walked her to the door, she paused before leaving. "Father," she said, feeling suddenly timid. But she had to ask. "About our mutual friend . . . how did the two of you . . . ever . . ."

His gaze flashed quickly to her face, a flash of cobalt like a blue jay's sudden taking to wing. "He has not told you about that?"

"No."

He lowered his lashes. "Then it is not my place to say."

"Forgive me, Father. I didn't mean to pry. Feminine curiosity got the better of me."

He looked at her again, but now his gaze was unwavering and stern. "Curiosity killed the cat."

The words, and the way he said them, shocked her. And as he took her hand to say good-bye, his touch was electric.

She felt the color drain from her face.

All at once an impossible idea took hold of her. This man was the same size and build as the Panther. He spoke Italian. He had a mission that needed to be financed. He came with an obstacle that definitively gave them no hope of a future together.

He was a priest.

The very idea that she might have been so intimate with such a man shook her to her Habsburg Catholic core.

The things she'd done—and learned—at the Panther's hands flashed through her mind, causing a flush of heat to burn her cheeks.

Dear Lord, no!

She snatched her hand away and all but ran from the room.

Father of mercies and God of all consolations, please let it be anyone but him!

Chapter 26

Jules was a wreck for the rest of the day. She snapped at Hudson for no reason. When DeRohan insisted on her having dinner with him, she took her place dutifully in the dining hall, but ignored him completely, picking at her grilled rack of lamb with garigue herbs and assorted Provençal vegetables, but tasting none of it.

In contrast, DeRohan ate with a hearty appetite. As he did, he told her some of what had transpired in his business dealings, but it was little more than she already knew—the Shah was returning soon and he would once again need her help—and she wasn't listening anyway.

She was too wrapped up in her own troubled thoughts.

As he munched on black grapes and cheese, he peered at her curiously. "You seem restless tonight, Juliana."

His tone—and implication that she should be raptly hanging onto his every word—irritated her. Distractedly falling into old habits, she said tonelessly, "Do I? Perhaps this forced domesticity is too much for me to stomach."

A voice deep within her whispered that she shouldn't antagonize him—not now. But she was too upset by her suspicions to be able to concentrate on any plan.

"I suggest you accustom yourself to this—forced domesticity, as you so prettily term it. Because I intend to remain by your side from this day forward. My absence doesn't seem to have done you much good. You're as pale as a ghost."

His high-handedness rubbed at her already frayed nerves. "Perhaps it isn't your absence but your return that has affected my complexion."

He stood so abruptly that the chair behind him clattered to the floor. Charging around the long table, he grabbed her neck with both hands and hauled her to her feet.

"And perhaps my return has merely put a crimp in your fun," he snarled, his thumbs pressing her throat. "Perhaps it's another man whose—forced domesticity you crave. What have you been doing, wife, while your husband has been fighting for his life?"

She felt herself choking. But she stared him down with all the dignity she could muster.

Her coolness infuriated him. He shook her so her teeth rattled. "Don't think I don't know that you've been off with other men during my leave. And don't look so surprised. You didn't really imagine I would go away without having you watched?"

"You're mad," she croaked defiantly.

He searched her face. "Perhaps I am. But know this, Juliana. If I ever catch you with another man—if I ever obtain proof of any kind—I will dispatch the sniveling coward as swiftly as I dispatched your precious Edwin."

She glared at him, hating him beyond words. "You needn't remind me. I know very well what you're capable of."

"Good." He dropped his hands and she swallowed the pain in her throat. "Now get out of my sight before I do something I might regret."

He turned his back and she left the room with her head held high, determined not to give him the satisfaction of seeing her flee from him. But once she'd bolted her door behind her, she berated herself. *What am I doing? I'm so flustered, I can't think straight.*

But if her awful suspicions were correct, what did any of it matter? If Father Siffredi *was* the Panther, how could she, in all good conscience, go through with the plan?

She paced her room restlessly. Four more hours until she was supposed to meet him in their room.

When he arrived, through the door leading from the beach tunnel, she was waiting for him, standing with her back to the single candle. He started toward her, then stopped, sensing her mood.

"What is it?" he asked. "Has something gone amiss?"

As she looked at him, so dark and mysterious, his mask covering the features that might give him away, all the careful words she'd rehearsed during the long hours of waiting fled from her mind. She blurted out, in a quivering tone, "Are you Father Siffredi?"

He stood stock still, regarding her quietly. Finally, he asked, "What makes you think that?"

"I don't want to think it. I've tried all day to convince myself it can't be true. I tell myself a priest would never do the things you have. He'd never steal. He'd never force himself into a woman's bedroom, never . . . do the things to me . . . that you've done . . ."

"And?"

"And then I say: but he's not a typical priest. He isn't meek or mild. He's faced down DeRohan—come after him—like a—"

"Like a what?"

She looked at him desolately. "Like a panther stalking an antelope. And then I think: if the Panther is a fantasy projection of someone else, what would the fantasy projection be of a handsome, virile, man-of-action priest but all the things his nature was screaming at him to be? The things he couldn't be in the daytime?"

"Ah. And yet, there's something you haven't considered."

"What's that?" she asked, hoping he could say something—anything—to relieve her mind.

"If this picture you've painted so vividly were true, why

would he go to all this trouble to throw you together with the priest? Why not simply say that he will requisition the aid of the man himself? Why make such a game of it?"

"Because you're fond of games, I think. And because perhaps you're no longer content with what you call borrowed snatches of time in the dead of night. Perhaps you're pointing me to your other self, making me a partner with you during the day. Because, like me, you long for more. And because that's all the daylight life we could ever have. If you love me, as you say, wouldn't you want that, too?"

"Yes," he said thoughtfully. "I might very well want that."

Was that a confession?

Sickly, she said, "But there's something *you* haven't considered."

"And what is that, *Cara?*"

"I'm a Habsburg. I may have been forced to convert when I married DeRohan, but I was raised a Catholic."

"I know that."

Her voice cracking, she told him, "I could never be with you again if I thought you were a priest."

He said nothing.

Desperately, she cried, "Tell me it isn't true!"

Her plea rang out, bouncing off the marble of the room where they'd shared so much passion. He let a silence stretch out between them before asking, "And if I lied because I wanted you in my bed?"

"Better that than that I knowingly—"

She drifted off, unable to say the words.

He crossed the distance between them, sleekly, like a cat. Taking her shoulders in his hands, he looked her in the eyes. In the dim light, she couldn't see their color, though she tried.

"Then you may rest your mind. I am not Father Siffredi."

"How can I believe you?"

"You can't. There's no reason that you should. Except that, to believe otherwise would put an end to—" He caught himself, then amended, "All our plans."

She didn't know what to believe. But his talk of their plans reminded her of the muddle she'd made earlier that night. She pulled away from him, pacing the room, avoiding the bed. "I may already have put an end to our plans."

"How so?"

"I had a row with DeRohan. I couldn't help myself. I was so worried—and I have never been able to be with him without losing my temper."

"I see." He moved then, seating himself in a nearby chair. She waited, expecting a rebuke, but instead he told her, "It may be just as well. If you were too welcoming of his return, it would surely arouse his suspicions. As it is, he'll be more likely to believe you when you tell him why you intend to help him. He'll think this latest altercation was the last straw."

She turned and looked at him again. "Why are you so forgiving of me when I make such a mess of things?"

"Perhaps because I love you," he said mildly. "And perhaps," he added with a mocking smile, "because I'm accustomed to giving absolution."

"Don't say that."

"Come, *Cara,* you must see *some* humor in the prospect that I might be masquerading as a priest."

She wanted to believe him. But could she?

He changed the subject. "What was the cause of this altercation with your husband?"

"He accused me of seeing another man. Or men, I don't know. He's had me watched. I suppose he was told that I went driving with Dev."

"And what was his reaction to this happy news?"

"He threatened to kill any man I might be seeing if he found out."

"And you believed him."

"How could I not?"

"And so you worry for my safety along with everything else."

"Of course I do. How can you ask such a question?"

"Then let me put your fears to rest. Given the state of your mind at present, I won't touch you tonight—as much as I might want to. I won't come to you again. We won't see one another until the plan is in motion. That way, there will be no mysterious absences for you to explain."

"And then?"

"Are you asking me about the future?"

"Yes."

"But *Cara*, we have no future. You've always known that."

When she didn't answer, he stood. "I've come back with a purpose. To see that your husband can never harm you again, to keep your house and jewels in your possession, to ensure that you may live independently. That's all I could ever hope for. I thought you understood."

"I don't understand any of this," she told him truthfully.

"No, I don't suppose you do. You don't understand how a man can love you so much that he'd be willing to give you up for your own sake."

She watched him, her body aching, wanting him even now, despite everything. "What shall I be without you?"

He came to her and kissed her forehead. "Free," he said simply. Then he turned to leave. But at the door, he looked back. "Don't think about the future. Concentrate on DeRohan now. Remember all the things he's said and done to you. Use your hatred of him to make you strong. Nothing else matters now. I can't do this alone. I'm counting on you to help me."

And then he was gone. The candle flickered as he closed the door.

Jules went to the bed she'd been avoiding, sitting on it now, not knowing what to think or feel.

But suddenly she was seized by a premonition she couldn't shake.

A premonition of doom.

Chapter 27

Just before midnight the next night, Jules approached the door of DeRohan's study at Rêve de l'Amour. He'd been sequestered here all afternoon and evening, on the telephone or meeting with emissaries that came and went from the far-flung corners of his faltering empire. Now the room was quiet, but she could see a ribbon of light at the base of the door, so she knew he was still hard at work.

She'd been jittery all day. She couldn't shed the feeling that something was about to go wrong. She'd been so excited when the Panther had first broached his plan. The chance to pull a heist with him again, as they had at the Carlton, had been intoxicating. Then, too, there was the prospect of the look on DeRohan's face when he found out he'd been bested. But in her haste, she hadn't thought it through. She hadn't realized their reunion was again to be only temporary.

The prospect of losing her lover at the end of this perilous process was dismal at best.

But she remembered what he'd said: *I can't do this alone. I'm counting on you to help me.* So she'd done as he'd asked, pushing aside her dread and applying herself to her assigned tasks.

Now she paused a moment, her hand on the doorknob, gathering her wits.

Concentrate on DeRohan. Use your hatred of him to make you strong.

She quietly opened the door and stepped into the room. DeRohan sat at the far desk, his coat off, the sleeves of his shirt rolled to just below the elbows, his face in his hands. Beside him was a carafe of brandy that had been full that morning but was now half-empty. There was an air of weariness about him. Unaware that he was being watched, he made a pathetic sight, sitting there in such despair. A far cry from the arrogant man who'd hauled her from her dining chair and threatened murder. But she steeled herself to feel no pity.

Remember what this man has done to you. Remember that he's perfectly capable of extricating himself from this mess and taking everything from you in the process.

He looked up slowly. When he saw her, the pained look hardened instantly. His eyes raked over her like a ravenous wolf. She felt naked suddenly, as if he could see right through her pink hip-waisted dress and into her soul.

"What do *you* want?" he growled, like a man so far in his cups that he didn't care what he said. "I don't suppose I dare hope you've come to ease my suffering with a little—wifely solicitude."

There was a strange sort of energy in the room, like the buildup of too much tension with no promise of relief. She could well imagine him rising from his chair to stalk toward her, intent on relieving his stress with some violent act against her, aimed at restoring his flagging male supremacy.

"I've come to put an end to your suffering," she told him as evenly as she could manage.

He gave her a nasty smile. "By all means, do go on. I can't wait to hear how you're planning to manage this marvel."

"You said you wanted me to help you make the deal with the Shah."

"I not only want it, I expect it."

She swallowed, stamping down her irritation with him—

and her fear. "I've decided that I might comply with your request."

"Have you now?"

"I think I may even be successful at it. In fact, I think I may be your only hope of bringing that man anywhere near the corpse of DeRohan Enterprises."

Without looking, he reached over and grabbed the glass of brandy at his side. He took a healthy gulp, then wiped his mouth with the back of his hand. "I'm genuinely touched by your show of wifely devotion. But I suspect you're about to tell me you want something in return."

She'd been holding some legal papers behind her back. Now she crossed the room and laid them on the desk in front of him.

He glanced at them contemptuously. "What is this?"

"Annulment papers." She'd had her attorney draw up the document that morning. It stated that their marriage had never been consummated. "Monsieur Breton has assured me that once we both sign it, he can quickly rush it through the courthouse in Nice, and we shall be free of each other within the week."

He replaced the glass on the table. "You'd love me to sign that, wouldn't you?"

"You'd love me to bring the Shah back into your good graces, wouldn't you?"

He sat for a long time, staring at the papers, weighing his options. Then, slowly looking up, he said, "All right, Juliana. You deliver the Shah, and once he gives me the oil leases, I shall give you your freedom."

"I'd prefer to have your signature before I approach the Shah. Now, if you please."

He leaned back in his chair. "I think you know me better than that. But once my deal is set, I'll sign your bloody papers. You have my word on it. Just leave them here with me."

"You'll forgive me, I'm sure, but I'm hardly about to trust the word of a man who has blackmailed and cheated and bullied his way to power."

He draped his arm over the back of the chair. "You've turned heartless, Juliana. I wonder that I've tried so hard to hold onto you all these years. But the fact is, these leases are more important to me than you are."

"Very well, then," she said. "I shall accept your word."

Of course, he had no intention of signing those papers. She'd just presented them to him so she would seem to have a reason for helping him with the Shah. He'd just put one foot into their trap.

As she left the room, she looked back to see if he might be eyeing her suspiciously. But he wasn't. He appeared to have blithely returned to his business.

Such gullibility wasn't in his character. It made her feel even more uneasy than before.

A stroll through the Flower Market in Nice was like a journey through a Monet painting. All around Jules were hundreds of stalls filled with the colorful blooms of Provence, lending their fragrance to the sultry summer morning. But the man walking by her side was so enraptured by her company that he didn't seem to notice the beauty of his surroundings.

She smiled at the Shah, dapper in his European suit with a bright red carnation at the lapel. "Your Imperial Majesty has been so patient with my husband in his time of trouble. I can't tell you how appreciative I am that you haven't given the oil leases to anyone else."

"Ah, dear lady, the Koran teaches us to be patient in times of crisis. But I am afraid that patience has finally reached its end. I have waited weeks for your husband to turn his financial situation around to the extent that I could still make accommodation with him. Unfortunately, that has not happened. So now I must find a new partner to help bring my country into the twentieth century."

"But the two of you seemed so well suited to one another. It seems such a shame."

"Very true, my lady. Your husband has an animal cunning

that I find particularly attractive in a partner. It is, indeed, a pity, but what can a forward-thinking man do but align himself with the worthiest candidate?"

She lowered her lashes timorously. "I flattered myself that you found me attractive, as well."

He stopped walking. With a flame lighting his dark eyes, he took her hand and brought it reverently to his lips, tickling it with his bushy mustache. "Oh, indeed, dear lady. More than you could possibly know. I have thought of you so many times."

She smiled her most captivating smile. "And I of you. I'm not sure if the servants' gossip has reached your ears, Your Majesty, but my husband and I are—shall we say, estranged? It's often quite lonely for a woman in such circumstances."

"Understandably so," he said, eyeing her as if to determine if she was saying what he thought she was.

"To me, that is the saddest part of this failed venture. Your proximity to my husband would have afforded us such a wonderful opportunity to ripen our friendship."

She reached into the nearest stall and plucked a deep red rose from the bucket, then kissed it and handed it to him.

Her meaning was now clear.

He reached for the rose, but instead grasped the hand that offered it. "Oh, dear lady . . . if I thought . . . if there was any possibility . . ."

"Naturally, I would never dream of asking you to do anything imprudent. I know the business world's confidence in my husband has been shaken. But if he could rise above his present troubles to seal the bargain with a substantial personal payment to you . . ."

"A *personal* payment, you say?"

"Yes. Delivered on the eighth of August, just after you sign the leases. In cash, so that it would be untraceable and might be easily distributed to whomever you might care to share it with."

"How substantial a payment are we speaking of?"

"Ten million pounds sterling."

He thought this over. Then he squeezed her hand, kissing it again. "But dear lady, for the promise of your—special friendship, I might not even need any such inducement."

"No, no, I insist. My husband should, after all, have to prove himself worthy of a man such as you."

He preened beneath the flattery. "And when might I anticipate the—consummation of our special friendship?"

She removed her hand from his with a sweet smile. "Once the deal is signed."

From the back terrace of Rêve de l'Amour, overlooking the French gardens, Jules could see DeRohan with a shotgun in his hands. To relieve his mounting stress, he'd taken to coming out here several times a day to shoot skeet. Even from the distance, he looked haggard.

As one of the gardeners sent the clay pigeon soaring into the air, DeRohan raised the weapon without bothering to take aim, pulled the trigger, and exploded the projectile in a blast that shattered the calm of the afternoon.

As always, his disrespect for the sanctity of her home irritated Jules. But she shook it off as she and Hudson walked down the steps and across the lawn to join him.

Hearing them behind him, he swiveled their way, inadvertently pointing the gun directly at Jules. Instinctively, Hudson shot between them, looking as if he might tear the weapon from DeRohan's hands and wrap it around his neck.

Amused by the action, DeRohan said, "Don't worry, old fellow, I'm not going to shoot your mistress."

"Especially now that I'm about to give him the thing he wants most in the world," Jules added.

DeRohan lowered the shotgun. "I take it you have news for me?"

"I've done just what I said I would. I went to see the Shah this morning. He's still eager to give you those concessions."

"Well. This *is* news."

"With one small stipulation."

"Oh?" he asked casually. "And what is that?"

She explained to him the bargain she'd made. The personal bribe. The time limit. The amount. Everything but her implied promise to sleep with the Shah.

He listened carefully, then asked, "How is that supposed to save me? Where am I to get ten million pounds by the eighth of August?"

She nodded to Hudson. He went into the house and moments later, returned, leading a man their way.

Father Siffredi.

She'd been stilted with the priest earlier in the day. She'd told herself over and over that he wasn't the Panther—he couldn't be. But she'd still caught herself looking for comparisons. The graceful yet manly way the priest walked . . . his large, expressive hands . . . He'd given her no indication one way or the other. But he'd noticed her agitation and had said, "My child, if you feel yourself in need of confession . . ." To which she'd told him quickly, "No."

Now she avoided looking at him, lest DeRohan read something in her eyes.

She'd expected her husband to explode upon seeing his enemy escorted across the lawn. But he just stared levelly as the priest approached. He didn't even seem particularly taken aback, murmuring to her instead, "You *are* full of surprises this morning."

"Father Siffredi is here to help," Jules explained.

"I fail to see how."

"He's arranged to have those Corsican miners call off their strike against you. You'll be able to sell all that gold ore that's been stockpiled there for the past year. For a hefty price, I should imagine. Perhaps even ten million pounds."

DeRohan's eyes narrowed on the priest. "A momentous concession from a man who's dedicated his life to exposing my supposed crimes."

Siffredi didn't flinch from DeRohan's daunting glower. "Your beautiful wife has shown me the benefits that might be had from a compromise. But please don't think I am doing you a favor. In exchange, you are going to compensate the miners for their time lost in the strike, substantially increase their wages, and instigate a lengthy list of safety measures."

"Am I?"

Jules said, "You are unless you know a better way to raise that ten million pounds."

He glanced from her to the priest. "Well, then," he said almost cheerfully, "I suppose I am."

As he and Siffredi proceeded to discuss the terms of this agreement in detail, Jules and Hudson just stood there watching. It had all gone smoothly—more smoothly even than she'd hoped. But inside, her instincts were screaming.

Because all through this exchange, she'd had the uncanny sensation that the Panther was here, taking part in it.

She could feel his presence.

Beyond that, the prey had walked into the trap just a little too easily.

Chapter 28

Dominic DeRohan sat in the stands of the seaside Monaco sporting complex, filled with a large, wealthy crowd who had gathered for the St-Ignatius Foundation Charity Tennis Tournament. His eyes scanned the pastel parasols that shaded the faces of most of the spectators.

At his side, under their own sun umbrella, his wife sat beside the Shah of Persia. The man hadn't even glanced at the athletic event transpiring below him. He was fawning over Jules and not being very subtle about it.

DeRohan could see that Jules was still making an effort to fulfill her part of the bargain—listening attentively to the man's stories, sitting tantalizingly close, smiling alluringly—but he could tell her heart wasn't in it. When she thought no one was looking, he noticed her restlessly searching the crowd, as if looking for something. Occasionally, he caught her glancing his way with an uneasy concern in her eyes.

She was clearly suspicious.

I shouldn't have jumped at their deal so quickly. I should have driven a harder bargain.

She couldn't know all of it, of course. But she might be thinking: *My husband, being the resourceful villain he is, might have somehow learned about my love affair with the Panther. He might know that the shipment of cash from Corsica is bait for our trap. He might have a counterplan to pull the rug out from under us at the last moment.*

DeRohan could almost hear the words in her mind: *We're in danger. DeRohan knows everything. He won't rest until the Panther is destroyed.*

Suddenly, as if sensing his thoughts, Jules shot to her feet. "It's so hot here, I think I shall go get something cool to drink."

The Shah rose with a show of gallantry. "But do not trouble yourself, dear lady. It would be my pleasure to fetch it for you."

She put her hand on his. "No, no. We can't have the Lion of the Aryans running errands for me. In any case, I need to powder my nose. I'm just wilting in this heat."

DeRohan watched her leave, a ravishing slim figure in a cool white dress, her golden bobbed hair peeking out beneath the chicly angled sun hat. As she moved up the aisle with her inherent grace, he saw heads swivel, watching her. There had never been a time when he was with his wife when people hadn't turned to stare. Today, despite her protestations to the contrary, she appeared as fresh and lovely against the backdrop of azure sky as a ship sailing into a deep blue bay.

He remembered the first time he'd seen her. He'd been a twelve-year-old boy working on the estate of Lord Beckingham in Cannes. He was wearing the suit her ladyship had just purchased for him, the first good clothes he'd ever possessed. He'd felt grand and proud, strutting along as if he owned the world, on his way to deliver a message for her ladyship—taking care to avoid the puddles in the muddy road left from an earlier rain, admiring the gleam of his new shoes in the sun. When all at once, the Habsburg coach-and-four had barreled past at a gallop, haughtily sweeping by everything in its path. He'd stepped aside and turned to look at it just as its wheels sent a spew of mud that covered him from head to foot. From the coach window, the face of a pretty little rich girl looked out and laughed.

It was the defining moment of his life.

Standing there, soiled, humiliated, he'd vowed to have his revenge. Someday he'd be wealthy enough so that no one would ever spray mud in his face again. And when that day came, he'd make those Habsburgs pay for that unbearable insult.

He'd fulfilled that vow. The incident had happened in front of the site that would later become the Carlton Hotel. Now he owned it. That, and the Habsburg brat who'd laughed in his face.

The Shah slid over to take the seat Jules had just vacated. "My British solicitors are currently drawing up the oil leases. They constitute a most complicated legal document, but they assure me they will be ready for our signatures at the end of the allotted time frame."

DeRohan barely heard him. He was still looking at Jules as she descended the stairs, thinking how he'd fulfilled that childhood vow and made that imperious little girl suffer. He remembered the look on her face when he'd told her he'd put a bullet through her lover's head.

"Good," he answered distractedly.

"And how are you progressing with my . . . signing bonus?"

"It's all going according to plan. The Americans are paying even more for the gold than I'd anticipated. They've agreed to pay in cash. One of my ships will be bringing it from Corsica. It will be here the eighth of August, as you requested. I've installed a new security lock on the door of the basement at the villa, so it will be quite safe until the signing that night."

The Shah was watching him. "You *are* a gambler, are you not, my friend?" he said with a sudden smile. "Sending out your entire future in the hold of one ship. You do realize, do you not, that should anything happen to that cargo, you would be completely ruined. As destitute as a Cairo beggar."

DeRohan angled back a sly smile. "Then I can't let anything happen to it, can I?"

Jules passed the refreshment stand and continued walking toward a long table where several staff members of the

St-Ignatius Foundation were scoring the tennis tournament, their largest fundraiser of the year.

Father Siffredi had just joined them. Jules spotted his arrival and made her way down to see him.

He was conferring with another priest when he saw her approaching. Excusing himself, he stood to meet her. "Signora DeRohan, how delightful to see you here today. I hope you are enjoying the competition as much as we are."

She gave a thin smile, saying, "We're having a most pleasant time, thank you, Father." She nodded a greeting to the other church officials who were perspiring in their liturgical robes. Under her breath, she added, "Walk with me. We must talk."

They headed back toward the refreshment stand where nuns were handing out citronade in paper cups. She kept her voice low, saying, "I have to be careful. DeRohan has been watching me closely."

"What's wrong?" he asked in an equally low tone.

"I think DeRohan knows."

"Knows what?"

"The plan."

"How could he possibly?"

"I don't know how. But every instinct in my body is telling me he does. He's just not behaving the way he should in this situation. There's a calculation in the back of his eyes that unsettles me. He's up to something. I can feel it."

"But our mutual friend is not concerned."

She looked up at him pointedly and said, "Perhaps our mutual friend *should* be concerned."

"What would you have him do? Cancel the entire operation? We have positioned your husband to become the most powerful man in Europe. Should we now drop everything and allow that to occur?"

"No, of course not. It's just that . . . I'm frightened."

"Nerves," he soothed. "I feel it as well. But everything is proceeding as it should. Try not to allow your fears to get the better of you. Try to remain calm."

That was easy for him to say. For the last ten days, she'd been telling herself that once they'd brought DeRohan to his knees, she and her lover would have one last poignant time together. But now she feared DeRohan would find some way to turn the tables on them, and that that final meeting might never take place.

She had to see the Panther. To tell him her fears and be close to him now. She'd been going crazy for the last ten days, missing him, wanting him.

At the same time, the possibility existed that this man standing in front of her might be . . .

No! She wouldn't allow herself to even think it.

She turned and looked into the eyes of the priest. "Our mutual friend . . . I must see him. As soon as possible. Tonight. Can you help me?"

She saw something flick in his eyes. "But Signora, I have no idea of how to reach him."

Part of her hoped that was true. "But you've had some sort of relationship with him before. You've learned to trust him."

"But I have no way of initiating a meeting. He has left me messages. Sometimes he has appeared in the dark to bestow certain . . . donations for my various causes. However . . ."

She glanced back at the stands to find DeRohan staring down on them. "My husband's watching us. I must go. But promise me that if any means presents itself by which you can get word to our friend, you will do it. I must see him as soon as possible."

"Very well," the priest said. "I promise."

Jules sat on the bed of their secret room, her hands pressed together in an attempt to keep herself still. Her frustration had reached a boiling point. She'd been pacing the confines of the room for hours, waiting . . . waiting . . . her desperation mounting as the minutes ticked by.

But she was determined to stay—all night if necessary. Back at the house, DeRohan would no doubt have asked where she was. But she'd told Hudson of her desperation and ordered him to tell whatever lie was necessary—that she was in bed with a headache, that her favorite cousin had died—*anything* to keep DeRohan from growing suspicious.

In the golden glow of the candle's light, the Roman statues in the room cast eerie shadows on the marble walls. There was a forlorn air about the place already, as if it were preparing itself for the emptiness to come. As if the statues were whispering to her that this would be the last time they would ever see her here.

Where was he? If, as she feared, he was Siffredi, then surely he would come. And if he wasn't . . . she prayed that somehow the priest could get word to him.

She was so confused. She didn't know what to think about anything. All she knew was that she had to see him.

Suddenly, like a gift from Heaven, she heard the tunnel door open. And there he was in all his dark glory—her phantom of the night.

Forgetting all her qualms, she gave a cry of joy and rushed into his arms. They tightened about her, lifting her feet off the floor as he kissed her—a deep, possessive kiss that felt as frenzied to her as she felt inside.

"I shouldn't have come, I know," he murmured. "But everything's set. The sale of the gold ore has been finalized. The ship will soon set sail from Corsica with the cash. My arrangements for its reception are all in place. And I can't think of anything but you."

He kissed her again. He felt so dynamic, so warm, so solid. She'd never felt so right as she did in his arms.

It terrified her.

"We must call this off," she told him. "I feel it even more than I did this afternoon."

"This afternoon?"

She tipped her head back to look up at him. Did he really have no knowledge of her conversation with Siffredi? Or was he merely trying to throw her off the scent? "I'm certain DeRohan's onto us. His manner is so sure, so smug. He knows. I can't explain how I know it, but I feel it. It's as if the very air I breathe is screaming at me to beware."

He pulled her to him, stroking her back. Quietly, he told her, "I respect your feelings and I trust your instincts. You may be right. It could be that we've slipped up somewhere and he knows. But even if he does, we can't back out now without doing what we can to stop him."

"Why can't we? Better to let him win than to risk your life on something that's doomed to fail."

"Because, *Cara*, he'd be winning more than just a business venture. He would be winning you."

"He could never win me, never have me."

"You're wrong. If he were to regain his power, there would be no incentive to let you go. He would hold onto you more tightly than ever before. I can't allow that. You're too good for this man. If I do nothing else, I won't let him have you."

"You can't know that he'd want me. He said himself that he didn't know why he's held onto me for so long."

"Then he lied."

"How do you know that?"

"Because I'm a man. And there isn't a man alive who—once having possessed you—would willingly let you go."

She pushed away, out of the safe haven of his arms. "*You* are letting me go."

"Not willingly."

"Then don't."

He turned from her, his shoulders slumped, taking himself out of the candle's glow. His hands at his sides balled into fists.

Jules's Habsburg pride was waging war with her desperation, cautioning her not to beg. But for once, she banished the training of her youth. What was her pride to her now? She had no pride where he was concerned.

"Please don't leave me," she begged. "I don't care who you are. I don't care what lies between us. Whatever it is, we can overcome it together. Our love is stronger than any obstacle in our path. These awful nights without you, I haven't cared about convention or right and wrong, or even what people might say. I've missed you so that I feel I'm losing my mind. I've wanted you in my arms so much that the longing is like a fever. Let's forget this doomed plan. Let's go someplace where DeRohan can never find us. I don't care where. Just someplace where we can be together forever, away from the eyes and judgment of the world."

He turned on her so savagely that she flinched.

"Do you think this is easy for me?" he ground out in a torturous tone. "Do you think I wouldn't love to rip off this mask and tell you everything? It kills me to think of never seeing you again. To never touch you—never have you really know me—never have you love me for myself. Do you have any idea of what that does to a man? How it's eating me inside?"

"Then don't do it."

"I have to do it."

"For what purpose?"

As he looked at her, she thought she could see the pain blazing from the eyes behind the mask. The air in the room was turbulent, explosive with the things he couldn't—or wouldn't—bring himself to say.

Finally, he did say, quietly now, "For you."

"For *me?*" she cried. "You're leaving me with nothing and I don't even know the reason why."

"I'm leaving you with the only gift it's possible for me to bestow."

"Then I don't want your horrible gift. It demands too much of a price."

"If there is a price, it's a price we both must pay. I more than you. I ask nothing of you but that you not make it more difficult than it already is. As it is, I'll spend the rest of my life wishing your *fantasia romantica* could be."

"But, it can't," she said dully.

"No. It can't."

She swallowed before asking, "Because you're a priest?"

"No, *Cara*. Because it's even worse than that."

"What could be worse?"

His voice sounding strangled, he told her, "You have to stop asking me that. Don't you see what you're doing to me? Don't you care?"

She felt stricken. "Of course I care. I love you. I've never loved another man. Not for a minute. God help me, I only used Edwin to spite DeRohan. But it wasn't love. Not like this. Not like you. I don't even have a name to call you, but I know I shall never love any other man. It will always be you. No matter what you do, you can't kill that."

He didn't say anything for a long time. She could see in the flexing of his hands the struggle that was battling inside him. Then with a flat air of finality, he said, "I'm not going to come to you again."

She felt her heart crack in two.

"If I do," he added, "I'll never have the strength to leave you."

"Then this is good-bye." Even to herself, she sounded like a lost little girl.

"This is good-bye," he repeated.

Unshed tears burned at her throat. "Then you must leave me with something. Something to remember through the awful years ahead."

Warily, he replied, "If I can."

She glanced back at the candle, then at him again. Memorizing his position by the bed, she went and snuffed out the flame.

The smell of lingering smoke was acrid in the air. Without the illumination, the subterranean room was pitch black.

Slowly, like a sleepwalker, she made her way around the edge of the bed toward him until her hands came to rest upon his chest. It seemed to her that the total darkness heightened her other senses. She could feel the chiseled muscles beneath her fingertips, hear the rasp of his breath through his chest.

"Take off your mask."

She felt the jolt of resistance pass from him to her.

"Please," she whispered, unable now to see even his silhouette in the dark. "You can trust me. I can't see you anymore than you can see me. But if you need it from me, I'll swear to you by all I hold holy that I shan't do anything to betray you. I won't feel your face. I won't touch your hair. If you can't bring yourself to trust me, then tie my hands behind my back. I only want one time with you without that cursed mask coming between us."

It was quiet for several moments as she felt the rise and fall of his chest. He didn't move. She knew what she was asking. She knew the battle going on inside his head.

And she knew the moment when he relinquished his fears. When his love for her outweighed his need to protect himself.

He put his strong hands on her shoulders and slid them down her arms until he had her hands in his. Then he lifted them and placed them on the mask on either side of his head. Together, their hands entwined, they slowly slipped it back and off his head. Then, taking one of her hands in his, he laid the silken headgear into her open palm.

It was a moment of such exquisite intimacy that the unshed tears sprang to her eyes.

For a moment, she caressed it with her fingertips. Then she put it to her cheek, lovingly, turning her lips to kiss the soft fabric that smelled ever so faintly of him. Tenderly, she laid it on the bedside table, then took his hand and placed it on the mask, showing him where it was.

She could sense that he felt vulnerable and exposed in a way he never had before. "Do you want to tie my hands?"

"No," he said hoarsely. "I trust you."

She brought his hand to her lips, kissing it, whispering, "Now there's nothing between us."

She unzipped her dress and let it drop to the floor.

"And now, *amore mio*," she whispered, "make love to me one last time. Let us love one another in such a way that the memory of it will carry us through all eternity."

* * *

Hours later, after he'd left, Jules went outside through the Venus Temple. It was nearly dawn. The last of the morning stars glistened in a milk-grey sky.

Her body was still humming from their shared passion. But she ached inside, because she knew she would never feel this way again.

She breathed in the fresh morning air, wondering if she would ever again welcome a new day.

She'd come out here because she'd wanted to feel herself a part of everything around her. But the beauty and peace seemed tarnished now. Empty. Her prize for giving up her love.

She walked back toward the house, shivering a little in the chilly breeze. And nearly ran into a man crossing the lawn.

Hudson.

He whirled, startled. "Highness!"

"What are you doing out here, Hudson, at such an hour?"

When he didn't answer, she pressed, "Another of your mysterious personal errands?"

He looked flustered. In the gathering dawn, he cast a glance toward the villa. "I think it best, Highness, that we go inside. I shouldn't want Mr. DeRohan to think there was anything unseemly—"

"Come now, Hudson. Even DeRohan wouldn't be so base as to think I was having a tryst with my butler."

Tartly, he replied, "Of course not, Highness. It was stupid of me to suggest."

He turned and left.

Belatedly, she recalled his war wound and cursed herself. She'd forgotten everything lately but her own quandary. This incident reminded her that life would go on without her lover. The days would come and go, and faithful Hudson would be by her side. She'd have to apologize to him in the morning.

It seemed she was causing everyone misery of late.

Chapter 29

Inspector Ladd was in trouble.

For some days now, it had been clear to him that the greatest victory of his career—the capture of the Panther—had turned to dust. No one else seemed to know this—no one but himself and Juan Cubatta: the gypsy devil he'd arrested and offered up to the world as the celebrated burglar.

But as the bugger's trial date approached, it would soon be obvious to everyone just how much of a blunder he'd made. Because the evidence he'd assembled against the man consisted of a token batch of jewelry from only two robberies committed two days apart. And Ladd's own investigation into the gypsy's activities during the past year had uncovered the embarrassing fact that the suspect had been in Spain for the first six months of the year—while the lion's share of the Panther's eighteen capers were occurring on the Riviera.

He was *not* the Panther.

He was some ruddy copycat.

And the infuriating thing was that, all this time, the fellow hadn't said a word in his defense. He'd remained as tight-lipped as a mummy in the British Museum. Until so much time had passed and Ladd was so committed to the idea that the man was the Panther, that the inevitable revelation that he was not—that the real Panther was still at large—was bound to be a colossal, career-damaging mortification for the inspector.

Why had Cubatta done this?

Because he knew something about the real Panther that he hoped to trade when the time was right. He'd let Ladd climb further and further out on a limb, until he found himself in serious trouble and would *have* to make a deal to the gypsy's advantage in exchange for whatever the man knew that might get him out of it.

As he stood hesitantly before the Nice police headquarters interrogation room where he had Cubatta cooling his heels, Ladd realized the criminal had him over a barrel.

Right, then. If that was the way he had to play it to extricate himself from this blasted tangle, so be it. He'd see what the man had to offer.

He entered the small austere room and closed the door behind him.

The gypsy was seated at a metal table across from an empty chair. His eyes flicked to Ladd but his face offered the same blank, mute intransigence he'd given him in all their previous interrogations.

This time, however, Ladd flopped down in the chair opposite him in a gesture of defeat. "All right," he said, "you win. What is it you want?"

For the first time in their relationship, the gypsy's lips curled into a smile. It seemed to say: all things come to those who wait.

"My needs are few, *monsieur l'inspecteur*. I wish you to drop *all* charges against me and I wish amnesty for any new charges that might come from anything I've done in the past."

Ladd pursed his lips in distaste. "And what do you offer in exchange?"

"The real Panther, naturally."

It was a bitter pill to swallow, but would be worth it—if the man could deliver. "All right, then, we have a deal."

"I am not so much of a fool as you take me for, Monsieur. I want your word as an English gentleman."

Bloody hell! Swallowing, he bit out the words, "You have it."

The negotiations at an end, Cubatta reached for the pack of Turkish cigarettes on the table. Lighting one, he took a puff and sent a smoke ring into the air. "I do not know his name but I know where he lives."

"Where?"

"Cap Ferrat."

"You're not serious."

Cubatta flicked an ash into the ashtray. "It sticks in your craw, does it not? That you have been combing the seedy streets of Marseille when he was living in luxury in the midst of his victims all the time."

"I'll thank you to keep a civil tongue in your head. How do you know this?"

Cubatta shrugged insolently. "I read the stories about him in the newspapers. I studied his work so that I might follow in his footsteps. I began to pull jobs in his likeness that everyone assumed was his own work. Then, one night—by pure chance, mind you—it happened that we both decided to rob the same place at the same time: the Villa Maryland. But he got there first and was leaving just as I started to enter. I followed him to his lair."

"And where was that?"

"Up the hill, a short distance away. That huge villa just north of it. The largest villa on the Cap."

"You don't mean—Rêve de l'Amour?"

"*Oui,* that's the one. I followed him into the estate and watched him vanish into the house—into the side servant's entrance. Your illusive Panther, *monsieur l'inspecteur,* is obviously in service there. A gardener, a maintenance man, a butler— who knows? But if you take those oh-so-diligent policemen who so gleefully came after me and make a search through the place, you would be sure to turn up the man. Along with enough incriminating evidence to once and for all put an end to your nightmare."

*   *   *

Preparations for the evening's signing ceremony began early on the eighth of August at Rêve de l'Amour. With more than a hundred guests expected—diplomats, business moguls from all over Europe, a large contingent of the press, and even a newsreel camera crew—Hudson had to make an extra effort to ensure that everything would be perfect. The trees and topiary hedges were all newly clipped, and the freshly mowed lawns were set up with tables that would hold hundreds of bottles of iced champagne under colorful striped tents that looked like a recreation of a desert oasis from *The Arabian Nights*.

By the central dancing fountain, a table had been set up where the contracts would be signed amidst the popping of flashbulbs and envious applause.

The ship from Corsica arrived at Villefranche harbor just after five PM, several hours later than scheduled due to rough seas off Cap Corse. DeRohan was waiting at the dock with a team of private detectives he'd hired to escort its precious cargo—three large boxes of British pound notes—the short drive to the estate. There, it was carried down to the basement and safely stored behind the newly installed lock until the Shah would take it off his hands later that same night, after the signing ceremony was over and the guests had gone on their way.

As dusk began to settle on Cap Ferrat, the guests began to arrive. With DeRohan acting as ebullient host, they milled around the back lawn, sipping champagne and nibbling on canapés until the Shah—making a grand entrance with his twenty-man entourage—arrived just after eight.

Finally, the moment had arrived.

As DeRohan raised his arms in the air and called for the guests' attention, the reporters crowded close to him with notebooks in hand, and the Pathé newsreel cameras began to crank.

DeRohan uttered a few self-serving words about the importance to humanity of this auspicious new alliance between his company and the ancient nation of Persia—soon to be called Iran, Land of the Aryans—and then he offered a toast.

The Shah reciprocated with a similar speech about how this

innovative new partnership would bring East and West together. Then they signed the contracts.

Standing a few feet away from her husband in this moment
of his greatest triumph, Jules watched the two men embrace.

At that very moment, she thought, the Panther must be heading toward the basement to relieve it of its treasure. The plan
was for him to enter the tunnel from its beach entrance, walk
down it past their love nest and up the other arm into the basement. He would carry the money in three trips back to the
beach where, just off the western shore of the Cap, Father
Siffredi would be waiting with another ship that would take
the cash straight back to Corsica. Once there, it would be
given back to the people from whom DeRohan had stolen it.

It was agonizing, knowing her lover was so close, not being
able to go to him. But—anticipating the temptation—he'd
made her promise not to before leaving Rêve de l'Amour for
the last time. All she could do was whisper a fervent prayer for
his safety.

That, and try to stamp down this pervasive feeling that
something was about to go horribly wrong.

All around her, there was much backslapping and hand
shaking, and more toasts before everyone headed for the tables
heavily laden with food. A string quartet began to play and a
buoyant mood gripped the assembly as the victorious DeRohan
was mobbed by well-wishers eager to curry his favor.

The night dragged on. It grew dark and things began to settle down. Couples danced on the portable dance floor set up
on the lawn. Champagne flowed freely. As the guests became
more inebriated, the Shah began to make his way toward
Jules, with the keen look of a man eager to collect his reward.

As he placed a claiming arm around her waist and popping
flashbulbs blinded her, Jules cringed inside. But she was making it through the next difficult hour by imagining the look on
her husband's face when he and his cohort opened that basement door and found the room empty.

Coup d'etat.

Justice.

Sweet revenge.

She intended to be there with them to witness that long awaited scene firsthand.

But at that moment, a shuffling broke out in the section of the crowd nearest the house. They began to part as if a battering ram was being shoved through their midst. The guests around Jules began to murmur. As a woman close to the house let out a startled yelp, someone behind her asked out loud, "What's happening?"

"It's the police!"

The crowd was growing more frantic.

"They're all over the place. What's going on?"

"I just saw a dozen gendarmes running into the house with drawn pistols!"

The Shah went pale. Jules herself had no idea what was happening. But she thought of the Panther, making his way through the tunnels even now.

The pushing and shoving crowd was in an uproar. Reporters raced toward the house to investigate.

Then someone yelled, "Look, on the roof!"

Jules looked up. In the glow of the bright lights all around them, she could see a dark figure running along the top of the house: a man dressed in black with a mask over his face.

"It's the Panther!" someone cried.

Jules's heart stopped. *What in the world was he doing up there?*

A volley of gunfire spit out from below as the police drew their pistols and fired. The figure clasped his side, tottered a moment on the edge of the roof, and fell to the ground—a drop of at least thirty feet.

Jules cried out in horror and raced toward the house. As she reached the back terrace, she saw Inspector Ladd. Around him were dozens of uniformed policemen, beating the bushes and pointing flashlights in search of their fallen prey.

Noticing her, the inspector explained, "Pardon the intrusion, Ma'am, but it turns out that gypsy we've been detaining is not the Panther after all. We've conclusively determined that the real man is one of your employees."

Employees?

The word wouldn't register, as if he'd spoken in a foreign tongue. She tried to comprehend what he was saying. And then, like a thunderbolt, she understood.

Oh, my God.

"In any case," Ladd continued, "we've got the real chap for sure now. He seems to be momentarily out of our clutches but he's been hit and he can't get far. We have the place surrounded with fifty men and we'll comb through every inch of the place until we arrest or kill him."

Through her shock, Jules realized that the bushes must have broken his fall and that he was trying to circle around the Florentine garden and up to the Temple of Venus, where he could find sanctuary in the room below.

But with all these people milling about, searching the grounds, he was sure to be spotted by someone before he reached the temple.

What can I do? I have to get to him.

All at once, she put her hands to her face and shrieked at the top of her lungs. A hundred faces looked her way.

The Inspector rushed to her side. "What is it?"

"The Panther! I just saw him crawling out a window on the east side of the house! He's going to escape through the front entrance!"

Ladd raised a whistle to his fleshy lips and blew a shrill blast. Then he raced toward the entrance as the gendarmes turned in their tracks and followed him.

Jules waited several moments, then, as inconspicuously as possible, began to slowly make her way back through the upset crowd toward the temple and its secret rotunda entrance to the world below.

As she did, she saw that the Shah was in a frenzy. He was, no doubt, sure that he himself was the object of the raid, that his bribe would be confiscated by the police, and that the reporters would broadcast it to the world. He grabbed up the signed contracts and tore them to bits.

It took some time to make her way through the buzzing guests and into the darkness beyond, skirting the long pool, keeping herself under cover of the pines, lest someone spot her. When she reached the rotunda, she tripped the mechanism that opened the door. As she closed it behind her and hurried down the spiral staircase, she heard heavy breathing in the darkness below.

At the base of the stairs, she snatched the flashlight from its holder and flicked it on. As the room illuminated, she saw the Panther lying on the floor, gasping for air, blood seeping from the wound in his side.

With a strangled cry, Jules rushed to him, throwing herself to the floor beside him as the flashlight fell from her hands. It clattered on the marble, rolling, then settled so that it cast a macabre spotlight onto them.

She threw her arms about him, cradling him, sobbing, "What have they done to you?"

He winced in pain. She shot up, looking at him. He was bleeding heavily, the red of it stark against the white marble. She could see at once how weak he was, how labored was his breathing. But he forced a smile and in a pathetic whisper, groaned, "*Cara.*"

Panicked tears streamed down her face. "Let me see how bad it is." Gingerly, she took his black sweater in her hands and peeled it back from where it stuck to his side. It was soaked, smearing crimson on her hands. The gash in his side was oozing blood. Sobbing frantically, despising the men who'd done this to him, she tried to think what to do.

"Don't move," she told him. "I'm going to help you."

She stood, looking down at her white dress. The entire front of her skirt was stained with his blood. Lifting it, she pulled down her half-slip and wadded it to form a makeshift compress.

Falling to her knees beside him, she pushed it hard against the gushing wound.

He gave a sharp intake of breath.

"I'm sorry," she told him. "I don't want to hurt you, but I have to stop this bleeding."

She bore down on it but it wasn't long before the slip was drenched. Sitting back on her heels, she felt her body wracked with sobs. "It isn't helping. What can I do?"

His voice a mere rasp, he grunted, "*Cara*, listen to me . . ."

She put her fingers to his lips to quiet him, but seeing the blood on them, drew them back. "I need something else."

She bounded up, ran to the bed, threw off the coverlet, and yanked off the top sheet. Balling it up, she knelt beside him again, pressing it to his side. But it, too, was soaked in seconds.

"I've got to get you out of here," she told him.

"No. I'm better off here. Listen to me." His voice was so faint, she had to put her ear to his mouth to hear him. "Siffredi—aborted the mission . . . his ship left the area—the moment the gunfire broke out—we agreed—to that—contingency—in advance."

She could see that every word was an agony of effort.

"But I can still get you out. We can find a doctor in Villefranche. We have to get that bullet out of you."

"We wouldn't—get five feet up the coast. They'll have—every inch—of Cap Ferrat—covered."

"You'll bleed to death. I can't just sit here and watch you die!"

"You can—stop it. I know—you can."

How could he ask this of her? She wasn't equipped to care for him. She didn't know how. But she had to try. So, finding a dry patch, she rebundled the sheet and renewed the pressure.

Please let it stop. He can't take much more of this!

"I could kill Ladd for this. What were you *doing* up there?"

"The police—surprised me. I had to—get out of there—the best way—I could."

"Ladd said the gypsy led them here."

He gave a bleak smile. "There is always—the unexpected," he said.

She concentrated her energies on caring for him, putting steady pressure on the wound, dying a little every time he winced in pain. It was tearing her up inside to see him like this—this vital man, lying at her feet, so weak and pale. But as the bleeding lessened, she poured all her energy into him, willing him well with every ounce of her resolve.

He was quieter now, deathly still. She couldn't tell if he was conscious. But the bleeding stopped at last. Her tense body slumping in reprieve, she shoved aside the bloody rags and carefully lay down by his side. Ignoring the stickiness of her hands, she wrapped her arms around him, holding him close.

Hudson.

Dear, loyal Hudson. The last man she ever would have envisioned.

Hudson, who'd listened to her tales of romantic heroes. Who'd donned a mask and had made those heroes come to life. Who'd always been there, quietly by her side, helping her, protecting her. Choking back the humiliation of playing her servant. Pretending he had a war wound so she would never guess.

She remembered the day she'd first met him, when he'd so miraculously appeared to save her from drowning. She'd looked up at him then, no doubt like a frightened child, revealing her vulnerability, saying to him, *I'm in a rather fragile state at the moment. I feel the need for someone who might—*

And he, in his quiet, efficient way, had answered for her: *Take care of you?*

How could she have been so blind?

He stirred, groaning softly.

"I'm so sorry this happened," she told him, tasting fresh tears. "I'd do anything to make it go away. Meeting me was the worst thing that ever happened to you."

He moved then, by a force of will, placing his hand on her face. Turning it toward him, he smiled faintly and in a draining whisper said, "Don't ever say that, *Cara*. You have been the *best* thing to ever happen to me."

He spoke like a man who knew he was dying.

Overcome with love for him, with helplessness and fear, her tears splashed on his hand. But she had to think of him. Comfort him the best she could. So she bent over and gave his lips a tender kiss. "Thank you for the way you've taken care of me."

"I thought it—was you—who was caring—for me." He smiled at his attempted jest, then suddenly threw back his head as pain ripped through his body. His hand convulsed to his side, and came away wet with blood.

She lunged up, checking his wound. It was bleeding again.

"I'm going up to get help. Better that you be caught and go to jail than to die in my arms."

His hand snaked out, grasping her wrist. But he couldn't hold it for long. His arm collapsed beside him again as he struggled for air. "No, *Cara*," he said between breaths. "Please . . . This may be our—last—moment—together. Don't ruin it by—betraying me."

In a fury of frustration, Inspector Ladd realized the villain had somehow escaped!

But where? And how?

By now, they'd covered every inch of the estate grounds twice.

He wasn't here.

They'd searched the entire area around the estate—all the way down to the beach on both sides of the Cap.

Nothing!

But Ladd wasn't about to give up. The villain was wounded. He had to be here somewhere, hiding under some bush or hedge or tree shadow.

Or . . . perhaps he'd gone back into the house.

He'd started back for the front entrance, and was walking

along its western side near where the Panther had dropped, when the flashlight he was using to rake the pathway in front of him revealed something.

He squatted on his haunches to see a few drops of blood. Keeping low to the ground, he followed them toward the side of the house and a small shuttered window.

Quickly, he ran around and entered the house from the front door and found his way to the other side of this window: a pantry just off the kitchen.

Below it, he saw more drops of blood. He tracked it down a narrow service passage, into a wider hallway, and out to a door. It appeared as if it might lead to the basement, but it was fitted with a formidable looking bolt lock—a secure model, his policeman's eye noticed, that looked brand new to boot.

He tried the handle. The door was firmly locked.

He went back outside and called several of his men to the scene. "Fetch me a hammer," he told them. "I saw a service shed out back." They scampered off and, minutes later, returned with a sledgehammer.

"Break in the door," he ordered.

It took half a dozen blows but the stubborn door was finally splintered and torn from its hinges.

Ladd descended the wooden stairs to the cool cement floor. One of the gendarmes behind him switched on a bare overhead lightbulb dangling from a chord.

The room was empty except for three large shipping boxes labeled "Fragile." And yet . . .

The trail of blood continued across the floor, past the boxes, and straight to a cabinet against the wall.

"What the deuce . . . ?"

The flashlight had dimmed, and, with a last defiant flare, had gone out completely. Jules lay in the darkness, her dying lover cradled against her side, his blood covering her dress and hands. Fighting with her conscience. Knowing she should go and call for help.

But suddenly she heard a scratching sound in the distance. The Panther jerked, hearing it, too.

The noises continued. They seemed to be coming from the tunnel leading from the basement.

She left his side to peer out the door. She could see the beams of several flashlights coming their way.

Returning to him, she said, "They've found us." She felt a crushing sense of relief. Now, at least, they could get help for him, save his life. As long as he lived, there was always hope.

But the Panther pushed himself up, his mouth twisted with pain. "I have to—get out." He tried to stand but couldn't. "Help me, *Cara*."

"It's no use, my love."

Through tightly clenched teeth, he ground out, "*I . . . must . . . get . . . out!*"

He struggled to his feet but an instant later crumpled to the floor on his side. She bent down beside him, stroking his back. "It's all right, darling," she told him soothingly. "I'm with you. Whatever comes, we shall face it together."

The door crashed open. Inspector Ladd and some of his men charged into the room, the beams of their flashlights sweeping the room, then coming to rest on the two figures on the floor.

"Jesus wept," Ladd said, surveying the scene.

Jules looked up at him, her hair falling in her eyes. "He's hurt, dying. You must help him."

"Looks to me, my lady, that the blighter has been getting quite a bit of help from yourself."

She couldn't believe his gloating tone. "What's the matter with you? Can't you see he's bleeding to death?"

"Have no fear, Ma'am. We'll get him to hospital soon enough. But before we do, there's one bit of unfinished business I need to take care of."

He came toward them, his heels clicking on the marble floor. Skirting the pool of blood, he crouched down beside them. Watching him, Jules suddenly realized his intention. It seemed to her then that he was moving in slow motion, like someone in a dream. As he nudged the prisoner onto his back . . . as he stretched out his hand, reaching for the Panther's face . . . as he slipped his fingers beneath the mask . . . as her lover's voice moaned feebly, "Don't . . ."

She dove for the inspector's hand, wanting—irrationally—to spare Hudson this final indignity.

But it was too late.

With a single callous jerk, Ladd ripped off the mask.

Revealing the Panther's face.

In that moment, Jules's world came crashing in around her.

Because the man lying there on the verge of death . . . the man she'd given everything to—her body, her heart, her soul . . . the man she'd trusted with her life against all reason . . .

. . . the man she'd *begged* not to leave her . . .

. . . wasn't Hudson at all.

He wasn't anyone she'd ever suspected.

He was the man she hated most in all the world.

Dominic DeRohan.

Chapter 30

She sat where she was, staring into his eyes.
DeRohan's eyes.

It was such a monumental transposition that her mind couldn't adjust to it.

And then, in one terrible instant, everything became clear. A whole alternate reality from the one she'd been living.

The Panther was a ruse.

A cynical manipulation aimed at her.

Knowing her penchant for tragic romantic outlaws . . .

Knowing the Shah's fascination with all things Habsburg . . .

DeRohan had created the Panther to use Jules to achieve his evil ends.

He would get the oil leases that would make him the most powerful businessman in Europe.

And in the process of getting them, he would remove the biggest thorn in the side of his empire—the Corsican strike.

He was so greedy, he even intended to steal back the money he was giving to the Shah as a bribe. Blame it on the Panther.

It all made diabolical sense.

DeRohan would have the oil leases, his strike ended, *and* the money from the gold all for himself.

But most loathsome of all, the scheme had allowed him to

take the one thing she'd vowed never to give him under any circumstance.

It had allowed him to trick his way into her bed.

The Panther was nothing more than a foul violation of her.

Even with the evidence staring her in the face, it still seemed impossible to believe.

This man who'd vowed to ruin her husband.

This man who'd told her the hatred of her husband would make her strong.

This man who'd plunged his fingers into her and said, "*This* is how you should be touched."

This man was . . .

Dominic DeRohan himself.

She heard more footsteps behind her. More people coming into the room. But nothing penetrated. It was as if her surroundings were but a fog swirling all around her. And all that existed in the world was the blaze of those icy eyes.

Two policemen came forth and hoisted the prisoner to his feet. She felt hands on her arm and a soft voice urging her, "Please, Mrs. DeRohan, you must leave."

The hands helped her stand. Inspector Ladd. She stared at him as if she'd never seen him before.

"We found some of the loot, sir, in DeRohan's bedroom, hidden in the floorboards." One of the new arrivals handed forth a small velvet pouch with an assortment of jewels. "We also found these. Apparently, he was using them to disguise himself." He showed the items: a specially designed false padding meant to strap around the waist to give the impression of bulk, and a costume beard and mustache.

Jules studied the disguise for a moment, then her hollow eyes moved to the prisoner. He was being held up by a policeman on each side, his feet dangling on the floor. Without the beard and false padding, he looked tragically handsome.

A Byronic hero in the flesh.

What a fool I am!

Unbidden, a memory flashed across her mind. A tall, mysterious man, masked and dangerous, standing before her in the moonlight. *I'm afraid there's only one payment I would consider for my services in this matter. You.*

She, humiliated, admitting a vulnerable truth: *I swore to my husband the instant the ceremony was over that I would never allow him to touch me. I've never broken that vow.*

And he, his voice husky, telling her: *If you were my wife, you wouldn't be able to give such a testimony. I can assure you that.*

A white heat flared through her.

"You incomparable *wretch!*"

Her words cut through the room, louder than she'd supposed. Wildly, she glanced around. The inspector was still standing by her side. But it wasn't his concerned face she was looking at. It was the pistol tucked into his belt. In a flash of rage, she grabbed for it, tugging it free, and leveled it on DeRohan.

With great effort, he raised his head and looked her in the eyes. He was pale and drawn. He couldn't stand on his own. His eyes were bleary with pain. But they showed no fear of her.

She was shivering violently. Her hand was trembling so badly, she had to join the other to it to steady the gun.

Beside her, Ladd said with the careful voice he might use with someone deranged, "Mrs. DeRohan, please . . . give me back the gun."

When he put his hand on her, she veered toward him. He stepped back. She had a vague sensation of dozens of eyes staring at her, wide with alarm.

"Let us handle this, Mrs. DeRohan," Ladd was saying. "We'll make certain the bugger gets what he has coming to him."

She turned the gun back on DeRohan. "*I* shall make certain he gets what he has coming to him."

"Mrs. DeRohan—"

She stepped toward her husband, keeping the pistol trained on him, her finger itching at the trigger.

With all the strength left in him, he held her gaze. His eyes were full, not of trepidation, but of a kind of mournful sorrow. They brimmed with tears.

It incensed her. She wanted to see something else . . . fear for his life. She wanted him to grovel. She wanted to see not this beaten corpse of a man, but Dominic DeRohan in all his malevolent splendor. That's who she wanted to kill.

Her hands shook terribly again and she tightened her grip, keeping it leveled on his chest.

Ladd's voice beside her was saying, "For heaven's sake, Mrs. DeRohan, try to get a grip on yourself."

DeRohan's head suddenly drooped toward his chest, his strength ebbing fast. Seeing that he was slipping toward unconsciousness, Jules abruptly stepped closer and shoved the barrel of the gun directly into his wound.

He convulsed with pain.

"I'm going to kill you, you sham of a human being. But before I pull the trigger, I want you to remember what you did to my father."

"If you do this, Mrs. DeRohan," Ladd warned, "the law will make no allowances for whatever outrages he may have committed against you. So, please just—"

She shoved the gun back into DeRohan's wound. His face went white. But his eyes looked at her as if they contained all the anguish in the world.

"You miserable swine. Before I blow off the top of your head, I want you to think of poor pathetic Edwin, who didn't know one end of the pistol from another."

"Mrs. DeRohan," Ladd said as he slowly extended his hand, "I'm going to very carefully take the weapon from you."

She swiveled on him. "Just try it."

He lowered his hand.

Yet again, she shoved the gun into DeRohan's side. This time he gave no reaction at all. But blood dripped onto the floor at his feet.

"Most of all, as I pull this trigger, I want you to think of how you took advantage of me. I want you to think of all those times we were together . . . the things we did . . . the things you made me do . . ."

His pained gaze softened on her face.

"Don't look at me that way, dammit!" she cried. "Show some fear. Arrogance. Anger. *Something!*"

Her voice broke on the last word.

His sorrowful eyes continued to burn into her soul.

And then she felt a movement behind her and a voice penetrated her fog. A voice she knew. A voice that had comforted her before.

Kindly, with quiet efficiency, the voice said, "I'll take that now, Highness, so you can get some rest."

She glanced toward the voice. A face swam before her eyes. Hudson.

He smiled gently. "You must be tired, Highness. We'll get you cleaned up and put to bed."

All at once, the sight of his face cracked through her delirium. Hudson. Hudson, who'd always been there for her.

But wasn't it Hudson behind the mask?

No.

It was DeRohan.

She looked down and saw her blood-smeared dress. Her hands—shaking uncontrollably, stained scarlet—held a gun. Her index fingers were positioned on the trigger, ready to pull.

She saw then—in the eerie beams of the flashlights—a circle of petrified police, and began to comprehend the sight she must present.

They think I'm crazy.

They think I'm going to pull the trigger.

Finally, she looked at DeRohan.

She could have sworn there was love in his eyes.

She dropped the gun. As it clattered to the floor, the vanguard of police leapt back, afraid it might go off. Ladd bent hastily and scooped it up.

"Very good, Highness," Hudson said. "Now, we'll go back to the house, shall we?"

As he was steering her away, Jules heard a thump. Turning back to look, she saw that DeRohan had lost consciousness and collapsed to the floor. The policemen on either side were bending down to pick him up.

"Get him out of here," she told them.

She felt Hudson's hand on her arm. "Come, Highness, I'll take care of you."

In that moment, a deathly calm settled over her. She looked at the throng of parting policemen. She looked at the blood on the floor. It all seemed to have happened to someone else.

"Thank you, Hudson," she said in a composed tone. "I can make it on my own. I don't need any help."

Her head held high, she left the room, the police and Hudson staring after her.

When she finally went to bed, hours later, she fell into a deep sleep and didn't move once during the night. She didn't think. She didn't dream. But when she awoke ten hours later with a blinding headache, everything came back to her.

Faintly in the distance, she could hear some sort of commotion. When it didn't cease, she decided to investigate. She slipped into the first robe she could find, noting idly that the bloodied clothes she'd left on the floor had been removed.

Hudson met her at the foot of the stairs. "Highness, I'll bring you a tray. I didn't know you were awake. I didn't want to disturb you."

"What is all that noise?"

"I'm sorry to have to tell you that the house is under siege. The story about the master was in all the morning papers. There is an army of reporters at the front gate, clamoring for more information. I've had to take the telephone off the hook.

A number of your husband's business associates seem quite desperate to talk to you. The police have also been by to take your detailed statement. I know you won't want to deal with any of this—"

But she shook her head. "No, it's fine, Hudson. I shall see them all, one at a time."

He gave her an odd look. "The priest from Monaco is also here. I asked him to wait in the study."

DeRohan's study.

"Transfer him to the salon and tell him I'll be in as soon as I'm dressed. Then bring me some coffee."

"Highness—"

"Was there something more?"

"No. Only . . . are you all right?"

With the same composure she'd shown the night before, she answered, "Quite all right, Hudson. Now please see to Father Siffredi."

When they met a few minutes later, Siffredi seemed shaken. "I cannot believe it!" he greeted her. "DeRohan of all people!"

She sat in a chair across from him, her back ramrod straight. "We've been the victim of a Machiavellian schemer."

"But to what end? It makes no sense."

"If his plan had succeeded, it would have given him everything. Don't you see? It ended your strike, earned him the deal with the Shah, *and* he would have pocketed the money from the sale of the gold."

"Yes, I can see how that would work for him. Except for the money. If the plan had worked, the cash would be arriving in Corsica now."

"No, it would be on its way to some other destination he'd picked for it, you can be sure."

"But Signora, there was only one ship out there last night, and I was on it. It was manned entirely by patriotic Corsicans that I handpicked myself. So I can assure you, had the police not shown up when they did, that money would have gone nowhere else."

Jules's acceptance of the dupe she'd been, and her under-standing of DeRohan's monstrous conspiracy against her, was giving her a strange kind of security that she needed to carry her through this ordeal. His words pricked at the edges of that security, but she wasn't going to allow it to destabilize her.

"Well, I don't know what his plan was," she said, "but we can be sure it had no altruistic end. In any case, as far as I know, the money is sitting downstairs. So, when that crowd at the gate thins down in a day or two, you may come and take it back to Corsica as planned."

"It is your money now, Signora. Are you sure you want to do that?"

But she shook her head. "It's not my money, Father. It was stolen from the Corsican people. It belongs to them."

"That is most generous, Signora." He watched her closely for a few moments. "This has to have been unbelievably diffi-cult for you. Is there anything I can do to ease your burden?"

"No. Thank you, Father. I'm determined to learn from this experience. It's high time I grew up."

That afternoon, she met with a delegation made up of high ranking executives from all three divisions of DeRohan Enter-prises. Their appointed spokesman, Mr. Mathews, had flown in from London by aeroplane. He laid a briefcase full of pa-pers before her and asked her to sign them.

"Me?" she asked. "Why should I sign them?"

"Because your husband is . . . indisposed. They say he will recover, but he is being held incognito at an undisclosed hospi-tal and we're not allowed to communicate with him. Since DeRohan Enterprises is a privately owned company, only his wife has power of attorney in such a situation."

"I have no intention of signing any papers."

"But Mrs. DeRohan, the company is falling apart! These measures are imperative if it's to be saved."

"What you don't seem to understand, Mr. Mathews, is that I don't want it to be saved."

He glanced nervously at his associates. "I realized your husband felt that way, but we were hoping you might feel differently."

Jules frowned at him. "What do you mean, my husband felt that way?"

"I don't know if it is a part of the illness that has come over him, but for the past year, he seems to have been deliberately destroying this great company he founded. We've tried to fight him, but—for reasons we have never understood—he has been determined to systematically destroy himself."

"Mr. Mathews, let me assure you, you have been as deceived as the rest of us. It was all a ruse. Whatever losses he manipulated in order to seem vulnerable, I'm certain the money was funneled into some other part of his company."

Mathews stood. "And let me assure *you*, Mrs. DeRohan, whatever his purposes, the losses are quite real. As his financial manager, I can testify that this company is at death's door. And the reason is that Mr. DeRohan knowingly made bad decisions that were sure to wreck it. Not overnight, mind you, but in little steps along the way. And all this time, after the Rothschild crisis, when we were endeavoring to salvage the company, he refused to cooperate. One might almost say the man had embarked on a crusade of self-destruction."

Again, she felt a prick against the bubble of security that had been sustaining her since that terrible moment when Ladd had ripped off the mask from DeRohan's face. But she stamped it down with an iron will. "I'm certain, sirs, that whatever self-destruction was involved was all part of his gamble to get those oil leases."

"Begging your pardon, Mrs. DeRohan, but it was the faltering position of the company that was standing in the way of his getting the oil leases in the first place. So there is no logic to your reasoning."

"Mr. Mathews—" She felt herself flaring up. Taking a breath, she continued, "I don't pretend to understand the man's psychology. And truthfully, I don't really care. Nor do I care about the fate of his company. But perhaps I shall change my mind about that. So, in the meantime, if my signing these papers will keep you going for a while, I'll do it."

As they left, they crossed paths with her own attorney, Monsieur Breton, a short elderly man with snowy hair who'd been her father's French representative in the old days. "I want to be with you when the police question you again," he told her. "It is most important that you answer only as I direct you."

"I don't think they intend to charge me with anything," Jules argued. "They realize I'm a victim of the man."

"Still, it is most critical that your reputation not be compromised in any way. Those animals out there"—he pointed toward the front gate where the reporters were still camped—"are out for blood, and we do not want to give them anything to chew on."

"I intend to give the prosecution my utmost cooperation. I *can* testify against him, can't I? Even though I'm married to him?"

He blanched. "But, Juliana, you are no longer married to him."

"What do you mean? Of course I am."

"But you are not. Do you not recall the annulment papers? They contained your signature."

The papers she'd given DeRohan. "He signed them? He sent them to you?"

"But, of course, my dear. Nearly two weeks ago. They have been accepted and filed. You have been a free woman for the better part of a week."

Chapter 31

A month later, Dominic DeRohan sat reading on the cot in his cell of La Pérouse prison in Nice. Once the bullet had been removed and he'd been stitched up and allowed a few days in the hospital to recover from the loss of blood, his journey through the French criminal justice system had been swift. He'd dismissed the solicitor that had been provided him, and at the arraignment had pled guilty to all charges. With no defense offered, the highly anticipated trial had taken all of fifteen minutes. The verdict was a foregone conclusion. The sentence was twenty years, to be served in French Guiana, in the most dreaded of the nation's overseas penal colonies.

Devil's Island.

He was scheduled to ship out tomorrow at two PM.

Kept in isolation for most of this period, he had little knowledge of what was transpiring in the outside world. He knew, because the prison guards taunted him with it, that DeRohan Enterprises had filed for bankruptcy and that he was penniless. He'd seen Jules at the trial and they'd exchanged a brief glance in which he saw, in her eyes, the strength of her hatred for him. But he had no idea what was going on in her life, other than the fact that she'd retained her villa, a maintenance fund, and the jewels from the wreckage of DeRohan Enterprises. He'd made sure of that.

He hadn't planned for things to end quite this way, but now that they had, he was resigned to his fate and a strange kind of peace had settled over him. All his life, he'd been driven by an overwhelming ambition that had brought him nothing but misery. And now that he was no longer under its sway, he felt the respite of a man who had no options to trouble him. He'd never had time to be much of a reader before, but he'd taken to checking books out of the prison library and found he enjoyed both the escape they offered and the stimulation they provided his mind. He was particularly enjoying the novels of Balzac. He wanted to finish *Père Goriot* before having to leave it behind tomorrow.

He heard a key turn in the heavy lock and the squeal of the door as it was pulled open. "Time for your exercise, *monsieur le chat*," the guard greeted him.

The guard accompanied him on the walk down the long cell block and into the wide open space of the cobblestone courtyard. Outside, he would also keep a careful eye on DeRohan every second. The warden was taking no chances that this particular cat might decide to scale a wall and escape.

It was a sparkling early fall day with just a hint of brisk coolness in the air. La Pérouse may be a penal complex, but it was a prison on the French Riviera. Commanding a position of secluded prominence, it was built on a cliff just past the old town, at the foot of an ancient chateau, and afforded dazzling views of the glittering Baie des Anges—Bay of Angels—and the curving coastline below. The same view the Fauve painters had immortalized. Surely the most magnificent setting of any prison in the world.

A far cry from the sweltering jungles of Devil's Island.

DeRohan joined a circle of convicts walking a continuous circuit of the yard. At first, given his notoriety, he'd been something of a *cause célèbre* among the prisoners. But he'd remained aloof and they'd soon learned to keep their distance.

On this day, however, a wiry man with the face of a weasel

sidled up to him as they walked. "Blimey. They told me there was another Englishman in this place. I hoped it might be you. Tough break, them sending you off tomorrow."

DeRohan recognized Leroy the Louse, a small-time criminal he'd used to run several shady errands for him back in London. He wasn't especially happy to see a face from his past, but he said mildly, "Hello, Leroy. How's the world been treating you?"

"No better 'n yerself, gov'na. I was involved with a nifty little smuggling gig over in St-Trop, until the flics wised up to us."

"Pity." DeRohan wondered how he was going to get away from this worm.

"But I've got some interestin' news fer you. You know them blokes in the Verdun League you used to run with back in the old days? Smitty Sullivan and them blokes? Looks like they're about to do you a good turn."

"Oh? How's that?"

"That Habsburg wench who sent you up the river . . . they're goin' to get 'er fer you. I have it on good authority that they intend to snuff out 'er candle once and fer all."

DeRohan stopped so abruptly, the prisoner behind him banged into him. "What are you talking about?"

"It's all set up. Takes place tomorrow, it will, at the dedication ceremony for that war memorial up in the hills. They've got some inside man who'll be waltzing her right into the middle of the bull's-eye. Like a lamb to the slaughter, eh? So at least you can go to that hellhole knowing that tart will be taken care of. Now ain't that a pretty bit of news? Worth a bob er two, mayhap?"

Without a word, DeRohan turned, left the circle of convicts, and stormed toward the guard. "I need to see the warden."

Surprised, the guard responded, "He's in Paris all this week. In any event, what business could you possibly have with him at this late date?"

"You must get word to him. There's something I have to tell him. It's imperative."

"Things always get a bit imperative when that date with Devil's Island starts edging up on you. Now get back in line if you don't want the taste of my club."

DeRohan stumbled back in line. But his mind was racing now. Everything had changed.

He had to get out of here.

Fast.

The next morning, Jules came downstairs dressed in an understated beige silk suit designed by her friend Coco Chanel, carrying her matching cloche hat and gloves. Hudson was waiting for her in the vestibule, dressed in his best chauffeur's uniform as befitted this occasion—the dedication of the Great War Memorial.

Over the past month, her life had finally taken on some semblance of normalcy again. The reporters had abandoned their positions outside her gate. Her friends had called, expressing their concern, but she'd assured them all, with that same sense of tautly reined control, that there was no need for them to worry. She was fine. She resumed her round of social activities as if nothing had ever happened, laughing at people's witticisms and chatting with such an air of amiable nonchalance that they were soon convinced she was actually better off for her tragic experience.

On August twenty-third, Rudy Valentino died unexpectedly in New York of blood poisoning following a perforated ulcer. He was twenty-six. As the world mourned, the plans for the movie version of Booth Devlin's novel were scrapped, ending his guaranteed future for his wife's care. Jules and Dev began spending time together again and, without telling him, she sold off one of her jewels—enough to set up a fund to pay his wife's long-term medical expenses—and gave the proceeds to Rex Ingram. He, in turn, presented the money to Dev with the explanation that he wanted to buy the property anyway, and hoped to make the picture at a later date with another star.

To the outside world, it seemed that Jules had everything—

her villa, her gems, her glittering Riviera social whirl, and her monstrous husband finally out of her life. Far from harming her, the publicity had given her a kind of cachet that made her the most coveted party guest of European society. Beyond that, her friends marveled at the new composure they saw in her. She seemed more mature in every way. Stronger as a person. Infinitely more independent. She'd stopped relying on Hudson to oversee every aspect of her daily life. She no longer confided in him as she used to, maintaining the more coolly formal relationship of employer to employee. When she went out, she drove herself in the Austin Clifton roadster. She assumed management of Rêve de l'Amour, seeing to all the details and making the decisions that kept it running smoothly. To everyone, she seemed a new person.

But inside, Jules had never stopped being troubled about all that had happened to her, and the puzzling inconsistencies in DeRohan's plot against her. As she went about her day, as she gracefully chatted with friends, even as she slept, she couldn't banish the memory of that moment in the secret room just after he was unmasked and she'd almost killed him—the mournful look in his tortured eyes. And again at the trial, when, before pronouncing sentence, the judge had asked him if he had anything to say. Instead of speaking, he'd turned to look at her. And there, once again, was that profound expression in his eyes. What was it? Regret? Contrition? Forgiveness?

Love?

She didn't know. But it pierced right through her. She'd sat there trembling as he'd turned back to the judge and replied, "I have nothing to say."

That look haunted her.

Many was the night she thought: *This unsettling confusion is driving me mad. I must see him before he's transported half a world away. I need my hate for him to be renewed. Because he was right. My hatred for him is what keeps me strong.*

But the better part of her realized this was likely just another strategy of his to undermine her—a most effective strategy. Because it *was* getting to her. So the best thing she could do was drive it from her mind and let him be gone and out of her life forever.

It was in this confused state of mind that she'd gone against her instinct and agreed to attend the opening of the Great War Memorial. Everyone had been at her to make an appearance—Nikki, Dev, Sara, and Gerald. Even her attorney, Monsieur Breton, came forward with the argument that a gracious appearance at the event would once and for all smooth over any damage that had been done to her reputation by the unfortunate incident with the Panther.

So, finally beaten down—because it seemed so important to everyone—she agreed.

But now that it was upon her, and she was just about to leave the house for the drive up to Mont Gros, she was once again overcome with a feeling that something was wrong. A return of the old reluctance, perhaps, as she still felt in her heart that to go there would be to admit Habsburg guilt. She kept thinking of her father, of how ashamed he'd be to know she was giving in on this point.

But Hudson was waiting. He'd insisted on driving her today. It would only be proper for such an occasion. So she headed for the front door.

But as she passed the table in the vestibule, she noticed the morning newspaper folded there. Hudson hadn't brought it with her tray. And then, the word jumped out at her. "DeRohan."

She picked it up and read the headline:

PANTHER OFF TO JUNGLE TODAY
DEROHAN LEAVES FOR DEVIL'S ISLAND

Something froze inside her. Dropping the paper, she said, "I can't go."

Hudson looked alarmed. "But Highness, they're expecting you. You're to be one of the guests of honor."

"There may be time to catch the committee chairman before

he leaves. Find me his number, please. I'll telephone with my apologies."

"Begging your pardon, Highness, but you just can't do that!" There was an edge in his voice she'd never heard before.

She wheeled on him angrily. "It's not open to discussion, Hudson. I told you that—"

"But you *must* go. It's extremely important to me that you be there."

"Important to *you*?"

"Yes. To me. I was in the war, too, you know, and that memorial is important to me. I can't explain exactly why I want you to be there, but I do. I've served you faithfully for some time now, and I've never asked anything of you before. But I'm asking this now. Please. Please go. For me."

He was so agitated that it startled her. This insistence wasn't in his character at all. But she supposed it had something to do with the war wound they'd never spoken of in any detail. Put this way, she could hardly refuse.

And perhaps it *would* be better for her to go. If nothing else, it would take her mind off the images that had sprung forth as she'd read the headlines. DeRohan shackled, being led onto the ship. Perhaps looking back for the last time.

That tragic, inexplicable look in his eyes.

By the time the long ceremony was over, he'd be gone.

"Very well, Hudson," she sighed. "Bring the Rolls around."

The guard's footsteps echoed in the long corridor that housed the solitary confinement cells. The day before, La Pérouse's most notorious prisoner, Dominic DeRohan, had been dragged here by five guards after making a determined effort to storm the administration building and speak to someone—anyone— in authority. The man had finally cracked. Obviously, the reality had set in that he was about to begin a future in hell.

When he reached the Panther's cell, the guard knelt down and shoved open the slot in the bottom of the door with one hand while balancing the tray of food with the other—an early lunch before the prisoner was transported to the dock. But as he glanced inside, his eyes widened with alarm. He had a clear view of the cot and its surroundings, but the cell's inhabitant was nowhere in sight.

Frantically, he dropped the tray and fumbled for his keys. Within a second he'd opened the door to find an even more incongruous sight: the bare-chested prisoner hanging from the overhead light fixture—the noose made from his ripped-up prison shirt.

The guard yelled for assistance, then stepped inside, pulled out his penknife, stood on the cot, and cut down the prisoner. As the summoned help came flooding into the room, he put his ear to DeRohan's mouth. He was still breathing, but barely.

His parched lips parted and the faint words emerged. "Just let me die."

The prison doctor was called for. He appeared a few minutes later with his medical bag. He lifted the eyelids, one at a time, noting the way the eyes rolled back in their sockets. Then he removed his stethoscope and placed it to DeRohan's bare chest.

"It has to be a trick of some kind," the guard said.

After listening for a moment, the doctor pronounced, "This is no trick. This man isn't going to make it. Get him to the infirmary."

They carried him out of the high-security building, across the courtyard, to the east wing of the administration building where the prison hospital was housed. There, they laid him on a metal table. Orderlies came and went, each one looking at him and taking his pulse, only to shake their heads and leave again.

DeRohan let a few minutes pass, then, the room empty, he leapt off the table, went to the door, and cracked it to see what was going on in the hallway. A guard was coming his way.

DeRohan waited until he was passing, then flung open the door and pounced on him. In quick succession, he rendered him unconscious, yanked him into the infirmary, stripped him, put on his uniform, and buckled the holstered gun about his own hips.

As he walked toward the guard station at the end of the hall, he realized he was still shaky from the minutes he'd hung there, lowering his body metabolism to the point where his pulse would be so faint it would barely be detectable—an old trick they'd taught pilots in the Royal Flying Corps in case of capture during the war.

The sentry was sitting at a table with a clipboard in front of him. He looked up as DeRohan passed. "Hey, you. You're not—"

In a flash, DeRohan's fist knocked him cold. At that moment, several other people entered the corridor and noticed the guard lying on the floor. DeRohan called out in French, "This man's had a heart attack. Come and help him. I'm going to fetch the doctor."

With that, he hastened out the front door into the prison courtyard. Fingering the pistol in the holster, he walked as calmly as possible out the gate and emerged on a busy street.

He had no idea how much time he had. He guessed he had no more than an hour to reach the dedication site. How to get there in time?

Suddenly the air was split by the wail of the prison siren. They were on to him.

With no time to think, he stepped into the street and held his hands high to stop the first auto that came along. A bald man rolled down the window and said, "Yes, Officer, what is wrong?"

DeRohan approached the open window, put the pistol to the man's head, and said, "Get out."

He opened the door and pulled the startled man out. As he drove off, he saw Inspector Ladd and two of his men drive past him. He'd obviously been told about the Panther's "suicide" and had rushed over. Ladd screeched to a halt and looked back, his face contorted in shock.

Dammit, he recognized me.

DeRohan put the accelerator to the floor. As he zoomed away, he looked in the rearview mirror and saw that Ladd had performed a hasty U-turn and was in frantic pursuit.

Chapter 32

The site of the Great War Memorial looked much changed since the last time Jules had seen it. The towering statue of the grieving mother and her fallen son was completed. Hundreds of people had made the journey for the dedication and were spread out over the site—many of them veterans in their old uniforms. Some of them had been terribly maimed—armless, legless, with patches over one eye, with scarred faces, with coughs that had never gone away after suffering the effects of mustard gas in the trenches. The idea that they'd come here in the spirit of reconciliation, not just from France, Germany, Britain, and the rest of Europe, but from all over the world—America, Australia, the Asian and African colonies—was unexpectedly moving. All these people wounded in some way or another, all needing whatever balm this day could give them. But as an usher led her to a seat in the front row with the other dignitaries, Jules was nervous. She had no idea what she was going to say when it was her turn to speak.

A band from the *USS Lexington,* berthed in Villefranche, played a medley of national anthems of the many countries represented here today. As they did, dozens of white doves were released from their pens to fly overhead. The French President, Raymond Poincaré, made a windy welcoming speech. Then, one by one, the invited speakers took the podium and gave their words of convocation, each in his own language as an interpreter translated into French.

As the speeches continued, the words washed over Jules.

In another hour, he'd be gone forever.

Once that ship leaves the shore, I'll finally stop thinking about him.

She looked around her at the brilliant day, at the rapt faces that took in every word of the addresses, at the grieving visage of the granite mother high above. All around her, she heard the sounds of sniffling, of sobbing, of the cleared throats of men pushing back raw emotions.

In the midst of all this, her mind wandered back to that day when she'd come up here with Booth Devlin—and how she'd thought at the time that he was the Panther. Looking back on it now, the suspicion seemed absurd. And yet, the truth was, she'd never *really* thought the Panther was Dev. She'd thought he was a separate identity that had emerged from him—the better part of him, a part that was so pure and heroic that it couldn't even exist in the light of day.

The same thing she'd thought about Nikki.

Even when she was convinced the Panther had evolved out of her childhood friend, she'd never really thought he *was* the shallow, aimless Nikki. She'd thought the Panther was his other, grander self.

It was the same with Father Siffredi—and even briefly with Hudson. She'd never really believed any of those men *were* the Panther, but rather their magical midnight persona. The part of them that was larger than the limitations and scars of their everyday lives. The secret self she could love.

And then she saw DeRohan's haunting eyes and the world moved beneath her feet.

It hadn't once occurred to her.

She'd been right all along.

Except that the Panther wasn't a separate identity that had

been secreted in these other men. He'd come out of the wreck of Dominic DeRohan.

The Panther was DeRohan's real self. The one he'd never been allowed to show. The one *she'd* never allowed him to show.

And in this identity . . .

DeRohan was everything she'd thought the Panther was.

Things he'd said to her—things she'd rejected before—came back to her now.

Once you let go of that compulsion to cling to the symbols of a past that is dead, you can simply walk away.

Break the curse. It's not the being, it's the doing that defines you.

Take your pain and find a way to use it, to do something with it.

He hadn't been using her after all!

Everything he'd said as the Panther had been sincere. And everything he'd done in that guise had been . . . for her.

The thought was so shattering that she lost all sense of her surroundings. She had no idea how long she'd sat there in the immobilizing grip of this revelation. But at some point, she faintly heard her name echoing around her, and then someone touched her arm and said, "It's time for you to speak, Mademoiselle von Habsburg."

She felt herself rise and walk up the stairs to the raised podium. In a blur, she saw the sea of faces staring up at her. The usher adjusted the microphone for her, and for what must have seemed an eternity, she just stood there in mute silence.

In her daze, she began to realize that the moment had become awkward for everyone. People were beginning to shift uncomfortably in their seats. She thought of DeRohan, perhaps even now being led onto the ship that would take him from her life.

And all at once, she knew what she was going to say.

What she had to say.

Finally, she leaned into the microphone. "I must tell you good people that I didn't want to come here today," she began in French. "I had to be forced into it. Once I had been, I dreaded it. Even as late as an hour ago, I was trying to get out of coming here. Because the truth is, I was resisting the idea behind this memorial, which is asking us to give up the grudges, the assumptions, the hatreds of the past. The fact is, I did not want to give up that past. Something in me needed to cling to it. I needed to hold on to my family and that dead world they represented. And I was afraid that, by coming here, I was accepting the idea that my family was directly responsible for the war."

As she spoke, her eyes were occasionally distracted by the glint of something in the distance. Gradually, the object came into view: an automobile racing up the Corniche at breakneck speed. Behind it, a line of police cars followed.

"But as I arrived, and saw how many of you had come here today to embrace this idea, I was suddenly ashamed of myself. Something is happening to me—I'm not certain I could even explain to you what it is. But I realize now that I have been profoundly wrong. Not long ago, a wise man came out of the night to tell me that I must give up the past—that I must free myself from it. That I was its victim and its prisoner. Who this man was, I do not know. Where this man came from, I do not know. Even if the clay from which he was formed was evil, the creation he became was noble, and his motive benevolent. And everything he did was in an effort to help me free myself from this crushing bondage. I wouldn't do it. I fought him, too. But he was right all along."

The auto in the distance and the cortege behind it had come closer and closer. She paused, thinking it must be some late-arriving dignitary being given an escort. The vehicle turned into the site on two wheels and pulled to an abrupt halt. As a uniformed man jumped out of the car and began to make his way toward the assembly, she turned her attention from him and continued.

"So I'm here to tell you now that, with you, I am giving up this past. I humbly apologize for my family's role in this devastating war. Whatever blame history wants to place on us, I willingly accept. And now I join hands with all of you in what I hope will be a new beginning for the world. My only regret is that I don't have the chance to tell that man how grateful I am. And that I love him—no matter where he came from."

As applause rang out, the late arrival was charging up the aisle. Abruptly, the applause stopped. On its heels was a collective gasp. It wasn't due to this man's disruptive presence, because they couldn't even see him. Rather, it was aimed at the stage, where someone had joined her at the podium.

Hudson.

Pointing a pistol at her head.

When he saw what was happening, DeRohan slowed his approach. But he kept coming.

Just then, a scuffle broke out in the audience to his left. Another man stood with a drawn pistol—no doubt, the intended Verdun League assassin—but in the wake of what was happening on stage, several of the former soldiers jumped him and he was quickly disarmed.

Hudson had seen DeRohan coming and, recognizing him, had panicked and put the gun to her head. He now looked dazed, as if he might already be regretting this impulse to save the assassination at all costs, but was now stuck with it.

He cocked the hammer.

DeRohan called up to the stage, "Don't do it, Harry."

He kept advancing, releasing the flap of his borrowed holster as he did. He'd been keeping his gaze on Hudson, but as he came closer, he couldn't help but take hasty stock of Jules. She was breathtakingly beautiful. She'd been looking at Hudson in shock, but when DeRohan had spoken and she realized who he was, she'd turned to him and a light came to her eyes.

He saw no fear whatsoever.

In fact, once she looked at him, she never took her gaze off his face.

Behind him, he heard the police cars squeal onto the site and the sound of slamming doors. Now his pursuers were rushing up the aisle after him. He didn't have long.

He heard Ladd's voice. "Freeze, DeRohan!"

Ignoring it, he walked up the steps to the podium, piercing Hudson with his glare. As he moved closer still, he lowered his voice so that no one but the three of them could hear. "For the love of God, Harry, how did this ever happen?"

Hudson kept the gun to Jules's head. "They found me out, Dom. Those bastards from the Verdun League. They forced me into helping them. They said if I didn't, they would tell the world my secret—and you know I would do anything to keep that from happening."

"You should have told me," DeRohan said. "We could have faced them down together, just as we did in the war. You should have had some faith in me—in our friendship. But I can still help. Put the gun down and we can figure this out together."

Sweat dripped from Hudson's brow. "It's too late. But if I go through with it, at least it will keep the world from knowing what I did."

"You'd kill my wife?"

"I have to, Dom, don't you see?"

DeRohan's temper flared. "You Judas! You swore to look after her for me. I trusted you. You were the one man in this whole bloody world I knew I could trust to protect her."

Hudson wiped the sweat from his eyes with his sleeve. But he kept the gun trained on Jules's temple. "I didn't want to betray you. You have to believe that. You're the last man in the world I want to betray. I want a way out of it, but I just . . . don't . . . know . . . what to do."

DeRohan could hear Ladd and his men on the steps below him. Within seconds, their presence on the stage would force the issue. He had to do something.

Now.

He lunged for Hudson's gun.

Hudson swiveled out of his way, then took a step back, pointing the pistol now at DeRohan. Tears were streaming down his face.

DeRohan took a step, putting himself between Hudson and Jules. "Now you can pull the trigger, Harry."

Hudson was sobbing by now. He raised the gun to DeRohan's chest and started to pull the trigger. But he just couldn't do it. Slowly, he dropped the weapon to his side. Then, remembering the position he was in, his eyes went wild. He put the pistol into his own mouth and pulled the trigger, blowing his brains out the back of his head.

The report echoed throughout the assembly. But instead of the outcry one might have expected, it left a deathly silence.

For some time, no one moved. No one breathed. Then, finally, Ladd and his men came forward and grabbed DeRohan by the arms. He didn't fight them. He let them disarm him. He offered his wrists for the handcuffs. He turned to Jules as they began to take him away.

But she quickly stepped forward and said, "I'm afraid you've made a mistake, Inspector."

He paused, giving her a quizzical look. "Yes, I have, but I'm about to correct it."

Once again, he began to pull DeRohan away.

"But you've got the wrong man."

Again, Ladd stopped. This time he fixed her with a shrewd stare. "Ma'am, it's late in the day and I have no patience for—"

"I'm afraid you're going to have to be patient for just a while longer. Because this man isn't the Panther. The Panther just committed suicide."

Ladd's eyes were clouded with a troubled mixture of suspicion and confusion. "Exactly what are you trying to tell me, Mrs. DeRohan?"

"I am trying to tell you, Inspector, that all these months, I have been the terrified prisoner of that villain lying there." She pointed at Hudson. "And now that I'm free of his evil grip, I can finally tell the truth. A terrible injustice has been committed. *This* man . . ." she put her hand on DeRohan's arm ". . . my husband . . . is completely innocent."

Chapter 33

Despite Jules's dramatic new testimony, DeRohan wasn't immediately released. He was taken back to La Pérouse, pending a reopening of the case. Two days later, a private hearing was convened, presided over by the same judge who'd sentenced DeRohan to twenty years of hard labor. Jules took the stand and elaborated on the story she'd told in the aftermath of the Great War Memorial tragedy: how she'd been the terrorized prisoner of her butler, the Panther. When Ladd attempted to poke holes in her story, she had an answer for everything, creating an alternate scenario that explained all that had happened.

"But my good woman," Ladd exclaimed, "we were there at the unmasking of the Panther when you were so angry at your husband's deception that you almost killed him!"

Calmly, she replied, "True, Inspector, but as you may recall, Hudson was in the room at the time, orchestrating my reaction to the unmasking."

"And just how, pray tell, do you explain the fact that Mr. DeRohan was on the roof, in the Panther costume, and wounded by one of my men?"

"When the police raided the house, Hudson knew he was about to be discovered. So he hatched the twisted idea of forcing my husband into his costume and sending him out on the roof, where he would be shot down and hopefully killed.

DeRohan would be blamed for the crime spree, and Hudson would go free and continue to hold me his prisoner. It nearly worked. But thankfully your police weren't the accurate shots Hudson had hoped. When my husband was arrested, he couldn't tell the truth because he knew I'd be killed. That's why he didn't put forth a defense. Then, when Hudson saw DeRohan coming to rescue me from his clutches at the ceremony, he panicked. And you know the rest."

Ladd didn't believe a word of it. But he was powerless. He had nothing to counteract it except his instinct. Besides which, hundreds of witnesses had watched the butler Harry Hudson point a gun at her head and had seen DeRohan gallantly save her life. It was clear to the world who was the villain and who the hero of this tale.

And whatever embarrassment this reversal might have caused to his career was offset by his capture of the Verdun League assassin who'd been overpowered by the crowd. After a full day of interrogation, Ladd had managed to break down the man and get him to divulge the names of all the members of the League. He'd cabled Scotland Yard, the conspirators had all been arrested, and were on their way to Wormwood Scrubs. The papers were lauding Ladd as a mastermind of detection.

So when, at the end of the hearing, the judge set DeRohan free, Ladd decided to let the matter drop.

As they walked out of the courthouse and into the early autumn sun, the inspector cleared his throat, then turned to DeRohan, saying, "Well, you're a free man again. You're entitled to one last ride on the French nation. Is there someplace I can drop you?"

DeRohan looked around him at the traffic passing in the street as if he hadn't thought about what he'd do once this was all over.

Before he could answer, Jules said, "I came by taxi this morning. Could I trouble you for a ride, as well, Inspector?"

"Of course."

"In that case, you may drop us both at Rêve de l'Amour."

DeRohan turned to her. Their eyes locked briefly, then once again he looked away at the street before them.

On the ride back to Cap Ferrat, no one spoke. The silence was heavy and uncomfortable. Jules stared out the window, watching the passing scenery—the flashes of blueberry sea, the palms swaying in the breeze, the green hills dotted with white villas—churning with a mixture of emotions. Relief now that it was over. Uncertainty as to where they would go from here. Dread at the thought of going back to the house with all its painful memories.

But drowning out all this was a barrage of unanswered questions. Why had DeRohan done all this? Who *was* this man, anyway? This man she loved, yet didn't really know except in two fractured guises.

Nothing could happen—no decisions could be made—until she knew everything.

It couldn't wait. She had to know. Now.

"Stop the car!"

Startled by her urgency, Ladd slammed on the brakes. The car screeched to a halt just short of the turnoff to Cap Ferrat.

"We shall walk from here," Jules told him.

Both men were looking at her with surprise.

After a slight pause, Ladd said, "Very well." Setting the hand brake, he turned in his seat. "Whether or not justice has been served today, I trust that the reign of the Panther is over."

DeRohan met his gaze. "I think you may rest assured that the cat has had his last prowl."

He and Jules got out of the car and, with a last shake of his head, the inspector drove off.

As the Peugeot sped away, Jules glanced at DeRohan, who, now clean shaven, looked tired but handsome in the dark grey suit she'd brought for him to wear to court. She suddenly felt very much alone with him. It made her nervous. She rubbed her damp palms together and said, "I can't bear the thought of going back to that house just yet. Let's go down to Villefranche and walk back along the beach."

"If you'd like."

"What I'd like is for you to tell me *everything*. Everything you've kept from me. Why you've done all this."

"There's a great deal to tell."

"We have nothing but time."

They set off down the road, meandering their way through the medieval village that clung to the steep hillside, down the stone steps, through the pleasant courtyard by St-Michel Church, past narrow alleyways filled with shops and cafes. There were flowers everywhere, vivid splashes of orange, red, yellow, and pink. Jules let him gather his thoughts as they walked.

They came out of the stone warren that dead-ended on the tiny Villefranche harbor. To their right was the Welcome Hotel, where the artist Jean Cocteau held court. To the left, down the street, was the sandy crescent beach where Jules had swum with Nikki a lifetime ago. Navy ships gleamed in the harbor, while closer in small fishing boats painted blue, red, and yellow bobbed with the tide.

They turned left, passing bistros where a handful of people dined outdoors. The smell of fish was pungent from the fish stalls along the quay. An old man wandered about, playing the accordion.

DeRohan walked beside Jules, his hands thrust deep into his pockets. He said nothing until they reached the now deserted beach. Until they'd climbed down from the quay, using the large flat rocks as steps, and had begun a slow stroll along the sand.

Before them, a half mile ahead, jutting out into the sea, was the peninsula of Cap Ferrat. Waiting for him to begin, Jules scanned it with her eyes. There, at the top, on the narrowest strip high above everything else, was Rêve de l'Amour, gleaming distantly in the sun. It looked so peaceful from here, yet it had been the site of so much strife between them.

"There's no way to tell it so you'll really understand without going back to the beginning."

"I told you, I want to hear everything."

He nodded, then started slowly, telling the tale of a little boy who'd spent his first years in the grinding poverty of London's East End. His father a petty rogue who'd been killed in a drunken brawl. His mother a good, hardworking woman who'd barely managed to make ends meet for Dominic and his baby sister Rose by taking in laundry. He spoke of how this boy, at the age of ten—determined to provide for the starving family— had stowed away on a departing ship for the South of France, where so many wealthy Englishmen had migrated. With no jobs to be had in London for a Stepney slum lad, he reasoned that a British aristocrat far from home might well covet the services of an enterprising English-speaking errand boy.

He'd judged rightly. When he presented himself at the villa of Lord Beckingham in Cannes, the impressed earl hired him on the spot. For two years, the boy thrived there. Discovering a natural affinity for languages, he quickly leaned both French and Italian from other workers on the estate. Then one day something happened. The boy, dressed in his first good clothes, given to him by the lady of the house, on an important errand . . . splashed by mud from a Habsburg carriage . . . unbearable humiliation . . . a little girl laughing out the window at him . . . Then, when he returned to the estate, drenched in mud, the important errand unfulfilled, the word reached him of his mother's death. The cause: tuberculosis complicated by malnutrition.

At this point, he paused, bending to take up a handful of sand, letting it slip through his fingers.

With a kind of horror, Jules suddenly remembered the incident he'd spoken of. "*You* were that boy . . . My God."

He tossed the sand aside. "Yes, I was that little bugger."

"And that was the genesis of your hatred of the Habsburgs?"

"The two events became fused in my mind. The humiliation . . . my mother's ignoble death. Malnutrition. Christ! She'd starved to death. That day twisted me. I vowed I'd someday have revenge, both for what had been done to my mother and the indignity I'd suffered. I became ferociously ambitious—

power mad, really—and I returned to London where the real money was being made. With Lord Beckingham's recommendation, and my knowledge of foreign languages, I found employment as an apprentice at a stock brokerage, where my talents turned out to be particularly well suited. When I came of age, I became a broker myself. I was in my element."

A seagull made a cawing dive in front of them and DeRohan took a moment to watch it pick up a sand crab and fly away.

"Anyway, I did quite well at Richards and Lloyd Ltd. Quite well, indeed. Then the war broke out. At first, it was called The Habsburg War, and that alone made me want to get in it. I signed up right away and managed to get into the Royal Flying Corps. I flew thirty-five missions over the Western Front and earned my share of decorations. But on my thirty-sixth mission, I was shot down behind enemy lines and ended up in a prisoner of war camp near Stuttgart. I was there for eight months. That's where I met Harry Hudson."

"You'd known him that long," Jules marveled. "Neither of you let on to me once."

"Harry had been there for almost a year before I arrived and he'd cracked under the pressure. He did something in that state that seemed to him—would seem to any veteran of the war—to be unspeakable. The guilt he felt over this crime crushed him. That's the real war wound he told you of. By chance, I found out his awful secret. I felt sorry for him. So when I escaped, I took him with me. When he learned that I knew what he'd done, he tried to kill himself out of shame. Put the gun right in his mouth, just as he did the other day. But I stopped him. We trudged together for two weeks before we reached the Allied lines. Harry was sick through much of that journey, and I carried him through half the way. After that, he was supremely grateful to me. He swore he just wanted to spend the rest of his life repaying the debt of gratitude he felt. This seemed crucial to him, as if by doing so he might make up for some of the guilt he still felt. And since his family had been in service for three generations, I simply put him to work for me."

"What *was* the awful thing he did?"

DeRohan had been staring out at the sea, but he looked at her then, assessingly. "Do you remember that moment in the Carlton when I offered to let you see the Rothschild letter? And you said we'd allow them their privacy?"

She nodded.

"I'll make you the same offer now. I shall tell you if you really want to know. But you'd be better off not knowing."

Jules considered the matter for a moment. "Then my answer is the same."

As she had that night at the Carlton, she saw the flash of respect in his eyes. But they were soon clouded again with some dark memory.

"The war took a terrible toll on everyone. I was no exception. The horror, the death, what happened to my sister Rose— it all served to make the twisted streak in me even blacker than it was."

"What happened to Rose?"

"She was in a building that took a direct hit from a zeppelin bomb."

"She died?"

"Not immediately. She managed to stay alive for a couple of months. It was after I'd made my escape and was back in London. I nursed her the best I could, but her internal injuries wouldn't heal. And she was horribly shell-shocked. Often, the slightest noise would set her off and she would scream for hours. Other times, the same catalyst would send her into days of catatonic withdrawal. Nothing the doctors did seemed to have the slightest effect. One morning, I came with her breakfast and found she'd died in her sleep."

"I'm so sorry," Jules said.

For a moment he didn't speak, the pain etched on his face. Once again he began walking. "The war only deepened my hatred for the Habsburgs. For a time, just after the Armistice, I even flirted with the Verdun League—before I realized they were a pack of lunatics. But most of all, it made me reckless, ruthless. Unscrupulous in my business dealings. Determined to become so powerful that I would be above all the misery I'd been mucking in all my life. I channeled all that drive and ambition into making myself so wealthy and powerful that I would be the master of my own destiny. Taught myself the things I'd need to succeed—how to pass myself off as a gentleman of fortune, how to speak, what clothes to wear. Began collecting the possessions I'd need to symbolize my transformation—symbols of status and privilege. Had myself tutored in the trappings of a university education so I could hold my own in any company. But it was all an act. I did it all with a cold and calculated purpose. I was every despicable thing you ever heard about me and more. I used women heartlessly, and when I grew bored with them, I tossed them aside. I cheated and blackmailed and cheerfully drove my competitors to ruin. After a while, everything I touched turned to gold, even when I wasn't trying. And the horror was, the more successful I became, the more miserable I felt. It began to dawn on me that, no matter how vast my empire became, it was *never* going to give me satisfaction or fulfillment. And Jules, I tell you, that's a scary realization for a man."

He'd never called her Jules before. She watched the flutter of emotions cross his face as he laid himself bare. "So what did you do?"

"I thought back on that boy with the mud on his clothes. I wanted to become him again. I thought: if I could just get back at the Habsburgs for him, for what they'd done to him, for what they would do to his sister—everything would be all right. That I'd find peace again. So I went back to the scene of the crime. I bought the Carlton Hotel. And I began to stake out that old man, your father, now himself humbled from what he'd been."

Jules stopped walking. She suddenly didn't want to hear what he was going to say.

As if reading her mind, he asked, "Can you take this?"

Chapter 34

It was the moment she'd been dreading most. She feared that hearing it would stir up all the old feelings, would spoil her resolution to listen with an open heart. But she knew she would never fully understand if he left out this critical portion of the tale. So she took a slow breath and told him, "If you can say it, I can take it."

He nodded, then slowly began to speak once more. "I became obsessed with finishing him off, crazed with the idea that this was the thing that would give me the satisfaction I sought. I got him involved in that baccarat game. I didn't cheat, but believe me, I would have if I'd had to. I won all his money, then I tricked him into going even further so I could take your house and jewels. And when even this didn't give me the balm I needed, I had a further inspiration. I'd take his daughter as well. The same daughter who'd laughed at the little boy I'd been. I'd force her to submit to me in the way generations of Habsburg women before her had been auctioned off like whores to conquerors and other royal houses—as a means of preserving and extending Habsburg power. The irony, the justice of it, just seemed too perfect to resist. So I married her."

Jules felt the need to sit. She stepped over to one of the large flat rocks fronting the beach and sat down on it, hugging her knees, waiting for him to resume—even though what was to come filled her with trepidation. Up to this point, this narrative had been *his* saga. But now, it was her story as well.

He stooped, picked up a handful of pebbles, and began flinging them toward the gentle surf.

"This marriage represented a moment of triumph and vindication for the little boy with mud on his face," he continued. "But then, just as I realized that it, too, wasn't going to give me the fulfillment I craved, an extraordinary thing happened. I fell in love with you. It happened in that instant, right after the wedding, when you spat in my face. Remember? You said, 'I did this for my father, but no matter what you do, I will never allow you in my bed. I will never live under the same roof with you. Mr. DeRohan, you may go straight to hell.'"

He turned and looked at her, and she could see the tenderness in his eyes. She vividly recalled the moment and the vehemence with which she'd cursed him.

"I can't explain it," he told her. "I'd never loved anyone in my life—outside my family. But I realized in that *instant* that you were the most magnificent creature I'd ever encountered, and I was madly in love with you. I have been ever since. In one way or another, it's determined every move I've made since that moment."

The breeze blew a strand of hair in her face. She brushed it aside, saying, "But you gave me not the slightest indication. Your manner was so cold . . . so uncaring . . ."

"I wanted to, but I didn't know how. I had no idea how to tell a woman I cared for her. Nothing in my experience had ever prepared me for that—least of all, a woman like you. To do so seemed . . . a contemptible weakness. Then things began to happen that would make any closeness between us impossible."

"My father."

"This is the part that's most difficult for me to tell, and I know, the part that you'll resist the most. All I can say is that verification for what I'm about to relate is on file in the Vienna police department. You can see it if you wish." He tossed another pebble toward the water. "I'm sure you've heard something of the Manheim Conspiracy. It was a plot hatched in 1922 by a deranged Austrian general named Gunther Manheim to return the Habsburg Dynasty to power. Part of this insane plan involved immobilizing the Vienna police force by dumping barrels of strychnine into the city's water system—never mind that it was going to kill much of the rest of the population as well. As you probably know, Manheim was arrested before he could carry out his mass murder. But what you didn't know was that he'd enticed your father into his scheme."

She shot to her feet. "No, it can't be true."

"You have to realize, Jules, that he wasn't himself. Manheim came to him and stirred his dreams of a new Habsburg glory, and in his deranged state, he grabbed at it. The Manheim ring was broken the same week of our marriage. I learned shortly thereafter that your father was soon to be arrested and extradited to Austria. That's when I went to him in his study. I closed the door. I gave him my pistol. I told him if he chose to do the honorable thing, I'd make sure his name was never linked to this unspeakable plot. I'd keep his shame out of the history books. He took me up on my offer."

A single tear trickled down her cheek. In her heart, she knew it was true. In the state he was in, her father would have been susceptible to the twisted dream of a man like Gunther Manheim.

"Can you hear more?" he asked gently.

She wiped away the tear and nodded.

"After that, you and I seemed to have no chance whatsoever. You held me responsible for your father's death, and I couldn't very well tell you the truth. First, you wouldn't have believed me. And second, I didn't want to destroy your pride and good feelings for your father. You hated me more and more with every passing day. And I loved you more. I'd tried to keep you close to me by stipulating in our agreement that you must live in London, but you found that damned loophole and moved into your own place. I rarely even got to see you, but I kept close watch on everything you did. When you took up with Edwin, it tore my heart out. But I did nothing until I discovered, through a private detective I had watching him, that he was a member of the Verdun League. I learned the details from some of my old contacts in the organization. Edwin Monahan had been sent to win your confidence any way he could and lure you to a concert at the Royal Albert Hall, where the Royal Family would be in attendance. He wanted to kill you, Jules. In the most public way possible. He was never a poet. He was an assassin."

Jules sat back down. Once again, she knew what he was saying had to be true. Now that she thought back on it, she was hit by all the little things in Edwin's character that hadn't added up. The things she hadn't wanted to see.

She'd walked right into the trap.

"I couldn't prove what I knew in a court of law. And I knew that if I stopped this particular attempt, there would soon be another. So the only way I could stop it for good was to sever their link to you: Edwin. I goaded him into a duel. Incidentally, the bastard was a dead shot, with numerous decorations for marksmanship during the war. I wasn't even sure I could outshoot him. Regardless, that night of the concert, I challenged him. I found him at a tavern gulping down courage before picking you up. I flung a drink into his face. He had a job to do and wanted no part of this, so I had to force him into it. I left him no way out. Whatever Edwin was, he considered himself a gentleman. So when I slapped his face and called him a coward in front of fifty people, he had no choice but to follow me to Hyde Park with the clientele of the pub clamoring behind. As you know, I came out best in that confrontation. Intending to explain, I went to you and said, 'I've just killed your lover,' but the hatred I saw on your face backed me down. That's when you went to France."

Jules thought back on Edwin's sweet words to her and the insincerity galled her. She suddenly hated him. She wished she'd been there to see the smirk on DeRohan's face when he'd put a bullet through his brain.

There was a drawn out silence between them. DeRohan picked up more pebbles and pitched them across the surface of the water. The sun was high in the sky.

"Go on," she prompted.

"When you left, it devastated me. You'd broken our contract and I could have forced you back to London, but what good would that have done me? I decided I had to leave you alone. But after Edwin, I was concerned about your safety. I dispatched Harry to Cap Ferrat with instructions to somehow ingratiate himself into your employment and watch out for you. We agreed that he should tell you he'd been injured in the war so you'd feel no threat from him."

Jules thought back on the day Hudson had so fortuitously saved her from drowning. He must have been watching her for weeks, waiting for his opportunity.

DeRohan crossed the patch of beach and sat down beside her. "I found in your absence that I'd lost all interest in my businesses. I was stuck with this insurmountable dilemma. I was in love with a woman who utterly detested me. I lay awake nights dreaming of ways to overcome the impossible. One night, it hit me. If I could break the hold of your Habsburg past— which was symbolized by your house, but mostly by your jewels—I might just have a chance with you. I could, of course, take the jewels away, because you'd broken our agreement. But if I did that, you'd hate me all the more. And they'd still exist as this thing I'd personally denied you. So the problem was: how do I get the jewels away from you without you knowing I had anything to do with it?"

"The Panther."

"One night, I was walking down the Strand in this tortured state, searching for an idea, when I passed a bookstall and saw this novel called *Man on the Roof*."

"Dev's book!"

He nodded. "I don't know what made me pick it up. Fate, I suppose. But I opened it and read the dust jacket and when I saw the words 'cat burglar,' this incredible plan leapt into my mind.

What if I could create this cat burglar character? What if he became famous for his burglaries all over the Côte? And what if, in the process of that spree, he stole the Habsburg jewels? It seemed perfect. It would take the jewels away from you, and you couldn't blame me—you'd blame the cat burglar. Then, in time, you'd be a different person. As DeRohan, I would be sympathetic and hopefully we could make a fresh start. I even had an alternate plan. If it didn't work, and you still hated me, I could miraculously rescue the jewels and give them back to you, and I'd be your hero. You'd feel grateful to me, and maybe from there we could build a life together. As crazy as it sounds, that's what I was thinking."

"Never realizing you were creating a character I was bound to fall in love with."

"No. That didn't occur to me until much later. At the time, I was just fired up by the brilliance and audacity of my scheme. It was like coming out of a dark tunnel. Suddenly, I had a mission in life. Because I'd been a pilot, the idea of heights thrilled me. As a kid, there were times when I had to nip to stay alive, so I knew how to steal. I put all my businesses in the hands of my associates. Spent nine months physically training myself, working with a gymnastics instructor from London University, making myself the perfect physical specimen for the task. Secretly came to the Côte and began a series of robberies— robberies meant to make the lifting of your jewels seem just one more heist. Harry, who knew of my plans—"

She interrupted him. "You mean to tell me that all those times when I spoke to Hudson about the Panther . . . he knew it was you all along?"

"From the beginning. He was my confederate. Anyway, it was well known that you kept the jewels in the bank vault in Nice. I was building the Panther's reputation so no one would be surprised when he crowned his career with a daring heist of the Nice Banque de Marchés. But then, the story reached me— the story you planted—that you'd taken the emeralds out of the vault and would be wearing them to the Richardson ball. It seemed Heaven sent. I knew the grounds of the estate. I knew you'd put them in the wall safe in the upstairs study so there was no chance of being seen by you. That was important, as I didn't know how my disguise would hold up to someone who knew me. You were never supposed to wake up, never supposed to see me. But of course, you had a plan of your own. Even when you surprised me that night, I had no intention of ever speaking to you. I tried to get out of there as fast as I could. But your proposition stopped me. You can imagine my shock when you asked me to kill your husband for you."

"You must have thought me dreadful, asking you to kill—yourself."

He smiled, but merely continued. "As you spoke, I realized my disguise was even better than I'd hoped—that you didn't suspect who I was. So I listened. And gradually, it occurred to me that this was an opportunity to see inside your mind, to understand what I would have to overcome if I was ever to win your heart. Then you told me your story. You spoke with such dignity and courage that it tore me up inside. And afterwards, I realized I could actually have you. I could make love to my wife. Just once, I could touch you the way I'd longed to for so many years. I could let you know my feelings, if not with words, with my body. Selfishly, I seized that opportunity. And it was more exquisite than I'd ever dreamt it could be."

He looked at her, his eyes shining with love.

"As you know, I tried to stay away from you. But I found I couldn't. So I began to come to you as the Panther. I was fairly certain I could keep up the masquerade since we hadn't spent much time together and I was basically a stranger to you. Meanwhile, I found myself playing out this perverse strategy. I discovered that the meaner I was to you as DeRohan, the more it pushed you into the arms of the Panther—and the stronger it made you. So I was playing this game. By day, I was punishing you as DeRohan so I could offer you sweet consolation as the Panther at night. Behind a mask, I could tell you all the things I really felt. I knew it had to end. I was doing so much damage to whatever future DeRohan might have with you . . . yet there could be no future with the Panther."

She smiled ruefully at him. "I can see your dilemma."

"Then," he said forcefully, ignoring her, "I got the idea of destroying DeRohan completely. I simply did not want to be that man anymore. And I decided if I was asking you to give up your past, I had to do the same. So I set out to commit suicide—or, more correctly, to kill your husband as you'd asked. Together, we destroyed him. First with the Rothschild letter, then by trashing his chances with the Shah. So in a manner of speaking, Dominic DeRohan really doesn't exist."

"Doesn't he?"

"He died in stages after he forced you into marriage. And now his empire is but a memory, never to be resurrected again."

A silence ensued. The story was over. It made so many things clear, and yet it left Jules with a wistful dissatisfaction.

"I'm honored that you shared all this with me," she told him softly. "I know it wasn't easy . . ."

"But . . . ?"

"But is DeRohan really dead?" Jules asked. "Can anyone really destroy his essential nature?"

"It's what I set out to do."

She turned toward him. "Let me ask you this: when you were playing the brute—when you were dominating me—can you honestly say some part of you wasn't enjoying it? After all, you were doing it *so* well."

He leaned forward, resting his elbows on his knees, looking up the hill toward Rêve de l'Amour. "I don't know. All I know is I had to do it to push you in the direction you needed to go."

"But how can I know it won't happen again? How can *either* of us know?"

"I don't have an answer. All I can say is I've done everything in my power to suppress him—to kill him."

"I know you have, and I love you for it. I'd love nothing more than to tell you I understand and forgive. That we can be remarried and go on happily from here. But the reality is, as much as you've embraced the Panther, you'll always be DeRohan, too. You can never really kill that part of yourself. How can we have a future together based on the idea that you've suppressed an essential part of your nature? A monster that might spring to the surface at any time and wreak the kind of damage that made our married life such hell? How can we base our future on such a dubious proposition?"

Chapter 35

Jules awoke with a start.

She was in her bedroom at Rêve de l'Amour. The French doors were open, the sheer white curtains dancing in the crisp October breeze. But all was still and dark.

Her heart was racing. She'd been dreaming about . . . what? Not a nightmare, not fear or dread. Something pleasant . . . Colorful buildings fronting a charming harbor . . . an enchanted blue grotto . . . a high promontory crowned with a storybook castle. Lovely images. Images of comfort . . . security . . . escape.

All at once, she remembered. And on the heels of the memory, the idea came to her with all its power.

She sat up, brushing the hair back from her face.

What time was it? She glanced at the clock across the room. Just after four AM.

A new day.

She leapt out of bed, all traces of sleep vanished. In her nightgown, on bare feet, she hurried through her bedroom, her sitting room, down the upstairs hall, making her way to the east wing. Barging through his bedroom door to shake him awake.

Alarmed, his instincts flaring, he shot up in bed.

"I know what we can do," she told him excitedly.

Groggily, he reached for the bedside lamp. The soft golden light cast a halo around the bed. He held up a hand to shield his eyes as he peered at her. His dark hair was tousled and there was a faint stubble of beard on his strong jaw. He looked rumpled and sexy.

"Do?" he repeated.

"Get up. We're going on a trip."

He looked over at the window, noting the darkness beyond. "Now?"

"You can still fly an aeroplane, can't you?"

"Of course. But . . ."

"Is there some place around here where we can hire a plane?"

"The Nice airfield will—"

"Then get dressed. I'll call ahead and make the arrangements, then get us some breakfast. We can go as soon as it gets light."

"Go where?"

She gave him a dazzling smile. "Italy."

In the distance, the coastline came into view. Sitting in the rear of the two-seated Vickers Vespa biplane, goggles shielding her eyes, the wind whipping her hair, Jules gazed down on the Ligurian Sea. The water was turquoise closer into shore, but out here, it was as blue as royal sapphires. She'd never flown before. But as she felt the engine surge beneath her, as she looked down on the panorama of the Italian Riviera stretching out before her, she knew what the Panther had meant when he'd said he'd never felt so alive as when he was in the air.

It was good to feel the freshening breeze in her face, the hopeful beating of her heart. It had been difficult to return to the house the day before. The awkwardness of the uncertain future. The bad memories at every turn. The heavy-hearted retiring to separate bedrooms. But now, with France far behind them, sustained by her new vision, she was on fire with possibility.

She refused to consider failure.

Despite the fact that he was a captive to her will, DeRohan

flew with resolute authority. There was a grace and confidence about the way he handled the machine that put her instantly at ease. She felt a part of it all, of the sea, of the sky, of the fluffy white clouds that occasionally fogged her view.

It wasn't long before the fishing village of Portovenere came into view. She'd been here before, of course, but she'd never seen it from this soaring perspective, spread out in all its tranquil glory. The picturesque harbor with its cluster of pastel-hued buildings; the medieval castle on the rocky promontory above the village; the verdant hills spreading out on all sides. All surrounded by cobalt water and azure sky. All sparkling in the golden wash of the Italian sun. More breathtakingly beautiful than her most idealized memories. More dreamlike than her dreams.

With swift efficiency, DeRohan dove in toward the harbor, cut the engine, swooped in over the fishing boats, then came to a bouncing landing on the crescent of white sand bordering the harbor.

A flock of young children scurried down from the town to gawk at them. As DeRohan helped Jules out, he tossed his goggles onto his seat and smiled. "This is your party. What now?"

"I'm going to show you around."

Some mothers had followed their children to the beach. More slowly, a succession of fishermen ambled up, their eyes squinted against the gleam of sun on the plane.

DeRohan reached into his pocket for a coin and flipped it to the largest of the boys. Winking at him, he said in Italian, "Keep an eye on the flying machine for me, eh, *ragazzo?*"

The boy snapped to attention and gave a salute. As Jules and DeRohan left, the other children swarmed down on him, examining the coin.

Jules led the way. To their left, the harbor was lined with an irregular row of tall buildings butted up against one another and painted in vivid, distinctly Italian tints—pink, mustard, terra-cotta, olive, and blue. Before them, on the street level, multicolored umbrellas decorated the fronts of shops and cafés. To the right of the harbor was a leafy tree-lined square where people lounged in the morning shade, speculating about the new arrival from the sky.

They crossed the square, returning the greetings of the citizens, and Jules took him through the arched medieval gateway that led into the old town. They strolled down a narrow cobbled street, passing small shops along the way. There seemed to be more cats than people. They graced windowsills, the walls and doorsteps of the shops, and peered down from the tiled roofs, their tails swishing lazily. Lounging, sleeping, creeping, stretching, their heads in bowls of milk, they gave the surroundings a homey atmosphere.

"Portovenere means 'Port of Venus,'" Jules told him as they walked. "It was a major galley port of the Roman Empire. Now, as you can see, it's a sleepy little village. Less glamorous than Portofino up the coast. But to me, it's much more special."

"I've been to Italy a dozen times and I've never even heard of it. It looks like a postcard."

She smiled, pleased. "I came here for the first time just after the war. It was a revelation—its simplicity, its lack of pretension, its spectacular yet effortless beauty—I'd never experienced anything like it before. There was something about the harmony of it all that touched something deep in my soul. It was as if the air itself hummed with a feeling of peace . . . contentment. As if nothing could ever go wrong in such a place. Just knowing it was here gave me solace. I thought of it the way other people think of Heaven . . . no matter what went wrong in life, there was always Portovenere." She glanced at him sheepishly. "I've never told this to anyone. It was my secret."

His eyes softened on her face. But still, she could see the curiosity, the waiting, as if wondering where all this was leading.

"Let's walk to the top," she suggested. "I'd like to show you something."

They came out from the shaded street into a bright empty

square. Beyond it was a network of steeply inclining pathways that led up the looming promontory to the castle. They began to climb, pausing occasionally to catch their breath and look down on the glistening vista. Gulls soared and dipped over the hills, pristine white slashes in the endless blue sky, the air warm and cradling.

Halfway up, they came to the village church with its faded yellow façade. Passing it, on the steepening path, they finally reached the massive shell of the abandoned castle—a vast complex of ruins dominating the crown of the hill. They climbed the stairs to the summit where she took him to a perspective she remembered well. Before them lay the sparkling panorama of the Mediterranean and the postage-stamp village far below.

"It's breathtaking," he said.

But she could still hear the question in his tone: why are we here?

Jules pointed into the distance. "See that island out there?"

He gazed where she'd indicated, a lushly wooden island alone in the midst of the sea with a hill rising majestically to one side.

"It belongs to me. I bought it after I left you in London, using one of the jewels as payment. I knew, at that point, that you could legally take everything away from me. If the worst happened, I wanted a place to which I could escape. I was in such a panic, wondering where it could be, and suddenly I realized this was the perfect place. I'd never told anyone about it, so no one would think to look for me here."

"So you bought it as an escape from me."

"Originally, yes. But now I think it could be our future."

He took in the vista before them. "It's peaceful here, I admit. Still, I don't see how even the most serene place on earth can miraculously wipe away the past. Or the doubts that plague us."

"Miraculously? Perhaps not. But I have an idea. It came to me in a dream last night. Sit down here and I'll tell you about it."

She eased herself down onto the bulwark wall and dangled

her legs over the edge. He sat down beside her, wary but poised to listen.

"There's nothing on the island right now," she began. "But it has its own water supply, a relatively deep natural harbor, and plenty of level ground to build on."

"Build what? A cozy little cottage for two?"

"More like a place for several hundred."

He looked at her sharply. "You want to build a hotel?"

"No. A hospital. A most extraordinary hospital. One that would specialize in helping shell-shocked victims from the war. We would take them in free of charge and lavish on them the best treatment medical science has to offer. We could bring specialists in from all over the world. Can't you see the beauty—the poetic justice—of it all? Two victims of the war building a citadel of healing designed to treat other victims of the war in the most tranquil setting in the world. We'll build bungalows for the doctors and patients to live in, so it feels more like a resort than an institution. We'll finance research that will help us to learn new methods of treatment. We'll do whatever we must to get the job done. We won't take no for an answer. We'll knock down all the obstacles in our path. And I just thought of this. We'll call it the 'Rose DeRohan Clinic.'"

He looked at her a moment, then away again. "It sounds wonderful. But aren't you forgetting something? We have no money. And no prospects. I'm a ruined man. I've burned my bridges."

"I'm going to sell Rêve de l'Amour and all the jewels. That will be enough to build it."

"You'd give them up?"

"For this? Gladly."

"Why *this?*"

"Because it's the path God has put before us. Because it's a way of assuaging the guilt my family must bear for the war—guilt I've always denied. Because of your sister Rose. Because of the damage we both suffered from the war. And because . . ."

When she faltered, he prompted, "What?"

She took a breath. "When you told me about Rose, I wondered if I hadn't been somewhat shell-shocked after the war myself. My fear of thunder—my need to hide from the world. You helped me with that, you know. You could help so many others as well."

He shook his head. "I don't know. We could probably build the place for the money you'd get. But how would we sustain it? It would cost a fortune to keep something like that in operation. Particularly if we took the patients gratis."

"That's where you come in. That's where the skills of DeRohan the Invincible take over. What if you were to direct all the drive, cunning, and ruthlessness that built the DeRohan empire into our hospital? Think of what we could do!"

He shifted uncomfortably. "I told you. I've rejected that man. I don't want to go back to being him in any form."

"But *that's* our problem. You *can't* reject what you are. And it's not DeRohan's skills or his drive that made him evil. It was his objectives. Directed toward the proper goal, all of his qualities would become the instrument of good. And that, in turn, would make him a good man."

He mulled it over for some time as she waited, watched, his expression difficult to read. Finally, he said quietly, "I never would have thought of this on my own. But now that you've proposed it, there's a part of me that longs for it so much it hurts. I can imagine how satisfying and healing it could be. I can even envision myself reentering the world of business and mobilizing all those dark skills toward that good end. But I have to tell you I'm also frightened by the idea. Because DeRohan was more than just an expedient business wizard. He was a man who did terrible things—terrible things to you. I'm afraid of him."

She put her hand on his. "I'm not," she told him. "I have faith in him."

They strolled back down to the village and had a quiet lunch at a sidewalk café that overlooked the harbor and fishing boats. Afterward, they rented a skiff and spent the afternoon on the island. Jules showed him spots that would be perfect for the main hospital building and its surrounding bungalows. "There's a small sandy beach where the patients could swim and rest in the sun. The soil everywhere is fertile. We could plant flowers, make the whole island into a garden full of scent and color. And there, up on the hill, we could build our own villa. Our *home*. Nothing fancy, just a cozy hideaway that we could manage ourselves, with plenty of windows to let in the light and the views of the sea and the sky and the hills. With a terrace where we could sit and sip wine and watch the sun go down. And at the end of the day, no matter how tired or frustrated we were by what had happened, we would have the satisfaction of knowing our efforts had been directed toward helping people. Do you remember what you once suggested? To take our pain and do something meaningful with it? You said I'd know the opportunity when I saw it. I realized last night that it was here all the time, waiting for us. Can't you feel how fulfilling that kind of life would be?"

She continued to lay out the ideas as they came to her, becoming more and more convinced with every word. She could see the wistful longing in his eyes. Yet, she could see, too, the reluctance: his fear of the man she was asking him to be.

As twilight began to signal the end of the day, they sailed back across the bay. A silence had fallen between them that began to alarm Jules.

The silence lingered as they had dinner at another café under the stars and sipped their chianti as they watched the villagers stroll by in their nightly *passeggiata*. Finally, as it became clear that he was hopelessly deadlocked in his mind, Jules took a breath for courage and said, "There's something else I want to tell you. I wasn't sure earlier if I should, but I think you need to know."

His eyes narrowed on her cautiously. "And what is that?"

She took a sip of wine. "In the carriage that day. The little girl who laughed at you. It wasn't me. It was my friend Therese.

She was a silly twit. She laughed at everything. She wasn't even a Habsburg."

His eyes closed. They stayed closed for a full minute. Then he opened them and said, "When I think back on the boy I was . . . that poor little bugger. All those years, propelled by an image that was false. Isn't that the definition of a tragedy?"

"But don't you see? It doesn't have to be a tragedy. All those traits that little boy developed in pursuit of an empty dream can now be turned toward a *good* end. It will have been for something. Because we need those traits now. We can turn that young boy's tragedy into a grown man's triumph."

For what seemed an eternity, he was unable to speak. He just drained his glass and looked off into the distance.

Her words had obviously had a huge impact on him, but she couldn't tell what he was thinking. She could see that the bitter irony of what she'd just told him was pushing him over the edge. But which edge?

Quickly, she said, "There's one more place I want to show you before we leave."

When he spoke his voice sounded strained. "It's been a long day. Let's see it in the morning."

The morning would be too late. It was now or never. "No, I want you to experience it in the moonlight."

He gave her a long, level look, then reluctantly stood, tossing some bills to the table. They walked along the waterfront to its end. Jules could sense the tempest of thoughts rushing through his mind, trying to settle into some pattern that would give him peace. She whispered a silent prayer.

Then, on the heels of it, she gave herself up to the magic of the warm Portovenere night. And as she did, it seemed to her that no air had ever been as soft, no stars as close, no moon as silvery bright. The languor of Italy began to seep into her soul, the sense of hope and possibility all around.

She wanted to take his hand, but sensed it was too soon. So instead she directed him along a path that led up another rise to the left. There, bathed in the moonlight, in the midst of the crumbling ruins of ancient rampart walls, was a stone doorway leading to an open space beyond. She paused before it.

"They call this Byron's Grotto. The Romantic Poets fell in love with this corner of Italy, and this was Lord Byron's favorite swimming spot. I've always thought it the most enchanting place on earth."

They came out through the doorway onto a spectacular sight. Dark grey terraced slate formed a natural series of wide steps down to the water far below. The grotto was small, enclosed on the sides by soaring cliffs, topped to the right by the castle, to the left by the remaining rampart walls. The water, emerald and sapphire in the day but now an inky midnight blue, pooled around giant rocks, then joined the sea to stretch out toward the moon-drenched horizon.

"I've always wanted to swim here," she told him. "Will you join me?"

Without waiting for his reply, she began to remove her clothing, dropping each piece to the rocky ledge at her feet. As he watched her, she could feel the shift in the energy around them, a spark of raw desire. But she didn't wait. She padded down the wide stone steps and into the water like Venus returning to the sea.

The water was cool at first, but she dove into it, then rose again, her hair dripping, her breasts bobbing on the surface. She turned and saw him standing still on the steps high above. But he, too, had shed his clothes and was standing, watching her. In the glow of the moonlight, his naked body looked sleek and virile.

And then he was descending toward her, moving with a cat-like grace, reminding her of the way the Panther had stalked toward her that first night and seized her for his own. And then it hit her: the one thing that had been missing in her vision.

She played with the idea in her mind, turning over the tantalizing possibilities as he waded into the water beside her. Without a word, they began to swim beneath the moon and the stars, out into the open sea. There was no current tonight

and the water was calm and refreshing. All was quiet and
serene. They floated on their backs for a while, silently looking
up at the splendor of the night.

"Dominic?" she said at last, her voice a breathy sigh.

He turned to look at her, catching the intimacy of the name
she'd used, sensing her excitement. "Yes?"

"You say you're afraid of DeRohan because he was dominant and forceful and ruthless—not just with his competitors,
but with me."

"We both know it's true."

"But there's one thing you've forgotten."

"And what's that?"

"When you were the Panther . . . when you were dominant
and forceful and ruthless with me in bed . . ."

"Yes . . . ?"

"I loved it."

He looked at her then, with an ember of passion in his eyes.
"I did, too."

"It wasn't debasing or humiliating. Every moment that we
were together, I felt the force of your love. But what I didn't realize at the time was . . . in those moments, when the Panther
was making love to me, it was really DeRohan expressing himself in a way he never could before. When we made love, all aspects of you came together with a power and perfection that
was . . . sublime."

"Sublime . . ." he repeated, turning toward her in the water.

"Dominic, I don't want a milksop in my bed. A penitent
man who's afraid to touch me, afraid to unleash his desires. I
want you to be the man nature intended you to be."

"A brute?"

"You weren't a brute to me in bed. Masterful, yes. But that
was thrilling! I loved it all. So come to me that way in passion.
But when we're done, leave it there. In all the other hours of
the day, cherish me. Let me be your equal, your partner, your
best friend."

He'd gone perfectly still. As the water lapped about them,

the moonlight played on the muscles of his chest. For some time, he didn't speak. But finally he said, in a tormented voice, "I want that more than you know. But . . . is it possible?"

She moved closer to him. "Look around. We're naked and alone in the most romantic spot imaginable. A setting that inspired Roman myths and made poets weep. So let's find out. I want you to take me, Dominic DeRohan. Here. Now. Love me as you've never loved anyone before. In all your ferocious glory. Hold nothing back."

For a moment, he continued to stare at her with doubt clouding his eyes. But when she smiled at him with impish enticement, the doubt vanished. "All right, then," he said, his tone decisive now. "Let's find out."

They swam back toward shore together, but before they reached it, he took hold of her wrist and headed toward a massive flat-topped rock jutting out from the water. He sprang up easily, then reached down to pull her up beside him.

Then, standing face-to-face, naked in the midst of the rocks and the water and the starlit sky, he gave her a commanding kiss, crushing her wet hair in his fist.

If you liked this book, you've got to
try HelenKay Dimon's
HARD AS NAILS,
out this month from Brava.
Here's an excerpt from
"This Old House,"
the first story in this three-novella anthology.

She dragged his mouth down and scorched him with a deep, drugging kiss. A kiss that wiped out good intentions and common sense. One that overpowered him, causing every nerve ending to flare to life.

Gone was the gentle assault. Restless energy radiated off of her. Her lower body cuddled against and inflamed his. Fingers tunneled into his hair as her hot tongue rubbed against his. Hot and wet, body against body, and mouth against mouth.

"Damn, Aubrey. Yes."

Air caught in his lungs, making breathing impossible. Every inhale hitched, every exhale caught and stuttered. When he finally broke off the kiss, he balanced his forehead against hers to hold on to the warm contact a few minutes longer.

"Better?" Her finger traced the outline of his jaw.

Damn, did she have to ask? "Magnificent."

"You do know your way around a kitchen."

"I'm pretty knowledgeable about every room of the house. Wait until you see what I can do with a shower stall."

Her laugh vibrated against his cheek. "I guess we can consider the kiss a down payment on my bill."

Her words hit him like a big bucket of icy water. If she wanted to kill the mood, she had succeeded.

He blew out a long, painful breath. "Aubrey, about that—"

"Maybe making these payments won't be so hard after all."

No way would he have her rolling over in bed tomorrow morning, looking up at him with those bottomless dark eyes, and accusing him of a new sin. Stealing was bad enough.

"Think of it more as a taste of things to come." He forced his hands to drop to his sides. The rest of his body shouted to stay right where he was.

"What are you doing?" A cloudy haze hovered over her eyes, and those sleek arms stayed around his shoulders.

"Stopping." He reached up and loosened her hold around his neck. Otherwise, she might choke him.

"Why in the hell are you doing that?"

Yep, haze gone. Anger firmly in place. He'd buried her desire all right. Scooped up the dirt and piled it on top.

Despite the strong pull he felt for this woman, the situation didn't feel right. Sex for a house. Sex to get out of trouble. Neither of those worked for him. Not on those terms. Sex for sex. Wanting him for him—not for the name or his finances— was the deal. For some reason, accepting less no longer sat right with him.

This doing the mature thing sure was a bitch.

"We need to call a halt," Cole said, as he separated their bodies the rest of the way.

"Are you a complete idiot?"

No mystery there. Yeah, he was. A master idiot. "I'm trying to be sensible."

"You're about to be killed." She shoved hard against his chest with both palms.

"That's not quite the reaction I was going for." Where was the gratitude for treating her like a woman and not just a body? For giving her the benefit of the doubt despite all of her accusations?

"What game are you playing? Clue me in so I know the rules."

"No game, Aubrey. That's the point. When we have sex—"

"You blew your chance on that one, stud."

She didn't have to sound so sure. "When we have sex—and we will, so stop shaking your head—it will be because we both want it. Not because you need something from me."

She pulled back as if he'd slapped her. "What do you think I need?"

"Money. The house."

Somehow those black eyes darkened even further. "That's the kind of male nonsense guaranteed to get a plate smashed over your head."

"It is?"

"You make it sound as if I proposed we trade sex for money."

Uh-oh. Somewhere along the line he had lost the upper hand in the conversation. "Well, I thought . . ."

"You better deny it before you end up wearing those dishes," she warned.

Red face and puffing cheeks. A damned angry expression for a woman supposedly seeking a quid pro quo.

Cole tried to regain lost ground. "Look, let's back up a step."

"You can back right out the door for all I care." Her chest rose and fell in rapid counts.

"You mean you weren't saying . . . ?"

"I was kissing, you idiot." The words shot out of her and into him like tiny knife wounds. "And you were what, Cole, dissecting my intentions?"

"I didn't mean to—"

"Deciding I had a motive other than putting my tongue in your mouth?"

He knew enough to keep his mouth shut this time. Didn't help though. Her rage kept spiraling.

"I admit I'm new at the one-night stand thing, Cole, but I thought kissing meant kissing, not that cash needed to be exchanged."

Something that tasted like regret boiled up from his stomach. He'd been so sure a second ago that she wanted something from him. At least that's what he thought right up to the minute he started thinking something else.

He mentally composed a convincing apology. He refused to beg, but he could admit some responsibility for their misunderstanding. Cooking her something to eat would play a role. He'll need all of his skills for this one.

The tension is electric in
THE BAD BOYS GUIDE TO
THE GALAXY,
the newest story from Karen Kelley,
out this month from Brava . . .

"Where's your dress . . ."—he waved a finger around—"thingy . . . robe, whatchamacallit?" He finally pointed toward her.

She raised an eyebrow. He didn't seem to notice the clean floor. Disappointment filled her. She'd hoped for more. Silly, she knew. After all, he was an Earthman, and she shouldn't care what he thought.

"My robe was getting dirty along the hem, so I removed it."

Her gaze traveled slowly over him, noting the bulge below his waist. It was quite large. Odd. She mentally shook her head.

"Your clothes are quite dirty. Once again, I've proven that I'm superior in my way of thinking," she told him.

"You're naked."

She glanced down. "You're very observant," she said, using his earlier words. "Did you know there's a slight breeze outside? It made my nipples tingle and felt quite pleasant. Not that I would be tempted to stay on Earth because of a breeze."

"You . . . you . . . can't . . ."

She frowned. "There's something wrong with your speech. Are you ill? If you'd like, I can retrieve my diagnostic tool and examine you." He was sweating. Not good. She only hoped she didn't catch what he had.

"You can't go around without clothes," he sputtered. "And I'm not sick."

"Then what are you?"

"Horny!" He marched to the other room, returning in a few minutes with her robe. "You can't go around naked."

"Why not?" She slipped her arms into the robe and belted it.

"It causes a certain reaction inside men."

"What kind of a reaction?"

What an interesting topic. She wanted to know more. Maybe they would be able to have a scientific conversation.

Kia had only talked about battles, and Mala had talked about exploration of other planets, but Sam was actually speaking about something to do with the body. It was a very stimulating discussion.

He ran a hand through his hair. "I'm going to kill Nick," he grumbled. "No one said anything about having to explain the birds and bees."

"And what's so important about these birds and bees?"

He drew in a deep breath. "When a man sees a naked woman, it causes certain reactions inside him."

"Like the bulge in your pants? It wasn't there before."

"Ah, Lord."

"Did my nakedness do that?"

"You're very beautiful."

"But I'm not supposed to think so."

"No, we're not talking about that right now."

She was so confused. Sam wasn't making sense. "Then please explain what we are talking about."

"Sex," he blurted. "When a man sees a beautiful and very sexy naked woman, it causes him to think about having sex with her."

He looked relieved to finally have said so much. She thought about his words for a moment. A companion unit did not have these reactions unless buttons were pushed, and even then, their response would be generic. This was very unusual. But also exciting that her nakedness would make him want to copulate. She felt quite powerful.

And she was also horny now that she knew what the word meant. She untied her robe and opened it. "Then we will join."

He made a strangled sound and coughed again and jerked her robe closed. "No, it's not done like that. Dammit, I'm not a companion unit to perform whenever you decide you need sex."

"But don't you want sex?"

"There are emotions that need to be involved. I'm not one of those guys who jump on top of a woman, gets his jollies, and then goes his own way."

"You want me on top?" She'd never been on top, but she thought she could manage.

He firmly tied her robe, then raised her chin until her gaze met his.

"When I make love with a woman, I want her to know damn well who she's with, and there won't be anything clinical about it." He lowered his mouth to hers.

He was touching her again. She should remind him that it was forbidden to touch a healer. But there was something about his lips against hers, the way he brushed his tongue over them, then delved inside that made her body ache, made her want to lean in closer, made her want to have sex other than just to relieve herself of stress.

And keep an eye out for Donna Kauffman's
THE BLACK SHEEP AND
THE ENGLISH ROSE,
coming next month from Brava . . .

"I only ask for one thing."

She arched a brow and decided to give him the benefit of the doubt. "Which is?"

"Until the sapphire is in our hands, we operate as a team. No secret maneuvers, no hidden agendas."

Her whole life was a hidden agenda. Well, half of it anyway. "And when we have the necklace? Then what?"

"See? I like how you think. When, not if."

"Which doesn't answer my question."

"I don't have an answer for that. Yet."

She laughed. "Oh, great. I'm supposed to sign on to help you recover a priceless artifact, in the hopes that when we retrieve it, you'll just let me have it out of the kindness of your heart? Why would I sign on for that deal?"

He turned more fully and stepped into her personal space. She should have backed up. She should have made it clear he wouldn't be taking any liberties with her, regardless of Prague. Or Bogota. Or what they'd just done on her bed. Hell, she should have never involved herself with him in the first place. But it was far too late for that regret now.

"Because I found you tied to your own hotel bed and I let you go. Because you need me." He toyed with the end of a tendril of her hair. "Just as much, I'm afraid, as I need you."

"What are you afraid of?" she asked, hating the breathy catch in her voice, but incapable of stifling it.

"Oh, any number of things. More bad clams, for one."

"Touché," she said, refusing to apologize again. "So why are you willing to risk that? Or any number of other exit strategies I might come up with this time around? You're quite good at your job, however you choose to label it these days. Why is it you really want my help? And don't tell me it's because you need me to get close to our quarry. You could just as easily pay someone to do that. Someone who he isn't already on the alert about and whose charms he's not immune to."

"Maybe I want to keep my enemies close. At least those that I can."

"Ah. Now we're getting somewhere. You think that by working together, you can reduce the chance that I'll come out with the win this time. I can't believe you just handed that over to me, and still expect me to agree to this arrangement."

"I said maybe. I also said there were myriad reasons why I think this is the best plan of action. For both of us. I never said it was great or foolproof. Just the best option we happen to have at this time."

"Why should I trust you? Why should I trust that you'll keep to this no-secret-maneuvers, no-hidden-agenda deal? More to the point, why would you think I would? No matter what I stand here and promise you?"

"Have you ever lied to me?"

She started to laugh, incredulous, given their history, then stopped, paused, and thought about the question. She looked at him, almost as surprised by the actual answer as she'd been by the question itself. "No. No, I don't suppose, when it comes down to it, that I have." Not outright, anyway. But then, they'd been careful not to pose too many questions of one another, either.

"Exactly."

"But—"

"Yes, I know we've played to win, and we've done whatever

was necessary to come out on top. No pun intended," he added, the flash of humor crinkling the corners of his eyes despite the dead seriousness of his tone. "But we've never pretended otherwise. And we've never pretended to be anything other than what we are."

"Honor among thieves, you mean."

"In a manner of speaking, yes."

"I still don't think this is wise. Our agendas—and we have them, no matter that you'd like to spin that differently—are at cross purposes."

"We'll sort out who gets what after we succeed in—"

"Who gets what?" she broke in. "There is only one thing we both want."

"That's where you're wrong."

She opened her mouth, then closed it again. "Wrong how? Are you saying there are two priceless artifacts in the offing here? Or that you can somehow divide the one without destroying its value?"

He moved closer still, and her breath caught in her throat. He traced his fingertips down the side of her cheek, then cupped her face with both hands, tilting her head back as he kept his gaze directly on hers. "I'm saying there are other things I want. Things that have nothing to do with gemstones, rare or otherwise."

She couldn't breathe, couldn't so much as swallow. She definitely couldn't look away. He was mesmerizing at all times, but none more so than right that very second. She wanted to ask him what he meant, and blamed her sudden lack of oxygen for her inability to do so. When, in fact, it was absolute cowardice that prevented her from speaking. She didn't want him to put into words what he wanted.

Because then she might be forced to reconcile herself to the fact that she could want other things, too.

"Do we have a deal?" he asked, his gaze dropping briefly to her mouth as he tipped her face closer to his.

Every shred of common sense, every flicker of rational thought she possessed screamed at her to turn him down flat. To walk away, run if necessary, and never look back. But she did neither of those things, and was already damning herself even as she nodded. Barely more than a dip of her chin. But that was all it took. Her deal with the devil had been made.

"Good. Then let's seal it, shall we?"

She didn't have to respond this time. His mouth was already on hers.